ENTER THE WORLD OF

COME SUNRISE

WHERE LOVE CANNOT ALWAYS ENDURE THE LIGHT OF DAY. . . .

AMY NORMAN. A beautiful innocent, she was cast away from her home and family, only to find a great love in the one man she could never have. . . .

(MORE)

LUKE WESTERMAN. Blond and charismatic, he returned Amy's love—but his heart and soul already belonged to God and the priesthood. . . .

COME SUNRISE

TOMMY WESTERMAN. As dark as his brother was fair, he wanted Amy for his own—even if he was the second choice. . . .

BEATRIZ ORTEGA. Strong and statuesque, she would keep her New Mexico range—at any cost. . . .

RICARDO IBANEZ. A handsome doctor, he could only love the married Amy from afar—until his passion grew too strong to deny. . . .

BEVERLY BYRNE

ROSA MADAGO. A voluptuous beauty, she wanted the good life—and she would become Tommy's mistress to get it. . . .

DONALD VARLEY. As Amy's guardian, he was to look after her best interests. But was he everything he seemed to be?

COME SUNRISE

Beverly Byrne

FAWCETT GOLD MEDAL • NEW YORK

Prologue

❧

O N THE SEVENTH OF MAY, 1915 TWO MEN STARED IN
disbelief at a clattering teletype machine. Its staccato
clicks and clacks and bells bespoke urgency in an
otherwise silent and deserted room.

Outside twilight made blue gray the New York
streets. It was after 8:00 P.M. and most of Tenth Avenue's warehouses and offices were deserted. A few
wharfs sheltered ships. They seemed lifeless and still,
suspended in that moment between night and day.
Dusk blurred to dark and a light winked here and
there.

In the Cunard office the older clerk wrenched himself into motion. He stretched out a hand and tore the message from the machine.

> *Lusitania* sunk off Irish coast by German U-Boat . . . this day fourteen-fifteen GMT . . . search and rescue underway . . . few survivors . . .

"Jesus Christ," the second man said. "There must have been two thousand people on that ship."

"Twelve hundred and fifty passengers," his companion said tonelessly. "About six hundred crew. Eighteen, maybe nineteen hundred."

"Jesus," the other one repeated.

"Bloody bastards. Goddamn Huns." The curses were spoken softly, respectful of the power of death. "A passenger ship, nobody on board but civilians. Oh, my God!" A rising note of hysteria crept into his voice. He fought it off and crossed to his desk, still holding the teletype message. Other, more senior, employees of the company must be notified. He had no desire to carry the responsibility for this ghastly news.

The younger clerk stared into the darkness beyond the window. "Do you remember a few days back, when she sailed?" he asked. "First real day of spring. Aren't they lucky, I thought. Going to England on a lovely day like this. Wish it was me." He shivered and said nothing more.

BOOK ONE

❧

1915–16

1

⁓

"THE *LUSITANIA* WENT DOWN IN FORTY-FIVE MIN-
utes, my dear. I'm so very sorry," Donald Varley said.

"But it's only two days." Amy Norman looked at
the man, uncomprehending. "We may get more news.
My parents may have been rescued. . . ."

The headmistress of Miss Taylor's School for Young
Ladies moved from behind her desk and laid her hands
on Amy's rigid shoulders. "My dear child, you mustn't
deceive yourself with false hope. We waited until now
to inform you for just that reason. All the survivors
are accounted for. There were very few, and your dear
parents were not among them."

Amy raised her brown eyes and stared at the woman. "You can't be sure," she said stubbornly.

"I'm afraid I can," Miss Taylor insisted. "Believe me, I wish desperately that I were not."

"Miss Norman—Amy—I do know how you feel. My sister and her husband were aboard too, you know. They didn't survive either." Varley fumbled with the briefcase on his lap, as if preparing to produce evidence to support that fact.

"Uncle Charles and Aunt Cecily too," Amy whispered. "Oh, God . . . " She hunched the spine she'd previously kept deliberately straight, as if to clasp close the pain of loss.

Miss Taylor hugged the girl and stroked her hair. Amy had black hair. Usually it was tied back with a grosgrain ribbon. Now the ribbon had come loose, and the shining hair hung forward over the girl's face. "Go ahead and cry, dear," the headmistress whispered. "It's best to face grief at such times."

Amy pulled free of the woman's embrace and stood up. "Thank you for coming to Boston to see me, Mr. Varley," she said woodenly. "If you don't mind, I'd like to go to my room now." Without waiting for permission she left the office.

Miss Taylor turned to the lawyer. "I think it best if Miss Norman is left alone for a bit," she said. "I'll go up to her presently. She needs time to assimilate the shock."

"Yes, of course." This time he did reach into his briefcase and withdrew a sheet of paper. "I believe you should have this. It's an extract from Mr. Charles

Westerman's will. As you will see, I'm named as executor for the estate of my late brother-in-law."

"Yes," she took the proffered document. "But I don't see . . ."

"According to the terms of Roland Norman's will, Charles was to be Amy's guardian in the event of her parents' death. Since both the Normans and the Westermans died simultaneously, in law at any rate, I am now Miss Norman's guardian. Until she's twenty-one."

"I understand. And what do you wish me to do, Mr. Varley? Are we to keep Amy here?"

"Yes, of course. For the present at least. The way things are there's certainly no question of her returning to the family home in Africa. And she must not be alone."

"Good, I think that a wise decision. One further thing Mr. Varley. Is there to be a funeral? I know the bodies have not been recovered." She swallowed hard. "But perhaps . . ."

Varley frowned. He was an exceedingly handsome man. The frown settled over his features like a mask donned by a superior actor. His clear gray eyes expressed troubled concern. "I'm afraid I'm at a loss to know what to do about poor Roland and Jessie in this regard. They weren't members of any church you see. As far as I know they had no religious beliefs at all. And there is no family apart from the child. My sister and brother-in-law were closer to them than anyone else. I only knew the Normans slightly."

"May I ask what your intentions are with respect to Mr. and Mrs. Westerman."

"There's to be a memorial mass at St. Ignatius' Church tomorrow. We're a Catholic family, so it's rather different.

Miss Taylor nodded her perfectly coifed gray head. Catholics had rules to guide them in situations of this sort. It was one thing she found to admire about them. "I believe the Westermans leave survivors apart from yourself?"

Varley managed a small smile. "Quite a few. There are two sons and a large assortment of other relations. We're a sizable clan."

And an influential one, Miss Taylor thought. She pursed her lips and looked speculative. "Perhaps I should suggest that Amy return with you to New York for the service," she ventured. Then, when Varley looked like agreeing with her, she added, "But I do not advise it. I don't know Amy as well as I might, she's been with us less than a year, but I know young girls. Amy is naturally in shock. I think it best if she remain here in familiar surroundings."

"I'll abide by your decision in the matter," Varley said, rising. "I'm a bachelor myself. I don't claim to know anything about children, certainly not girls."

Miss Taylor extended her hand. "Please allow me to offer my sympathy for your own loss, and to thank you for coming."

He left her his address and telephone number and proceeded to South Station to catch the *Yankee Clipper* to New York.

*   *   *

Miss Taylor went to Amy's room within half an hour of saying good-bye to Donald Varley. She knocked softly, then let herself in. Amy sat in a stiff chair by the window. She didn't turn her head when the headmistress entered.

There was a jumble of boxes and ribbons on the bed. A bunch of long stem roses lay wilting on the floor. Miss Taylor looked at the things and remembered that today was Amy's seventeenth birthday. The presents must have arrived just a short time ago.

She stooped and rescued the roses. A vase stood by the washstand already full of water. Amy must have been preparing to arrange the flowers before she was summoned to meet Mr. Varley.

"I'll just put these here for now," Miss Taylor said. Then she picked up the crumpled wrapping paper and neatly folded the discarded ribbons. A framed picture caught her eye. It was done in watercolors and showed a huge sprawling house surrounded by verdant greenery. A pony stood in the foreground. "Is this your home in Africa?" she asked softly.

Amy turned and acknowledged the woman's presence for the first time. "Yes, that's Jericho. Mummy painted it. She liked making watercolors of the house. This one's always been my favorite. That's why she sent it to me for my birthday."

"And is this your horse?"

"My pony, Sheba. I've had her since I was six." There was a flicker of animation on the girl's face.

"She must miss you," Miss Taylor said, then bit her lip. "Oh, look," she added hastily, "here's a present you haven't opened." She held it out, but Amy didn't take it.

Miss Taylor opened the small box. A diamond ring winked up from a velvet cushion. "Oh, Amy, it's exquisite. You must look."

The girl finally stretched out her hand, and Miss Taylor slipped the ring on her finger. Amy looked at it in silence, then she said, "This was the first stone my father found in Africa. He always promised I'd have it for my seventeenth birthday. It's not very large, only two carats." She spoke as though she were repeating a lesson learned by rote. "It's perfect though. A perfect blue-white stone. They arranged all the presents before they sailed. They made sure the things would be delivered today."

She stopped speaking and stared at the older woman. Then she looked around the simple bedroom with its schoolgirl decor and its single window looking out on unfamiliar, unloved Boston. Her tears began as a silent flood, but soon became wrenching sobs that shook her small frame and made the curtain of black hair tremble around her white face.

Amy spent a few days in the infirmary, then returned to her classes and the normal routine of the school. But looking at her, as she frequently did, Miss Taylor recognized the taut control for what it was, a thread being pulled tighter and tighter. Eventually it must snap, and what would be Amy's hold on reality then?

The girl's only outward sign of mourning was the

black serge dress she wore. More poignant was her zombielike behavior. She had never been an enthusiastic student, nor had she made close friends among the other girls. At first Miss Taylor put it down to Amy's exotic background. Now she gave up hoping that time would make the girl more like her classmates, or give her a share in their world. In early June she rang Donald Varley in New York.

"As you know," she told him, "I had arranged with Mr. and Mrs. Norman for Amy to spend this summer at a camp in Maine. We thought she'd enjoy the outdoor life. I'm no longer sure that's a wise plan." She went on to try and explain her concerns. "Amy needs people to whom she feels close, Mr. Varley. People with whom she can express her feelings. I fear that she'll do herself great damage keeping everything locked inside this way."

Varley had no suggestions to offer. "I'll think about it and call you back," he told Miss Taylor.

There was no return phone call, but a letter came a few days later. Varley had discussed the problem with other members of the family. Perhaps Amy would like to join them at their summer home in Cross River. Both Luke and Tommy Westerman would be there. Amy might take solace from being with the boys. They had, after all, sustained an identical loss.

"Where is Cross River?" Amy asked when Miss Taylor told her of the plan.

"In Westchester County, New York. A charming town. I was there once many years ago. Do you know the Westerman boys well, Amy?"

The girl shook her head. She'd taken to wearing her

black hair in a severe bun, and it accentuated her high cheekbones and her piquant heart-shaped face. The brown eyes looked enormous now that she was so thin. "Not well," she answered. "We've met a few times over the years, and I saw them last summer with . . ." She stumbled, then went on. "With Mummy and Daddy. There are a lot of Westermans. I don't really know who all the others are."

Miss Taylor glanced at Varley's letter. "Your hostess would be Miss Lil Westerman, the late Mr. Charles Westerman's sister. She and her brother are also spending the summer in Cross River. It would all be quite correct, my dear. I think you should go."

"Can't I just go home?" Amy asked. She sounded as if she knew what the answer must be.

"I'm afraid that's impossible," Miss Taylor said softly. "At least until this wretched war is over and you're a bit older. Won't you consider accepting this very kind invitation?"

"Whatever you say," Amy agreed. "It doesn't matter."

2

"AMERICA'S GOING TO GET INTO THE WAR," TOMMY announced. He didn't look up to see how his remark affected the assembled company, just continued his complicated task at the small table serving as a bar. He was squeezing oranges, and his aunt avoided looking at the acid stains forming on the polished wood.

"Any idea when this catastrophe is to come to pass?" Warren Westerman asked. He made the remark with little movement of his lips, and without removing the stem of his pipe. Neither did he lift his head from the book he was reading.

"Soon maybe," Tommy said. He poured a portion

13

of champagne into five stemmed crystal goblets. "Wilson doesn't want it of course. The privilege of being gassed in a trench isn't one of his New Freedoms. But after the *Lusitania*, well, someone's got to put the Huns in their place."

Amy's head jerked up. Tommy didn't seem at all embarrassed by mentioning the ship in her presence. But then, why should he be? His parents had gone down with the *Lusitania* too. If it didn't bother him, why should it offend her?

She glanced round the room. It was large and square with a high ceiling and book-lined walls. There was a big fieldstone fireplace, filled with greenery on this late June evening, and a deep bay window looking out over an expanse of lawn. Luke Westerman sprawled on the windowseat. His long legs were stretched across the flowered cushions, and his white duck trousers were bright against the vivid pink cretonne. He was leaning against the wall, and his blond hair contrasted with the soft green paint. Only his face was dark, but the frown seemed to have little to do with what Tommy said. Luke wasn't paying any attention to his younger brother.

Amy looked away and her eyes met Lil's—Aunt Lil, she'd asked to be called. "You're among family here," she'd told the girl when she arrived a few days ago. "Or at least near enough as makes no difference." Amy was grateful for the gesture, but she still didn't feel at ease.

"Do switch on the lamp, Amy," Aunt Lil said. "You'll hurt your eyes sewing in that dim light."

The girl did as she was bid, and returned to her

embroidery. Tommy added cherries to his creations and lifted the tray of drinks to be admired.

"*Voila!* The TWS is ready for your delectation."

"What does TWS mean?" Lil asked.

"Tommy Westerman Special." He walked with the tray toward his aunt, and Amy caught her breath slightly, afraid he'd spill the drinks. His limp was pronounced at this time of day. The specially built-up shoe he wore on his right foot always seemed less effective by evening. None of the others offered to help him. Amy had guessed that he resented assistance. Now there was no accident, despite her concern. Lil took one of the glasses, and Tommy moved to where Amy sat.

"Your evening libation *memsahib*." He bowed with exaggerated deference.

"I've never had anything but sherry before. And do stop calling me that." She laughed nervously as she reached for her drink.

"Why? It's what you're used to, and we want you to feel at home. Don't we, Luke? And isn't that what everyone called her when we were there?"

Luke turned and smiled for the first time that evening. He had an incredibly sunny smile that lit his face. "You're forgetting, I wasn't along on that trip to Africa. Had to go to summer school if I was going to get into Hotchkiss." He laughed and walked over to collect his own drink. "This little brat tormented me for the next year about all I'd missed," he told Amy. "You should have heard his stories. Lions and tigers and giraffes eating out of his hand. Black men bowing

and scraping and calling him *b'wana* for all he was the
ripe old age of eleven."

"They did," Tommy said. "And they called Amy
memsahib. And she couldn't have been more than
six."

"Seven," Amy corrected. "But it doesn't mean anything. It's just their way."

"Damned right too," Tommy said. "Keep the natives in their place and all that sort of thing. Wot?"

His British accent was very good, and he produced a
monocle from the pocket of his vest. Luke wore a
blazer and an ascot, but Tommy, as always, was in a
three-piece suit and bow tie. He held the tray with one
hand while he fitted the monocle and crossed the
room to deliver a drink to Uncle Warren. Now he was
Jeeves rather than an African.

Amy giggled in spite of herself. Luke sat down on
the arm of her chair. "Don't be fooled by him. It's not
humor. It's delusion. Stark mad, my poor brother.
Fancies himself Napoleon every time there's a new
moon."

Tommy turned to face them. "Yes, too bad isn't it?
And the lad showed such promise too. Never had to
go to summer school, that one. Straight A's and never
seemed to do a lick of work."

Amy heard the undertone of bitterness in Tommy's
voice, but she saw no answering anger in Luke's blue
eyes.

"This is really quite good, Tommy." Lil sipped her
drink with appreciation. "Isn't it good, Warren?"

"Mmm, yes, all right if you say so." He returned to
his book. Neither his sister, his nephews, nor their

guest fascinated him. He didn't try to hide the fact. "Fellow here says he's had marvelous results by leaving roses unpruned. Extraordinary. Have to write to him."

Luke smiled ruefully at Amy. "We must all seem a little mad to you," he said softly.

"Why do you say that?" she asked.

Luke started to answer, but Tommy came back to where they were sitting and occupied the other arm of her chair. Amy could see his heavy leather invalid's shoe where it gleamed in the lamplight. "I've arranged for the car tomorrow morning," he told her. "I'm taking you on a tour of the countryside." To his brother he added, "Care to join us?" His voice now held none of the hostility of the moment before.

"Sorry," Luke said. "I've some letters to write that can't wait."

Amy had not thought it would be so easy to laugh again. She still wore black, as did Lil, but the house in Cross River was not a place of mourning. The Westermans were deft at handling their grief. It was acknowledged in tiny silences and the occasional bittersweet comment about what Charles or Cecily might have said or done were they there. Sadness was an interstice in the pattern of life. They all seemed to accept that eventually the gap would silt over and only memory remain.

Amy felt guilty. She did not understand such an attitude, nor was she sure of her right to share it. But her guilt was a sometime thing, deep and poignant when it surfaced, but often forgotten.

Cross River was a leafy haven near the Connecticut border where rich Manhattan folk had summer homes, and the locals seemed to be born in spring and die in autumn. The next day Tommy took her outside its privileged environs to the rural countryside.

He drove slowly past perfect little farms with red barns and shining silos and pacific cows that seemed placed by an artist with an unerring eye. Once they saw a couple of pigs wallowing in a muddy puddle by the roadside, truants from an enclosed yard most likely. Tommy regaled her with an endless story of a pig that won so many prizes at the country fair that the proud owner moved into the sty and gave the pig the run of the house. She laughed until the tears rolled down her cheeks.

On the way home he felt less obliged to show her the sights, and he drove very fast instead. The Pierce-Arrow could do better than thirty miles an hour, and Tommy pushed it to its limit. After lunch Amy said she wanted to take a walk. Tommy didn't offer to join her—rambling through the countryside was one of the things he couldn't do—and Luke had already disappeared, so she was alone.

The guilt came over her in waves then. Crying, she walked only as far as the duck pond and sat there, solitary under the willow trees.

Luke appeared from the direction of the tennis courts. Amy knew how well he played. She'd watched him a few days ago. He moved across the grass with a dazzling blend of speed and elegance. The neighbor who was his frequent opponent was good too, but Luke always won. "As good as young Bill Tilden," the loser said. Amy heard talk of Luke's entering the national championships, or competing at Wimbledon. The suggestion always came from someone else. Luke only laughed. "I play for my own amusement, that's all," he'd told her.

Now he dropped the racket and came to sit beside her. For some seconds neither of them spoke. "Would you rather be alone?" Luke asked finally.

"Yes, no . . . I don't know. I'm sorry."

"Don't be. I feel the same way lots of times. That's the nice thing about being a girl. You can cry and no one thinks less of you for it."

"I didn't think any of you ever felt like crying."

He looked startled. "What ever gave you that idea?"

Amy wiped her eyes with her handkerchief. "The way you all act," she said. "Laughing, making jokes, playing tennis. It's just two months since it happened."

"Maybe it's because we know that's how Mother and Dad would have wanted it." It was a lame explanation and he knew it.

"That's got nothing to do with it," she said. "I'm not just crying for them. I'm crying for me, because I want them back. I want things to be as they were before we came here. I want to be at Jericho and I want them there too. Do you understand?"

"Of course I do. You're very wise for such a young girl." He reached for her hand, and Amy let him take it. "You're honest about your feelings. That's a long way toward mastering them."

"I don't care about mastering my feelings. Just about

making it different. Making the *Lusitania* never happen."

"Can't be done, I'm afraid," he said softly. "Amy, if I talk to you about the will of God, will you try and understand?"

She pulled her hand away. "I'm not a Catholic, you know that."

Luke chuckled. "That's not what I mean. The will of God is a bigger concept than any one religion."

Amy shook her head impatiently and he dropped the approach. "Would you like a change from Cross River?" he asked suddenly.

"What kind of a change?"

"I have to go into the city day after tomorrow. I plan to leave right after breakfast and be back around dinner time. Why don't you come?"

She turned to him with a smile, although her enormous dark eyes were still shiny with tears. "Yes, I'd like that. Will it be just you and me? Is Tommy coming?" She felt her cheeks redden. He'd think she didn't want to go anywhere without Tommy.

"Nope," he said. "Just you and me. Ok?"

"Fine."

"Good. I'll tell Aunt Lil."

They arranged to take the 8:00 A.M. train. The night before their departure Lil came to Amy's room when she was preparing for bed. "I've a couple of errands that need doing in the city. Would you mind, darling?"

"No, of course not. I'm not very good at shopping,

though. Mummy took me with her a few times when we first arrived, but I'm not used to big stores."

"I know you're not, poor thing," Lil said indulgently. "How could you be after all those years in the bush?" Her tone indicated what a deprivation she considered a girlhood in Africa, but Amy didn't bother to correct the notion. "It won't matter," Lil continued. "They're very helpful at Altman's and they know me. It's just these gloves. I've lost two buttons, and they've nothing to match them in the shops here."

She handed over a pair of white kid gloves missing two tiny pearl buttons and a note with the name of the sales clerk for whom Amy was to ask. It struck the girl that she'd never seen Lil wear the gloves. Not even on her Sunday trips to the local church. "Is there anything else, Aunt Lil?"

"Well, if you're near a Schrafft's, get one of those gorgeous fudge cakes. Bessie is a terrible baker. Warren likes cakes from Schrafft's best of all." Her attention suddenly switched. "You like Luke, don't you?"

Amy was startled. "Of course I do. He's been so kind to me. You all have."

"I don't mean that," Lil said. "It's just that Luke is such a golden boy. While Tommy . . ." Her voice trailed off.

"Tommy is very amusing," Amy said. She felt obliged to defend the younger Westerman boy, though she didn't know why.

"He's brilliant, you know that don't you? Tommy's going to make his mark. Politics, I imagine. He's really extraordinarily intelligent. Charles always said so."

Lil wore a double strand of pearls, and she kept toying with them while she spoke. Her hands, Amy noticed, betrayed her fifty plus years as none of the rest of her did. They trembled slightly and blue veins showed against crinkled skin. "Tommy's quite strong you know. Despite his leg. He does special exercises, and his arms and shoulders are powerful. He can lift anything."

"Yes, Aunt Lil, I know. I think both Luke and Tommy are wonderful. And I'm very grateful . . ."

"Shh." She leaned forward and put her hands on the girl's shoulders. "I don't want you talking about gratitude. Your mother and father were Charles and Cecily's best friends. We love you, darling, and we're overjoyed to have you with us. Particularly just now. That's not what I mean at all."

"What do you mean, Aunt Lil?"

The older woman smiled. "I'm a silly old maid who's still a romantic at heart. I mean nothing, darling, ignore me. Have a nice day tomorrow."

Luke had to go to Donald Varley's office to sign some papers, one of the reasons for his trip, so he took Amy to Wall Street first.

"You know Uncle Donald, don't you, Amy?" Luke asked when they were shown into the lawyer's presence.

"We've met," Varley said. "I'm glad to see you looking so well, Miss Norman. May I call you Amy? Good. The country air must agree with you." He pushed some papers toward Luke while he spoke. Luke hesitated for a moment and exchanged a look with his uncle. Then he signed them quickly, without bothering to read the contents.

"I had a note from your headmistress the other day, Amy," Varley said. "She's concerned about you. You should write to Miss Taylor."

"Yes, I know I should. I will, this week. I promise."

"That's fine. Now, can I offer you two young people lunch? I've a regular table at Lüchows. The food's quite good."

"Thanks, but we've errands to do," Luke said quickly. "We'll get something later."

They rode uptown on a bus, sitting on the open upper deck, and Luke accompanied Amy on the foray into Altman's. Then they went to Schrafft's for lunch and bought a fudge cake on their way out. It had been cloudy during the morning; now the sum came out and it grew hotter. Amy felt the weight of her black serge dress.

"You're looking tired," Luke said solicitously. "I have to go up to Sixty-sixth Street. We'll take a taxi." He hunted until he found one of the few remaining horse-drawn cabs, and Amy sat beside him in friendly silence, watching the city pass by. In twenty minutes they pulled up by a large gray pseudo-gothic building. St. Vincent Ferrer's Church, a sign said. Dominican Priory.

"What does that mean?" Amy asked.

"The Dominicans are a religious order. Priests who follow after St. Dominic. He lived in the twelfth century."

"Then they've a long way to follow," she said.

He smiled his sunny smile, as if her wit were magnificent. "I have to see someone here. Would you mind waiting? You can sit in the church. It's cool and no one will bother you. I won't be long."

"I don't mind."

He ushered her inside. Amy just stood, but Luke genuflected and knelt in a pew for a few moments. After he left she sat on one of the wooden benches and studied the long nave and the elaborate statuary. She had no eye for art, but she recognized what was here as being better than the pink and white plaster figures scattered around the house in Cross River. Soon Luke returned and they went outside into the sunlight.

"Look," he said as if the idea had just occurred to him, "would you mind visiting one more church? I'd like to show you something."

"Can we walk?" she said. "I'd like to."

They headed further uptown and in half an hour reached Eighty-third Street and Madison Avenue. This church was different from the first. It was of gray stone too, but it had no gothic pretensions. The letters A.M.D.G. were carved over the door. "This is a Jesuit church," Luke explained. "They're another religious order. The initials stand for their motto. Latin for 'To the greater glory of God.' It's our parish church. Our house is nearby."

The interior was bigger and brighter than that of St. Vincent Ferrer. Luke directed her to a side altar with a statue of the Virgin Mary, drew her to the wall and pointed to a marble plaque. It was obviously new, and bore the names of Charles and Cecily Westerman.

'Lost at sea and safe with almighty God' it said. Then the letters R.I.P.

"I just wanted you to know it was here," Luke said. "I don't know why it seemed important. Crazy, I guess."

Amy felt a sudden sense of the most terrible and agonizing desolation. In seconds she was wracked with sobs.

"Oh, lord! Amy, I'm sorry. I didn't mean to upset you. I thought you'd find it comforting. The same's true of your parents. It has to be. Oh, please stop crying. I'm so very sorry."

"It's all right, it's not your fault," she managed to say. He handed her his handkerchief, and she blew her nose and looked around. Except for themselves, the church was deserted.

"I didn't have any funeral for my parents," she whispered. "I thought about it, but nobody said anything and we aren't religious so . . ."

Luke looked horrified for a moment, but he masked the reaction quickly. "We can still arrange something," he said. "I'll help if you like. You're Protestants, aren't you?"

"No," she shook her head. The sobs were still threateningly close. "We're not anything. Maybe it could be here. They could have a plaque next to this one. They were such good friends . . . " Her voice trailed away when she saw the look on his face.

"I'm sorry," Luke said. "It's not allowed. Because they weren't Catholics. But I'm sure we can find another church. I'll talk to someone right away."

She shook her head again. "No, that's all right, it's a silly idea. They were never religious. Neither am I."

They spoke little on the journey home. Luke tried to bring up the subject again, but Amy forestalled him.

When they were on the train she remembered the chocolate fudge cake. They'd left it behind in the church. In her mind's eye she could clearly see the white box with its blue lettering. She'd left it on the velvet cushion of the kneeler in the side chapel, below the plaque to the Westermans. She wondered what the next visitor would think of such an offering.

3

"WHAT HAPPENED IN NEW YORK?" TOMMY flipped a flat stone into the pond and some ducks squawked angrily.

"Why do you think anything happened?" Amy trailed her hand in the water. It was warm and felt slightly slimy. She withdrew her fingers quickly.

"Because you and Luke haven't said a word to each other since you got back," Tommy said. "Are you angry with him? Hard to imagine good old Luke being anything but a perfect gentleman."

"Oh, no!" Amy said. "It wasn't anything like that."

"But it was something. What?"

She'd been trapped into granting his premise. "He took me to a church to see the memorial plaque to your mother and father."

Tommy looked at her. "Why'd that make you mad?" he asked in wonder.

"It didn't. It upset me, that's all." She told him what had happened.

"My brother's an ass," Tommy said. "Sorry, but it's true."

"You mean I could have a plaque for my parents? Next to the one for yours?"

Tommy threw another stone, this time with more force. A duck just missed being hit. "No, he told that one straight. Against church rules."

"Well, it doesn't matter," she said, just as she had to Luke. "I don't believe in God anyway."

"Then why worry? If I could forget about hell, I wouldn't worry about anything. It's all a damn sight easier if you convince yourself there's no God."

Amy shook her head and the sunlight glimmered on her hair. She'd been wearing it up all summer. Now it fell loose down her back in an ebony curtain. "I'd like to think I'll see them again. I just can't make myself believe it."

Tommy whistled softly through his teeth. "You shouldn't play about with philosophy. Women aren't suited for it. C'mon." He rose and pulled her up after him. It was always a shock to Amy to discover how strong he was.

"Where are we going?" she asked.

"To church."

"No, Tommy, I don't want to. I'm sick of being dragged into churches, first by Luke and now by you."

"Will you stop chattering," he said angrily. "Just come along." He pulled her behind him; his grip on her wrist was unbreakable. Their progress across the field and up the garden path was marked by Tommy's arhythmic movements.

He pushed her into the Pierce-Arrow and started the motor and they headed toward the village.

Sacred Heart Church had been built only a few years earlier. It was a small white clapboard building that existed to serve the Italians and Irish who worked on the nearby farms. "Father O'Reilly won't be here," Tommy said. "He always goes to the racetrack on Friday afternoons. But he never locks the church."

Tommy did however. Once they were inside he threw the sliding bolt on the door and walked over to the side entrance to make sure it was locked too. Only then did he genuflect before the flickering candle near the high altar.

Amy stood in the dimness and watched him. She felt fear, but didn't know of what she was afraid. Not of Tommy certainly. Just of his bizarre behavior perhaps.

"Right here," he said, pointing to a bare piece of white painted wall beneath an elaborate stained glass window.

Amy looked up and saw a notice. It said that the window had been the gift of Mr. and Mrs. Charles Westerman. "Right here what?" she asked.

"Here's where we're going to put up a memorial to your parents." Tommy grinned at her in his lopsided boyish way. He had a spattering of freckles across his nose and cheeks; they stood out in the dim interior. "You'll be hedging your bets, so to speak." he said. "In case we're right and you're wrong, and there is a God after all."

She couldn't keep from giggling. "That's ridiculous."

"Of course it is," he said. He was laughing too. His hair was brown and curly. A lock of it was always falling untidily over his gray eyes. Tommy had a habit of sticking out his lip and blowing upward to clear his vision. He did it now. "It's nuts," he agreed. "But we're going to do it anyway. Wait a minute."

She watched him move off toward a small door beside the altar. It was locked, but he knew where the key was kept. He disappeared for a moment, then returned with two candles, a brass dish filled with water, and a peculiar wandlike implement.

"We're going to do this right," Tommy said. He placed the candles on the floor and lit them. Then he sprinkled water on the wall using the wand that he said was called an agpergillum. "It's holy water," he explained. "Specially blessed. Maybe by the pope, I don't know. But I know the drill." His voice became solemn. "In the name of the Father and of the Son and of the Holy Ghost," he said, sprinkling the wall with water once more. "There, now it's consecrated."

Amy watched him in fascination. He fished out a pocketknife and stepped closer to the space he'd chosen for the inscription. "How did your folks spell their names exactly?"

She told him, but he got no further than the J in

Jessie. "The wall's stone. I'm not making any impression."

"Here, use my ring." She pulled it from her finger and handed it to him.

"This is real, is it?" he said in surprise. "But then it would be. The Norman Diamond Mines. I forgot."

"It was a present from my father for my seventeenth birthday. It's the first stone he took out of the mine."

"Good, it'll do the job and it's appropriate." He carefully etched the names Jessie and Roland Norman on the wall. "What else do you want to say?"

"Nothing, only their names, that's all."

"You sure? How about the date of the sinking?"

"No, nothing more."

"Not even R.I.P.?"

She shook her head and he nodded in agreement. "Ok. But we'll say a prayer." Tommy gave her back the ring and once more donned an air of studied solemnity. He lifted the agpergillum and flicked holy water at the rough inscription. "Lord," he said softly. "You know what we have in mind. May they rest in peace. Amen." He looked expectantly at Amy.

"Amen," she said.

"Good girl."

Afterward, when they'd put everything back in the sacristy and left, she asked him about the priest. "Won't you get into a lot of trouble?"

"No. I'll square it with O'Reilly. He drinks like a fish, a couple of cases of Scotch will do it."

It was close to dinner time when they got home. "I have to hurry and change," Amy said.

"Ok. And listen, how about giving up black? We've

had a proper memorial service for them now. That should end your official mourning, shouldn't it?"

Amy smiled. He had exorcised for her more than the ghost of that stark moment with Luke in New York. "All right," she said. "No more black."

That evening she came downstairs in a pale cream dress of cotton lace. It made the warm pink tones of her skin glow. "How very attractive you look, my dear," Lil said. "I am glad to see you wearing ordinary clothes again. You're far too young and pretty for mourning."

A couple of days later Tommy reported. "Father O'Reilly's hung a holy picture over the inscription so no one will notice and ask questions. You don't care, do you?" He looked at her anxiously. "We know it's there."

"Yes," she agreed. "It's all right, I don't mind about the picture. I hope it's a nice one."

He grinned with relief. "It is." He didn't bother to tell her the painting was entitled "Our Lady Star of the Sea."

August was a yellow month; a time of buttery sunshine, and goldenrod blooming in the fields. The sumac trees began to turn color and hint of autumn. It was very hot, but Amy was used to that. She didn't mind the heat now that she'd given up the black serge. Slowly her emotional paralysis ebbed.

The Cross River house was a Victorian folly of turrets and gables and sprawling porches to which an earlier owner had given the name Balmoral. It was a self-contained universe, surrounded by seven acres of grounds, and possessed of a resident staff that Charles and Cecily had kept on when they bought the place. Balmoral was isolated by its location, but more effectively by the fact of the Westermans' religion. The local population were Yankees, and the other summer residents wealthy New Yorkers of the Protestant elite.

It had been perverse of Charles to buy in Cross River. He should have chosen a vacation home on Long Island, Far Rockaway or Southampton, where his fellow believers congregated. His objection was that those people, the MacDonalds and the Murrays and their ilk, were Irish. The Westermans were vague about their ancestry, but they were decidedly not Irish. In his lifetime Charles Westerman did business with men of every class and shade of belief, but he was more fastidious in selecting a place to live.

It was this very isolation which restored Amy. There was a sense in which life at Balmoral harked back to Jericho. It was a rural fastness without any rural inconveniences. Every comfort was provided, but no strangers came and went. She did not have to look from the windows at crowded city streets.

Slowly she came to life. It was not merely a return to the state before Donald Varley told her of her parents' death. When she left Africa Amy had suffered a mortal wound. The ship that sailed out to the Indian Ocean through the strait between Dar es Salaam and Zanzibar severed her roots. Jessie and Roland knew that she was sad about leaving, but they assumed that, as they would, Amy would be secure about returning. She was, however, a child—without control of her own destiny—and she was gripped by the irrational fears of childhood.

In the months at Balmoral she began to stop being a child. It was tragedy that achieved her coming of age, but she needed to absorb the pain of the loss before she recognized her adulthood. Tommy and the long golden days of that summer allowed her to do so.

Toward the end of August Luke was called to the telephone during breakfast. He returned looking sober and sad. "I'm sorry, bad news," he announced.

Everyone stopped eating. "We have to leave here right away," Luke said. "Balmoral has been sold, and the new owners want immediate possession. That was Uncle Donald on the phone. He's promised them we'll be out in three days."

"Sold," Lil spoke the word as if it were a foreign tongue. "Why ever did you sell it?"

Warren cleared his throat noisily. He had spent summers here for the past fifteen years. "My garden," he muttered. "What about my garden?"

Luke looked pained. "It's best for the estate. I am sorry."

"You could have warned us." Tommy's face was deathly white except for two spots of color in his cheeks. Amy looked at him and realized with shock that it was fury, not sorrow.

"I never thought it would happen so quickly," Luke said. "I thought we'd have this summer. Then I'd tell you, and there'd be the whole winter to get used to the idea."

Lil acted as if she'd not heard his explanation. "Why sell Balmoral? We've always been so happy here. What will we do next year?"

"Go to the poor house, no doubt," Tommy said, rising quickly. He knocked over his chair and the noise made a welcome diversion.

Amy felt herself an awkward witness to a drama in which she had no place. She responded, nonetheless, to the shock in Lil's face and in Warren's.

"I'll help you, Aunt Lil," she said. "I know there will be a lot to do. And can't we take cuttings in the garden, Uncle Warren? My mother used to do that all the time. You can make new plants from all the old ones."

He nodded in her direction. "Yes, cuttings. It's the right time of year for most things. Thank God for that."

Later Luke found Amy in the linen room where she was counting table cloths. "No need for that," he said softly. "The place has been sold fully furnished. I've just explained to Aunt Lil. We don't have to move anything but our personal belongings."

She put down the stack of lace and damask but she didn't look at him. "Luke, is it what Tommy said? Are you poor?"

"Don't be silly," Luke said brusquely. "This is just a good move for the estate. I told everyone that. There are long term advantages in realizing some capital at this moment."

"I'm sorry. I didn't mean to pry."

"Of course you're not prying. You're family as far as we're concerned. You know that. It's what I came to talk to you about actually. What do you want to do for the next few weeks until your school reopens?"

"I'm not sure." She was, but she hadn't the nerve to say so outright. "I've been thinking about it."

"Well, you could go to that camp in Maine for a while, if you want to. Or you could stay with Aunt Lil and Uncle Warren in New York. I've already talked to Aunt Lil about it. They have a nice apartment overlooking Central Park. It's just a few blocks from our house. New York's still beastly hot, of course."

"I'm used to heat," Amy said.

"Yes, that's right, you are. You'll come with us, then?"

"I'd like to," she said shyly. She had never intended to do anything else.

4

A HOLY STATUE IN THE FRONT HALL WAS APPAR-
ently *de rigueur* for the Westermans. There'd been
one at Balmoral and there was one in Lil and Warren's flat. It was of white porcelain with gilt trim. A
candle holder of dark red pimpled glass, and more gilt
trim, stood next to it.

Lil reached up and flicked a switch as soon as they
came in the door. "I always light Our Lady's vigil light
first thing we come home," she said. It wasn't a candle, it was electrified. "Now, Amy, we only have one
guest room, so I can't offer you a choice. I hope you'll
be comfortable."

She led the girl to a room of polished mahogany
furniture and blue and white flocked wallpaper. The
drapes and bedspread were of rose-colored silk. "It's a
lovely room, Aunt Lil, thank you."

"I'll send Maureen to help you unpack. Dinner is at
seven-thirty." She kissed the girl lightly on the cheek.
Lil always smelled of jasmine. Jessie Norman had
worn the same scent, and Amy inevitably felt a catch
in her throat after one of Lil's embraces. "Welcome,
darling," Lil said. "We want you to be completely at
home."

Quite soon Amy did feel at home. She had feared a
return to city life, but she found that she could adjust
here as she had not been able to in Boston. They
were on the eleventh floor. The apartment was something of an aerie. It reminded her of the nests built by
birds in the high cliffs near Jericho, and she liked it.
Her determination not to return to Miss Taylor's school
strengthened.

She'd made up her mind about that the morning at
Balmoral when the precipitous departure was announced. Now she wanted Tommy to help her mount
the campaign, but he was unwilling.

"It's crazy," he said when she told him about it.
They'd been to the movies, "the flicks," Tommy called
them, to see the Keystone Kops. Now they were sitting in Central Park. Tommy kicked at some fallen
leaves while he spoke. "You've got to finish your
education. I'm going back to Georgetown the end of

this month. I'm a senior, another year to go. I'm not wild about Washington either, but it has to be done."

"It's different for you. I'm a girl. I don't need to know anything they can teach me at Miss Taylor's. And it's horrid. The other girls are such idiots, Tommy. They don't know anything."

He shrugged. "I know it's different for girls. Still . . ."

"Anyway, I'm going to return to Jericho as soon as this war's over. It can't last much longer. I just want to stay with your aunt and uncle till then. Besides, I can ride here." She nodded her head in the direction of one of the park's bridle paths. "Miss Taylor doesn't allow young ladies to ride."

"What does Aunt Lil say?"

"I haven't asked her yet. I hoped you'd do it with me. She thinks you're quite the cleverest thing alive, she'll listen to you."

"Not a chance." He shook his head emphatically. "It's nuts, Amy, and I'm not going to help you."

She was forced to try Luke. She telephoned and asked him to meet her at Schrafft's the next day. ". . . so there's no reason I shouldn't stay in New York," she finished. Then she looked at him closely. "You're not surprised."

"No, Tommy warned me."

"Warned you not to help me, you mean."

"It's not like that, Amy. Tommy just thinks you're being unwise. I think he's right."

"Rubbish!" She slammed a gloved hand on the marble-topped table, and the spoon in her ice cream dish rattled. "Why is everybody against me?" Luke had never seen her like this before. He stared in fascination.

"I'm not some silly schoolgirl like those twits at Miss Taylor's. I was breaking horses and riding in the bush when I was six. In Africa I visit every *shamba* for miles around by myself. Sometimes I'm gone for days. Miss Taylor doesn't think girls should leave the grounds without a companion. She . . ."

"What's a *shamba*?" he interrupted.

"A farm. A homestead."

"Oh."

"Is that all you can say, Luke Westerman? Oh? I thought you were my friend."

"Of course I am."

"Then why won't you help me? My father and yours grew up together. They helped each other all their lives."

Luke wondered how much Amy knew of the basis of that friendship. She'd never mentioned any of it. Perhaps she'd never been told the sordid details. Suddenly he felt more than ever sorry for her. She was so alone. "All right," he said at last. "I'll go with you and we'll talk to Aunt Lil. In the end it will be up to Uncle Donald though. He's your guardian."

"I know that. I just want it all settled with Lil before I tackle him."

Lil proved quite amenable to the idea. "But I'd be delighted to have you stay, darling! Such good company. We'd both be delighted, wouldn't we, Warren?" As usual she didn't wait for her brother to reply to her rhetorical question. "Tommy's going back to school of course." Lil bit her lip and looked at Luke and Amy in perplexity. "I suppose that part can't be helped. Never mind, it will be great fun."

When Amy looked up she saw that Warren was staring at her. She waited, but he didn't say anything.

Donald Varley was even easier. "Very well, if that's what you'd prefer, my dear. I don't see much sense in elaborate schooling for girls myself. By the way, perhaps we can talk again soon. I'm beginning to sort out your estate and there are some things we must discuss."

Amy threw her arms round Luke's neck when they were alone in the corridor outside Donald's office. "Hooray! We've done it. I shall write to Miss Taylor tonight. And what will that prig Tommy say now!"

Luke disengaged himself. He was as red-faced as if she'd kissed him. "He'll be hopping mad."

"But why, for heaven's sake?"

"I don't know. I guess just because he's got to go back to school and now you don't."

"Luke"—she changed the subject abruptly—"what are you going to do now that you're through college? Are you taking over your father's business?"

He studied a mural on the wall. It was an artist's conception of Lincoln reading the Gettysburg Address. The scene was the middle of a battlefield and there was lots of blood and gore. "Funny picture for a public place. Yes, I'm to work in Dad's office. At least for a while."

"What did he do exactly? I only know he was a businessman."

"He was an investment broker, a financier. Frankly

I don't know too much about it. Tommy's the one with the business head. Dad had two partners though, and they've offered to help me learn the ropes."

Only later did she wonder why he'd said he'd be in his father's business "for a while."

Toward the end of September Tommy left for his last year at the Jesuit university of Georgetown. Things had been strained between them since Amy's scheme succeeded. Still, she went to Pennsylvania Station to see him off. He seemed pleased she'd come. He'd insisted that none of the others bother, and the two of them were alone.

"I'll be home for Thanksgiving," he said. "You behave yourself until then. Don't forget me just because I'm away and Luke's on the spot."

Amy's eyes opened wide. Suddenly she understood many things, and she realized that she possessed some power over Tommy. She had, however, been armed unawares; as yet she had no idea how to use the gift. "Of course I won't forget you. How could I? Besides" —she flushed prettily—"Luke doesn't make me laugh the way you do."

Tommy looked as if he'd just won the sweepstakes. "That's good," he said. "That's great in fact!" Impulsively he leaned forward and kissed her on the cheek. "You take care of yourself, Amy Norman. And you write to me."

"I will, I promise." Her last sight of him was hanging off the train waving his gray fedora in her direction. As long as he wasn't walking, she realized, no one would guess that Tommy was a cripple.

Donald Varley came to see Amy a few days later. "I thought it best if I came here, my dear. These are rather personal matters, and I'm sure you'd prefer we be alone."

He belonged to a generation that didn't expect a young lady to travel the city unescorted. They were in Lil Westerman's small but charming drawing room. Varley crossed to the door and closed it. "I realize you understand nothing of these things. I'll try to explain. You are the only heir to your father's estate. However, with things as they now are it's difficult to determine the exact value of that estate. Letters to Africa take many weeks. Sometimes they don't arrive at all."

"Yes, I know about that." She had written to old friends in Dar es Salaam, and to the workers on Jericho, and had no replies.

"Then you'll understand that I can't give you exact figures. And of course we must face the fact that after this war is over the value of things may be entirely different."

"Of diamonds you mean?"

"No, not that exactly. But foreign holdings, such as your father's. If the Germans win, they may conscript everything. It may develop that you have no rights to the Norman mines."

"But Daddy bought the land from the Kaiser years ago."

"War is a terrible thing, child. It turns everything

topsy-turvey." He shook his head and his mane of silver gray hair held Amy's gaze. He had a small, neat moustache, and he stroked it while he spoke. "There's another sad fact. Near as I can make out, the Jericho Diamond went down with the *Lusitania*. Your poor dear mother had it with her apparently."

"But that was only a copy!" Amy said at once. "Mummy and Daddy used to laugh about it all the time. She never traveled with the real Jericho Diamond."

"I see. Well, that's fine if it turns out to be true. And if we can find the stone after the war. Seventy carats, isn't it?"

"Seventy-two. And it's perfect. It's in a bank vault in Dar es Salaam." She could see that bank as she spoke. It was an enormous place with marble walls and huge fans whirring overhead. It was impregnable. Of course the jewel was safe.

"Well, then, that makes me hopeful that everything will work out for the best," Varley said heartily. "Meanwhile there are your expenses to consider. Of course Lil and Warren are happy to have you as their guest, but . . ."

Amy blushed. It was the first time the thought had occurred to her. She was taking charity from the Westermans. She had never offered to pay her way. "I never realized," she stammered. "It just didn't cross my mind. Of course, I should pay some kind of rent or something."

"Nonsense, child! We're happy to help you, for your father and mother's sake. All of us. And I've arranged a long-term loan with a bank here. The interest is very fair, and they're content to wait for repayment until your affairs are settled. It makes it possible for me to give you a small allowance to meet your personal needs." He smiled at her conspiratorially. "I'm just an old bachelor, but I know a thing or two about ladies."

He'd succeeded in making her feel dreadful. "I don't really need any money, Mr. Varley," she said in a hoarse whisper. "I just need a place to stay until I can go home."

"Now, my dear, you mustn't take that attitude. And we can't say when you'll be able to return to Africa. Not the way things are. I don't want you to worry. You're to have twenty-five dollars a month. And I'm sure we'll be able to repay the bank as soon as we settle your estate."

That same afternoon Lil suggested that she should have some new clothes. "Oh, no," Amy said quickly. "I don't need anything."

"Yes, you do, darling. If you're going to spend the winter in New York, you'll need a few new dresses at least. And a new coat as well. I thought of fur, but you're still so young."

"I'm in mourning," Amy said in desperation. "I shouldn't buy any new clothes yet."

"Nonsense! I thought we settled all that this summer. Believe me, your poor mother wouldn't want you going about the city looking a frump. That's the last thing Jessie Norman would have wanted."

"But . . ."

"I'll telephone Donald and arrange that the bills be sent to him," Lil said firmly. "And I'll make an appointment at the dressmaker. We can try Altman's, but in the end I think you'll have to have most things made. It's this awful war. Nothing at all in the shops."

Amy was terrified by the debts she was running up, but she didn't know how to stop Lil.

The following week there was an engagement party for a Westerman cousin. Amy found herself surrounded by dozens of strangers who took her hand and murmured condolences. Then they drifted away across a barrier forged by intimacy she did not share.

Eventually Luke joined her. "You looked dazed."

"All these people! Are you related to every one of them?"

"Just about, except for the prospective groom's side. Daunting, isn't it?"

"Incredible." Someone jostled her arm and a trickle of punch stained the front of her new blue dress. There were hasty apologies, and Luke led her off to find the powder room. A young Irish maid repaired the damage quickly. Luke was waiting in the hall when Amy emerged.

"All fixed?"

"Yes, thank you. It's fine."

"Do you want to go back in there?" He nodded in the direction of the drawing room. "They'll be serving supper soon."

She shook her head.

"Me neither," he said. "Let's go for a walk."

They escaped to Fifth Avenue and a soft mild evening that belied the October date. "Indian summer," Luke said. "Sure you're not hungry? We can probably find somplace open."

"No, I'm not. Tell me about your family. Who are all those people?"

"Not one by one!" He laughed and took her arm and drew it through his. "I'll give you a potted history. Grandpa Westerman was in the fur trade, an agent for the Hudson Bay trappers. He married a French Canadian girl, that's the Catholic connection, and settled in Fort Covington. It's a tiny town on the New York-Canadian border. They had sixteen children."

"My God!"

"Exactly. I told you, Grandma was a Catholic. Anyway, eleven of them survived. My dad was the youngest, by the way. Eventually Grandpa was selling more and more furs in New York City, so they moved down here. Apparently Grandma was pretty sharp too. She bought property, most of it up here around the eighties. It was considered the back of beyond in those days, and she got it cheap. What with one thing and another they died very rich. Of course the estate was cut up eleven ways. Still, nobody did too badly."

"And they all live in New York?"

"Most of them. They married well, except for Lil and Warren, who didn't marry at all, and most of that lot you met back there are either doctors or dentists. That was Grandma's idea of respectability. She steered all her kids into medical training or a medical marriage. Dad was the only one interested in business."

"How come Warren isn't a doctor?"

Luke grinned at her ruefully. "Family skeleton. Failed medical school because he couldn't stand the sight of blood. Lil wanted to be a nun, I'm told. Grandpa wouldn't hear of it. She didn't defy him, but she wouldn't marry either. So they live together on their share of the original spoils. Now you know it all. Not very exciting, is it?"

"Maybe not, but it's overwhelming. Don't you feel" —she groped for a word—"stretched, pulled apart by having so many relatives?"

"It's never occurred to me. They've just always been there." His laugh echoed in the semideserted street.

They passed a doorway sheltering a couple locked in embrace and Amy averted her eyes. "How come so many of them seem to have known my father?" she asked. "They were all very sweet and sympathetic, and they sounded as if they'd known him."

"But they did," Luke said in surprise. "He was brought up by my grandparents. Didn't you know?"

She shook her head and felt embarrassed. "Daddy never talked about his childhood. I guess because Mummy was raised in an orphanage. It was very unhappy for her, so the subject was avoided. Anyway, when you live in Africa I think you forget about the past. Africa is so real that nothing else seems to be. Do you understand that?"

"I think so."

He drew her arm tighter through his own, and Amy was conscious of his warmth beneath the black dinner jacket. They stopped by a street light and her eyes searched his face. Luke looked almost godlike in the glow. His perfectly chiseled features reminded her of the ancient Greeks pictured in Warren's leather-bound books.

"Listen, Amy," he said. "Don't you start worrying about the past." There was an odd hint of urgency in his voice, and of protectiveness. "You've got your whole life to look forward to."

5

AMY BEGAN TO SEE MORE OF LUKE. HE CAME TO THE apartment for dinner two or three times a week, and took her to plays or concerts or for long walks in the park. They talked endlessly, mostly about themselves, and she realized that Luke was unhappy in his father's firm. "I'm not very good at it," he told her ruefully.

"But you'll learn. Just be patient."

"I will if I have to," he agreed.

Amy didn't see how he could avoid it, but she didn't press. Luke needed time to adjust to being a business-man rather than a student.

Literature was a safer subject. She discovered po-

etry and wasn't afraid to argue vehemently her prefer-
ences. Luke's taste was austere, and he denounced
hers as romantic and sentimental. She developed a
passion for Christina Rossetti; he tried unsuccessfully
to interest her in William Blake. "We'd better switch
to novels," he said one Sunday afternoon. "We'll never
agree about poetry."

"Wuthering Heights," she said instantly.

"Middlemarch," he retorted. "Bronte can't hold a
candle to Eliot."

They looked at each other and laughed.

They laughed a lot together, unless, as sometimes
happened, they were trapped into discussing the war.
The Times introduced a new process called rotogra-
vure. Like the rest of New York, Amy and Luke lived
their lives against a background of graphic death. Exotic battlefield names such as Sulva Bay and Gallipoli
and Loos were made real by sepia-tinted photographs
of horror, served up with breakfast.

Tommy had the paper sent to him at college, and he
wrote worshipfully of the news photographers report-
ing from the front lines. One letter announced that
he'd spent six dollars on a camera, Kodak's new fold-
ing pocket-size model, and was practicing. "I'm not
very good yet, but I'm snapping everything that will
stand still, and I'm getting better."

She worried that he was nursing some crazy dream
of going off to war, but she wrote less frequently.
Three letters a week shrank to one every ten days or
so. She didn't disguise the reason. "Sorry I haven't
been in touch for a while," Amy wrote at the end of
October. "Luke's been taking up my education. Lots

of plays and things. We saw Mr. Cohan's *Hello Broadway* Tuesday night and on Saturday we're going to the opera to hear *Faust*. It will be my first time . . ."

Tommy didn't answer that letter.

November came bringing swift and sudden cold. A freezing wind stripped the last of the leaves from the trees in the park, leaving black branches silhouetted bleak and severe against a leaden sky. Two days later there was a blizzard, the earliest anyone could remember, and Amy stared out the windows at a world of white.

"What's the matter?" Luke asked, coming into the drawing room the day after the storm. "You look terrible."

"I hate it," she said with unexpected passion. "These winters of yours are awful. I hoped New York would be better than Boston."

"It isn't much different." He crossed and took both her hands. He smelled of sunshine and cold fresh air. "It's not so bad once you get used to it. It can be a lot of fun."

"I don't see how. The streets get icy and it's impossible to walk. Then when it melts everything's filthy and soaking wet and . . ."

"Whoa! Slow down. It's not my fault, I don't make the weather. Blame God if you must."

She looked away. She didn't want to revive the time when each of their conversations ended by being about God. "What is there that's fun about it? Tell me, I'm longing to be convinced."

"Well, sleighing for one thing. And building snowmen. And snowball fights."

"I've never done any of those things."

"Then it's high time you did. Get your coat. Do you have snow boots?"

"Yes, Aunt Lil made me buy them weeks ago."

"Let's go then."

They entered the park at Seventy-ninth Street and turned right into the big open field skirting the Metropolitan Museum of Art. It was full of laughing children watched by prim governesses. Nearby was a steep hill. Small boys hurtled down it on shiny wooden sleds that reached breakneck speed.

"We're too old for that unfortunately," Luke told her. "Too bad. It was great. I've still got my old sled somewhere at home."

"You can save it for your children," she said.

For a moment it appeared he was going to say something serious. Instead he grinned. "Let's find a place to build a snowman. I suspect you're going to be the artistic type."

They walked deeper into the park, beyond where the paths were shoveled, and the children's voices faded into the distance. Luke selected an enormous drift beneath a bewhitened pine. "It's easy," he said. "You begin with a snowball. Then you start rolling it to make it bigger."

Amy handled the snow gingerly. It was dry and powdery and still very clean. The icy cold stung through her thick woolen gloves. She tried to imitate his expertise, but she was clumsy. Her attempts produced lumpy misshapen spheres that wouldn't hold together.

Luke made her a starter ball. "Here, begin with this." He was intent, as if he were giving lessons in some art necessary to survival.

"Don't take it so seriously," she said laughing. "I thought it was supposed to be fun."

"Might as well make a good snowman if you're going to make one at all."

She got the hang of rolling the original snowball along the ground to make it grow. Soon it took both of them to control the enormous result.

"Ok, that's his lordship's body. Now we need another one."

In a while they had a smaller round on top of the first, and Luke put his bowler on the snowman's head. "He needs a face."

Amy plucked a couple of pine cones for eyes. Then she removed a tortoise shell comb from her hair and used it as a mouth. The snowman was grinning. "How's that?"

"Perfect." He took her hand. "Miss Norman, may I present Lord Frostbite. Seems a cold type at first, but he's warmhearted once you get to know him."

They laughed and suddenly he reached down and pelted her with a handful of snow. "I told you about snowball fights, didn't I?"

"Not fair! You have to give me time to make some!"

"Three minutes, not a second longer. Then you're fair game."

They stockpiled their efforts a few yards apart. "Time!" Luke called suddenly and hurled a snowball at her.

He'd made more than she, and his aim was better. "Give up?" he shouted after a few seconds.

"Not a chance!" She landed a hit.

He charged across the distance between them brandishing an enormous snowball and shouting lustily. She ducked and he tripped over her skirt, and they were rolling together in the soft snow, giggling like children in a tickling match.

Then he kissed her.

He'd done so before, in an avuncular fashion that bespoke the five years between them, little affectionate pecks on her forehead or her cheek. This was different. His mouth covered hers and remained so for a long time. When he lifted his head they stared at each other in silence. "Sorry," Luke said at last. "I'd no right to do that."

She didn't answer, because she didn't know what to say, and because her heart was pounding and her breath was coming in short hard gasps not caused by the exertion of the snowball fight.

He drew her to her feet and brushed the snow from her coat. It was of plum-colored wool, with a fox collar, and she wore a matching hat. Her face, surrounded by the silvery fur, was an ivory cameo flushed pink. Her large brown eyes looked at him questioningly. Luke leaned forward and kissed her again, on the forehead this time.

"Come along, little one," he said softly. "I'll take you to Schrafft's for hot chocolate and cookies. Good little girls always get a treat."

Warren Westerman had turned his study into a greenhouse. He nursed there the myriad cuttings taken from the garden at Balmoral. "I think this rose is going to root, Amy," he told her with enthusiasm. "I didn't think it would. Roses are difficult."

She looked carefully at the fragile stem. A tiny new shoot was emerging from the tip. "Yes, I'm sure it is. Congratulations, Uncle Warren. That takes skill."

He moved the plantlet closer to the light. He had abolished the drapes and pushed the furniture to one side to make room for a long table in front of the windows. It was covered with pots and jars and an assortment of kitchenware pressed into service as containers for greenery. "They will almost all be ready for planting out next spring."

Amy wondered where he intended to make his new garden. Perhaps he and Lil were buying a summer home of their own. Before she could ask he said, "Did you have roses in German East Africa?" It was the first time he'd ever asked her a direct question.

"No roses," she said. "Mummy tried, but they didn't thrive. Have you ever seen a flame tree?"

He admitted he hadn't, and she described the beautiful trees with scarlet blossoms lining the long avenue to Jericho. "You and Aunt Lil must come and visit as soon as I go home. You'll love it."

"Are you planning to go home after the war is over?" he asked, adjusting the position of a jam jar filled with privet sprays.

"Yes, of course." She was surprised that he didn't know. "Everyone at Jericho will be waiting for me. The servants have all been with us for years. And all Mummy's and Daddy's things are there."

"Your mother and father were happy in Africa, I believe."

"Oh yes, and so was I. You'll come and visit, won't you?" She was suddenly full of tenderness for this taciturn, sere old man.

"I don't travel much," he said softly. "It's kind of you to invite me, however."

"But I owe you both so much! I know you were Daddy's friends, and you've been such good friends to me. I want you to come."

He looked away. "I knew your father of course, for many years. I cannot claim to have been his friend. He and Charles were very close always. But I was older and . . ."

"And what, Uncle Warren?" She wanted to hear more of her father's youth. The subject had begun to prick her curiosity of late.

"And less tolerant," he said.

It struck her as a strange remark. "I don't quite follow you."

He favored her with one of his rare smiles. "Never mind, it was all a long time ago. You get on well with Luke, don't you?" he said, changing the subject abruptly. "You see a lot of him."

"He's very kind to me." Amy fingered the velvet leaf of a clump of potted violets.

"Luke's a nice boy." Warren seemed to be forcing out the words, as if mentioning Luke's virtues was painful. "He's very religious you know. I think it's because he almost died when he was a small child."

"I didn't know that."

"No one ever mentions it now. But he was very ill. For many weeks. Cecily was beside herself. I remember it well."

"I'm glad he recovered." She didn't know what else to say.

"Yes. Such things have consequences though. You must realize that."

"Luke seems perfectly healthy to me."

"Oh, he is of course." Warren changed tack abruptly. "Tommy's coming home for Thanksgiving, isn't he?"

"I suppose so. I haven't heard from him lately."

"I'm sure he's coming home. Lil told me. This week I think. It will be nice to see him again."

Amy agreed and escaped to her own room. The atmosphere in the makeshift greenhouse had become disturbing.

She went with Luke to meet Tommy's train. He was reserved, and his limp was pronounced. "Did you hurt yourself?" Luke inquired anxiously.

"No, I bloody well didn't! I'm just tired that's all. Had to stand most of the way." He flung his case into the back of the taxi and sat up front with the driver so they had no further opportunity to talk.

That was on Tuesday. Amy didn't see either Luke or Tommy again until Thursday noon when they arrived at the apartment for Thanksgiving dinner. They seemed barely on speaking terms, and the conversation during the meal was strained, despite all Lil's efforts.

Later Lil played the piano. She had all the latest sheet music, Berlin's "Araby" and "When I Leave the World Behind," as well as Amy's favorite Cohan song, "Give My Regards to Broadway." Amy wanted very much to dance with Luke. In the past Tommy had always been good-natured about the things he couldn't do, but he looked surly and black this afternoon. Luke didn't ask her to dance.

They were expected at one of the other aunt's for a holiday tea. At the last minute Tommy refused to go, so they left him behind.

The tea party was crowded with relatives. Donald Varley was there, and Luke spent a long time talking to him. Amy was involved in a conversation with the girl who had recently become engaged. It centered on bridal dresses and honeymoon plans, and she felt stupid and young and tongue-tied.

When they returned to the apartment Tommy was gone and the decanter of brandy on the table was almost empty. Luke left right away, without saying when he'd see her next.

The next day Amy felt guilty, as if she were to blame for Tommy's bad temper and the way it had spoiled the holiday. Lil was regretful too. "Why don't you ring up the boys," she said anxiously. "See if they'd like to come for supper and help eat the leftover turkey. It's always better the second day."

Amy tried the number, but there was no reply. "No one seems to be home," she reported. "Not even the maid. Isn't that odd?"

Lil fumbled with the fichu of lace at her throat. "Not really. I believe Luke manages with only a weekly cleaning woman now. He's on his own most of the time, and he has so many of his meals here," she added hastily.

They didn't mention the boys again. Amy went riding on Saturday afternoon. The rest of the time she kept to her room and read.

On Sunday morning Luke arrived alone. Only Amy was home. "Lil and Warren are at church," she explained. "How come you're not?"

"I couldn't sleep, so I went early. Lots of maids and bus drivers and people like that. Quite nice, really."

She knew that it was customary for all the Westermans to attend the eleven o'clock high mass at St. Ignatius. Tommy had once described it to her. "Mustering the forces for a full dress parade," he'd called it. She thought of that every Sunday when she saw Warren depart in his morning coat and striped trousers and spats. She had wondered if Luke wore the same formal attire on those occasions. He certainly wasn't dressed like that this morning. He was wearing trousers and a sweater. The casual clothes emphasized his long, lean body.

"Is Tommy coming here after Mass?" she asked. "I should tell Maureen if there's going to be extras for lunch."

"Tommy's gone back to Washington. He left yesterday."

"But he didn't even come to say good-bye! Lil and Warren will be hurt."

"I know. He can be a sod sometimes. And we had a row, which made it worse."

She felt again that uncomfortable sensation of guilt. "I've never seen you and Tommy fight seriously."

"This was a humdinger. Don't look like that. It will blow over. Things are a little tense just now, that's all. And his leg was hurting, for all he denied it."

"What did you fight about?"

Luke flashed his incomparable sunny smile. Amy had begun to suspect that he used the smile and his good looks as a way of keeping others at arm's length. "We disagreed about some suggestions Uncle Donald has made about financial matters. That's all."

She moved closer to him. Luke hadn't kissed her since the day in the park three weeks before, not even a brotherly peck on the forehead. Now she stood on tiptoe and kissed his cheek. "You mustn't worry about anything," she said. "And you must never fight with Tommy about me."

"You! My dear girl, you're getting too big for your boots! Fight about a mere child, indeed." He laughed at her and tweaked her nose. "Maybe when you grow up. Certainly not now. Let's have some music."

He could play almost as well as Lil, and she sat next to him on the piano bench and turned the pages. Sometimes they broke off and practiced a dance step. Luke was a superb dancer. He held her masterfully and moved with the same effortless coordination he displayed on the tennis court.

6

SARAH, THE ENGAGED WESTERMAN COUSIN, WAS
launched on a series of prenuptial festivities. Amy was
usually invited. She listened to endless talk of wed-
dings. Visions of white satin and filmy lace began to
fill her mind.

Luke collected her from a tea party at the home of a
relative on Sixty-first Street. "Shall we walk or take a
cab?"

"Let's walk. It's early yet."

They strolled up Lexington Avenue in the wintery
dusk, past St. Vincent Ferrer's Church where she had
waited for him that summer's day when they came

together to the city. The memory was unspoken, but acknowledged, between them. "I know you so much better now," she said. "It seems like we were strangers back then."

"Amy, listen. I want to tell you something. . . ."

She couldn't see him clearly in the half-light, but she turned her face expectantly.

He stopped walking. "You are a little beauty you know," he said softly. "You'd thwart the resolve of a saint."

"I don't know what you mean."

"No, I know you don't." He was so much taller that she had to bend her head back to look into his eyes. He raised his gloved hands and trailed his fingers along her arched neck. It rose with a grace above the fur collar of her coat. "I know you don't understand," he said in a whisper. "That's what makes it so hard."

"You think I'm a child. I'm not. Girls grow up faster in Africa. Anyway, your cousin Sarah's not nineteen yet, and she's getting married in February. She said it had to be then or not until Easter."

"Yes, Catholics can't get married in Lent."

She didn't know what Lent was, but to ask would switch the subject from marriage. "I'm not a child," she repeated. "I'll be eighteen in May."

"Oh, Amy, precious little girl." He sounded as if he wanted to cry, and she didn't know what comfort to offer. Then he smiled, and she thought she must have imagined the incipient tears. "We'd better get moving. Aunt Lil will think I've kidnapped you."

Lil, however, was not conscious of the time they'd been out. She was instead pale and distraught, but offered no explanation. The apartment was heavy with tension. Warren too was weighed down with it, and Maureen looked baleful while she served dinner. Amy glanced questioningly at Luke, but he only shrugged his shoulders in puzzlement.

They had coffee in the drawing room. Suddenly Lil looked up, as if newly aware of her nephew.

"Shouldn't we ask Luke what he thinks, Warren?"

Lil's hands fluttered at her pearls, twisted an embroidered handkerchief, and finally spread in a gesture of appeal. Warren said nothing. He'd ignored his sister's rhetorical questions for so long that he no longer imagined any reply necessary.

"Luke must know about such things now that he's working," Lil added. Warren grunted. Lil took it as assent. Amy saw the way the older woman was readying herself to explain, and felt fear.

"Warren wants to buy a summer cottage on Long Island," Lil blurted out. "Of course, it wouldn't change anything here." This last was spoken with a look at Maureen's retreating back. The maid carried the coffee tray from the room with the air of a martyr.

Amy wanted to giggle, but she repressed her laughter. She'd expected disaster and it was only this. Instantly she felt herself on Warren's side. "What a nice idea! Does it have a garden, Uncle Warren?"

It was the one question guaranteed a response. "Not really, but there's a nice bit of ground out back."

So there would be a home for his tenderly nurtured cuttings from Balmoral. That explained his motive.

"Where on Long Island?" Luke asked.

"A little town, just a village, I guess," Lil stammered. "Atlantic Beach." When Luke looked blank she added, "It's out beyond Far Rockaway and Lawrence. Isn't that what you said, Warren?"

"Not beyond," Warren said. "Across from. They're separated by East Rockaway Inlet."

"There's no church in Atlantic Beach," Lil said. The words tumbled forth in a rush that was almost a wail. "And no permanent settlement. We'd never be able to find servants."

"Maureen can come with us when we go," Warren said.

Now Amy understood the cause of the maid's hostility. Customarily Maureen spent summers with her sister in the Bronx and returned to Manhattan when her employers did. A new arrangement wouldn't suit her at all, but that couldn't be Lil's main worry. "How far is the nearest church, Uncle Warren?" Amy asked.

"There's one in Far Rockaway. It's no problem."

Lil shook her head. "But you told me we would have to cross a bridge to get to the mainland. In bad weather we could be cut off." She looked close to tears.

Luke ignored her distress and turned to his uncle. "How much are they asking?"

Finally Warren took the initiative. "Not they. He. A builder. He's completed three houses, and he's working on a fourth. It's going to be a flourishing community some day. We're getting in on the ground floor."

"How much?" Luke repeated.

"Two thousand seven hundred," Warren said.

Luke looked thoughtful—and something else. Amy

thought about it. Masterful. Yes, that was the word. Her heart gave a funny little thud. She kept watching his face. He said gravely, "It sounds reasonable. Depending on the house, of course. Why don't you go take a look at it, Aunt Lil? After that you can make up your mind."

Amy saw Warren shift in his chair and open his mouth as if to say something, then close it again. It was Lil who asked, "Would you come too, Luke? I'd feel better if you saw it."

Warren didn't react to the implication that his judgment was unreliable. Amy felt a twinge of impatience at his placid acceptance of Lil's dominance.

"I'm rather busy just now," Luke said.

Obviously Luke didn't want to be in the middle of a feud between his aunt and uncle. Amy was annoyed with all of them for making such a fuss and at the same time hiding so much emotion. "We could go on a Sunday," she said. Nobody had invited her, but she included herself. It would mean a whole day with Luke.

Lil looked at her gratefully. "Oh, that would be nice! But Saturday, not Sunday. That way we wouldn't have to worry about Mass. You don't work on Saturday, do you, Luke?"

"Half a day," he said. Both women were watching him and he relented. "I guess I could take one morning off."

"We'll bring a picnic lunch," Amy said. "You'll see, it will be fun."

*   *   *

Despite his early reluctance, it was Luke who made it fun. He borrowed a big Lincoln touring car from one of his relatives. There was room for all five of them. Amy had suggested that they take Maureen, and Lil had seen the wisdom of the idea. Besides, the maid was useful because they had so much luggage. They were only going for the day, but Lil believed she was setting forth into the unknown. She'd brought two hampers of food and an assortment of wraps and galoshes and blankets—just in case.

The freak November blizzard had been replaced by an early December thaw. The sky was deep blue and there were few clouds. The winter-distant sun created an illusion of warmth. Amy looked over the shiny black hood of the Lincoln at a city basking in false spring.

Pushcarts and taxis and bicycles clogged the traffic. Heading east on Fifty-ninth Street they crossed the path of streetcars jammed with passengers who hung out open windows and tipped pale faces to the sun. Luke didn't mind driving through the melee. He began singing, "Daisy, Daisy, give me your answer do . . ." His rich baritone filled the car and bounced off the elegant red leather upholstery. Amy joined in. She was very happy.

Then they crossed the Fifty-ninth Street Bridge and it took her breath away. She didn't look down. Nothing in nature frightened her; but this feat of technology, this city-bred phenomenon arcing through space on perilously slender steel cables, made her dizzy.

"Are you all right?" Luke reached over and touched her clenched hands.

"Yes, fine." She spoke in a small whisper, embarrassed lest the others know she was afraid, and acutely conscious of the light touch of his fingers.

Long Island City, where the bridge debouched, was grim and ugly. It was an excrescence belonging in spirit neither to Long Island nor Manhattan. Amy was glad when they left it behind and moved out into the countryside.

Someone mentioned being thirsty. Lil glanced at her watch and said that it was time to stop for a snack. Luke fouund a spot overlooking a meadow and parked the car. Maureen rummaged in one of the hampers and produced a Thermos flask of hot coffee and some bread and butter. Amy took her cup and wandered a short distance up the road. Nearby two old horses grazed peacefully. She leaned on the fence and watched them. Luke came up beside her. "They look like candidates for the glue factory to me."

"Yes. Old plough horses that have no further use, I expect. Luke, do you think it's a good idea for Lil and Warren to buy a place out here?"

"I'll tell you a secret," he confided. His voice was pitched low. "It doesn't matter what any of us thinks. Uncle Warren's already bought it."

Amy's eyes opened wide. "But what if Lil hates it after she sees it?"

"I don't know." He shook his head. "I don't think they've ever had a serious disagreement. Lil always does what she wants, and Warren goes along. We've just got to convince her the house is marvelous. Otherwise there's going to be a devil of a scene."

"She should like it." Amy said with conviction. "It's beautiful here in the country. Why do they live in New York anyway?"

Luke chuckled. "Some people prefer the city, you know. Anyway, Warren only intends them to live here in the summer."

"Do you prefer the city?" She searched his deep blue eyes for an answer. "Would you be unhappy living away from New York?" He couldn't know how important his answer was to her. She didn't take her eyes from his face.

"I like New York," he said. "But I don't think where you live is important, as long as it's where you're meant to be."

"You mean fate or destiny? Something like that?"

His smile broadened. "I mean God. And there you go getting that tight look you get whenever I mention the word."

"You're teasing me."

"You're very teasable. I like the way your eyes spark when you get mad." He reached into his waistcoat pocket and took out his watch. "Almost eleven," he said. "We'd better go. I think there's still an hour or more to drive." They'd left the house at seven. Lil really would think she was traveling to the end of the world.

It wasn't as warm on Long Island as it had been in New York. Amy buttoned the jacket of her blue wool suit and nestled more comfortably into the plaid lap-robe Luke had arranged over her knees. The road cut across brown salt marshes, thick with reeds and birds. It reminded her of the area north of Boston. "It's a bit like New England," she said.

"Geologically Long Island is part of New England," Warren said. He explained, a rather long speech for him, but the technical terms and references to the long-ago Ice Age bored Amy. Her mind wandered. Warren lapsed into silence and no one else spoke. Luke wasn't singing any more. With every mile they put between themselves and Manhattan the tension increased. Amy could feel it, emanating from Lil, and being silently but stubbornly ignored by Warren.

A little past noon they reached Lawrence, and could look across a small bay to Far Rockaway. The big summer houses were all closed and boarded over. They stood like hulking sentinels, exposed by leafless trees that skirted long impressive drives.

"The bridge to Atlantic Beach should be on our left." Warren said.

"Have you been here before, Uncle Warren?" Amy asked.

"No, I've seen pictures. And a map."

So he had bought the house sight unseen. Amy marveled at the audacity of it, but when she remembered the cuttings she understood. If Lil didn't agree to join him, Warren was quite prepared to spend his summers there alone. Sometimes, Amy realized, people are absolutely determined to have their own way. She mulled over the notion and decided she approved of it. Her estimation of Warren was growing by the minute.

Luke found the bridge that spanned the narrow tidal channel known as East Rockaway Inlet. He drove the Lincoln across, and they had arrived. But where? Atlantic Beach was nothing. Not even a village. Off to their right was a distant coast guard station, with a high tower that interrupted the expanse of sea and sky. In front of them was the breakwater that divided the inlet from the ocean, and a long sandy beach. That was all.

Amy turned to look at Lil. The older woman was very pale, but she said nothing. Beside her Maureen sniffed and pressed a handkerchief to her running nose. Warren stared straight ahead, refusing to acknowledge the desolation. Luke finally broke the silence. "Where's the house supposed to be, Uncle Warren?"

"To the left. One hundred twenty Montgomery Street." It sounded absurd. Where were the other one hundred and nineteen? Amy swallowed a giggle.

They drove along a dirt road. Finally they saw a cluster of obviously new houses and a few weather-beaten shacks. There was a crude grid of streets, apparently laid out by someone with more faith than realism. One bore a signpost that said Montgomery, and they followed it to three finished houses and a half-constructed fourth.

Number one-twenty was on a corner of sorts, close to the beach and the ocean. It was a sizable two-story house built of white stucco with a red tile roof. There was a screened entry porch. The door leading to it was locked, but Warren produced a set of keys. He stood aside for his sister to enter.

"I'm going out back to see the yard," Warren said when they were all huddled together in the cold and silent foyer.

Lil stared after him. Amy took her hand and tugged her toward the stairway. "Come, Aunt Lil, let's start at the top and work our way down." They left Luke to cope with Maureen, who was still sniffling loudly.

There were four bedrooms and two baths. Amy remarked on the nice size of the rooms and the pleasant views. Lil said nothing. She followed the girl around on stiff wooden legs.

"Here's the maid's quarters," Amy said. They were in a rear suite comprising two rooms and a bath. "You know, I think Maureen will be impressed with this. After all she only has one room in the apartment." The rooms were small, and the view was only of the neighboring house. Still, the fact of two separate rooms was likely to strike Maureen as luxury. "I think we'd better get her up here to see this right away," Amy said. "It may stop her moaning."

"It's so empty, so far from everything," Lil whispered. "I couldn't live here. Warren just has to see that."

Amy studied the pale, crumpled face. Then she made a hasty decision. "Listen, Aunt Lil, he's afraid to tell you himself, but Warren's already bought the house."

"No! He couldn't do that. Not without my agreement. We've always done these things together. Why when we bought the apartment . . ."

"He's desperate for a garden, you know that. And this place was offered at a price he could afford."

"No," Lil said again. But with less conviction.

"It's true, Luke told me." She took the older woman's hands in hers. "Warren means to live here alone if you won't join him. That would be a shame, Aunt Lil. You'd both be so lonely."

"Alone? Without me?"

"I think so, yes. But I'm sure he'd much prefer it if you'd live here with him."

Lil walked to the window and stood looking at the

wall of the next house. Finally she turned back to Amy. Slowly a change came over her features. She had been ghostly pale; now she flushed. The thin lips trembled for a moment, then set in a half-smile. It was forced, but firmly held in place. "Of course if Warren's made up his mind . . . These other houses are sure to be sold soon. And more will probably be built." She turned and hurried out of the maid's suite to a large bedroom with a superb view of the sea. "This could be my room. I could paint it pale blue. What do you think, Amy? Is blue too cold a color?"

"I think it's a lovely choice for a summer house."

Lil nodded and looked at her watch. "Goodness! It's after one. We'd better have our picnic lunch."

All the while she nibbled roast chicken and picked at potato salad Amy thought about the lessons of the morning. Getting what you want is largely a matter of determination, she decided. And knowing whether you want it badly enough.

"How about a walk on the beach before we start back?" she said after they'd eaten.

"You two youngsters go do that," Lil said. She sounded like her old self when she added, "I want to measure some of these windows. It will take forever to get the curtains made. Warren, you must tell me whether you mean to have the bedroom next to mine, or the one across the hall."

"You decide," he said. "It doesn't matter to me." He left to go back to the barren yard heaped with builder's rubble in which he planned to make a garden.

Luke grinned at Amy, and they slipped out the door and headed for the beach. "Now, tell me what you said up there," he demanded. "When Lil went upstairs with you she was horrified. When she came down she'd given in."

"I told her the truth. That Warren had bought the house and meant to spend his summers in it. With or without her."

Luke stopped in his tracks and stared at her. "Little Amy," he said softly, "you are a very tough lady."

She shook her head. "No," she said. "But sometimes I understand how things are."

They walked the length of the deserted beach. The tide was out, and the ocean was a lacy froth trembling in the distance. Amy turned and looked back the way they'd come. "The houses are little dollops of cream on the horizon."

Luke took her hand. "Don't look back, Amy, look forward."

She was not quite sure what he meant. "What does that look like to you?" She nodded toward the coast guard station. The spit of land that was Atlantic Beach narrowed at this point, and the building was close behind them. They could see the boat ramp reaching into the inlet and the tower high above.

"I don't know," Luke said. "I've no gift for metaphor."

"Cyclops, the one-eyed giant."

"He wasn't very nice."

"No, let's forget about him." She had left her hat at the house and a soft breeze ruffled her dark hair. December was still pretending to be May. "It's beautiful here. If I were Lil, I'd never want to go back."

He smiled and took her upturned face between his hands. "Don't be Lil. Don't be a spinster, Amy. You're meant for love and marriage and all the happy things."

Their eyes caught and held. Amy's lips parted slightly. She felt his fingers lightly touching her cheeks. Tentatively, she put her hands on his arms.

"Oh, God," Luke whispered. It was half-prayer and half-curse. Then he was holding her tight and his mouth was on hers and it was like that day in Central Park, only more so. This time they tasted each other avidly, hungrily. Their tongues probed and their bodies locked so close it was as if there were no layers of clothes separating their flesh. His hands moved down her spine. He was feeling, groping, seeking. She shivered beneath his touch. Her fingers tangled in his thick blond hair and held his face against hers. The kiss went on and on. Luke's hands were on her buttocks pressing her even closer. She felt him move. His hard taut body seemed to imprint itself on the softness of her belly, her thighs, and her breasts.

Finally the kiss ended, but neither of them moved out of the embrace. Amy buried her face in his shoulder. She nuzzled his neck and smelled the warm spicy maleness of his skin. She heard him moan and sensed the increased urgency of the movement of his hips. Her tongue licked his flesh. She wanted to bite, to devour the essence of all that was Luke. He made a sound deep in his throat that ended in a gasp. It was like nothing she'd ever heard. There was something elementary in that cry. It frightened her and pleased her at the same time, and Amy could interpret neither feeling.

Suddenly he let her go and almost pushed her away. "Oh, God," he said again.

Luke turned and walked some distance from her. Amy stared after him. His shoes raised little puffs of sand, then he stood still and stared out at the ocean. She put her hands to her face. Her cheeks were hot, but she was shivering. For some unaccountable reason she wanted to laugh aloud. She wanted to strip off her clothes and run into the icy sea. She only smoothed her skirt over her hips and adjusted the collar of her jacket. A few minutes passed. Then Luke returned to where she stood.

He reached out to touch her again, then drew his hand back, as if she were fire and he would be burned.

"Listen to me," he said, his voice low and urgent. "What happened, what we, that is, what I did. I don't want you frightened."

I'm not frightened, Amy thought. You are. She didn't say anything, just kept looking at him.

"It's natural and even beautiful," he said, "but only when you're married. This way it's all wrong. That's not your fault, it's mine. You're too young and innocent to know better."

She didn't know what he was talking about, but she didn't care. Married, he'd said. She had watched his sensitive mouth form the word. Married. Two people joined together for always; sharing a home, their hearts, the very air they breathed. Married. Mrs. Luke Westerman. Yes, Amy thought. Oh, yes!

Don't say anything, Eve-like instinct warned her instantly. Not yet. "It's okay," she whispered. "Don't worry." She smiled at him, and all the sunshine of her seventeen years was in that smile. "Come," she said quietly. "The others will be waiting."

He nodded and they retraced their steps along the beach toward the new houses thrust so incongruously into the primitive landscape. "They don't look as if they belong at all," Amy said. Luke merely grunted. He was still lost in his own thoughts. Amy didn't mind. She understood everything with her pores, her nerves, and her instinct. Married, her blood sang. Married, married, married.

For a day or two she worried that he might start avoiding her because the truth she perceived so clearly was a worry or an embarrassment for him. "Men can be very difficult," her mother had sometimes said with a sigh. Usually the comment followed some obstinacy of Daddy's or some small quarrel. But Jessie had smiled knowingly at her daughter, and in a brief time the cloud, whatever it may have been, was lifted. Amy had learned the lesson well, without ever realizing that she'd learned it.

She took to washing her hair every other day, so that she would look her best whenever Luke appeared. Each morning she dressed with special care, grateful for the pretty new things Lil had made her buy and no longer worried about the expense. After four days her patience was rewarded.

"Luke's coming for dinner this evening," Lil said on Wednesday. "Shall we have pot roast or chicken?"

"Whatever you think," Amy said. What did she care about food? Luke was coming. Lil, accustomed to never getting answers to her questions, went to the kitchen to confer with Maureen. Amy danced around

the room and hummed the wedding march, silently, so
that only she could hear.

That night Luke was relaxed, animated, and charming. He was his old self. While she dressed, Amy had
worried just a tiny bit. Perhaps he'd be stiff or embarrassed because he had half proposed, and now he
didn't know how to finish it and make it official. I'll
have to find some way to put him at his ease, she'd
thought. But it wasn't necessary. He laughed at her
and teased her and complimented Lil, and as always
the whole apartment seemed alive and new just because he was there.

"I saw an old friend of yours today," Luke mentioned to his aunt. "Father Clement at St. Vincent's.
He sends you a big hello."

"How nice," Lil said. Then, to Amy, "I knew him
years ago before he was a Dominican. Joe Devereaux
he was in those days. How did you happen to see
him?" she asked Luke. "I'd heard he was sent to the
missions."

"He was. Caught some tropical disease and had to
come home. He's ok now. He was hearing confessions. Just coming out of the box when I got to church."

Amy had a mental image of a man stepping out of a
coffin. Catholics certainly had some weird ideas. "What
are confessions?" she asked.

Luke laughed and patted her hand. "The sacrament
of penance," he said. He was off on a long explanation, but she only half heard. She was watching his
face. The way his mouth moved, the smile in his deep
blue eyes. He was happy and peaceful. She could tell
by the way he looked and sounded. It did not occur to

her that his calm was related to his visit to church and this thing called confession. Luke, she told herself, was beginning to know what she knew.

"I've got two tickets for the Saturday matinee of the new Cohan review," Lil announced over coffee. "I meant them as a surprise for Amy. Now I don't see how I can go because I'm so busy with plans for the new house. Can you take her Luke?"

Amy flushed. Lil made her sound like a child that needed a nurse. "It's all right if you've something else planned," she said hastily.

Luke hesitated for only a fraction of a second. "Never too busy to be your escort, princess."

He brought her chocolate truffles to eat at the theater and they had a box and the show was marvelous. Amy was excited and very happy. She kept casting sidelong glances at Luke and comparing him to all the other men in the audience and on stage. No one was as handsome or as wonderful. Luke moved with more elegance than the dancers, and there was something else that at first she couldn't put a name to. It was power, she decided. Luke was so tall and lean and self-assured. When he helped her off with her coat or conferred with her over the program his every move was perfect. Once she glanced up and caught sight of the two of them reflected in a gilt-framed mirror. Luke so blond, she so dark. We're a handsome couple, she told herself. Even when we're old we'll look beautiful together. Together, married . . . her blood was still singing that new and irrefutable truth.

They were together almost daily for the next week. Errands to be done for Lil, meetings at lunchtime to go to the library and find a book he wanted Amy to read, dinner at the apartment. It was as if Luke somehow knew what she loved most in him and acted accordingly. He was more sure, more graceful, more Luke. His manner seemed to lose the trace of shyness and hesitancy he'd previously had with her. Amy decided that the day on the beach had confirmed things for him too. He knows, she told herself. Now it's just a matter of the right moment. When that moment came they would speak aloud their love. They would become engaged.

The weather relinquished its pretence of spring and turned bitterly cold. Amy didn't mind; she was warm inside. Lil was deep in Christmas preparations. Amy debated about what she'd give Luke, and dreamed that he might present her with a ring. Christmas would be a lovely time to get engaged.

Close to five one Monday evening Lil knocked on the door of Amy's room. "Darling, I've been such a fool. I saw a nice scarf for Warren at Macy's this afternoon, but there were so many people at the counter I didn't want to wait. Now I'm afraid it will be gone by tomorrow. They're open until six and I was wondering. . ."

"Of course, Aunt Lil. I'll go right away."

She was leaving the building just as Luke arrived. He was earlier than usual. "The heating in our office broke down," he explained, "so we closed early. Where are you off to?"

"Macy's. Aunt Lil needs something." She saw the way he looked at her, and she was conscious of her hat. It was green velvet with a fur trim. She knew it made a ravishing frame for her face. "Care to come?" she asked.

"I'd love to. I haven't seen Macy's window this year."

All the way to Herald Square he regaled her with stories of when he was a kid and he and Tommy were taken to see Macy's Christmas window. By the time they reached the store Amy was filled with anticipation. Mr. Macy didn't disappoint her. The window was a gold and white and red fantasy. The theme was Santa Claus's workshop complete with all the elves. Lots of the parts moved, and there was a clock that chimed every quarter hour and opened miniature doors to display within a group of dancing figurines.

"It's gorgeous," she said with delight, turning her face up to Luke. "I've never seen anything like it."

"Nothing like this in Africa, eh?" He grinned and tweaked her nose and added that they had to hurry or the store would close before they got the scarf.

When they came out the streets were even more crowded and a few snowflakes had started to fall. "Let's be extravagant and take a cab," Luke said. "The streetcars are horrible at this hour."

The taxi was warm and dark and snug, and it moved slowly because of the traffic. When it turned the corner of Forty-second Street it lurched slightly on the wet road, and Amy was thrown against Luke. She stayed there, loving the closeness of him and the smell of his damp overcoat mingling with the smell of him.

Luke stiffened. Men could be difficult, just as Mummy used to say, and stupidly shy and blind. She reached up and laid her gloved hand on his cheek. He moaned and covered it with his and then he was kiss-

ing her again and it was as it had been on Long Island.
The same urgency, the same rightness. They couldn't
press together as they had on the beach, not in the
back of a taxi, but his hands stroked her and his
mouth moved against hers.

"Oh, God, Amy," he muttered when the kiss ended.

"It's all right, Luke," she whispered. The assertion
was drawn out of her without her knowing how or
why. "We're right."

"I don't know. I just don't know."

"Here you are sir, Seventy-sixth and Fifth," the cab
driver said. His voice broke the mood.

After that she didn't know how he'd be during dinner, but he was wonderful. He seemed almost eu-
phoric. Gay and witty, and seeking opportunities to
touch her hand or find her eyes when no one else was
looking. Tonight, she thought. Tonight he's going to
propose! If only Lil and Warren would leave us alone
for a bit.

But they didn't. They seemed almost to conspire to
avoid the very thing Amy longed for. After dinner
neither brother nor sister left the drawing room as
they usually did. Finally it was eleven and Luke said
good night and left. Bitterly disappointed, Amy didn't
sleep well.

That night she had a strange dream. She was in
Africa in a grove of trees beside a river. She knew the
place well; it wasn't far from Jericho. There was a
waterfall and behind it a small cave. Amy knew that
too. She'd explored it years before, when she was
small. Luke was with her and he didn't believe the
cave was there. "Come," she said in her dream, "I'll
prove it to you." They took off their clothes, as if it

was the most natural thing in the world, and she felt
no shyness because a white cloud enveloped them
both. Then they plunged into the river and swam to
the falls. The next instant they were in the cave, and
the covering clouds had melted away. "Now we're
clean," the dream Amy said. The dream Luke nodded
and took her in his arms. His hips moved against hers
the way they had on the beach, but when she looked
over his shoulder she saw an enormous lion watching
them from the other side of the river. It was distorted
by the sheet of falling water, but she knew it was the
biggest lion in the world. Amy waited for Luke to gasp
the way he had before, but she awoke before it happened. She was shivering and a lump of tears choked
her throat.

The next evening Luke was entirely different. He
was expected for dinner and he came, but he was
withdrawn and almost cold. And now, when he was
like this, Lil and Warren did what they hadn't done
the night before, they left them alone.

"I have to talk to you," Luke said.

No, a voice shouted in her head. Not when he's in
this mood. "I have a headache," she lied. "I think I'll
go to bed."

"Please," he said. "It won't take long."

She looked around for an escape or an interruption.
She felt like an animal trapped in a pit. The hunters
were waiting and their spears were sharp. "You're
wonderful, Amy," Luke said. "I enjoy being with you
so much. But. . ."

"I really don't feel well," she said. Her voice was too loud, and she forced herself to lower it. "I'm sorry, I must go to bed."

"Sometimes I'm not sure," he continued as if he hadn't heard her. "Sometimes I think maybe I've been wrong all along, and you've been sent to prove it to me. Other times I know it's just a test."

"Sent by whom?" she demanded. "A test of what?" As soon as she asked the questions, Amy knew that she'd made a terrible mistake. Now she really was ill. She would faint if she didn't get out of this room. She left him without another word, ran to her bedroom, and closed the door hard behind her. Then she stood leaning against it, trying to catch her breath and to hear what was happening in the apartment.

There was the sound of low voices. Soon the outside door opened and shut. Luke had said good night to Lil and left. A minute passed and she began to feel a little calmer. Nothing irrevocable had been said. She would have to think and plan. Then she'd find a way to make it all right again. A light tap on the door intruded on her thoughts.

"It's Aunt Lil, darling. Luke said you were ill."

"It's nothing really." Amy knew that she should be polite and open the door, but she couldn't make herself do it. "Just a headache. I'll be fine in the morning."

Lil made sympathetic noises and offered her tea.

"Nothing, thank you. I just want to sleep."

Finally she heard Lil's footsteps moving away. She threw herself on the bed fully dressed. He doesn't love me, she thought. But she knew he did. She'd seen it in his eyes, felt it in his touch. She was young and inex-

perienced, but she couldn't be mistaken about that.
Then why was he resisting her and his own desires?
His religion perhaps. But that was mad! What did she
care about religion? She would become a Catholic too,
if that was what he wanted. She must find some way to
let him know that. She'd ask questions about his church,
and this time she'd really listen to his answers. And
she'd stop telling him she didn't believe in God.

Satisfied that she had some new insight into both
the problem and the solution, Amy got up and undressed. She was glad that she'd managed to forestall
tonight's conversation. At least she had gained time.
She told herself that everything was going to be all
right, and finally she slept. But she had the same
dream, and this time the lion seemed closer and even
more menacing.

It was late when she woke. There was a message for
her. Donald Varley wanted to see her as soon as
possible, today if she could arrange it. She telephoned
his secretary and made an appointment for the same
afternoon. There was no word from Luke, and she
was glad that he didn't arrive for lunch as he sometimes did. She needed more time.

When Amy was seated by Varley's desk he told his
secretary to bring tea. He insisted that Amy have a
cup right away, as if she'd braved an exhausting and
perilous ordeal to join him. She thought of telling him
about riding alone through the African bush, but decided against it.

"I understand you are very friendly with my nephew
Luke," Varley said. "You like Tommy too, don't you?"

Amy nodded at him over the rim of the teacup. Her
large brown eyes grew wary.

But Donald Varley didn't sound a warning. Instead he said, "I think it's a fine thing, considering how close your parents all were. Fine to see that kind of loyalty continued. Gives me hope for the modern world."

She set down her cup and waited.

"Amy, I must speak very frankly, and in a manner no gentleman likes. If your poor mother and father were alive, none of this would be necessary. But since they aren't and you're alone, I have no choice but to do my duty."

She stiffened her spine. She was ready to flee or deny or fight back—whatever was required. There was a shining inside her, a fire of love and wanting. Nothing Donald Varley could say would extinguish it.

He cleared his throat. "Before Charles died he made some unfortunate investments. My brother-in-law was brilliant, but on this occasion he was unlucky. It means that he died in straitened circumstances. Do you understand, my dear?"

"You're referring to money," Amy said. Relief flooded up from her toes to end in a bright flush on her cheeks.

Varley interpreted the blush as embarrassment. "I am. It pains me dreadfully to discuss such a matter with you. Please forgive me, but. . ."

"Are Luke and Tommy in some difficulty?" she interrupted quickly. "You must tell me if there is any way I can help." She was thinking of her ring. She could give it to him to sell. It was only two carats, but it *was* perfect. She had thought of it as her own insurance against the dreaded debts at the bank.

"How easy you make it, my dear child. Bless you.

Yes, they're in a tight place, and yes, you can help. I want to make some investments for them. If I do, their future will be more secure. But there's simply no cash available in Charles's estate. I had to use the proceeds of the sale of Balmoral to pay off past debts." He poured another cup of tea while he spoke. "I've examined every option I can think of," he continued. "The only solution I see is to borrow funds to make these investments. I'm wondering if I dare ask to use your estate as collateral for such a loan."

"But of course you can!" she said instantly. "That would be a splendid solution." She thought of Tommy's black mood at Thanksgiving and the fight about business matters Luke confessed. It must have been about their poverty. Now that source of friction could be eliminated. Then she remembered something else.

"But you said my inheritance was uncertain. You said after the war I might not have anything."

"Ah, yes, so I did. And how happy I am to say that things look much better on that score. The British have secured Dar es Salaam. Almost all German East is in their hands. The British can be relied on to deal honorably. Quite a different case from the Huns."

"I knew lots of German people at home," she said softly. "They were all fair and honorable too."

He patted her hand, and she noticed that he wore a large gold signet ring. "Don't you worry about any of that. Just leave it to me. Now, do I have your permission to go ahead? Good, then there are just a few things for you to sign."

He pushed some documents across the desk. Amy scrawled her name hastily, without bothering to read them. She was conscious only of doing something to help Luke. Not until she was out of the office and descending the stairs did the true implication of the conversation dawn on her.

How could she be so stupid! This was the explanation of everything, not just Tommy's bad temper. The rush of understanding made her dizzy. Amy put out a hand and steadied herself against the wall. Luke believed that he had limited prospects, and was in debt. No wonder he didn't think he could admit his feelings, much less take a wife. He was a man of honor, and more than a little stubborn. He must think he'd be asking her to wait for years. But it wasn't like that at all! Not now that Donald Varley believed her inheritance secure.

By the time she reached the street Amy was laughing with excitement. A few passersby looked at her strangely, but she ignored them. No one in the whole world mattered except Luke. She wanted to shout his name aloud, to run and dance. She was alive to joy, every nerve in her body tingled and sang.

Her mood hadn't changed when she let herself into the apartment.

"There's a message for you, Miss Amy," Maureen said. "From Mr. Luke."

"Oh, thank you! I'll call him back right away."

"Ah, there's no need for that. Sure didn't he just say he hoped you were feeling better, and he'd be seeing you at dinner tonight."

"Thank you," Amy repeated. Then, impulsively, she planted a large loud kiss on Maureen's cheek. "Thank you for everything. You'll make something specially good tonight, won't you? Something Mr. Luke likes. It's a sort of celebration," she added shyly.

"And aren't all my dinners good?" Maureen demanded a trifle huffily, but she smiled at the girl.

Amy took a long bath before she dressed. The newly modernized bathroom adjoining her bedroom had a deep porcelain tub, and the walls were covered in shiny black paper splashed with pink lily pads. She gazed at the flowers through the haze of steam and hummed softly to herself. The tune was a Kikuyu lullaby. One of Amy's earliest memories was being rocked to its rhythm in the arms of a huge African woman.

She seemed to see Jericho in the bubbles of the tub, and she lifted the shimmering mirage in her fingers and saw herself and Luke walking hand in hand up the avenue lined with flame trees. "This is my husband," she would tell the servants. "We've come home to stay."

She dressed with great care in a gown of ecru silk trimmed with brown velvet—Lil and the dressmaker confirmed what Mummy always said: Cream was her best color. She had few jewels except her ring, so she tied a brown velvet ribbon around her neck and pinned a gold locket to it. Amy knew she looked beautiful and she was glad. She wanted to be perfect for Luke.

She waited in her room until she heard him arrive. The timbre of his voice told her his mood was nothing like it had been. This was a more familiar Luke, without the hardness and the anger that had lurked behind his words the previous evening. Amy took a last look at herself in the mirror, then went to join him.

"How lovely you look," he said.

There was the faintest catch in his voice, and when he looked at her his eyes were filled with longing. Luke could never hide what he was thinking. "We should be going out someplace special," he added, gesturing to her gown.

"Oh, no, I want to stay right here." He mustn't imagine she required a lot of expensive outings. "I'm just feeling happy. A little like celebrating." She glanced at him from beneath demurely lowered lashes, hoping he'd respond to her barely disguised excitement before he knew its source. Instead he turned away, and she saw his shoulders tense as if in pain. Don't worry, she wanted to say. I understand, everything's all right. Instead Maureen announced dinner and Amy said nothing.

She was conscious of his eyes on her all the while they ate. Lil and Warren disappeared soon after dinner. "You two young people must excuse me," Lil said. "I've a couple of letters to write." For a moment before she left the room Lil looked disturbed and a little sad. Amy put it out of her mind. She had no time for Lil's vagaries tonight. Warren muttered something about his cuttings. The door to the drawing room was left ajar, but she was alone with Luke.

Amy drew in a deep breath and mustered all her courage. She had decided to speak, and she didn't intend to back down. Still, her hands trembled where they lay folded in her lap. "I saw your Uncle Donald today," she began.

"Oh, what did he want?" Luke seemed surprised.

Amy had rehearsed this part carefully. She knew exactly what she wanted to tell and what she should keep secret. She and Mr. Varley had agreed that the Westerman boys mustn't know about the loan or the new investments. That would embarrass them. "He wanted to tell me that my inheritance appears safe now," she said. "The English have taken control of Dar es Salaam, and they've promised to deal honorably with all the foreign business interests in German East. So I'll have the mines back as soon as the war is over."

"That's wonderful, Amy, I'm glad for you. Listen, I want to talk to you about something else. . . ."

"Not just for me," she interrupted. "It's wonderful for both of us, Luke." Nervous excitement made her rise and walk to where he stood by the fireplace. A log sputtered into flame, and she leaned forward and prodded it with a brass handled poker.

"Here, let me do that. You'll burn yourself." He took the poker from her and their hands touched. The poker dropped unheeded on the hearth. It seemed to Amy that sparks rose from their joined fingers.

"You must come with me to Africa just as soon as we can travel," she said breathlessly. "You'll love Jericho. I know you will. And you can manage the mines. I think you'll like that much better than the work you're doing now. I know you don't like the finance business."

"No," he said softly. "I don't. And you are very sweet and generous. But I can't do that, my dearest Amy. I would if I could."

"Why can't you? Oh, Luke, I know how things are. I'm trying to tell you it doesn't matter. The Norman mines are very profitable, and they belong to me. At least they will."

He drew his hand from hers and walked to the sideboard and poured himself a brandy. This was unusual, because he seldom drank. She remained where she was and stared at his rigid back.

"Listen," he said. "I was very sick when I was a kid."

"I know, Uncle Warren told me. He said you almost died. He said that's why you're so religious now. Is it because of your religion, Luke? Is that why you don't want to come to Africa?"

"That's not what I'm talking about. The sickness I had . . . Oh, Lord! This is impossible!" He turned to her in anguish. "No, don't move. Stay over there. It's easier to say this if you're not close. I thought of asking Aunt Lil to tell you, but I'm afraid she'd faint with shock if I suggested it. Amy, I had mumps. A bad case."

"But you're fine now. I've known you for ages and you're never sick."

"Not the way you mean." He tossed back his head and downed the brandy. "I can never be a father, Amy," he blurted out. "I'm sterile."

She stared at him for a long moment, then she laughed. "Oh, Luke! Is that all? I don't care and it's nothing to do with running the mines, so I suppose" —she grinned at him with gamine wiles—"you're finally proposing to me."

He didn't respond to her laughter. He was pale and

his face was stiff with pain. "No," he said. "That's just what I'm not doing. I'm trying to tell you I intend to be a priest. I told you the other thing because I hoped it would help you understand."

"A priest . . ." Her voice was a whisper. "But why? Catholic priests can never marry. Aunt Lil told me that."

"Yes, she was trying to prepare you. She's always known my plans. Please forgive me, Amy. I should have told you sooner. At first there just never seemed a right time. Then, when I realized how you felt, how we both felt . . . I simply couldn't bear to hurt you."

Amy's face burned with shame, but every instinct told her not to give in. "Then you admit you feel something for me."

"Something! Oh, Amy, I care for you very much. If I were going to marry anyone, it would be you, if you'd have me. For a while I thought maybe you were a sign and I was kidding myself about having a vocation. Sometimes I was high as a kite just being near you, and other times I'd get so damned mad I couldn't see straight. I've been going to confession over and over, and getting the same answer. Pray to know the will of God." He ran his hands through his hair in a gesture of despair and poured himself another brandy.

Amy seemed to hear him through a dark tunnel, as if he were far away. Her mouth felt full of cotton, but she struggled to speak. "How can anyone know God's will?" she managed to say. "Do you have visions? Or do priests tell you?"

"You just know. I've tried to fight it for years. I'm an ordinary man. I feel things." He turned red and didn't meet her pleading eyes. "You know I do. When I touch you I explode inside. I don't even want to be a priest. But I can't fight it anymore. The Dominicans have accepted me into their order. I begin the novitiate right after Christmas."

She thought about throwing herself into his arms, making him feel what she knew he'd feel, and forget all these mad ideas. But she knew it wouldn't last. Whatever he said or did now, in a little while he'd change again. His church had a stranglehold on him. She couldn't fight it anymore than he could. When he stretched out his hand she put up her own in self-defense. His words were whips flailing her flesh; she could not bear his touch too.

"Get out," she said. "Go away and leave me alone. I never want to see you again."

7

A MY FELT BATTERED, PHYSICALLY BEATEN. SHE LAY
awake for hours each night and slept only to wake to
agony once more. Worst of all was the shame. When
she remembered how she'd thrown herself at Luke she
grew nauseated. She spent endless time in the bathroom, crying and retching by turn. Twice Lil tried to
speak to her, but Amy met those attempts with stony
silence and Lil backed off.

Amy realized that Warren and Lil might not know
the details, but they certainly knew what had happened. Even Maureen must know that Luke didn't
want her. She'd made a fool of herself while everyone

else saw perfectly well that Luke Westerman wasn't
interested. He wasn't like other men. He wanted to be
some kind of holy monk. And she'd gone blithely
ahead with her childish fantasy while they all watched
and laughed behind her back.

Humiliation was the worst of her torments, but it
wasn't the only one. Amy kept remembering the way
she'd felt when Luke was near and the way her mouth
tasted after he kissed her. It was unbearable to realize
that she'd never feel that way again. Months before,
she'd thought that she would never get over her parents' death and the separation from Jericho. Then
Luke had filled her life. Now, once more, she had
nothing.

She was dimly conscious that while she remained
closeted in her room, the rest of the household continued its normal routine. Six days passed. Then one
afternoon she heard the doorbell ring. No one answered, but it didn't stop. Apparently she was the only
one home. It must be Thursday, Maureen's day off.
She tried to ignore the summons, but it went on and
on. Amy dragged herself to the foyer and opened the
door.

"Hi, *memsahib*, how's tricks?" Tommy was wearing
his jaunty gray fedora. It was pushed back on his
head, and his coat and white silk scarf were open. He
leaned against the wall. "Aren't you going to ask me
in?"

"Of course." She stepped aside. "I didn't know you
were back from school," she said dully. Tommy must
know too. Now he'd come to gloat.

"Just got in this morning, Christmas vacation started

early this year." There was irony in his voice, but she was too preoccupied to notice. He tossed his hat at the clothes tree in the hall and shrugged off his coat. "Where's the clan?"

"I don't know. Out I guess."

"Good," he said. He stared hard at her. "You look like hell. I'm not going to apologize. That *is* what you look like."

"I haven't been feeling well." Her voice sounded tinny and far away.

"So I've heard. Good old brother Luke, I gather. Don't deny it. He left town a few hours ago. He admitted that he finally told you about the priest business. A real charmer my brother. Set 'em up and knock 'em down, that's his motto."

"Please, Tommy, I don't want to talk about it. I can't."

"Read this." He took an envelope from his pocket and handed it to her. "I was asked to give it to you. Go on, read it."

She opened the note with trembling fingers, conscious that Tommy was watching her. It was written in black ink, like a letter of condolence.

My very dear Amy,
I'm more sorry than I can say about hurting you. Believe me, it is the will of God, and best for both of us. Someday you'll see that. By the time you read this I'll have left for the Dominican novitiate. It seemed wise for me to go early. Please remember that you will always be in my prayers. God bless you.
Luke.

"Where is this Dominican whatever it's called?" she asked.

"Dover, a little town south of Boston. You planning to chase after him up there?"

She gasped. "How dare you!"

"Oh, my God!" He pounded his fist on the table and a cut-glass bird fell to the floor. "You're going around like a heroine in a Greek tragedy and you're mad at me. Look at yourself!" He grabbed her shoulders and spun her around so she faced the mirror over the mantel. "Is it my fault you feel like you do? What did he say anyway?"

Tommy snatched the note from her hand. Amy remained staring into the empty fireplace. They never had a fire on the maid's day off.

"The supercilious bastard." Tommy took a gold lighter from his pocket.

"Don't burn it," she whispered.

"Why not? So you can sleep with it under your pillow? No chance, *memsahib*. I'm not going to let you pine away for brother Luke. He's chosen the arms of holy Church. So to hell with him. Or to hell with us. What difference does it make?" He lit the corner of the note and dropped it on the bare stones between the andirons. It flared up, then curled into black ash. "Over," he said. "Done. Finished. Now you and I are going out."

She shook her head.

"Damn it, lady, I'm not asking you, I'm telling you. Get your coat."

She didn't move, so he got it for her, yanking it from the hall closet and buttoning her into it as if she were a helpless child. "Move. Come on or I'll carry you."

They went by cab to the Plaza Hotel, and he led her to the most conspicuous table in the Palm Court. He ordered champagne, and when it came he made her drink two glasses in quick succession. "Now," he said, pouring a third for each of them and signaling for another bottle, "you listen to me. You are the best-looking girl in this room. And every man here is wishing he was me. You got that, *memsahib*?"

She nodded.

"Good, keep it. And something else, there's only one way to handle things like this. Don't get mad. Get even."

"How can I do that?"

"By having a good time. By being happy. Leave the sackcloth and ashes to my brother. That's what he's after, isn't it? Let him have the lifetime of penance, and you and I will have the fun. Now for heaven's sake, smile. C'mon, do it or I'll punch you right in that turned-up little nose."

She raised her eyes and looked directly at him for the first time that afternoon. A smile began, a stiff effort at the corners of her mouth.

He was watching her anxiously. His recalcitrant curls fell over his forehead as usual. Tommy stuck out his lip and blew them away in the familiar, funny gesture. Amy's smile reached her eyes.

"That's better," he said, grinning. "Drink up *memsahib*. You and I are going to do a little advance celebrating of the holiday. In fact, we're going to get discreetly blotto."

She had a terrible hangover next day, but the cold ache in the pit of her stomach began to subside.

Amy drank a lot of champagne in the next weeks. Tommy's idea of having fun in New York was different from Luke's. He knew many more people, and they all gave parties. She was led through a succession of drawing rooms filled with what the society pages called "smart young things." When they weren't being entertained in someone's house they joined them in hotels. They went to the St. Regis, the Sherry Netherland, or the Plaza for a late afternoon "tea dance," followed usually by dinner at Delmonico's. Tommy never seemed to pay for these excursions, though sometimes she saw him sign a bill. He always did it with a flourish and a smile.

At first she danced with some of the other men; then she realized how much that upset him and she stopped it. It wasn't that Tommy wanted her always at his side. "Circulate, sweetheart," he told her. "Have a good time." But she mustn't seek any pleasure that was, by its nature, forbidden to him. She didn't really mind.

"You and Tommy are having quite a whirl," Lil said.

"We are rather, aren't we?" Amy smiled even though her head ached from the wine of the night before. "Tommy says I mustn't tell anyone how old I am. Because I haven't 'come out' officially."

Lil toyed with her pearls. "There's that," she said.

"You're too young to be in society. And it's not a year yet, you know."

Amy flushed. "You said I wasn't to mourn, that none of us were." She didn't admit that being with people helped her forget her disappointment. When she saw Tommy and other men look at her admiringly the sting of rejection eased.

"No," Lil agreed. "I don't want you to mourn. I suppose this is better."

December twenty-fifth finally came. Amy didn't let herself remember the dreams about becoming engaged to Luke on Christmas Day. She gave Tommy a cashmere scarf, and he presented her with a small evening purse covered in bugle beads. She had seen similar things in Altman's and she knew the gift had cost a great deal. For Tommy's sake she was glad that apparently Donald Varley's new investments were successful. Never mind that they hadn't helped her get what she wanted. She'd put all that in the back of her mind.

The round of parties grew yet more hectic in the week between Christmas and New Year's Eve. Sometimes there were two or three in one day. They welcomed 1916 at a ball in the Sherry Netherland, and went from there to a dawn breakfast in someone's Fifth Avenue home. As was often the case, Amy didn't know the name of her host or hostess. Having a good time, fun—those were the only bonds between herself and these New York socialites.

When she and Tommy walked home it was New Year's Day and the sun was shining. Amy giggled. They were still in evening clothes and the milkman was making his rounds.

"Decadent," Tommy said. "That's what we are. Wouldn't brother Luke be mad." He was a little drunk; otherwise he wouldn't have mentioned Luke. It was a subject they avoided.

Amy felt a remnant of the old pain begin to surface. She probed, as if it was a sore tooth. "What's he doing right now do you think?" She must be a little drunk too.

"Praying of course. Kneeling on a cold stone floor and berating himself for his sins."

"What sins? Luke's holy, haven't you heard?"

They turned into the entrance of Lil's building, and the doorman wished them good morning, as if arriving home at breakfast time was quite normal. "Yeah," Tommy said. "People like Luke leave the sinning to the rest of us. But they feel guilty just the same. They like feeling guilty."

She was suddenly too sleepy to talk. "It's all too complicated for me," she said, covering a yawn with a gloved hand.

He left her at the elevator. "I'll call you later, *memsahib*. Get some sleep."

She did, until Maureen came and woke her and said that Mr. Tommy was on the telephone.

"What time is it?"

"Five o'clock." Maureen didn't actually sniff, but she might just as well have.

"Five o'clock in the afternoon?"

"Yes."

"Good lord!" She pulled on a robe and went to the telephone in the hall. "Hello, Tommy, did you just wake up too?"

"No. I've been awake a long time. I feel awful. And there's no one here. I want you to come over."

"Come to your house?" She had never been there. "I don't think Aunt Lil would like that. You know, appearances. Why don't you come here?"

"My leg hurts," he said. It was the first time she ever heard him complain or use his leg as an excuse. "Just come," he said. "You can be home in time for dinner."

Amy walked the eight blocks to the Westerman house on Eighty-third Street between Park and Madison avenues. It was a narrow five-story town house with four steps leading to the front door. Tommy must have been watching for her. He appeared before she rang the bell.

He looked awful, unshaven and still in the clothes he'd been wearing the night before. There was a stain on the front of his dinner jacket, and he'd removed his tie and loosened his collar button.

"Have you been sick?" she asked anxiously.

"Awful. I still am."

"I'll make you some tea. Where's the kitchen?"

It was on the ground floor at the back. It looked as if no one had prepared a meal there for ages. "The cleaning woman comes a couple of times a week," he said. "But there's no cook now."

"I can cook a little," she said, opening the ice box. "You have some eggs."

"I'm not hungry."

"You must eat something. Go take a shower and change while I get this ready."

He came back in a few minutes, shaved and wearing

a dressing gown. They put the tray of food in the dumb waiter and collected it in the butler's pantry on the floor above. Amy noticed a madonna and child of carved wood on a pedestal on the landing. "Your family always has something like this, don't they? This one's beautiful."

"Mother found it in France years ago. It's an antique. I guess it's beautiful. Don't blame me if all the Westermans are religious fanatics."

Tommy carried the meal to a small breakfast room, gay with chintz and blue and white tiles. Cecily Westerman had indeed possessed good taste.

"I like your house," Amy said. "It's charming."

"Yeah, charming." He ate quickly, as if he was suddenly ravenous. "Thanks," he said when he finished. "I feel better."

"You need looking after," she said with concern. "You should hire a housekeeper."

He grinned. "That's one way. Or I could take a wife."

She didn't meet his eyes. "When are you going back to school?" she asked.

"I'm not."

"What do you mean? You have another two terms before graduation."

"Well, I've changed my mind. This war is spreading, we're bound to get into it. They drop bombs from planes now, in case you didn't know. The whole world will probably be blown up. I don't see any point in the groves of academe." He rose from the table abruptly. "I'll show you the drawing room."

His limp was very pronounced. He had not been lying about his leg.

The drawing room was decorated in soft shades of beige and pale yellow. It was lovely, and Amy said so.

"Yeah," he said. "Mother was good at decorating. She liked modern things as well as antiques."

"Do you miss her a lot?" Amy asked softly. "Can you get used to the idea that you'll never see her again?"

He knew that she was voicing her own feelings. "There's nothing else to do. We have to get used to it."

He sat on the sofa and took a cigarette from a box on the table. "I want to ask you something," he said.

Amy watched him and waited.

"You've had a good time these last few weeks, haven't you? Do you still miss Luke?"

"I've had a marvelous time," she said quickly.

"What about the Luke part?"

"I don't want to talk about him." She got up and walked to the window. It was dark and a few stars winked down on the brownstone houses. "Why do you keep bringing up Luke lately?"

"Because I have to know. Damn it, Amy, you must see that."

"I don't know what you're talking about."

"I'm talking about us. You and me." He crossed to where she stood and put a hand on her arm. "I love you," he said softly.

"I don't think we should be talking like this," she said.

He spun her around and pulled her close. She was very stiff at first, but she didn't pull away. He bent his head and kissed her, gently at the start, then with more urgency. His hands moved along her spine, and he held her even tighter until she could feel her breasts pushing against his broad chest. Her hands fluttered at his shoulders, then came to rest behind his head. She tangled her fingers in his thick curly hair. It's like it was with Luke that day on the beach, she thought. She waited, but she did not feel again what she'd felt before. Her blood didn't sing. She did not tremble. It was Tommy who broke off the kiss. He took her arm and tried to lead her toward the sofa.

"No," she said. Her voice sounded strangely dead in her own ears, but Tommy didn't seem to notice. "I have to go," she said. "Aunt Lil's expecting me."

"Ok." He dropped her hand with an air of resignation. "You go home if you want. I'll see you tomorrow."

As she walked through the darkened streets she speculated that Luke would not have allowed her to go home alone.

"I understand Tommy isn't returning to Georgetown," Lil said at breakfast a few days later.

"That's what he says." Amy cracked the top of her boiled egg. "He claims it's because of the war. But I don't know why that makes any difference."

"This war's getting worse," Warren said. "Look here." He passed over the *Times* and Amy read the headline about Verdun.

Lil didn't want to talk about the war. "Tommy shouldn't interrupt his education," she said. "I told Donald he was mad to allow it." She grew more upset as she spoke. "Tommy has such a brilliant future. He's making a terrible mistake. Can't you talk to him, Amy?"

"I tried, Aunt Lil. He won't listen."

"No, probably not to me either. He's always been stubborn. I think we should get in touch with Luke. He should come home and try to make Tommy see sense."

"I don't think that would help." Amy stared at the tablecloth.

"Maybe not." Lil reached out and patted Amy's hand. "Anyway, I'm sure you're a good influence, my dear. You must do what you can."

She told Tommy a bit about the conversation. "Aunt Lil's very disappointed that you aren't going back to college. She thinks you're throwing away a brillant future."

They were watching the skaters in Central Park, and he flipped the butt of his cigarette toward the lake. It lay sputtering on the thick ice. A skater looked angrily in their direction. "Let's go," Tommy said. "This place is getting me down. I hate winter."

"So do I." She was remembering the first snowfall and the sounds of laughing children and the snowman called Lord Frostbite. "I wish this war would end and I could go home."

"That's what you want, is it?" He took her arm and steered her toward the exit from the park. "Home to the black natives and the diamonds and the hot African sun."

"You should be a writer," she laughed.

"No point in being anything these days. No future
in it. Don't you read the papers?"

"The war has to end sometime."

"I guess so. Everything ends, doesn't it?"

"You're making me depressed."

"Welcome to the club."

Tommy was supposed to have taken a job in Charles
Westerman's old firm, the post Luke had vacated, but
he never seemed to go to the office. He spent most
days with Amy, but she didn't return to the Eighty-
third Street house and he never tried to kiss her, or
talk about his brother. By mid-January society parties
were less frequent. They filled their time with "flicks"
at the Regent or the Rialto. Twice he took her to see
Ziegfeld's Follies on Broadway.

Amy was embarrassed by the scanty costumes of the
Ziegfeld girls, but she loved comics like W.C. Fields,
Eddie Cantor, and Fanny Brice. Tommy laughed at
her objections to the gorgeous chorus line and said she
mustn't be old-fashioned, but when she mentioned
bobbing her hair he objected and she gave up the
idea.

They didn't drink much when they were together,
but sometimes he was a little drunk by the time she
saw him. And he was morose, not so much fun. Amy
decided that she had to say something. She chose an
afternoon when he was at the apartment. They were
alone in the small sitting room at the back of the
house, sipping hot chocolate and saying very little.

"What's wrong, Tommy?" she ventured finally.

"You've been so down since New Year's. Are you sorry about not returning to Georgetown?"

"Not about that."

"What then?"

"Besides the *Lusitania* and the war and the state of my finances, you mean?" He leaned his head back wearily against the chair.

"I didn't know you were worried about money. I thought that was all settled."

"Oh, it's settled. I don't have any."

"But Mr. Varley said he was making some new investments, for you," she said without thinking.

He sat up quickly. "Have you been discussing me with Donald Varley?" There was a tic at the side of his mouth, and she knew he was furious.

"Not the way you think. It came up months ago. When I was talking to him about my own inheritance. He just said . . ."

"Forget it." He cut her short. "I didn't tell you what else I'm depressed about. You."

"Me! But why?"

"Why? Because nearly three weeks ago I said I loved you and you've never mentioned it again. Not a word or a look or anything. What do you think I am, Amy? What do you think I'm made of?"

"But what could I say? There's the war, and everything's so uncertain. And we're both so young." She wanted to cry. The look of pain and unhappiness on his face wrenched her heart.

"I'll be twenty-two next week. And we can't do anything about the war. Besides, that didn't hold you back with Luke."

She turned bright red. "That's a mean thing to say."

"Yes, well, I'm tired of playing second fiddle to the golden boy."

"I don't think of you like that at all."

"How do you think of me?"

She stared at her folded hands. The knuckles were white. "I don't know. I'm confused." Her voice was a tiny whisper.

Her uncertainty gave him confidence. He moved to sit beside her and put his arm around her shoulders. "I'm sure. Enough for both of us."

She shook her head. "I just don't know."

He tilted her face and leaned forward and kissed her. It wasn't demanding and urgent like the kiss on New Year's Day. There was gentleness in it. She responded to that. Her lips trembled beneath his and he pulled her closer. Their bodies pressed together on the soft down cushions of the sofa. "There," he said when he released her. "You don't mind me kissing you, do you?"

"I like it," she admitted shyly. And this time she did. It wasn't the same as with Luke, but it made her feel warm and protected and wanted.

Tommy smiled. It was that soft warm smile of last summer which she'd not seen in many months. "I do love you, you know," he said. "And we're a good combination. We ought to get married, *memsahib*. Right away before this damn war ends the world."

"Maybe we should," she whispered. *I won't be alone,* she thought. *I'll be a married lady.*

He kissed her again. They were still kissing when they heard Lil clear her throat loudly. She was standing in the doorway staring at them. "I'm sorry," she murmured. "I just thought . . ."

"It's all right, Aunt Lil," Tommy told her grinning. "Amy's just agreed to marry me. Right away."

8

~

THAT AMY WASN'T A CATHOLIC PRESENTED SOME
problems. She grew tired of endless, painfully tactful
conversations with Lil and Warren. "Why do we have
to have a church wedding?" she asked Tommy. "Why
can't we just get married?" Amy had her own reasons
for preferring such a scheme.

"I can't do that." Tommy kicked at a smoldering
log. Outside it was bleak February, and Lil kept a
constant fire on the hearth.

"Because of your family."

"Not just them. I can't do it. Don't ask me to
explain."

"You don't want to 'live in sin.' Isn't that the expression?"

"Amy, please don't tease me about it. I wish I felt differently, but I don't." He paused a moment, then added, "The family all want you to convert. I told them to forget it. I said it was your business and nobody else's." He paused again. "There is something you have to do though."

She flipped idly through the pages of *Life* magazine, pretending she didn't care and pretending to forget that she had planned to become a Catholic for Luke. "What is it?"

"You'll have to promise to bring up any children we have as Catholics. It's rather awful, they make you sign a paper." He looked miserable.

Amy turned pink at the mention of the family they might have. In Africa such things were just a part of ordinary life; here they had a mysterious and slightly sordid air. "I don't mind," she said.

"You're marvelous." He smiled at her and the look of despair vanished. "We're going to be very happy, you know."

Amy nodded and promised herself it was true. She would be a perfect wife. That was her part of the bargain.

The wedding was to take place at St. Ignatius on May ninth, Amy's eighteenth birthday. She thought it was to be the same type of ceremony as Sarah Westerman's, the cousin who was married in February.

"No, thank God," Tommy explained. "All that

hulabaloo is called a nuptial high mass. We can't have one because you're a heathen and I'm tainted."

"What?" She stared at him wide-eyed.

"Because you're not Catholic and I'm marrying outside the faith," he said. "We're a mixed marriage, so we don't get all the frills."

Amy would have preferred even fewer of them. Months before she had dreamed of satin and lace and orange blossoms. Now she just wanted to get married and be done with it. There was no chance of that. The Westerman clan rallied round, and she had the usual assortment of prebridal parties. Not quite as many as Sarah, nor as lavish, because Amy's engagement was during Lent, but enough of them to keep her busy. They also netted a great many useless presents.

Lil took charge of the trousseau arrangements and accompanied Amy to numerous fittings. The reception was to be a wedding breakfast at the Plaza, the guests largely family members. Only a few of the people with whom she and Tommy had partied over Christmas were put on the list. "They're just people I know," he said. "I don't want to ask them to my wedding."

She was glad he had lost interest in the "smart young things." Amy was feeling grown-up and ready to take on new responsibilities. She liked the feeling, and the fact that Tommy now went regularly to the office of his father's former partners.

By April the last of the snow melted and daffodils bloomed in Central Park. Tommy brought her an illustrated brochure of Niagara Falls, where they were to honeymoon.

"Isn't this all very expensive?" Amy asked.

He looked uncomfortable. "Uncle Donald says it's all right, we can afford it."

"But I thought you said . . ."

"Let me worry about finances. I'm the one that's supposed to be in charge of things like that."

She didn't mention money again.

Three days before the ceremony Luke came home to be his brother's best man. Amy had known it would be thus. As it turned out she saw little of him. She was busy with last-minute trips to the dressmaker and the final ladies' luncheon Aunt Lil gave. It wasn't until the afternoon of the wedding rehearsal that Amy had to face Luke. It was surprisingly less painful than she expected it to be.

Luke stood in the vestibule of the church when she arrived with Lil and the cousins who were to be her bridesmaids. He was as tall and handsome as ever, a little thinner, perhaps, and he wore ordinary clothes. She had thought he might be dressed in the white habit of the Dominicans.

"Hello, Amy. You look radiant. You know how much happiness I wish you both." He took her hand, leaned forward and kissed her lightly on the cheek. When they drew apart he looked at her for a moment, then turned away.

The stiff note of congratulations he had sent when the engagement was announced had not prepared her for the pain she now saw in his blue eyes. A small thrill of triumph shot along her spine. After that she was sweet and charming to him, and completely in control.

*   *   *

The hotel at Niagara Falls had been built by the
Victorians with their usual love of opulence. The public rooms were grand, and the bedrooms spacious. The
newlywed Westermans had a suite.

Amy felt relief when the bellhop closed the door.
"Peace at last," she said. "I'm worn out." She un-
pinned her hat and flung it on the sofa. Her traveling
costume was a beige suit of sheer wool, with a tight
ankle-length skirt, slit almost to the knee so she could
walk. She wore a matching silk blouse and the pearls
Tommy had given her as a wedding present.

"Shall I order some champagne?" Tommy asked.

"Not for me. You have some if you like."

"I don't need it," he said, taking her hand. "I'm
drunk with you."

Amy smiled, then pulled away. "It's nearly six. Why
don't we change and go down for an early dinner?"

They ate at a table overlooking gardens filled with
soft spring dusk. Birds sang an evensong chorale and,
the scent of early honeysuckle came through the open
window.

It grew darker, and a waiter lit the candles on their
table and brought the sauternes Tommy had ordered to
go with dessert. Amy drank thirstily. She had drunk a
lot of wine at dinner, despite refusing the earlier offer
of champagne. Her glance darted around the dining
room. Tommy strained to say funny things about all
the other guests. Both their minds were filled with the
previous night.

Their wedding night at the Plaza had been a fumbling saga of embarrassment and ineptitude that resulted in a perfunctory, and barely successful, deflowering. Tommy had been quite drunk, Amy overwrought and nervous.

The results were probably predictable, but no one had warned them. Now they both dreaded a repeat performance.

After dinner they strolled through the lobby and ventured into the garden, but it had turned chilly and Amy noticed that Tommy's limp was bad, so they stayed out only a short time. In the lobby a large placard announced a concert of chamber music to be held in the Washington Suite. Tommy asked if she wanted to go. She shook her head. There was nothing left to do but go upstairs.

The second night of their marriage began with Amy emerging from the bathroom in a pale blue lace peignoir and Tommy sitting on the side of the bed in striped pajamas stiff with newness. "I wish you didn't look so different," he said.

"What do you mean?"

"I keep looking at you and thinking," 'that's my wife.' You don't seem the same Amy any more. It scares me."

"I'm the same. So are you. Nothing's any different."

"Yes, it is." He groaned and reached out and pulled her down beside him. "You're so damned beautiful," he said. "I almost wish you were ugly. I wish you looked like Aunt Lil's maid."

Amy giggled at the thought of herself as the ugly,

thick-set Maureen, with a mole and hairs growing out of her chin. Tommy giggled too. When he kissed her both their mouths were open.

His tongue probed hers. She ran her hands along his arms to his shoulders and noticed again how strong he was. He moved his hand to her breast and fumbled with the buttons of the peignoir. When he opened it her nightdress was still between them. He tried to get his hand inside the fabric.

"You'll tear it," she murmured.

"Take it off then. Please. I won't look."

She stood and removed the things she was wearing and folded them carefully over the back of a chair. Then she scurried under the quilt.

"Ready?" he asked.

"Yes."

He took off his pajamas and crawled into the bed. Before last night she had sometimes wondered if he wore his invalid shoe when he slept. Now she knew he didn't, and that when he lay beside her his short leg was undetectable.

The night before they had barely managed to feel each other's bodies. Now he stroked her hip and trailed his fingers over her midriff to cup her breast. Amy felt the nipple tighten and swell, the way it did when she was cold.

"Touch me too," he whispered. "I want you to."

She put her hand on his back. He kissed her neck and her shoulder and dropped his mouth to her breast. He moved again, and he was lying almost on top of her, pinning her to the soft mattress. Tommy's body was compact and steellike, and the hardest thing of all was the appendage he was thrusting between her legs.

Amy knew it was wrong of her to resist. He was her husband and this was his right. She let her thighs relax and open. There was a moment's fumbling, and she wondered if it was going to be like last night after all. But it wasn't. This time he quickly penetrated, and she felt a bit of soreness, but nothing like the pain of the first time. His motion grew more intense and more rapid. She lay very still and waited, because she didn't know what else to do. It took about half a minute before he groaned loudly and rolled off her.

After a short time he turned to her again and kissed her cheek. "That was better, wasn't it? I was ashamed of myself last night. I'd had too much to drink. Are you all right? Did I hurt you?"

"No, I'm fine."

"So am I. I'm marvelous," he said, chuckling as if at some private joke. "Good night, *memsahib* darling." He kissed her again and fell asleep with one hand holding her breast.

They moved into the house on Eighty-third Street. Aunt Lil had insisted that Amy must have a maid and a cook, and engaged them. There was nothing for Amy to do but hang up her clothes.

She put them in the dressing room she still thought of as Cecily Westerman's, and tried to find places for the wedding presents. In the end she packed most of those away. The practical things were redundant in the well-equipped house, and the *objets d'art* only seemed to spoil the perfect decor.

By unspoken mutual consent both she and Tommy were determined to prove themselves mature. They lived quietly and Tommy was always anxious to go to bed early. Once there he would possess her with quick and apparently satisfying enthusiasm, then fall asleep.

Tommy rose before her in the morning. Delia, the black maid, brought coffee at seven, and Amy could hear her husband straining at his exercises in the dressing room. He lifted weights and chinned himself on a metal bar, and the sound of his exertions was the beginning of her day.

Tommy left the house at nine and returned at dinner time, but he never mentioned anything that happened at the office. Once she suggested that they invite the firm's partners to dinner, but Tommy vetoed the idea. Amy spent a lot of time reading *Life* or *Ladies' Home Journal* or the *Saturday Evening Post*.

The stories about different American lifestyles particularly interested her. Amy had seen nothing but the east coast; the magazines told her that there were other parts of this country, and she realized that some of them, the West for instance, were more like her beloved Africa. All the same, it was silly to dream about that. Tommy's world was New York, and she had chosen to share it when she married him. So she turned the glossy pages of the magazines and fought off any doubts about the wisdom of decisions that now seemed irrevocable.

Sunday was Amy's only day that was not outwardly serene. Tommy donned striped trousers and morning coat and joined his family at the eleven o'clock high mass. She refused all suggestions that she accompany him.

"I'm not saying you should be Catholic," he insisted. "Just come along. I want to show you off."

"No. I'm sorry, I don't want to do that."

He went without her. The rest of Sunday was often tense and pointless. In June they received an invitation to the Dominican Priory in Dover. Luke was to be "clothed in the habit of the order."

"What does that mean?" Amy asked.

"He's a full-fledged member of the club. Dressed up in the white robes. A bona fide man of religion."

"Is he a priest?"

"Not yet. That takes years. Six or seven with the Dominicans, I think."

Amy didn't want to go. The affair was bound to be ostentatiously Catholic. Recently Lil had invited her to join some of the women's organizations at St. Ignatius. Amy didn't feel she could refuse, and she'd gone to a few meetings. She found that she hated being among pious believers. She certainly didn't want to go to Dover.

At the last minute she pleaded illness and said they should go without her. "I can't stay home," Tommy said. "Lil and Warren are counting on me to drive. It's too far for Uncle Warren to manage alone."

"There's no reason you shouldn't go," she said. "Delia will look after me." So he left her in the care of the maid and went.

They were due home by suppertime Sunday night. When nine o'clock came Amy rang Lil's apartment to see if Maureen had heard anything. Lil herself answered the phone.

"But he dropped us off here at quarter to six," she said. "He must have had some place to go and forgot to mention it." Lil went on to tell Amy about the ceremony at Dover. "Luke looked marvelous in the habit. And so deeply prayerful. We were all touched."

Amy hung up, worried and angry.

Tommy returned after midnight. He was very drunk. Amy put him to bed and thought he was asleep, but he grabbed her arm and wouldn't let her go.

"Sorry," he muttered thickly. "Damn fool thing to do, get drunk."

"It's all right," she said. "Just go to sleep now."

"Oh, no, sweetheart, it's not all right. Damn shame. Everything all messed up. Everybody wanting what they can't have."

He sounded so very sad. Amy forgot that she was mad and pushed the brown curls back from his forehead with gentleness. "I don't know what you're talking about," she laughed softly. "Neither do you. You're too far gone."

Tommy spoke with sudden and surprising vehemence. "I bloody well do know. Never was fooled by old Luke. Everyone else, not me." He tightened his grip on her wrist. "Kept asking about you, wanting to know why you didn't come. Me too. Why didn't you go, Amy?"

She tried to pull away. "You're hurting me. I told you why I didn't go, I had a headache."

"Yeah. Old Luke, he's got a headache too. Or a heartache maybe. Too late. He lost and I won." He sat upright and yanked her closer. Amy lost her balance and sprawled across his lap.

"You're mine," Tommy said. "My wife, not Luke's."

"Stop it. You're drunk, Tommy. Let me go and just sleep it off." She was desperate to end this discussion, for her sake as well as his. "Please, darling"—her tone became placating—"let me go and I'll get undressed." He released her wrist, and she rubbed it while she went into the bathroom and changed into a nightdress.

Amy guessed that he would want to make love to her, and she was prepared to endure what must be a drunken fumbling attempt. But when she joined him in the big double bed he was snoring, and she knew that he'd not wake before morning.

9

A FEW DAYS AFTER THE TRIP TO DOVER TOMMY returned early from the office. "Where are you, darling?" his voice boomed up the stairs.

Amy had been resting. She left her bedroom and went to the landing. She wore only a negligee, and she clutched it to her in embarrassment when she saw that Tommy wasn't alone. Two couples stood with him in the foyer. Delia was busy taking the men's hats and the light summer wraps of the ladies. "I'm so sorry," Amy managed to say. "I didn't realize we had guests."

"That we do," Tommy said. "Get dressed and join us."

When she went to the drawing room all five had cocktails in hand. "You remember Kitty and Charlie, don't you, darling?" Tommy's voice was hearty, and he was grinning. She'd not seen him look like this since before their wedding. "This is Lou Rheingold, and his friend Suzy Randolph," he said.

Amy smiled and nodded. She had a vague recollection of meeting these people at parties the previous winter, but they looked decidedly alien sitting in her house. And this time she was in the unaccustomed role of hostess. She walked to the bell by the fireplace while she made some reply to the greetings. When Delia came Amy asked that hors d'oeuvres be brought. Delia rolled her eyes and implied trouble, so Amy followed her into the hall.

"Cook say she ain't gonna feed six people without no more notice than this," Delia announced. "Don't know if she's gonna produce no fancies either." Delia announced the crisis with satisfaction.

"Just tell her to send up some cheese and crackers," Amy said. "And don't worry. They won't stay for dinner."

Tommy paid no attention to Amy's domestic maneuvering. After about an hour they'd all had quite a few of Tommy's champagne cocktails, and finished the crackers and cheese. He said, "You'll stay for dinner of course."

Amy said anxiously "You're forgetting, I gave the servants the evening off." She flashed him urgent messages with her eyes. He grinned at her over the top of his glass.

"So you did. No matter, we'll all go to Delmonico's."

When the lavish, laugh-filled evening was ended Tommy signed the check with a flourish and waved aside the objections of the other men.

"You look terrific," he told Amy later. "I haven't seen you with so much color in your cheeks in weeks. We need more of that."

"More of what?" she giggled. "Color in my cheeks?" Amy had drunk a lot of champagne.

"No, silly. More good times and friends. We've been living like a couple of hermits."

She stretched her arms over her head in a feline luxurious gesture. The thin voile of her beige gown drew tight over her breasts, and the spangles at her hips danced in the glow of the soft lamp on the dressing table. "It was fun," she agreed.

Tommy was sitting on the side of the bed. "Come here," he said hoarsely.

Amy executed a twirling dance step and hummed under her breath. The movement brought her within reach of his powerful arms, and he drew her down beside him and kissed her hard. His hands roamed over her body. He searched her curves and crevices as if they were new to him. "You're so beautiful," he murmured huskily. "And you're mine."

"Wait, I'll get undressed," Amy said.

"No, I don't want to wait." Tommy pushed up the long skirt of her gown. The sheer fabric bunched in his hand and made more sensual the feel of her leg and her hip. He kissed her again, and tasted the champagne in her mouth while he fumbled with her delicate lace panties. They slid down as far as her knees, and his fingers explored the little rubber grips of her satin garter belt and her silk hose. The assembly was too complicated for him to remove with one hand. Then he felt the gentle rise of her flesh beneath his palm, and knew he didn't have to bother.

When he touched her Amy fought off the desire to pull away. She told herself she had no right to resist, that if she was a good wife, she'd welcome her husband's caresses. If only he wasn't always in such a hurry, if only he'd give her a little more time. . . . "Wait just a moment," she whispered again. But Tommy jerked open the buttons of his trousers and rolled on top of her.

His climax came seconds later. He didn't kiss her afterward, or say nice things in her ear. He almost never did. He just got up and staggered into the bathroom.

While Amy was getting undressed Tommy lay with his arms folded behind his head and tried to think. He wasn't drunk anymore. There was only a bitter taste in his mouth and an unsettled feeling in his stomach as reminders of the evening. He listened to Amy running the water, first the taps, then the shower, and to the small female sounds that had become familiar to him since marriage. And he pondered his reactions and hers.

He'd felt guilty about the scene when he came home from Luke's clothing ceremony. That's why he'd sought out Charlie and Lou and their dates and brought them home. He'd told himself Amy needed a bit of fun, some break in the domestic routine. Well, she'd had it all right. And then she tried to resist his lovemaking.

He knew why. Because she didn't want to be married to him, she wanted Luke.

Whore. The word came into his head unbidden. Tommy pushed it away.

But the word wouldn't disappear. Whore. He heard her humming softly, and he knew that she was brushing her thick black hair. He could picture the graceful gestures. Amy brushed her hair one hundred strokes a night; by now he had seen it often. But was it him she wanted to please? No, not the way she acted.

When she got into bed and snuggled up to him, murmuring endearments, he patted her arm perfunctorily. He didn't sleep at all. He kept thinking about this girl who was his wife, and about her exotic past, and he wondered how much part that played in the truth he was beginning to recognize.

The dinner at Delmonico's took place on Wednesday evening. Friday morning Amy's telephone rang.

"Hi, it's me, Suzy. Don't you remember?"

Amy summoned up an image of a tall willowy blonde with bobbed hair, saucer-size blue eyes, and a permanently vacant expression. "Oh, Suzy," she said with more enthusiasm than she felt. "Of course I remember. How are you?"

Suzy was fine. She was calling to see if Amy would join her for lunch and a bit of shopping. Amy's first instinct was to refuse, but she found herself agreeing to a time.

It was a pleasant afternoon. When she went home Tommy was waiting and mentioned that he had accepted an invitation to a party the following night. They were launched anew on the same hectic whirl they had known during the winter.

The dinner for twenty-four given by the Westermans two months later in August rated three paragraphs on the society page of the *New York Herald*. ". . . eleven exquisite courses and decor of the utmost chic," the columnist gushed. "Mrs. Westerman chose an Arabian Nights theme . . . footmen dressed as blackamoors, candlelight and incense . . . the most ravishing music provided by a foursome from abroad. Heaven knows where the clever young things found them!"

Amy flushed with pleasure. The party had been fearsomely expensive, but wonderful. And attention like this was good for Tommy's career. Too bad she hadn't talked more to the wife of his boss, but never mind, it had all been a huge success. She folded the newspaper and laid it on her breakfast tray. Then she looked at the mail. There were some bills, which she set aside for Tommy without opening them, and a few thank-you notes and invitations.

There was also an envelope with the return address of the doctor she had consulted last week. Amy's fingers trembled slightly when she opened it.

The news was positive. She was expecting a child. Slowly she lowered the sheet of stationery and looked out the window. The sun was pouring in through the sheer curtains. It would be hot again, but after today she and Tommy wouldn't be in the city. They were going to Long Island to spend the weekend with Lil and Warren. For a moment Amy regretted the plan. She would much rather tell Tommy her news here in their own home. She was fairly sure he would be pleased. Sometimes when they passed children on the street Tommy remarked that it would be nice when they had one of their own. Not that he ever said a lot about it. These days it seemed to Amy that they talked very little. How could they when they were always in the midst of people?

She stretched out her hand and touched the embroidered linen sheet. They were alone here, of course. But it wasn't a place where they talked. Tommy made love to her often, but he never spoke to her afterward. He only rolled over and went to sleep. Sometimes she suspected he took her more in anger than love. That was crazy, wasn't it? Why should he be angry?

Amy pressed her hands to her stomach and smiled. He wouldn't be angry about this. Pregnant. She said the word over in her mind and decided that she preferred it to any of the euphemisms women sometimes used. That's what she'd tell him as soon as the opportunity arose. I'm pregnant. And she would watch him smile his crooked smile and look the way he had last summer, when they were both so much younger.

She dressed with care. A white linen dress with navy blue trim made her look cool, even if she didn't feel it. No jewelry, just her rings and an elegant gold watch which Tommy had given her a few weeks earlier. When she was satisfied with her appearance she clipped the newspaper column describing their party. Then she put it and the doctor's letter in the dressing table drawer. She'd show Tommy both things when they returned from Atlantic Beach.

Her watch had a cover of blue enamel inlaid with

pearls. Amy flipped it open and was surprised to see that it was nearly eleven. Suzy Randolph was coming for lunch in an hour. Then they were going to tea with some other friends. At five she was to meet Tommy at Pennsylvania Station, and they would take the train to Long Island. On impulse Amy opened the drawer and put the letter and the clipping in her pocket. They didn't know too many people on the island. Maybe they could take a walk on the beach, just the two of them, and she could share her news.

She opened the bedroom door to find Delia standing with her hand raised, ready to knock. "You has a visitor, ma'am."

"Miss Randolph! But she's early."

"No ma'am, ain't Miss anybody. It's a gentleman."

Amy opened the drawing room door and saw him. He stood with his back to her, a tall slim figure who had lost neither his elegant catlike grace, nor his aura of intensity. She hesitated on the threshold and swallowed hard. He was staring out the window, one hand propped casually on the wall, the other tucked in his pocket. She took a deep breath, then said, "Hello, Luke."

"Hello, Amy." He didn't turn around.

"Tommy's at the office. We didn't expect you."

"I haven't come to see Tommy."

"I see."

"I doubt that," he said softly. "I doubt that you see anything at all."

He still hadn't faced her. Amy closed the door and moved forward. The room was pleasantly cool, and scented with lavender from a bowl of potpourri on the coffee table. She stood for a moment and waited. He didn't move. "Would you care for coffee? Or a sherry perhaps? I can ring for Delia."

"I don't want anything."

At last he spun round and looked at her. If anything, he was more handsome than she remembered. There was a tautness to him now, a kind of honing of all his features. He was more himself than ever.

Luke was aware of her scrutiny. "Am I so changed?"

"Not really. I'm just surprised to see you. And I didn't think you wore ordinary clothes anymore."

He smiled for the first time. It was the same devastatingly beautiful smile which gleamed white against tanned skin. "We don't wear the habit outside the priory," he explained. "Certainly not on a visit to New York."

"You're visiting, then?" Her voice cracked, making something unusual of the prosiac question.

"Not exactly. I've been ill, a persistent grippe. Father Prior sent me to see a doctor here."

"And what did he say?" She reached for a cigarette and fumbled with the table lighter.

"Here." Luke ignored her question and took the lighter from her. He lit it with one flick of his finger. "When did you start smoking?"

"A while ago." Amy inhaled gratefully.

"Just like all the 'clever young things,' eh? Exquisite, ravishing, chic . . . those are the operative words in your set, aren't they?"

She flushed. "You saw that silly article."

"This morning, in the doctor's waiting room."

"They aren't my 'set,' as you put it. They're just people we know."

He shrugged. "I didn't come here to talk about that anyway."

They sat down. Amy chose a chair across from him, far enough away so perhaps he wouldn't notice her trembling hands. When Luke had come to the wedding she had been strengthened by the foreknowledge of his arrival. This was different. "Are you staying long? Tommy will be sorry he missed you." She was speaking too quickly, betraying her nervousness and hating herself for it.

"I'm supposed to return to Dover tonight," he said. "And I told you, I didn't come to see Tommy."

She raised her eyes and studied his face. "Why did you come, Luke?"

"To see you."

She didn't know what to say. She leaned forward and stubbed out her cigarette. Luke moved at the same time and took hold of her wrist. His grip was vicelike.

"I'm supposed to make my first temporary vows next week," he said in a struggled voice. "I can't. I keep thinking about you. No matter how much I pray, I can't get you out of my mind."

"Maybe you're not saying the right prayers," she said. "Try another formula." She wanted to hurt him, and she could see that she had.

He let her go. "You never used to be cruel."

"Perhaps I've grown up. I used to believe that everyone was sincere and honest."

"Meaning that I'm not."

"Meaning whatever you want." She stood up and walked away. An ormolu French clock on the mantel chimed the quarter hour. "I have a luncheon guest coming in fifteen minutes. Will you join us? I'll have to send word to the kitchen."

"Oh, for God's sake! Damn your bloody luncheon guest. Amy, don't you understand anything I'm saying? I'm talking about my whole life, my soul, in fact."

"Your life, your soul," she repeated softly. "What about mine, Luke? Were you concerned about them when you allowed me to believe something that wasn't true? Are you worried about them now?"

"I imagine I deserve that," he said. "But you're wrong. I didn't understand. I thought you were just a test, an infatuation. I didn't realize I was falling in love with you."

Amy stood very still. She felt suddenly fragile. If she moved too quickly, she would shatter into bits.

"Were you in love with me?" she asked in a whisper. "Are you now?"

"Yes, God help me."

Amy exhaled slowly. She had not realized that she'd been holding her breath.

He rose and crossed to where she stood and put his hands on her shoulders. "You must listen to me," he said. The blue eyes were burning stars in his thin face. He sounded desperate, almost crazy. "There are ways to put things right. It's complicated. The rules about church annulments are difficult. But if you married Tommy without really wanting to, only because of me, it might be grounds. We can't live our whole lives paying for one mistake."

"What about the priesthood?" she said. "Have you changed your mind about that?"

"Yes." He hesitated, then said very softly. "I think so. I don't know anything more."

Amy felt the weight of his hands on her shoulders. He wore a navy linen blazer, and she could see the pronounced weave of the fabric. It was mesmerizing. She made herself raise her eyes and study the clean firm lines of his jaw, and his sensitive, mobile mouth. Then, unable to stop herself, she tilted her head and waited for his kiss.

Luke touched his lips to hers with infinite gentleness. They stayed thus for a few moments, then he groaned and pulled her closer, clasping her head against his chest and burying his face in her hair. When he spoke again he sounded more normal, as if her kiss had restored his sanity. "Amy, oh, my dearest Amy. How did we make such a mess of things?"

"We just did," she whispered, her words muffled against his pounding heart. "But what can we do about it now?"

He groaned again. "I've thought about nothing else, but I simply don't know. What I said before, about a church annulment, I'm only kidding us both. You'd never get one. Maybe it doesn't matter. You can get a civil divorce. We can go away. To Africa perhaps. We'll start a new life."

Amy closed her eyes and let the vision take possession of her for a brief moment. She and Luke together at Jericho the way she had dreamed it would be. Then she drew away slightly and leaned her head back so

she could look into his face. "There's something you
have to know. I'm going to have a baby."

He let her go and stood with his arms hanging
limply by his sides. She could read his thoughts in his
eyes. In the sight of God, his God at any rate, she was
his brother's wife.

"It doesn't matter," Luke managed to say. The
words were faltering and without conviction. "It doesn't
change anything."

The last bit of hope died inside her. "It changes
everything," Amy said. "You'd never be able to forget that the child was Tommy's."

"Would you?" he asked. His voice was hoarse with
pain.

"I don't know. But it wouldn't be the same for me.
I'd feel bad about Tommy and what I'd done to him.
But I wouldn't think I was going to hell. I don't
believe in hell, or in 'forever and ever, world without
end. . . .' "

He lifted one finger and traced the line of her cheek.
"You're wrong about that, but in other ways you're
very wise for one so young."

"I've told you before, that's what growing up in
Africa does."

"Yes," he agreed. "You've told me before." The
clock chimed noon. "I have to go."

She nodded and walked with him to the door of the
drawing room. "Don't come any further," he said.
"I'll see myself out. I want to remember you in this
room, here like this."

*　　　*　　　*

Luke was deep in thought when he walked down the front steps to the street. He didn't notice the blonde girl until she said, "Oh, hello! Don't I know you?"

He made an effort to struggle free of his preoccupations. "I don't think so," he said. Then he walked away.

Suzy Randolph stared after him in puzzlement. The man was Luke Westerman, Tommy's brother. She'd met him a few years back at a debutante party.

Later she thought more about it, and wondered why Amy had seemed so peculiar at lunch, and why she never mentioned her brother-in-law's visit.

10

~

AMY WALKED ATLANTIC BEACH ALONE. SHE HAD
forgotten her plan to do this with Tommy, and tell him
they were going to have a baby. Instead the sound of
the breaking surf provided a chorus for her agony. She
kept seeing and hearing Luke. She relived every moment of that extraordinary hour, everything he had
said. It was mad, cruel! Why did he come and tell her
these things now? Why did he wait until it was too
late?

"Too late." She spoke the words aloud. A lone gull
squawked raucously in reply. Too late for what? To
marry the man she loved, rather than take his brother

as second best? Yes. But was it? Perhaps they could salvage something from the wreck they'd made. She could get a divorce. Luke could tell the Dominicans that he was not going to take vows and become a priest. Everything could be put right if they simply saw enough lawyers and spent enough time in the courts.

She walked as far as the coast guard station and looked at the spot where she'd stood with Luke. She felt again the urgency of his embrace. The old memory mingled with the more recent one. And pain was a wound reopened after she'd thought it healed. The tide was going out and the sand was hard packed and damp, the way it had been that December day.

Amy studied the imprints of her bare feet and watched them disappear beneath the lapping waves. They faded without a trace. Maybe she could make the last six months fade away in similar fashion. The gull circled and swooped, and its cry was laughter. Tommy's child was growing inside her. It would be an ever-present reminder of what had been, whatever she and Luke did. So would his religion.

Amy threw back her head and looked at the empty blue sky and the sun. "You up there!" She shouted. "God, or whoever you are! You won't let him go, will you?" Her voice died without an echo.

Tears stung her eyes. She blinked them away, but they kept coming. It was true, and she knew it. That's the way it was in this country. It wasn't like Africa where the gods were part of nature, beings to be wooed so the rains would come and the crops would grow and the women be fecund. Here God was some kind of tyrant who demanded that people separate themselves from their humanity, their right to love and be loved.

Whoever he was, this God in whom Luke believed, he would never give up. If Luke left the Dominicans for her, he would be enslaved by guilt, and trapped by her and by Tommy's child.

Amy knelt in the sand. She doubled over in pain and stopped fighting the tears. If she prayed for anything, she who knew nothing of prayer, it was that this place would cease to exist. She wanted to raise her head and look around and see the shining grasslands of her childhood, with the snow-topped peak of Kilimanjaro in the distance.

It did not appear. That dream was as impossible as the notion that she and Luke could turn back the clock and do things differently. "Too late," she repeated. Then she wiped her face and washed it in the cold Atlantic waters, and headed back to the house.

Tommy was waiting for her, worried because she'd been gone so long. She saw him pacing anxiously in the front yard, and she knew a moment of tenderness, overlaid with guilt. "Sorry," she said. "I walked a long way and forgot the time."

"Doesn't matter, as long as you're all right. I thought you might be lost."

"No chance," she smiled. "It's just a long straight beach." She felt awful because he was looking at her with love, and he knew nothing of what had happened or what she had contemplated doing. All at once it seemed like a good time to tell him about the baby. A peace offering, despite the fact that Tommy didn't know about the war.

"Would you like a short drive?" she suggested. "Just the two of us?" Warren kept a Packard motor car at the house.

"No can do," Tommy said. "I invited some people. They'll be along in about twenty minutes. Tomorrow maybe."

"Yes, tomorrow maybe. I'd better go and change and see if Lil wants any help with the preparations." She went inside without saying any more.

The next day there was no opportunity for a drive. Tommy, Lil, and Warren went to Mass in Far Rockaway and brought home more guests. After they left it was time for Warren to drive them to Lawrence where they caught the train for New York.

In her bedroom that night Amy stared at the watercolor of Jericho hanging by the dressing table. The old longings surfaced with new poignancy. There was such an empty place inside her. Only one thing would fill it. She must go home; she must get away from this alien city where everything conspired to cause her pain.

She went downstairs in the morning thinking that she was in control of her emotions. But when she opened the *Times* it was filled with hateful, hurtful news that reminded her of her captivity in this place.

"I hate this damn war! I hate it!" Amy flung the newspaper and its reports of the tank battle of the Somme across the breakfast table.

Tommy was shocked by her intensity. She was white and trembling, and her breath came in short, sharp gasps. "Hey, it's ok sweetheart. It's ok." He moved

quickly to her side and held her head against his chest.
"It's got to end pretty soon." He believed no such
thing, but Amy need not know that. "What do we
care anyway? Let the Europeans blow each other up.
We're safe."

"Don't you understand?" she wailed, sobs choking
her words. "I want to go home. I want to have my
baby at Jericho."

"Baby! Oh, lord!" He dropped to his knees and
turned her face so he could look at it. "Are you
pregnant, sweetheart? Is that what you're telling me?"

She nodded her head and didn't stop weeping.

"That's great! Aren't you pleased?" He fished his
handkerchief from his pocket and wiped her eyes and
made her blow her nose. "No reason our baby can't
be born right here in New York, *memsahib*," he said
smiling. "We may not be Africa, but we have doctors
and hospitals here in the wilderness too."

She couldn't help but laugh. "I know," she said in a
voice still harsh with tears. "It's just that I want our
child to be born there. I want my nurse Naduta with
me, and my own things around me."

Tommy looked at her for a long moment. Then he
stood up and poured a cup of fresh coffee and handed
it to her. "Here, drink this. You still feel like a stranger
here, don't you?"

She nodded.

"One other thing, what about me? Do you want me
too? Or just you and the kid in the bush?"

Amy's brown eyes opened wide. His question made
her wince with pain. How much could Tommy know?

"Of course I want you! You're my husband. You're the baby's father."

He looked at her. "Ok, I just wanted to get that part straight. Listen, darling, the war will end. Maybe not as soon as we'd like, but sometime. It has to. If nothing else, they'll run out of poor bastards to send to the trenches." He looked grim and patted his pocket for a cigarette.

She reached for a box of them on the sideboard and passed it to him. "Would you consider it, Tommy?" she asked. "Would you be willing to give up your work here, and this house and move to Africa?"

"Sure," he said quickly. "Why not? I think it'd be great to have lots of little black boys running around calling me *b'wana* and waiting on me hand and foot. Who wouldn't?"

"You could manage the mines. You're so clever, Tommy, you'd learn about diamonds in no time."

"Yeah. Clever, that's me. That's what everyone says."

Amy guessed that he knew she'd once offered the same arrangement to Luke, but he didn't mention that. He smiled at her instead and said he'd take the day off.

They spent the morning walking in Central Park and the afternoon at the flicks, just like in the old days. When they went early to bed he made love to her. She tried not to resist, not to allow her guilt and disappointment to show, but it was difficult, and afterward she couldn't tell if she'd succeeded. Tommy didn't say anything, but she sensed disapproval in the stiff way he lay beside her when it was over.

*   *   *

Amy began to scheme to find a way they could go home before the end of the war. According to reports, there was a minimum of German resistance left in East Africa. Only one general, Von Lettow-Vorbeck, still led a small guerrilla force deep in the interior. If they could just find safe transport, they could go. She wrote countless letters to her father's former attorney in Dar es Salaam. He was an American, he must still be there. If she mailed enough letters, one of them was bound to get through.

When she talked of Jericho and the way things would be when they returned, Tommy listened quietly. At the same time he grew wary of having sex with her, said it might somehow harm the child. Instead he slept with his hand protectively resting on her belly. They continued to give parties and go to them, but Amy was only going through the motions. She was waiting.

One mellow day in late September she was composing yet another letter to Africa when her ink ran out. She went to Tommy's desk to see if there was a bottle there. The desk top was bare and clean. Tommy was always neat, but envelopes spilled onto the rug when she opened the drawer. It was crammed with paper, and she shook her head over the uncharacteristic mess and bent to tidy it. That's when she saw that most of the letters had never been opened.

They were bills. Masses of them, and all unpaid.

Amy spent fifteen minutes examining the material, then she put on her hat and gloves and took a cab to Wall Street.

"I'm sorry to arrive without an appointment, Uncle Donald." She had called him that since her marriage. He'd insisted on it.

"Not at all, my dear. I'm always happy to see you. Now, what can I do?"

She folded her hands in her lap and tried to speak calmly. "I feel some concern about our financial situation, Uncle Donald. I imagine that's foolish. It's my condition perhaps." She smiled shyly and glanced up to make sure he had understood.

"I see! Well, that's marvelous news, Amy. I'm delighted. And certainly you shouldn't worry at such a time. Have you discussed this with Tommy?"

She shook her head. "I don't want him to think I don't trust him. I do, really. It's just that we're both so young. I think we should consult you and take your advice, and I'm afraid Tommy will be too proud to do that."

"I understand." He drummed a finger on his desktop. "Actually, Tommy has been to see me a number of times. We've discussed the question of your future often."

"Then there's no reason for me to worry?" she asked.

"Now, Amy." He looked uncomfortable. "I'm not saying everything is exactly as it should be. There are one or two things . . ."

"What things?"

"Tommy has borrowed rather heavily against your

estate. I am a little concerned about that. We mustn't jeopardize your being able to take control once this war ends. Don't want the bank to end up owning the mines now, do we?"

Amy wanted to scream. She only said, "How real is the danger, Uncle Donald?"

"Oh, not at all real yet! It's just the pattern that concerns me. Perhaps you should suggest that the two of you live a little more frugally for the time being. You ladies are good at that sort of thing, I'm told."

"Yes, I'll do that. Thank you."

The scene was terrible. They said things neither of them would ever forget. "You're a cheat and a liar and a fraud!" Amy screamed after they'd been arguing for almost an hour. "You're not the man I thought you were at all."

"Not Luke, you mean." Tommy shook with rage and clung to a small mahogany table, as if to keep himself from striking her. "Not the saintly golden boy. That's what's bothering you, isn't it? You're just sick with wanting it to be Luke's baby inside you!"

"That's crazy! Luke has nothing to do with this. He's only part of it in your sick mind. You're afraid to face up to your responsibilities, so you spend money we don't have and don't pay the bills! And since you brought it up, you're right. Luke would never do such a thing."

"Aagh!" He screamed the wordless cry of anguish and struck out at the innocent bibelots on the table.

They crashed to the floor at his feet, and he slammed out of the room.

He didn't return for three days. When he did they made it up and promised each other it would be different in the future. Amy had paid all the bills in the meantime.

"How'd you do that? Uncle Donald?"

She shook her head. "No, that would only have made it worse. I sold my diamond ring. I got four thousand dollars for it. There's still a few hundred left."

He reached for her hand to confirm the story. There was a little white space where the ring had been. "Oh, Jesus," he whispered.

"It doesn't matter. When we go home there are lots of diamonds. They're in a vault in the bank in Dar es Salaam. I told you that." She tried to sound gay.

Tommy didn't say anything, but he examined her other hand and saw that his grandmother's sapphire, the ring he'd given her to mark their engagement, was still in place. So were the pearls around her neck. He reached up and fingered them. "You could have sold something else," he muttered.

"Those were presents from you to me," she whispered. "The diamond was my own. It's different."

Later they talked about living on just his salary. Amy hadn't known until now how much it was.

"Seventy-five a week," he told her. "Until I learn the ropes and have clients of my own. It's generous of them, I suppose, but I want to do better. They keep telling me to be patient, that I'm too young to take charge of any accounts."

She did some rapid calculations with pencil and paper. "We should be able to live on seventy-five a week." She frowned and nibbled on the eraser. "Maybe we should let Delia go and just keep the cook."

He took the paper and pencil from her and lay them aside. "Let me worry about all that. You just concentrate on keeping you and the baby healthy."

They stopped the socializing. Amy suspected it was as much a relief for Tommy as for her.

The first time Amy saw the advertisement in the *Times* was a day in October. She had taken the paper and gone to the park to sit in the sunshine. She did that a lot lately. Among the trees bright with autumn and the laughing children watched over by sturdy governesses, it was possible to let her thoughts drift. She dreamed about Jericho and about her baby. She was in a kind of limbo, waiting only for a letter from Dar es Salaam. Somehow, Amy convinced herself, her links with reality would then be reestablished. She could go home.

On this particular morning a girl stood on a nearby soapbox and preached about giving women the vote. The speaker looked to be about her own age, and Amy wondered what it must be like to be able to spare thought for problems outside oneself. The notion was depressing, so she pushed it away and opened the newspaper.

She liked to read the real estate section. There were always a few columns devoted to properties outside New York, and she'd invented a little game in which she compared them to Jericho and was pleased because they never measured up. Today one almost seemed to do so. It offered for sale not a country house in an eastern town like Cross River, but a piece of the fabled American West.

"New Mexico," the announcement read. "Youngest State in the Union and Land of Enchantment. Ranch for Sale. Amazing Opportunity." There were more details. A cattle spread was being offered, nearly three thousand head of prime beef on the hoof. "House and numerous ranch buildings," the advertisement promised. "Heartbroken owner must sell at a loss due to ill health. Don't miss out. Act now."

Amy remembered how she'd once thought of the West as being like Africa; then she turned the page.

The next day the advertisement was repeated, and the next. After that it disappeared and she assumed that the property had been sold. The following week she was surprised to see the advertisement again. This time she cut it out carefully and tucked it beneath the velvet cushion of her jewelry box.

That afternoon she went to the library on Eighty-sixth Street and read everything she could find on New Mexico and the Southwest. One book had a colored drawing of golden grasslands, fringed by the snow-topped Sangre de Cristo mountains. She looked at that picture and felt a stab of pleasure that was almost pain. It looked remarkably like the Africa she had known.

Amy walked home carrying the book and staring pensively at the pavement. Her body was growing a little heavy, her sense of balance changed by the life within. She moved slowly and had time to think before she reached her front door.

That night she slept with the book about New Mexico under her pillow. She was a little afraid that Tommy might find it, but he didn't.

Two days later she went to the *Times* office on Broadway and spoke to the advertising manager. She wanted to know if the ranch had been sold, but he couldn't tell her. "Our only instructions are to run the announcement three days a week until further notice." He ruffled through some papers. "The gentleman paid for a month's worth of insertions. Why don't you write to him?"

A dozen times she took up her pen, then put it down again. The idea wasn't just outlandish, it was a kind of dying. The rancher was asking fifty thousand dollars for his spread. To get that kind of money she must forfeit Jericho. It was too much to ask; she couldn't do it. She put her writing things away, then returned the book to the library.

Next morning the papers were full of the news of more allied losses in Europe and, for the first time, serious speculation that Wilson was considering taking America into the war. Amy read the reports and the columns carefully after Tommy went to the office. Africa seemed to be receding into the distance. It was moving beyond her reach because of events totally outside her control. She put aside the newspaper and sat down and wrote to the man who wanted to sell a ranch in New Mexico, the land of enchantment.

11

~

"T HIS IS THE LATEST LETTER." AMY PUT TWO SHEETS
of flimsy stationery on Donald Varley's desk.

The handwriting was large and open and marked by
many flourishes. In some places the ink had blotted
the paper. Varley held it to the weak November light
of the window, then made a noise of impatience and
switched on a lamp. He read in silence. "Did he send
the photographs you requested?" he asked finally.

"Just one." Amy handed him a speckled gray card-
board folder. It opened from the top and had one of
those flap arrangements that allowed it to stand by
itself. The picture was of an enormous black steer,

151

staged against a gray and white desert. The beast had curved horns and massive shoulders, and it looked at the camera with malevolence.

Varley snorted, "Not much help is it? One bull posed to have its picture taken."

"Mr. DeAngeles says it's representative." She leaned forward and ran a black-kid-encased finger over the letter lying on the desk. "He says all the stock is of the same high quality."

"Yes, and that the land is magnificent and the houses likewise. Do you believe him, my dear?"

Amy shrugged. "It's a gamble, I know that. But surely he wouldn't ask fifty thousand dollars if it weren't all true?"

Varley smiled. "It's not the asking that's difficult. It's the getting." She looked pained. "I can do some independent checking," he added hastily. "I'll ask around and find a reliable attorney in Santa Fe. Then we'll have an unbiased report."

Fifteen days later Amy returned to the office. Varley produced a manila envelope from the bookcase behind his chair.

"Will you read it, or shall I summarize?"

"Tell me what he says."

"Quite a bit. A lot more than Mr. DeAngeles. First, and most important, there's water on this . . . what's the place called?" He rifled the pages searching for the name of the ranch.

"Santo Domingo," Amy supplied. She sat primly on the edge of her seat, tense with expectation.

"That's right. As I said, there's a waterhole. Extremely reliable, my colleague says. It's on DeAngeles land, but shared by treaty with two other ranches. That's not uncommon apparently. And at the last count"—he ran his finger down the page searching for numbers—"there were three thousand head of cattle. That's certified by the government. We've been lucky there."

"I don't understand."

"Four years ago, when New Mexico was admitted as a state, the federal government sent in assessors to make a survey. That's the source of these figures." He tapped the manila envelope. "To continue, there's a main dwelling of ten rooms and various outbuildings. They're in need of some repair because the present owner has been ill. 'But basically sound' . . ." he read aloud. " . . .'And once a true showplace' . . ." Varley looked up and smiled at her. Amy glowed with pleasure.

"Oh, yes," he added. "There's water laid on to the house. The report stresses that. Not unreasonable when you come to think of it. Water must be the key out there."

"I saw the Sahara once," she said enthusiastically. "I went on a trip with Mummy and Daddy when I was five or six. It was beautiful."

"But can you imagine actually living in a desert?" Varley put down the report, leaned forward and took her hand. "I want what is best for you, my dear, I mean that most sincerely. This ranch sounds excellent, but the Southwest is still a frontier. Conditions are bound to be primitive. Have you really thought about all that?"

"Yes," she said firmly. She withdrew her hand from

his and sat up very straight. "I've considered it most carefully, Uncle Donald. I'm sure it's the right thing to do." Her tone changed and she rummaged in her handbag for a handkerchief. "You were never in Africa, so you can't understand. But the moment I saw those pictures in that book I knew. It's the closest thing to home I'm going to find."

She blew her nose, but she did not cry.

Varley said, "I admit that's my one remaining reservation. How would you two get on so far from the family and civilization? What does Tommy say?"

"I haven't told him."

"But, Amy, we agreed! After your last visit we agreed you'd discuss it with Tommy before we went any further. Really, my dear, I cannot pursue this matter without the consent of your husband. Apart from the legalities, it simply isn't right."

Amy took a deep breath. It was imperative that she enlist Donald Varley as an ally. To do so she would have to tell him at least part of the truth. "Tommy has always been a little insecure because of his handicap. He worries that I don't really love him."

"I see," Varley said. "And do you love him?"

She hesitated. "I care very much for Tommy. I believe we can be happy together. But not unless we leave New York. We need a new life, a new challenge. If things were different, we could go to Jericho. I would give half my life if we could do that. Apparently we cannot. This is the next best solution."

"You've thought it out carefully, haven't you? I grow more and more amazed at your maturity, my dear. Somehow I didn't expect it."

"I've said before that girls grow up more quickly in Africa. Perhaps now you'll believe me." Amy put the handkerchief away and closed her bag with a decisive snap. "You haven't told me the conclusion of that report."

Varley smiled. "If you were a man, my dear, I should make you a trial lawyer. Very well, according to my Santa Fe colleague the asking price for Santo Domingo is not unreasonable. It is perhaps a bargain."

"That settles it then—if I can raise fifty thousand dollars."

Varley stood up and walked to the window. Wall Street was a narrow ribbon, bepurpled by the long shadows of the setting sun. "I wish to consider the question of the money a little longer," he said. His voice sounded strained.

"Do you think it can be found, Uncle Donald?" Her words were a plea. "Will I be able to buy Santo Domingo?"

"I wish to consider the matter," Varley repeated. He turned back to her. "In the meantime you must find an opportunity to discuss this affair with Tommy. We can do nothing final until you have his agreement."

"I will," she said. "I promise."

She got up to go, and he didn't escort her out as he usually did. Instead his voice stopped her before she reached the door. "Amy, I had a letter from Luke yesterday. He's just taken his first vows. He's well on his way to the priesthood now. Did you know?"

She froze for a moment, realized the evidence her stiff back was providing, and willed herself to relax and speak normally. "No, I didn't. We haven't had a letter yet. The post probably."

"Yes, probably," Varley agreed. "You must tell Tommy about that too."

"I'll tell him everything," Amy said. But she wouldn't of course. Not quite everything.

"Are you crazy?" Tommy stared at his wife. Then he looked down at the papers and pictures she had spread before him on the dining-room table. "What is all this stuff? Where did you get it?"

"I told you, I've been corresponding with Mr. DeAngeles for a month, and Uncle Donald has written to a lawyer in Santa Fe. His report was very favorable. There's water on the property, you see. That makes it a good ranch."

She was wearing a pink chiffon tea gown, trimmed with feathers. The color cast flattering highlights on her creamy skin. She looked to Tommy infinitely desirable, more so because the soft clinging fabric betrayed the small sweet mound where once her flat belly had been. Her pregnancy was a mark of his possession, an affirmation of his manhood.

"Listen, I don't want to upset you. Sit down. We'll talk about it."

Amy pulled a chair close to his so they could look together at the papers.

She found the picture of the steer and stood it open on the table between them. "Isn't he a marvelous-looking brute? And there are more than three thousand of them! Look at this picture." She pointed to the book. "That's New Mexico, but it could be German East. Do you remember the grasslands? You saw them that one time you visited. Remember how they were all golden in the sun and stretched on and on with Kilimanjaro in the distance?"

"You're beautiful. Your eyes shine when you get excited."

She pushed away the hand he placed on her arm. "Please listen, Tommy. And look at all these things. It's very important. It's our whole future. Ours and the baby's."

She hadn't meant the gesture as a rejection, nonetheless he saw it so. "You listen," he said in the hard voice of a stranger. "Looking after our future is my job. And I'm not doing as badly as you seem to think. You're ok aren't you? This house and a couple of servants, it's not too much like poverty, is it?"

"Tommy, I never said that. I don't think it. It's just that this is such a wonderful opportunity."

He stood up and limped a few steps away, standing with his back to her and his hands plunged into his pockets. "Are you sorry you married me? Is that what you're trying to tell me?"

"No, of course not!" Her palms were sweating. Tommy was skirting close to the truth, and that meant disaster for both of them. "This is such a challenge," she said with forced brightness. "That's what I'm trying to explain."

"Little Miss Explainer, that's my Amy. Done a lot of it, haven't you? Probably even to sainted brother

Luke. Have you written to him about this new scheme?"
He turned to face her. The tic beside his mouth pulsed
wildly.

She couldn't bear the fury in his eyes. "No," she
whispered. "Why would I do that?"

"Yeah, why?" He put his hands on the table and
leaned forward. She could feel his breath when he
spoke. "Maybe because you're still regretting that you're
not married to him. But it's too late, baby. Luke took
vows last week. He wrote to tell me all about it."

"I know," she said. "Uncle Donald told me. Why
are we talking about Luke? It's you and I that matter.
Please, Tommy . . ." She reached for him, but he
pulled away.

"I know something else," he said. "Get ready for a
big surprise, sweetheart. That kid you're carrying could
never be Luke's, no matter how much you want it to
be." He laughed, but it was a sound without mirth.
"He's a eunuch, my holy brother. Sterile. Never could
be a father, so he's turned saint instead. How do you
like them apples?"

"I know," she said hoarsely. "He told me before he
went away. It's nothing to do with anything."

"Told you? Luke told you the sordid details of his
sex life. Oh, Jesus! What a fool I've been. I thought
you were little Miss Innocence when I married you.
Now it comes out you had a nice intimate relationship
with my big brother." He thrust his hand beneath her
chin and yanked her face up so he could look at her.
"When did he first have you, *memsahib*? Tell me all
about it."

Amy wrenched free of his grip and backed away,

clutching at the pink tea gown as if it were protection. "You know there wasn't anyone before you! Luke told me because he wanted me to understand about his being a priest." She felt as if she couldn't breathe.

Tommy looked from her to the books and papers on the table. "Shit!" he said, sweeping the pile to the floor with one savage motion. "That's what this whole thing is. Just shit! You and Luke and all the rest. Well, you aren't doing it on me. Not me, baby! You got that?"

He moved to where she stood. She was doubled over in fear and pain and grief. Tommy grabbed her shoulders. "Stand up! Stand up, you bitch whore, and look at me so I know you're listening!"

She tried to see his face, but it was lost behind a red haze of anguish. She couldn't see anything. Pains shot up her back and into her belly, cramping pains that kept her from standing upright. "Don't," she moaned. "Oh, Tommy, please don't do this."

"Me!" he shouted. "I haven't done a thing. You've done it all."

He pushed her away and she stumbled against the small loveseat that filled the space between the dining room windows. She tried to sit down, but managed only a half sprawl between the seat and the floor.

Tommy was screaming. It was as if she wasn't there, and his anger was directed at some unseen enemy. "Don't think I can't see what's going on! It's always been the same. Poor crippled Tommy. Needs looking after. Needs the family to manage his affairs. And you! You're my wife, but you played right into their hands. New Mexico for Chrissake! Exile. Banishment so Tommy will stay out of trouble. Oh, they must love it. It's perfect. I'm a cripple and you're part Indian. New Mexico's goddamn perfect!"

He started for the door, and she stretched out her hand to hold him back. "Tommy, I'm sick. Don't leave me. Please . . ."

He didn't seem to hear.

Delia found her an hour later, lying unconscious in a pool of blood. An ambulance came and took her to Lenox Hill Hospital on Lexington Avenue, but she had already miscarried. For a few hours the doctors thought she might bleed to death. She did not. Amy opened her eyes twenty-four hours later to a room filled with flowers and a smiling nurse.

"There, Mrs. Westerman, that's better. Feeling a bit peaky? Nevermind, you'll soon be well."

"My baby?"

The nurse shook her head. She wore a starched and ruffled cap that looked as if it must soon take flight. "Don't you fret about that, child. You're young. There will be plenty of babies yet. Just a little hiccup in the production line," she said cheerfully. "That's all this is."

"Where's Tommy?"

"I believe Mr. Westerman will be in to see you later," the nurse twittered. "Your aunt's waiting outside now. I'll just tell her you're awake, shall I?"

She didn't wait for her patient to agree. In a moment Amy was wrapped in the familiar jasmine-scented embrace.

"Oh, darling, you frightened us so! Thank God, you're all right. How do you feel?"

"Fine, thank you," Amy said. She smiled weakly at the inanity of her response. "I mean, not too bad. Where's Tommy, Aunt Lil? We quarreled. I'm worried about him."

"He's fine. He'll be here this afternoon. You mustn't worry about anything. Just get well."

The nurse came back and said that Mrs. Westerman must rest. Lil kissed her again and left. Finally the nurse left too. Amy put her hand on her empty belly and wept.

Tommy sat by her bed, but he didn't look at her. He stared at the floor. "I suppose you must hate me."

"It wasn't your fault."

"Yes, it was. I made you upset."

"That had nothing to do with it. The doctor told me these things are always for the best. It's nature's way of protecting people."

The doctor had filled her head full of images of deformed children and idiots, whom nature aborted as a kindness. She knew that he had meant to comfort, not alarm. She didn't want to share those terrors. "Are you all right?" she asked.

"Oh, I'm great. Feel like a million bucks, I do. What can you expect?" He pointed to a vase of long-stemmed roses. "Those are from me. I looked all over

New York, but nobody had any African flame flowers. At least these are red."

She smiled. "I didn't think you remembered the flame trees. You've never said anything."

"I remember." He leaned forward and clasped his hands between his legs. "Look, I've been thinking. Maybe this New Mexico thing isn't so crazy after all. I haven't had a chance to look at the stuff yet. After I left you"—he swallowed hard remembering that leave-taking—"I went out and got drunk. Uncle Warren found me this morning and told me what happened. I went back to their place to straighten out."

She had a vision of timid Warren searching for Tommy in all the New York bars. It made her want to cry again, but she swallowed the tears. "I guess everything's still at the house. You can look at it later."

"Yes. I'll go home right after I leave here."

"That's good. Tommy, I want to ask you something. What did you mean when you said I was part Indian?"

He looked startled. "Don't you know?"

She shook her head.

"Jesus, chalk up another one for me. I thought you did but just never liked to mention it."

"Tell me about it," she said.

"Some other time. After you're feeling better."

"No, I want to know now."

He shrugged. "Ok. I don't think it means anything anyway. It's different today." He reached for a cigarette, then changed his mind.

"It's all right. Smoke if you like."

He lit up and inhaled gratefully. "When they first

got married my Westerman grandparents lived in a little town way up north. Place called Fort Covington. It seems their maid got herself pregnant and local gossip said the father was an Indian. It was during the Civil War. There was a lot of feeling about things like that in those days."

"My father was born in 1863."

"Yeah, so was mine. That was part of it. Grandma Westerman had a son the same time as her maid did. Only the maid was being hounded by everybody. Grandma felt sorry for her and she believed there was some connection between the babies. She let the maid stay on and keep her son with her. Then, when the Westermans moved to New York, Grandma took them both along."

"Her last name was Norman then? My grandmother."

"Guess so. It must have been. The way dad told it she died when her son was around ten. Roland lived with the family until he went away to college."

"So your grandfather brought him up. He must have paid for Daddy's education, too."

Tommy looked uncomfortable. "I'll bet he got it all back. Your father certainly did well enough."

"Yes," she said. "I'm sure Daddy must have paid him back. How come your grandparents didn't make him a Catholic?"

Tommy grinned. "I asked the same thing when my father told me the story. The maid was a Methodist. A real bible thumper, despite everything. She thought the pope was the Antichrist and all Catholics were going straight to hell. Never mind what Grandma did for her. In the end I guess your father just figured, 'a pox on both your houses.' Or something like that."

The nurse returned and told Tommy he'd have to leave. Then she gave Amy a sedative and made clucking noises about Tommy's cigarette. He stubbed it out obediently and kissed his wife good-bye.

Amy wanted to think about the things he'd told her, but the sedative sent her swiftly to sleep.

12

WHEN TOMMY RETURNED THE NEXT MORNING SHE was sitting up in the bed brushing her hair. "I suppose that's why it's so straight and black," she said.

He looked puzzled at first. "Oh, the Indian business, you mean. Nothing was ever proved, you know."

"I don't mind," Amy said. "At least I don't think I do."

He grinned. "That's the spirit! Don't let the bastards get you down." He flushed slightly. "Sorry, didn't mean to be vulgar."

The memory of the curses he had hurled at her came to Amy's mind as the dull ache of remembered pain. "I have to ask you," she said, looking at him with sudden intensity. "Did you mean the things you said the other night? Is that what you believe?"

"Oh, God! Of course I didn't. You know what I'm like when I get mad. I don't mean any of the things I say." He dropped to his knees beside the bed and lay his head on the sheets. "I don't know why you should forgive me. But I hope you will."

She stroked his hair and the brown curls twined between her fingers. "It doesn't matter," she said. "Just so long as you don't really believe it."

"Please," he whispered. "Say you forgive me. I want to hear you say it."

"I forgive you."

He looked up and took her hand in his own and kissed her palm. "Thank you. It's going to be all right, darling. I called Uncle Donald this morning. I told him I thought we should try to buy that ranch. We're going to have a new start, just like you said. Maybe I'll go out there and have a look, later, when you're well."

Varley came to the house in deference to her health. Amy received him in the drawing room. It might have been planned as a backdrop for her. The pale creamy colors were just those that suited her best. When Varley bent over the sofa to kiss her he saw that her brown eyes had little gold specks in them, and that her black hair was tinged with auburn highlights.

"You look surprisingly wonderful. Where's Tommy?"

"He had to go to the office for a little while. He knows you're coming, and he'll be back soon."

"Good, I want all three of us talking together this time."

"Yes," she agreed. "That's the way it's going to be from now on."

Varley smiled. "I'm glad you're recovering so well. What does the doctor say?"

"That I'll be up and around before Christmas. Truthfully, I could be now. I'm just lying here so everyone will be sympathetic." She patted the cashmere blanket spread over her legs. "Sit down, Uncle Donald. Delia's bringing coffee."

The maid came in and put the tray where Amy could reach it. There were three bone china cups, each sprigged with rosebuds and edged with gilt. "Ask Mr. Westerman to join us as soon as he arrives, please, Delia."

"Yes, madam. I'll tell him."

They talked about the weather, surprisingly mild for December. Varley's briefcase sat beside his chair. They both looked at it frequently. Amy felt fear begin as a small cold knot in her stomach. What if Tommy didn't come? What would Uncle Donald do or say if Tommy changed his mind about this venture. What would happen to all her plans and dreams?

She heard his steps in the hall with a sense of relief.

"Hello, sorry I'm late. Beastly traffic. Christmas shoppers already taking all the cabs. How goes it, darling?" He kissed his wife and shook uncle's hand. "Coffee for me too, I hope. It's turning cold. Winter arriving at last, I'm afraid."

She filled another cup and held it out. "We haven't talked any business yet," she said. "We were waiting for you."

"Right." Tommy turned to his uncle. "Let's get to it then."

Varley picked up his briefcase and set it on the table next to the coffee tray. "I'll give you the bad news first," he said. "But I want you to know there's good news to follow."

Amy braced herself.

"I've talked to half a dozen banks. None of them wants to consider the loan. It's the war of course. Bankers become very tense when the world is so unsettled. I expect you understand about all that, Tommy."

Tommy nodded. "Money's tight all over the city. I have clients that are climbing the walls to raise a few thousand. Men that would have had no trouble doing it six months ago."

"Exactly. And all the latest news is bad. This chap Lloyd George who's taken over in England, people don't trust him."

"Bit of a socialist, one hears." Tommy said. "May turn out to be like those madmen beseiging the Russian Tsar."

"Please," Amy interrupted, "what's the outcome, Uncle Donald? How can we raise the money if the banks won't agree?"

Varley stood up. He took a cigarette from a slim silver case and offered one to Tommy, but not to her. Then he began pacing the room, puffing smoke between each word. "I have spent some time and thought on this matter. It isn't just an ordinary business arrangement. How can it be? I'm executor of your father's estate"—with a nod to Tommy—"and until you married, I was your legal guardian, Amy. Moreover, Tommy is my sister's son. I've known him since the day he was born. All that changes things. You do understand?"

The couple nodded their agreement. Amy thought Donald different than she'd ever seen him. There was great strain on his face. Normally he was a man made handsome by perfection. The silver hair and the small moustache, the erect bearing and the exquisitely tailored clothes—all bespoke sureness. Today he seemed inexplicably frayed at the edges.

"I have decided to give you the money myself," he said abruptly. The announcement dropped into the void between the three, and remained there awaiting comment.

"We can't let you do that," Tommy said finally. "It's too much to ask. We're taking a risk with this venture. Both Amy and I know that. Neither of us knows anything about ranching."

"Yes," Varley said. "So the banks pointed out. But you see, I know the two of you. The bankers do not."

"You mean it's our wonderful track record so far," Tommy said, leaning forward to place his empty cup on the tray. "Our history of success? Come on, we all know better."

"Uncle Donald's being extraordinarily kind," Amy said quickly. "Don't talk to him like that."

"It's all right, my dear. In fact, it illustrates my point. Tommy has brains and spunk. And you have both courage and imagination. I am prepared to believe that those qualities will prevail over the odds against you."

"What terms are you suggesting?" Tommy asked. His voice was expressionless.

"I am prepared to buy Amy's inheritance rights. For the amount required to purchase Santo Domingo—plus an additional ten thousand to give you some working capital. Sixty thousand dollars in all."

"I take it you mean an outright sale," Tommy said. "Twenty-five thousand acres of New Mexico, in exchange for the Norman Diamond Mines. Is that it?"

"Yes," Varley agreed. "If, of course the Norman mines exist after this damnable war ends. And if they are not conscripted as the spoils of victory by some triumphant government. I'm taking risks too."

"I'd have to see the New Mexico property first," Tommy said. "You understand that, of course."

"Of course," Varley agreed.

Amy listened to the voices of the men. They seemed to come from far away. She had known it would be thus since the day she clipped the advertisement from the *Times*. It had seemed to her obvious that the only way she could buy a ranch in New Mexico was to sell Jericho. Then Donald and Tommy had begun talking about a loan. For a brief time she had thought perhaps she could have both.

Now she lay on the couch and watched them, the older man and the younger one. They were united by blood, and by familiarity with a world of which she knew nothing. Business had a code of its own; it had laws and a language. Tommy and Donald knew the rules and the tongue. She did not.

She rested her head on the arm of the sofa and studied the ceiling. Where it joined the walls there was a cornice. It was a simple trim of white wood, and it ran completely round the room. Amy stared at it and knew that she must leave this place. If she did not, all the rest of her days would be just like the cornice— featureless, with neither beginning nor end. Tommy would be embittered by jealousy, and she would always think of Luke and what might have been. She would grow old in this city crammed with buildings and people, all clustered around a pathetic park imitating nature.

Tommy and Donald were discussing interest rates and foreign exchange. She cut through their words without apology. "Give me the papers, Uncle Donald. I'll sign them."

"Amy, wait," Tommy said quickly. "I've got to go to Santa Fe and have a look at this ranch. We can't buy it sight unseen."

"I can't wait," she said. She looked at him with pleading eyes that said, *I cannot bear another disappointment.* "Please, Tommy, try to understand."

He understood all too well. Guilt was a sour taste in his mouth, and love of her an ache in his gut. Tommy looked at his uncle. "You tell her," he said.

Varley knew what he was expected to say, but it was not the conservative prudent lawyer who spoke. "We've had an excellent unbiased report," he said. "And Amy has been through so much . . ."

Tommy's eyes narrowed. He glanced from his uncle

to his wife and saw that the two of them had formed
an alliance. He couldn't oppose it, not after what he'd
done. "You're sure you're willing to sell Jericho outright?" he asked Amy.

"I'm sure," she said.

Varley's palms were sweating inside his suede gloves.
His hands had trembled when he wrote the check, but
he didn't think they'd noticed. Now he clung to his
briefcase as if it were life, and didn't set it down
during the cab ride to Wall Street.

The receptionist at the bank recognized him and
sent him through to the president's office. He was
shown in immediately. He put the briefcase on the
other man's desk. It made a satisfying thump.

"From the look of you I assume your niece agreed."

"Yes."

"That's fine. If you'll just give me the papers. . . ."

Varley handed them over. "They're all in order."

The bank president smiled a wintry smile. "Yes, I'm
sure they are." He glanced through the documents,
making little sounds under his breath. ". . . and all
related holdings," he read aloud. "Yes, this will do
nicely. I'll see that the transfer to your account is
made immediately. One hundred and fifty thousand
dollars. As agreed. Of course there's the matter of my
commission and your overdraft, and the sixty thousand paid to Mr. and Mrs. Westerman. Still, you'll be
in credit to the tune of thirty thousand or more. A tidy
sum."

Varley felt weak-kneed, pulled between self-hate

and relief. "It's not a tenth of what the Norman holdings are worth," he said softly. "You realize that."

"Of course. But you're forgetting the element of risk. The world is a dangerous place just now. We bankers are willing to take chances, but we expect to be paid for them."

Tommy scowled at the assortment of toilet things on Amy's dressing table, as if the black enamel objects offended him. "I think we've been had," he said. "I think Uncle Donald's pulled a fast one. You should have waited until I had a chance to talk to some people. I should go out and see that place before we buy it."

"No," she moaned. "I don't want to wait that long; I can't. Please, Tommy . . . We have sixty thousand dollars. It's what we need. That's all I care about." Her face was white and drawn where it lay against the bed pillows. She was staring at the watercolor of Jericho, and it was obvious that she cared about a great deal beside.

"It's my fault," Tommy muttered. "Jesus, why do I make such a mess of things? If you believed you could trust me, you'd have waited. If you hadn't lost the baby you might never have gotten this crazy idea."

She was terrified of his guilt. She knew how much was really her fault, not his. "You're not to blame about the baby. You mustn't think so. But we have to get away from here. Please, can't we try to be happy?"

"Yeah, sure," he said, managing a grin. "We're going to be happy. Why the hell not? I'll go downtown and get some train schedules. We can plan the trip. You'll like that, won't you?"

"Very much. What did Western Union say? How long will it take for Mr. DeAngeles to get our telegram?"

"A few hours, that's all."

"Tell me the message again."

He fished a scrap of paper from his pocket and read aloud the wire he'd sent after Donald Varley left the house. "Agree to purchase ranch immediately. Please, confirm."

Confirmation arrived the next morning, after Tommy left to go to Pennsylvania station for more railroad information. Amy read the words on the pale yellow paper. Then she slowly climbed the stairs to her bedroom.

She went to the picture of Jericho hanging on the wall and removed it. Then she carried it to the window filled with thin, cold sunlight. The painting was covered by glass and the watercolors looked as fresh as the day Jessie Norman had stroked them delicately onto the paper. Some of the proportions were less than perfect. The long veranda framed in teak was actually broader than it appeared in the drawing. The roof had a gentler pitch. Amy smiled gently. Sheba, the pony, was badly done. "Mummy could never draw horses," she murmured. "She kept trying though."

There were two faces in one of the ground floor windows. You had to look closely to see them. One was supposed to be her. The black hair and oversize brown eyes were recognizable. The other was Naduta, her nurse. It was just an ebony blob without detail. "I didn't do Naduta well at all." Jessie had said, laughing when she held the picture out for her daughter's inspection. Amy remembered that long-ago day. She remembered the sun and the sounds of the bush, and her mother's voice.

"I don't care, I love it. It's the best picture ever," she'd said then. "The best picture ever," she repeated now.

She wrapped the painting carefully in a flowered silk scarf and put it away to await packing.

BOOK TWO

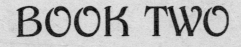

1917–21

13

~

AMY WORE HER BEIGE SUIT FOR THE DEPARTURE. THE one she'd worn on her honeymoon. She had a new coat of brown Persian lamb trimmed with mink. Lil had given it to her as a going-away present. Amy was glad of its warmth on this first day of February.

Lil and Warren came to the station to see them off. They huddled together by the platform gate, using chatter and forced humor as proof against nerves.

At last a man walked beside them announcing, "*Silver Arrow,* track twenty-two. Pittsburgh, Chicago, and points west. All aboard, please."

"That's us," Amy said.

Their redcap came by. "Right this way, Mr. and Mrs. Westerman. I'll show you to your carriage."

There was time only for hurried kisses and softly spoken blessings.

They followed the porter and his wheeled cart down the long open platform to a car marked "Pullman" in golden letters with elaborate scrolls. "Dining car's three forward," the black man said. "Club car right behind you. Here you are, compartment fourteen." Amy had a swift impression of pristine order and faultless comfort.

Finally they were alone and the train inched forward. Amy looked out at Pennsylvania Station, and then at the blackness of a tunnel.

"Good-bye New York," Tommy said. "C'mon, let's go to the club car and celebrate, or hold a wake. I'm not sure which is called for."

Dawn of the journey's third day carried them across the Mississippi into St. Louis. Tommy had planned the trip for a minimum number of train changes, but they could not avoid one there. With a small sense of loss Amy packed her case. Compartment fourteen had become comfortable and familiar.

They drank coffee and ate pancakes and cornmeal muffins at a Fred Harvey restaurant in the station. Then they followed another redcap across a bustling expanse of gates and platforms to the boarding point for the Atchison, Topeka and Santa Fe line.

The train was a duplicate of the one they'd been on. The Pullman car had the same lavish and comfortable appointments of mahogany and brass and starched white linen. Only when they chugged forth from St.

Louis did Amy slowly realize that she had entered a different world.

By late afternoon she was sure of it. They reached Kansas City and moved out across the fat flat plains of Kansas. The land was planted with winter wheat, short and straw colored and asleep; still the power of boundless fertility rose up and engulfed the passing train.

"Breadbasket of the nation," Tommy murmured.

"It's so . . ." She groped for the word. "So precise."

"God's always doing geometry," he said. She smiled with delight, and he added, "Not original. Plato said it first."

That night Amy couldn't sleep for excitement. When the porter knocked softly to announce, "Topeka in half an hour folks," she was up instantly.

They had to change trains once more. This time there was no Pullman car. In the deep dark before dawn they boarded a coach train that turned south into a sky streaked with pink and red, then hurtled into a mantle of sunlight spread across the border lands between Kansas and Oklahoma. As the vast empty spaces unfolded Amy felt reborn.

Tommy watched her glowing face, but did not share her joyous excitement. Instead he stared straight ahead and drummed his fingers nervously on the armrest between them. At one point he produced a silver hip flask. "A little brandy soothes the nerves," he said, offering it to her.

"No thanks. I'll have a cigarette though."

He lit one for her and for himself, and she kept darting glances at him through the smoke. Tommy took a long pull of the brandy, then put the flask away. She wondered about his mood, then concentrated on the scenery.

For two days they rode thus. Then, in the sunsoaked early morning of the sixth day since they'd left New York, they started to climb. Amy's heart pounded wildly and her breath came short and sharp. In an hour they had scaled the cliff and were poised on the edge of a canyon looking into the Raton pass.

She closed her eyes because it was too beautiful to look at, then opened them because it was too beautiful to miss. The train started downward. It passed miraculously unharmed between sheer, tawny rock faces; it hurtled through a landscape honey-dipped and bejeweled and glittering, beneath a fiery red sun in a limitless blue sky. They had arrived in New Mexico.

At Lamy, ten miles southeast of Santa Fe, they were met by the lawyer who had reported on the ranch to Donald Varley, and subsequently handled the purchase. His name was John Lopez. He was a small dark man who wore a white linen suit and a narrow braid around his neck in place of a tie. The braid was held together by a silver clasp. It flashed in the westering sun. So did his glasses. He seemed to shine. Amy was conscious of her rumpled suit and Tommy's trousers, which no longer had a crease.

"Mr. and Mrs. Westerman, welcome to your new home!" They shook hands, and he asked them about the journey and at the same time took the stubs for their luggage and handed them to another man slouching in the background. "Diego will get your things and load them on the buckboard. Don't worry about any of that. You must be exhausted. Too late to go out to your place today. I've reserved a room in a hotel in town."

He led them to his Model-T Ford. "Railroad passed by Santa Fe years ago. We have to drive from here."

The men chattered during the journey. Amy was silent with awe. By the time they drove into the fabled plaza, she was dizzy with excitement.

"It's small for a place with so much history." Lopez said. "Are you disappointed? Folks sometimes are."

Amy was unable to answer. She looked at squat adobe structures painted white and etched with black shadows where dark wooden beams thrust through their walls. Gray-green cottonwood trees hugged the buildings close. A brown-skinned woman squatted by the roadside guarding a pile of decorated clay pots. Across the way a similar figure hovered over a collection of brightly woven blankets. Familiarity was a wordless song in Amy's head, a sense of homecoming that made her tremble.

"Sometimes folks get here and they think about the Santa Fe trail and the old Camino Real, and they're disappointed because the plaza is so small," Lopez repeated.

"What does Camino Real mean?" Amy demanded. She felt that she must learn everything right away, that nothing in this place must remain strange to her.

"Royal road," Tommy supplied. "It's the name given to the route the conquistadors traveled up from Mexico. Like the Santa Fe trail, it ended here."

"Well, I'm not disappointed," she told the lawyer breathlessly.

"Good, good! Real glad to hear that. Hope you pass a comfortable night. Diego will take you out to your spread in the morning."

That night Tommy made love to her for the first time since she left the hospital seven weeks earlier.

All during dinner the intensity of Amy's excitement showed in flushed cheeks and shaking hands. She sat beside her husband in the hotel dining room and picked at fried chicken and thought, *I want to have a baby. Right away. I must have a baby in this place. Then it will belong to us.*

In their small nondescript hotel bedroom she took Tommy's hand and laid her head against his chest. "I'm so happy," she whispered. "I feel so alive now that we're here."

"Yeah, I know. I'm glad you're happy." He kissed her and murmured something about getting undressed.

She removed her clothes with fingers suddenly clumsy, and didn't wait to put them away, but dropped them on the floor and turned to him. She was quivering all over, and he picked her up and carried her to the bed.

Amy pulled him down on top of herself, and wrapped her arms tightly around his neck and spread her legs. When his climax came she was exultant. She almost believed that she could feel conception happening inside her.

Tommy turned away from her and faced the wall

and suddenly said, "Why did Luke come to see you in August?"

She was so startled she almost denied it. Then she thought about Tommy's recent mood and understood. It was too late for denials. "How did you know?"

"I ran into Suzy Randolph a couple of weeks before we left New York. She made a point of telling me she'd seen him leaving our house."

"She would," Amy said. Her mouth was dry and her brain was racing. "Look, he was in town to see a doctor. He came to talk to us because he was having doubts about staying with the Dominicans."

"Us?" Tommy questioned with a small laugh. "Come off it, baby. He knew I wouldn't be home during the day."

"He planned to wait," Amy said. She struggled to make her tone normal. "We talked a bit, and he saw that his doubts were silly. Just nerves. He wanted to go back to Dover right away. And he made me promise not to tell you. He was ashamed of himself."

There was silence when she finished this explanation. Amy couldn't bear the thought that they would begin their new life with a fight about Luke. "Please," she said, stretching out her hand and touching his shoulder, "believe me, that's all there was to it."

"Ok," he said tonelessly. "Whatever you say."

14

⌢

LOPEZ HAD TOLD THEM DIEGO WAS AN INDIAN FROM
Pueblo Cochiti. He came to the hotel while they were
having breakfast. "I'm ready when you are." His speech
was marked only by the slow southwestern drawl Amy
heard everywhere.

They followed him outside. Their trunks were piled
high on a rickety buckboard. Tommy inspected the
vehicle. "Is this what we travel in?"

"It belongs to Santo Domingo," Diego said.

"Are the horses ours too?" Amy studied the two
animals. They were big and looked strong, and their
coats were shiny.

"Yup."

She smiled with satisfaction. She started to climb aboard, but Tommy told her to wait. He looked up and down the street, then spotted what he wanted. "Stay here a minute. That's Lopez's office, according to the sign. I want to see him."

He hurried across the road and Amy waited, studying the beauty of the mountains all around them. "This is the Sangre de Cristo range, isn't it?" she asked.

Diego nodded.

A procession of half a dozen burros led by a small man in a serape and sombrero came into view. The animals were laden with wood. "Piñon logs from the mountains," Diego said. "For firewood."

Before Amy could answer, Tommy and Lopez emerged from the office. They stood in the road beside Lopez's black Model-T Ford. Amy went to join them.

"Good morning, Mrs. Westerman," Lopez said with a broad smile. "I trust you're rested from your travels. Mr. Westerman here is trying to buy my motor car. I keep telling him there aren't many roads out to your place. And none of 'em is paved."

Tommy signaled to the Indian. "Diego, come here a minute." He joined them. "You know anything about the Model-T?" Tommy asked.

"A little."

"Go anywhere, right? You can drive it over anything?"

"That's what they say."

"What do you think? Will it make it to Santo Domingo?"

The Indian sucked in his cheeks, and Amy saw his eyes dart to Tommy's built-up shoe, then back to the car. "Yeah, I think it might."

"Good. I think so too. How about it, Mr. Lopez?" Tommy took out his wallet and withdrew two hundred-dollar bills. They crackled with newness. "Almost as much as you paid for her."

"This flivver is practically new. I just went down and got her from Albuquerque four months ago."

"And she cost you . . . what? Three-fifty?" Lopez nodded. Tommy took out another hundred. Amy swallowed hard. Their working capital had just shrunk by three hundred dollars.

Lopez stared at the car and the money. "Okay, you're a nice young fella, and you're just starting out. I'll take it."

There were handshakes all around. On their way out of town they stopped at the telegraph office and sent a wire to Lil and Warren. "Arrived safely. Everything beautiful," it said. Then they set out on the last leg of their journey.

Amy rode in the buckboard with Diego while Tommy followed behind in the Model-T. They came down through the foothills into the desert, and she didn't try to absorb it all because she knew she couldn't. For now, it was enough to sense the vast bronzed land through which she traveled. Later she would become as intimate with it as once she'd been with the African bush.

Soon Santa Fe became a smudge to the north, and

the sun grew hotter. Amy removed her jacket and opened the neck of her silk blouse. Diego reached behind and gave her a tattered parasol. "Used to be a canopy on this thing," he said. "It got torn."

"Well, we'll have to replace it right away," Amy said. Then she wondered if Diego was in her employ. "Do you work for us?"

"When DeAngeles was the owner I was foreman."

"And now?"

He shrugged. "Up to you."

They rode on in silence across a flat mesa studded with cacti and low scrub, and roofed by the blinding blue sky. In some places the vegetation was thicker than in others. Once they saw a huddled mass on the horizon which Diego identified as Pecos Pueblo.

She wanted to ask him about the pueblos and if he lived in his or at the ranch. Just when she had decided to broach the subject Diego signaled a halt. They stopped and Tommy joined them by the buckboard. "She's doing fine. I knew the flivver wouldn't let us down. How about you?" he asked Amy. "Sun too much?"

"Not for me. I'm used to it, remember?"

"You been out here before?" Diego asked, handing them a drink of water from the canteen he carried. "I thought you was eastern folks."

"I was brought up in Africa," Amy explained. Diego look blank. "It's a lot like this," she added. "And it's just as hot."

He nodded. "I stopped here so's you could get your first look at the place," he said.

"Our place, you mean?" Tommy asked, surprised.

"Yup. Your land begins at that line of cottonwood trees."

"It's not exactly a well-defined border," Amy said softly.

"Fences are no part of the code of the Old West," Tommy said. "Isn't that so, Diego?"

"Mr. DeAngeles had a fence once. Least his pa did. It ain't been up for years."

They took their places and began traveling again. The next time Amy checked her watch it was after one. When she looked up there was a shadow in the distance ahead of them. "That's it," Diego told her.

The arch was of wrought iron, and it stood un-marked by time, a surreal incongruity on the earth. Whatever fence it had once been part of was gone without a trace. The words "Santo Domingo" were carved deep in a wooden sign swinging from the apex of the arch.

They passed beneath the useless thing, as if going around it would break some ancient taboo, and pulled up by a clutter of deserted buildings. "That's the main house," Diego said pointing. "Ain't been no one living in it for years."

"I thought Mr. DeAngeles left just a few weeks ago," Amy said.

"Yeah. But far back as I can remember, Mr. DeAngeles lived in there." Diego pointed to a small shed standing a few feet away.

Amy ignored his pointing finger and took a step closer to the structure he'd identified as the main house. It was made of adobe, like everything else, and turned to the world only a long blank wall pocked with ruin. It had been washed pink some time in the past. Now it was faded to a dark earthy terracotta. "It's a beautiful color," she said to Tommy. "I'm going to have a look." Her voice was slightly shrill.

"Wait a minute," Tommy said. "Don't go alone."

She paid no attention, but walked in her high-heeled patent leather city shoes across the pebbled ground.

There was a single opening in the wall and she pushed at a door of splintered, sun-bleached wood. It fell backward off rotted hinges. Amy had to clamber over it to make her way inside. Then she was in a small square room with doors in all the walls. She hesitated, then turned right. Tommy's step sounded on the newly formed wooden bridge. "In here," she called.

He came up behind her, and they walked from room to room, neither touching nor speaking. The house was built as a quadrangle. Each space led to another. One corner room had a second story, but the staircase had long since rotted away and only the opening in the ceiling remained.

"This must be the kitchen," Tommy said when they arrived at a place with a big chimney in one wall and a waist-high shelf running around the other three. "Here's the famous 'Water laid on to the house.' " He touched a rusty pump handle and it fell apart in his hand.

"There's a patio," Amy said. "We haven't seen it yet." The center of the quadrangle was occupied by an open area, still showing the chipped remains of a tile floor. In the middle, dominating all else, was a massive gray-trunked tree that spread its branches across the roof. Diego sat beneath the tree waiting for them.

"This here's special," he said patting the trunk. "Mr. DeAngles told me to tell you about it, so's you'd understand. His grandpa went to Spain once and brought the tree back with him. It was about two feet tall when they planted it. Then they built the house."

"It's a eucalyptus, I think," Tommy said, gazing up into the leafy branches. "Can't say for sure which one. They're called gum trees."

"This is the only one in New Mexico," Diego insisted. "It ain't got a name."

"Of course it has a name," Tommy said in disgust. "Everything does."

Amy was surprised. She had not known that Tommy knew anything about trees. "Does it flower?" she asked him.

"Can't say without knowing the variety."

"It has flowers in the spring," Diego said sullenly.

"What color are they?" Amy asked. She was holding her breath.

"White. Very small, but they smell sweet."

She tried not to show her disappointment. If he had said the flowers were red, everything else might not have mattered so much. "We were told the house was furnished," she said—as if that were the only deception she had noted among so many.

"There's some stuff in there." Diego jerked his head in the direction of one of the rooms.

Amy went to look. She discovered a few pieces of heavy carved oak. They were thick with dust and pushed far back into a dark corner. Much of the house was dark and cool, for the windows were small and few.

"We can't live here," Tommy said when she came back and reported on the furniture.

"The shed's got a bed and a few things," Diego supplied.

Tommy looked at him with loathing, as if it were the Indian's fault that they had bought a crumbling ruin. "Show me," he said briskly.

They went outside and Amy waited while Tommy made an inspection of the shed. "It could be worse," he told her when he came out, "but not much."

"We'll just have to wait until we can have a good look around," she said as brightly as she could. "Then we'll figure out how to get all this in shape." She turned to Diego. "Tell me, where are the cattle?"

He looked at her in puzzlement.

"The cattle," Amy repeated. "Where are they?" In Africa they had kept their livestock in a large fenced stockade behind the house. She craned her neck to look for such a structure, but saw nothing.

"You passed most of 'em," Diego said.

"I don't understand." Her brown eyes studied his brown face.

"The open range," Tommy said through clenched teeth. "The cattle are running free on the range. Isn't that it, Diego?"

"Yeah." He didn't meet their eyes.

"Anybody out riding herd on them?"

"Ain't nobody working the place now. Not since Mr. DeAngeles left."

"And for how long before that?" Tommy asked softly.

"A year, maybe two," was the muttered reply.

"Oh, sweet Jesus." Tommy took his silver hip flask from his pocket and uncorked it. "Here *memsahib*, have a drink. We're going to need it."

She shook her head, and he looked at her and laughed without mirth. Then he took a long deep swallow.

15

"**W**HY DO YOU SUPPOSE LOPEZ LIED?" AMY asked. She smoothed the threadbare blanket over the cot. Her nails snagged on the shredded wool.

"Don't know." Tommy put down his razor, wiped the last of the soap from his face, and carried the chipped enamel basin to the door. "But I sure as hell mean to ask."

"Don't!" she called swiftly.

"Don't ask?" He turned to her in amazement, still holding the basin.

"Don't throw out the water. We have to conserve. Here, I found this bucket to collect slops."

He stared at the dirty water. "Am I supposed to wash in this again?"

She managed a despairing laugh. "No, I'll use the second-hand water for cleaning this place."

It was a two-room adobe shed; low-ceilinged, dirt-floored, with a cot, a table, and a chair in one of the rooms, and a rudimentary kitchen in the other. An outhouse out back provided the only sanitary facilities, and near the splintered and sagging front door a hollow scooped in the earth held evidence of past cook fires. It was the home DeAngeles made for himself when he left the rotting hacienda. Now it was theirs.

Tommy dumped his offering into the tin bucket she indicated, and went back to stare at the sunrise.

Finally he turned his back on the splendor of the morning. "I'm going into Santa Fe. Lopez will have to help get our money back."

"Do you think he will?"

Tommy shrugged. "I don't know. But I can threaten him with disbarment. Lawyers can't practice if they get tossed out of their private club."

"Well," she said, "it's worth trying. And I'll give you a list of things to get in Santa Fe."

"Listen, let's talk about that some more. The hotel in town isn't bad. For God's sake, Amy, you can't mean it about staying here."

They had spent all the previous afternoon and most of the night arguing that question. Now she squared her shoulders as resolutely as she had yesterday. "I mean it," she said. "We made our bed, Tommy, and we're going to lie in it until something better comes along. At least I am," she added quietly. "I can't make you stay."

"I can't very well leave you here alone. You're not offering me any real choice."

Amy didn't bother to answer. She went to the open trunk in the corner and looked for something to wear.

Tommy made a gesture of disgust, then walked off to check the gasoline tank in the flivver. It was low, so he topped it off from the spare can on the running board. Amy came out. He looked up from his task and stared at her in astonishment.

"Clothes from home," she said. "What all the ladies wear in Africa. What do you think?"

She was dressed in buff-colored cotton twill. The blouse was simple and loose-fitting. She had rolled up the sleeves and left the neck unbuttoned. The skirt had a center seam that divided it into wide-legged trousers.

"You look like you're wearing pants. Like a man," he said.

"It's practical. You're always having to climb over things in a place like this. Good for riding too."

He busied himself with some adjustment to the car. "You ride well, don't you?"

"I've done it all my life."

"Yeah." He wiped a tool with an oily rag. "Good for you. Any chance of getting some breakfast around here? Or don't you do that sort of thing when you're dressed like one of the boys."

She started to say something, then changed her mind. "It will be ready in a few minutes. Tommy, you mustn't go bare-headed out here. Never. It's the first thing people have to learn in a climate like this." She touched the broad-brimmed straw hat she wore. It was styled like a nineteenth century pith helmet. "I've got another one of these you can have."

"No thanks. I don't fancy looking like a fugitive from Zulu land." He went back inside and came out wearing his fedora. It looked ridiculous, and she bit her lips so she wouldn't laugh.

"You could get some clothes while you're in Santa Fe," she said over coffee and the watery gruel she had produced in an attempt at cereal.

"I'm not ready to dress up in cowboy clothes," he said. "You may enjoy this charade, *memsahib,* but I don't." He spat out a mouthful of coffee, and it made a dark stain on the parched earth, then disappeared. "God, this stuff's awful."

"I'm not much of a cook yet. I'll learn. I promise."

He grinned at her. "Sorry I'm being so foul-tempered. It's not your fault. None of it."

"Yes it is," she said softly. "You wanted to see the place before we bought it. I wouldn't wait. It is my fault."

"You had your reasons," Tommy said. "Good ones. Besides, Uncle Donald said we could trust this guy Lopez. Don't worry." He smiled. "It'll all come out ok."

She returned his smile gratefully and he added, "How come you had those African clothes with you? They can't have been your idea of what to bring to a girls' school in Boston."

"They were. I packed all my bush clothes. Then Mummy found out and made me leave most of them

behind. She thought it terribly funny. I remember the
way she laughed." Amy picked up a pebble and fingered it. It was a perfect oval, red brown and beautiful. "She only let me bring this one outfit as a
concession. It's the first time I've worn it."

"I don't wonder," he said, looking at the flat-heeled
sturdy boots that came halfway up her calf. Her legs
looked slim and elegant despite them. "They look
good," he admitted. "But I don't exactly see them as
suitable for Fifth Avenue."

She stood up and gathered the soiled dishes. "I
wonder if I dare wash these in second-hand water?
Maybe I can put it through some kind of strainer."

He looked at her anxiously. "The water butt's full,"
he said, pointing to the storage barrel under the roof
of a nearby shed. "I checked. Don't go drinking that
used stuff."

"Of course not."

"You're sure you're going to be all right while I'm
gone? You could at least ride into Santa Fe with me.
We'll come back right after I've seen Lopez."

"I'm staying here," she said firmly. "There's a lot to
do. I've got to make a start."

"That Indian must be around here somewhere."
Tommy looked, but there was no sign of Diego. He
had disappeared the previous afternoon. "What about
the horses?" Tommy asked suddenly.

Amy gazed in the direction of the corral. "Don't
worry, I'll look after the horses." She tipped out the
remainder of the inedible cereal. "I know more about
them than cooking."

He got ready to leave, and she made a list of things

they needed to flesh out the meager supplies Diego had brought on the buckboard. "How long do you think you'll be?" she asked before he left.

"I can probably do the trip in about three hours when I'm not following that damned buckboard. Still, there's Lopez. And I've got to go to the bank." He patted his breast pocket. It held the certified check that represented most of their working capital. "We've got to get this in an account so we can draw on it. And there's your shopping. Not until nightfall, I'd guess."

"All right." She looked at him, then looked away, lest he see fear in her eyes. "I'm counting on you," she said softly. "I'll be waiting."

He flushed and jerked angrily at the Model-T's spark and throttle lever. "Stop worrying. I'll be back."

There was one outbuilding she hadn't inspected. It turned out to be a tackroom of sorts. The structure was as delapidated as the rest of the ranch, but the two saddles she found were well oiled and carefully hung. She took one from its peg and studied it, noting the features she wasn't used to. Then she carried it toward the corral.

The horses were penned some distance from the main house, behind high adobe walls. There was a door, the only piece of wood on the place not rotted and splintering. Eight horses grazed peacefully inside. Amy selected a gray about twelve hands high and started toward him, carrying the saddle and making clucking noises under her breath.

"I'll catch him for you," Diego's voice said from behind. She turned to see him sitting on the wall.

He looked the same as he had yesterday. He had straight short black hair framing a round face, and he wore a faded chambray shirt and tight blue-denim trousers. There was a beat-up Stetson in his hand. He jammed it on his head when he jumped down into the corral. "You know how to ride?" he asked.

"Of course."

Amy stood her ground until Diego had hold of the horse; then she went forward. He took the saddle from her and fitted it expertly. Neither of them said anything.

Amy led the gray to a nearby rock, obviously used as a mounting block, and swung easily astride. Diego continued to watch in silence. "Open the gate, please," she said.

He did as she bid. Amy didn't look at him. She knew well the shape of the small drama they were enacting, and she was neither cowed nor alarmed. "When you go to a strange land and take what belongs to another man," her father had told her years before, "you must convince him you are worthy. And you must do it according to his rules."

Amy prodded the gray lightly. He moved forward. She walked him for a few yards, getting the feel of his gait and the unfamiliar saddle. After a minute she urged the horse into a trot; then she stopped and pulled on the reins to see how well he backed. The gray was obedient. Amy started to canter and soon to gallop. In minutes she had left the ranch behind. She was no longer performing for Diego's benefit, but for

her own. This was riding as she had been born to it,
wild and free, with nothing but herself and the horse
and endless open earth and sky. It had nothing in
common with prancing along a bridle path in Central
Park.

She returned in an hour. Diego was waiting for her
by the corral. He helped her to dismount.

"You're good," he said. "But I was afraid you'd get
lost. You went pretty far."

She looked at him scornfully. "Not without sighting
landmarks," she said. "I've been doing this, in a place
every bit as tough as this one, as long as you have.
Since I was born." She adjusted her hat and tucked up
a couple of strands of hair that had come loose. "Water
him," she said. "And the others while you're about
it."

"I already watered the others."

"Very well. Take care of the gray. Come see me
after you've put the saddle away."

He joined her while she was trying to make some
order out of the scant supplies. "You didn't bring
enough food with us," she said. "And where did you
disappear to yesterday?"

"I figured your husband didn't want me around.
And I didn't bring more 'cause I didn't think you'd
stay."

"Mr. Westerman," she corrected. "Don't say 'your
husband.' And we are staying. Do you want to work
for us?"

"Sure, why not?"

"What did Mr. DeAngeles pay you?"

"Sixty dollars a month and my keep."

"We can't afford that. Not until things are sorted out. Fifty dollars."

"And my keep?"

She grimaced. "That's not worth much. I'm a terrible cook. Where do you sleep?"

"Bunkhouse out back." He pointed to yet another delapidated adobe hovel.

"Very well. We have an agreement, then. You can begin by telling me how we find these cattle that are supposed to be ours."

He went away and came back with a long-handled branding iron. He stamped it into the sandy earth, and Amy studied the imprint. "That's your mark," Diego said.

The brand consisted of the letters SD, enclosed in a circle of punctated dots.

"Your cows are marked on the right hip," Diego explained. "And their right ear is notched."

"But where are they?"

He looked exasperated. "I told you. On the range. Have to have a roundup if you want to get 'em counted. Take a lot of men."

The enormity of it depressed her. Maybe Tommy would have some success with Mr. Lopez. "Where did you get the water to fill the butt?" she asked, changing the subject.

"There's a well 'bout a hundred yards away. Mr. DeAngeles's pa drilled it a long time ago. I ain't never seen it dry. This is the best place for water between here and the Pecos river. No cause to complain 'bout that."

*   *   *

Tommy reported a similar reaction from the lawyer in Santa Fe. He told her about it as he stood near the small fire she'd made against the evening chill, drinking her terrible coffee. "Lopez practically laughed me out of his office when I mentioned complaining to the bar. According to him he told Uncle Donald the exact truth. Plenty of water, three thousand plus cattle at the *last official counting* and structures in need of repair due to Mr. DeAngeles's recent illness. Lopez still insists we got a bargain."

"Diego said the same about the water. We're lucky in that respect apparently."

"I take it he came back."

She told him the story and motioned to the bunkhouse where Diego slept. "We need help. And he knows the place. May as well keep him on."

"Yeah, I guess so. Particularly now he's so impressed with your skill as a horsewoman."

She felt a moment's regret at having told him that part of the story. "I'll help you unload," she said, starting for the car.

"Don't bother, I'll do it."

She insisted on helping. When they'd transferred the flour and bacon and canned goods Amy saw another box at the rear. She dragged it toward the car door. It was three cases of pure malt whiskey.

16

Tommy took to sitting at the far edge of the ranch buildings, his back propped against an adobe wall, and silently staring at the land from dawn to dusk. He kept a bottle of whiskey by his side, but he was never reeling drunk. When Amy asked him about the future all he said was, "Leave it to me. I'm thinking about it."

That first week Amy began clearing the debris from the main house. She wanted to believe that when she removed the crumbling clay, the vermin droppings, the discarded nests of creatures long grown and gone, and the tin and paper and glass rubbish of former human occupation, then there would be a transformation.

Diego provided old burlap feed sacks rescued from one of the outbuildings. After she filled them with refuse, he hauled them away. Lizards and snakes and nameless insects scurried ahead of her onslaught. Diego warned her about scorpions. She listened gravely and made him describe in detail the appearance of the poisonous ones.

"What about snakes?" she asked.

"Most of'em won't harm you none. Course, if you see a rattler, you'll know it. You just stand real still and . . ."

"I know how to deal with snakes," she interrupted. "It's just the local varieties I'm unfamiliar with."

He looked at her speculatively and watched with disbelief her exhausting attack on the house. It remained as much a ruin clean as it had been dirty.

A few times Amy discovered some entrancing architectural detail of carved wood or inlaid tile that indicated what once had been. She ran to call Tommy. Each time he came slowly, looked, and said little.

On the fourth day Tommy announced that he was going again to Santa Fe. He put a bottle of whiskey in the car and drove off with no further explanation.

That day Amy worked more rapidly as an antidote to anxiety and despair. The effort made her arms and legs leaden with fatigue, but it didn't divert her. Tommy returned at nightfall, no more inebriated than usual, and still offered no excuse for his journey.

He brought with him a letter from Lil, collected at the Santa Fe post office. It was full of chatter about relatives, including Luke, who was said to be well and happy in his priory.

Lil added that there was yet no sign of a buyer for the Eighty-third Street house. Amy knew that; they'd also had a letter from Donald Varley. She thought Tommy had received one from Luke, but he didn't offer to let her read it.

On the first day of their third week on the ranch Diego suggested that he and Amy ride. "You should see the waterhole and some of the boundaries, so's you know where they are," he said.

She packed a lunch, and he stowed it in his saddlebag. Then she mounted the gray, and they rode off. Amy had told Tommy she was going, but she didn't think he heard.

"What's this beauty's name," Amy asked, patting the gray's neck with affection.

"Always just called her the gray."

"I'm going to call her Sheba. It's the name of a pony I had back home."

They rode east. Amy wanted to see the Rio Grande, but it was seventy miles west of the ranch, and not the area Diego wanted to show her. Gradually the vegetation became thicker and greener. "Good grazing land here," Diego said. "Up ahead is Pintada Creek."

Amy searched for a sight of the cattle she purportedly owned, but only once did they see the dust of a herd off in the distance. "Thought maybe I could find a stray and show you the brand," Diego said, patting the rope at his waist. "No luck. Take a couple of days if we set out to do it purposeful-like."

The waterhole was a broad hollow sump, filled with murky brackish liquid that looked undrinkable. Amy's disappointment was plain on her face.

"It ain't never been dry since I knowed it," Diego explained. "Maybe you don't realize how important that is. Must be an underwater spring here. It ain't a gusher, I'll grant you that, but it's steady."

She nodded and looked again for cattle, but saw none. They rode back along a route Diego identified as a portion of Santo Domingo's southern border. Amy sited the landmarks carefully, but with a sense of despair tempered only by her delight in the infinite horizon and the endless space.

"Where the hell you been?" Tommy's speech was heavily slurred. He was crouched by the gate of the corral, clutching an empty bottle.

"I told you before we left. We went out to see the waterhole." Amy slid quickly from her horse and tossed the reins to Diego. "I'm sorry if you were worried. Come up to the house. I'll get some dinner ready."

He pushed off the hand she laid on his shoulder and staggered to his feet. "You told me nothing. And I want something . . ." He faltered as if his tongue were too thick to form the words. "Something clear. My wife doesn't go off with any Indian. Never!" His voice rose to a shout. "Never, you hear me?"

Amy looked at neither him nor Diego, but walked toward the house. Tommy stumbled after her. "I'm talking to you, lady! Don't you walk away from me!"

He caught up with her and spun her around. "Where did you go?"

"I told you. To see the waterhole."

"Waterhole? Twelve miles due east of here? That's where it is, isn't it? Answer me, damn you!"

"I guess so," she murmured. "I didn't keep track of the miles."

Without warning he slapped her hard across the face. Amy clutched her stinging cheek and stared at him speechless. It was the first time he had ever struck her. In all the terrible scenes of their nine months of marriage he had done nothing like that.

"Don't start showing your Indian blood, you bitch!" he hissed at her. "You act like a decent white woman, and keep pretending you're a lady, or I'll kill you!"

She turned and ran for the shelter of the shed. She knew that she could outrun him, and she had some half-formed idea of barricading herself in the room where they slept. By the time she reached it, sobbing and panting, she realized that he wasn't following. She heard the motor of the Model-T.

She changed direction and ran to where the flivver was parked. "Tommy, for God's sake! You're too drunk to drive. You'll kill yourself. Where are you going?"

"Get out of my way, bitch. I'm going to see this famous waterhole. Going to take a look myself, and see if it's worth fifty thousand dollars." He drove off in a cloud of dust.

By morning he had not returned. Amy was sick with worry and disgust and something akin to hatred. It didn't prevent her from going toward the corral carrying Sheba's saddle. She couldn't leave him alone out there, no matter what she felt.

"I'll go," Diego said, taking the saddle from her limp hands. "I know the country better."

"He said he was going to the waterhole. He seemed to know exactly where it was."

"Yeah, I heard." He didn't look at her. "Flivver probably got stuck somewhere. I'll bring him back. Don't worry, just wait here."

He returned three hours later with an unconscious Tommy slung over the front of his horse. "Car's stuck in the sand. He's all right, just passed out." He carried his employer into the shed and dumped him on the cot. "I'll go dig the car out and bring it back."

"Can you drive?"

"If I have to. You going to be all right?" He looked at Tommy.

"Yes. Go ahead, I'll be fine."

After that Tommy was constantly drunk, too much so to pay her any attention, let alone abuse her. Sometimes he stayed at the ranch, sitting in his customary place until he passed out and fell over and Diego carried him back to the shed. On other occasions he drove away. At first she thought he must be going to Santa Fe, but later she found a matchbook with the address of an Albuquerque bar in his pocket. Tommy often stayed away for days at a time, but she felt better knowing that he wasn't in Santa Fe. Even an animal doesn't foul its own nest, she told herself.

By early April she was sure she was pregnant. She sat one night in the door of the shed, unable to sleep, and stared out at the stars. They floated low in the blue velvet sky. Amy remembered the hotel room and their first night in New Mexico.

Tommy was gone at the moment, and she had no way of knowing when he'd be back. She resolved to go into Santa Fe in the morning and see a doctor. John Lopez could recommend someone. Dawn reddened the horizon by the time she pulled herself wearily to her feet and started to make coffee. Then she heard the motor of the car coming toward the ranch. "Oh, God," she muttered, "Why do you come back, Tommy? Why don't you just disappear?"

Amy brushed her tears away impatiently and added more water to the pot. The car stopped some distance away. She waited a while, then walked out.

He had parked by the corral and the gate was open. She saw it swinging on its hinges and started to run. The last thing she needed now was runaway horses. She thought of shouting for Diego, but he had heard the car. He appeared from the direction of the bunkhouse, casually hitching up his trousers. Then he too saw the open corral gate, and broke into a run.

They arrived at the enclosure at the same moment. In the half-light of dawn Amy and Diego stared at the scene within. Tommy was on a horse. He had no saddle. He merely lay along the animal's back, and clung fiercely to its neck, laughing aloud like a madman.

He'd chosen a black mare that neither Amy nor Diego ever rode. She was on the small side, but fractious and difficult. The mare bobbed her head from side to side, prancing and whinnying and trying to dislodge the annoyance plaguing her.

"You're not going to throw me, horse!" Tommy

shouted. "You're a lousy, dumb animal, and I'm clever Tommy Westerman who knows all the answers. You're not going to throw me!"

He was roaring, raving drunk. His muscles, loose and flaccid, rolled with the horse's motions. His built-up shoe slapped against the mare's flanks, and his body kept to her rhythm in a wild improbable grace.

"Jesus," Diego said under his breath. "I ain't never seen anything like that. Never thought no cripple could sit a horse."

"Shut the gate," Amy said, "before the horses realizes it's open, Diego."

He jerked into motion and closed the three of them and the eight horses inside the corral. Tommy continued his ride. Nearly two minutes passed before he noticed his wife and the Indian watching him.

"Good morning," he called as he passed by. "I'm learning to ride. Only way to get around out here. . . ." His voice was lost in the neighing and stomping of animals infected by the unhappiness of the black mare.

"Get down!" Amy shouted. "We'll take her out of the corral and you can try again. There's not enough room in here, Tommy. Too many other horses. Get down!"

For a long time he paid no attention, but finally he slid off at their feet, laughing and gasping for breath. "Ok, that'll do for now, I guess."

Diego helped him to his feet and half carried him to bed.

Amy left Tommy sleeping and drove the buckboard to Santa Fe. It took her four hours and was not an easy journey, and she realized that for her own good she must learn to drive the Model-T. Her amber linen dress was crushed and dusty by the time she stood outside the doctor's office, and she felt irritable and unsure of herself.

Lopez's secretary had told Amy how to find this low white complex of buildings perched on the edge of a canyon north of the plaza. Amy went through a painted green gate in a high white wall, and found herself in a courtyard filled with the scents of spring and the sound of trickling water. In front of her was a two-story house with carved wooden balconies fronting the upper windows. She looked left and spied a smaller structure with an open door and a sign that said, "Ricardo Ibañez, M.D." Underneath was the word, *entrada*. She knew no Spanish, but it wasn't difficult to guess the meaning. Amy entered.

"Good afternoon, señora. May I help you?" A woman dressed in nurse's white looked at her with little curiosity.

"I'd like to see Dr. Ibañez. I'm afraid I don't have an appointment."

"Don Rico will see you, señora, but he is very busy. You must wait please."

The nurse had a faintly foreign accent and a harried expression. She opened the door to the waiting room. It was jammed to overflowing with patients. Men, women, and children were everywhere. They sat on all the chairs, perched on the wide windowsills and wedged themselves into the corners. Amy looked at the scene and murmured. "I'm sorry, I seem to have picked a bad day."

"It is like this every day, señora," the nurse sighed. "You must just wait."

"Of course. Thank you."

A man rose to give her a chair, and she took it gratefully. He and many of the others looked to be Indians. A few women, like the nurse, looked vaguely foreign. Amy spotted three ladies more like herself, and didn't feel quite so out of place. She settled down to wait, adopting the air of patience the others exhibited.

In an hour and a half most of the throng had disappeared through the door to the doctor's office, but just as many had replaced them. The nurse came to where Amy sat, brandishing a pad of paper and a pencil, and took her name. The waiting continued.

Finally, after nearly three hours, it was her turn. She walked into a room lined with books and freshened by two vases of flowers. The doctor sat behind a large table of carved oak. When she came in he rose and extended his hand.

"Good afternoon, Señora Westerman. I am Don Rico. How can I help you?"

She had expected someone older. This was a man of perhaps thirty, tall and slim with smiling dark eyes and black hair that swept back from a pronounced widow's peak. His teeth were very white in a sun-bronzed face, and he had a deep cleft in his chin. He exuded vitality and frank maleness.

Amy took the hand he offered, and blurted out, "I think I'm pregnant."

"Ah, but that is always nice to hear. I am glad you are not ill, señora. Please," he ushered her to another door. "I will examine you."

When the examination was finished they left the treatment room and returned to the gracious office. Amy perched on the edge of her seat. "Well?" she asked.

Ibañez smiled. "I think so yes, but it is too soon to tell for sure. You have other children, señora?"

She explained about her miscarriage. "In New York the doctor said such things meant the baby wasn't normal. That's why I was anxious to see a doctor right away."

"New York! You have come a long way to consult me, señora," he said, smiling broadly. He glanced down at the notes on his desk. "But of course! I didn't make the connection right away. Westerman. You're the young couple who just bought Santo Domingo. Congratulations. And welcome to New Mexico." He pronounced the *x* as if it were an *h*, and didn't wait for her to reply but added quickly, "And stop worrying. There is no reason for you to lose this baby—if you are pregnant, that is. You must take sensible precautions, that's all. Plenty of rest, and the proper diet. My nurse will give you a list before you leave."

"I've been wondering if it's all right to ride," she said shyly.

He looked at her in mild surprise. "You ride? I didn't expect it. Forgive me, that is stupid and prejudiced of course. Out here we have stereotyped ideas about New Yorkers."

Amy explained that she had learned in Africa.

"Then, since it is an activity to which you are long accustomed, you may ride. But only for another month or two," Ibañez said. "And you must come to see me once a month. One other thing," he added. "No soaking in hot baths. Sponge baths only. It is a small precaution in view of the last time."

Amy thought of the chipped enamel basins and the water butt. No hot baths indeed. "Thank you." She rose to go. "I'm not sure, do I call you Dr. Ibañez or Don Rico?"

"Whichever you prefer," he said laughing.

There was a separate door for leaving, so she did not have to walk through the waiting room again. He escorted her out to the courtyard. "Wait here," he said. "I'll tell my nurse to give you the instructions I mentioned." He turned to go, then turned back. "Listen, I just thought. I go by your place every few weeks on the way to see patients in the pueblos. I'll call at the ranch. No need for you to come into Santa Fe."

She thanked him, but she was disturbed by the idea of this handsome and elegant stranger seeing her in the ruin that was her home.

She had left the buckboard in the plaza. When she walked back to the center of town she saw a noisy crowd standing by the telegraph office. Amy moved toward its fringe, trying to see what all the excitement was about. She craned her neck, but couldn't read the notice in the window. "What is it?" she asked a man standing nearby. "What's happened?"

"War, that's what's happened. News just came. President Wilson's asked congress to declare war on Germany." He pointed to the crush of people trying to get inside the telegraph office. "All these guys is trying to send wires to Washington. Want to volunteer to give ole Kaiser Bill what he deserves. Makes you proud to be an American."

She stood in the doorway of the shed, with the setting sun behind her, and told Tommy the news. He was bent over the table they used as a washstand, pale and red-eyed, but sober.

"War," he said quietly. "So it's come at last. I always knew it would sooner or later." He pushed by her and went outside, and stared at the sky as if he expected to see German planes zooming in from behind the fiery desert sunset. "War," he said again. He sounded thoughtful, not alarmed. "It makes sense."

Amy thought of the killing and the death that had filled the New York papers. "I don't think it makes any sense at all. It's just useless slaughter. I don't even know what they're really fighting about."

"That's not what I mean. Sense for us. For my plans."

"What plans?"

"I'm not ready to talk about it yet." He turned and stared at her, as if suddenly aware that she'd just returned after a day's absence. "What were you doing in Santa Fe? How come you went all that way alone?"

"I had to see a doctor. You certainly weren't in any condition to accompany me."

"Are you sick?" There was an anxious expression in his gray eyes.

"No," she said. "I'm going to have a baby."

He reached out as if to touch her, and she pulled

away. "Don't come near me. And don't start making
noises like a loving husband, as if nothing's happened.
I've been planning all the way home to tell you this. I
only hoped I'd find you sober enough to listen. You
are for the moment, so pay attention. Get this into
your alcohol-soaked brain."

Amy spoke through clenched teeth, with a fury that
nearly choked her.

"You hit me last month. You probably don't remember, but you did. It was the first and the last time,
Tommy Westerman. If you ever lay a finger on me
again, I'll leave you. No excuses and no warnings. I'll
just go. And I won't hesitate to tell your precious
prominent family in New York why."

She shook with rage, as if the abuse had just happened, and she was facing the shock for the first time.

Tommy looked at her silently. The swift desert night
already shrouded her features. "That's all you want to
say?" he asked at last.

"That's all."

"Ok. Let's eat. I'm hungry. And I've got a lot to do
tomorrow."

The next day Tommy disappeared for a few hours.
When he returned he emerged from the flivver wearing a striped chambray shirt, blue denim trousers and
a Stetson. The clothes, already covered with the dust
of the road, didn't look new, and despite his built-up
shoe, Tommy didn't look odd in them. Extraordinarily
he looked as if he'd been born in such an outfit.

17

Among the crates shipped from New York to Santo Domingo was one containing Tommy's exercise equipment. Each wooden box was carefully labeled in Amy's neat hand; silver serving dishes, china, glassware, linen—the still unused bounty of the showers and the wedding. Tommy pawed through them until he found what he was looking for; then he set up the chinning bar and the weights in the patio of the old house. He adopted a routine of rising at dawn, and in the morning cool, under the shade of the gum tree, he slowly and agonizingly began rebuilding muscles withered by alcohol and neglect.

Amy would stealthily creep as far as the wall of the house and listen to the sounds of his struggle. They made her hope. So did the untouched bottles of whiskey in the shed, and his harrowing riding sessions.

She offered to teach him, but he would accept no instruction. "At least let me show you how the saddle works. Why must you be so stubborn? This just happens to be something I know about. Why won't you let me help?"

He muttered something about doing it his own way, and refused to discuss it further.

Tommy never changed his original choice of a horse. The temperamental black mare was his unwilling partner in heroics. He mounted her by himself, alone behind the wall of the corral. Sometimes it took an hour or more. Diego and Amy, as instructed, waited by the gate. They could only listen to Tommy curse, and eight horses whinny and stomp and paw in response.

"For God's sake!" Amy shouted once. "Let Diego catch her. We'll lead her out on a tether. Tommy, do you hear me? This is mad, you'll kill yourself!" He didn't answer.

Eventually Tommy yelled, "Now!" Then she and Diego had a role to play. They pulled open the gate of the corral and closed it after Tommy rode out on the black.

He came as they had seen him that first drunken time, lying almost full length on the horse's bare back, his arms around the animal's neck, clinging for dear life. The mare would cavort wildly in an attempt to throw him, and Amy and Diego would dash from one strategic spot to another to head off any mad plunge into open country. This went on until Tommy slid to the ground in exhaustion. Then Diego would catch the horse and lead her back to the corral.

At the end of a week Tommy sat upright on his mount. Amy's offers of help had been refused, but on the eighth day she noticed a blanket between Tommy and the horse. At least Diego had some influence. The Indian watched Tommy's struggle without comment, but sometimes Amy saw something in his eyes. It was respect, hard won and grudgingly given, but permanent.

A few days later one of the saddles from the tackroom replaced the blanket. The stirrups had been carefully altered to accommodate Tommy's built-up shoe. "Thank you," she said to Diego.

Diego didn't look at her. "He was ready, so I did it. No thanks needed."

"You approve of the way he's learned to ride, don't you? Even though he wouldn't let either of us help?"

"In the old days, the Apaches and the Comanche were the greatest horsemen in the world. Nobody ever born could ride like them. That's how they taught their kids. Just put 'em up on a horse and let 'em go. You get a feel for the animal doing it that way. It's better."

It was a long speech for him. "What tribe are you?" Amy asked. "Are you an Apache?"

He didn't look disgusted, but he sounded it. "The Pueblo Indians were here before any Apache ever saw this country. And long before any Anglos came."

Amy found herself wondering what tribe her grandfather had belonged to.

*   *   *

Toward the end of the month Ricardo Ibañez called to see her. "I'm early, but I was in the vicinity, so I came. I hope it's not inconvenient."

"No, of course not. It's most kind of you. Please come in." Because she had no choice, she stepped aside and motioned for him to enter the shed.

Ibañez made no comment about their living conditions. He examined her and waited outside until she dressed and joined him.

"Well," he said. "You *are* pregnant."

"I know. I've been sure for some time."

"And in excellent health. You mustn't worry. Everything's going to be fine, Mrs. Westerman."

"Please call me Amy, Don Rico."

"Thank you. I'm Rick to my friends."

She smiled at him. "Rick and Amy, then. It's a lot easier."

Tommy had taken the Model-T and gone into Santa Fe for supplies. Diego was off somewhere. They were alone. "Would you like a cup of coffee? It's not much good, but it's hot and wet."

He grinned and she noticed the way his eyes crinkled at the corners. It was typical of the men of this territory, a characteristic born of a lifetime under the sun. "It will taste like ambrosia to me," he said. "I've been out to Santo Domingo pueblo. My motor car can't handle those dirt roads. It's a long ride on horseback."

She poured the thick black brew into a tin mug, the only thing available, and watched anxiously while he tasted it. He didn't seem to find it too bad. "I wonder if this ranch was named for the pueblo," she said. "Or vice versa."

"Neither," Rick told her. "They were both named for St. Dominic. That's what the name means in English. But you probably know that."

She shook her head. "No, I didn't, I've just never asked. It's funny actually. My husband's brother is studying to be a Dominican priest. He's in their novitiate back east."

Rick looked surprised. "You're Catholics? I didn't know."

"My husband is. I'm not much of anything. Are you a Catholic?"

"Nominally," Rick said. "Like you, I'm not really much of anything." He turned and studied the crumbling wall of the main house and changed the subject. "I remember this place in the old days. It was beautiful when I was a child. Once we came here for a fandango."

"What's that?"

"A dance, a fiesta. A big party with everyone for miles around."

"Have you lived here all your life?"

"Oh, yes." He put down his empty mug, and they strolled slowly to where he had tethered his horse. "My nine-times-great-grandfather is supposed to have been the natural son of Don Diego Vargas, a great conquistador and one of the first governors of Santa Fe. According to the story Don Diego sent his love-child to Spain to become a physician. Later the boy returned, and the men of my family have had the job every since."

He smiled at her, and she noticed his eyes again. He had dark thick lashes. "We are perhaps without ambition. We just keep doing the same thing."

"I don't think I'd describe it that way," she said. "Did you learn medicine in Spain? I hear traces of it in your speech."

Rick chuckled. "No, nothing so romantic. Johns Hopkins in Maryland. As for my speech, my mother was from Mexico City. When she married my father she spoke no English. Later she learned, but we used Spanish at home. It was my first language."

Rick untethered his horse, and Amy held the reins while he swung into the saddle. "Just keep doing what you're doing," he told her. "You're thriving, so it must be the right thing."

"And I can keep riding?"

"For a while longer, yes. I'll be back in a month, perhaps less. We'll talk about it again then."

"Rick, before you go, there's one more thing I want to ask." She bit her lip and he waited patiently. "DeAngeles," she blurted out. "He must have been your patient. He said he was selling because of ill health. Was it true?"

Ibañez looked from her to the ruined house and back again. "Doctors aren't supposed to discuss their patients. I'm sorry." Then, when he saw her embarrassed expression: "He wasn't sick, not the way you mean. But he was sick in his heart."

Rick wore a broad-brimmed black hat that tied under his chin. He pushed it to the back of his head.

"DeAngeles was born here in the last of the old, great days, when Santo Domingo was known simply as *el rancho*, the ranch. It was a magnificent spread and the men who owned it, Señor DeAngeles' father and grandfather, they were kings. When the son's turn came it had all changed. Government regulations, trains instead of cattle drives, everything was different. So he moved in there"—Rich nodded toward the shed—"and let it all fall to pieces around him. He really was sick, but it was nothing I could cure with tonics or treatments. Do you understand?"

"Yes, I think so. And thank you. I want to know everything about this place. It's very important to me. Some day I'll tell you why."

"I will like to know," he answered quietly. "And in the meantime, if you need me for anything at all, send Diego. I will come. Adios, Amy."

She watched him ride away until she could see nothing more. Then she turned and studied the house and tried to imagine what it must have looked like when it was full of beautiful happy people come for a fandango.

Later she found an opportunity to question Diego. "Don Rico is a very good doctor, isn't he?"

"In the pueblos the old ones think he's a god."

"And do you?"

"He's a good doctor. And a nice guy. Been here all his life."

"Yes, so he told me. He must be married. Is his wife a local girl?"

"She was. She's dead. Died three years ago. He has a daughter. Estella, I think her name is."

"How old is she?"

"Three, I guess."

He looked away, and Amy realized that he didn't want to say that Don Rico's wife had died in childbirth. Diego must know she was pregnant. Talk of the doctor had apparently given it away. In fact, she thought, there are few details of our life secret from Diego.

"Diego tells me some doctor came to see you," Tommy said that evening after they had eaten. "Are you sick?"

"No, I'm pregnant. I told you that."

"I haven't forgotten what you told me."

They had not mentioned the baby or her ultimatum again. Amy didn't know if her threat had influenced Tommy's subsequent efforts. "Listen," she said, "I want you to know I admire what you've done."

"Oh, what's that?"

"The way you've learned to ride, the exercises. I realize it's not easy. I'm grateful."

"Don't be," he said. "I'm doing it for myself. Don't kid yourself about that."

His voice was cold and hard. Amy felt tears sting her eyes, and she blinked them away.

"We've got to make some money out of this place," Tommy continued. "We can't just sit here, living on capital. It won't last long."

"I'd like to help," she whispered. "I would if you'd tell me what to do."

"I don't need you to do anything, sweetheart. You've

done quite enough already." The endearment was spoken in the same distant tone as the rest of his words.

He kicked out the fire without saying anything more. She started to gather up the dishes. "Leave those for the morning," he told her. "Come to bed."

"It's early. I'm not tired."

"Neither am I," he said very low. He stood aside and waited for her to precede him into the low-ceilinged hovel that was their home. Then Tommy lit the oil lamp, and Amy smelled its acrid fumes and stared at the black streaks it made on the wall.

"Get your clothes off," he said. "I want to have a good look at you."

"Why are you so angry with me?" she whispered. "What I said that night, I was desperate, frightened. Surely you can understand that."

"Oh, yeah, I understand everything. You're my wife. Do what you're told."

She unbuttoned the buff twill blouse. These days she wore it outside the skirt because her waist was thickening rapidly. She removed both pieces of clothing and stood in her panties and chemise.

"Everything," Tommy said. He slouched, arms folded, against the wall.

Amy hesitated, then looked at Tommy's expression and thought of the whiskey bottles still in the next room. She did as he asked.

"You're showing quite a bit," Tommy said. "More than I remember the last time. How far along are you?"

"Three months." She tried to make her voice normal, even bright. "The baby's due in November. They say it always shows faster after the first time."

"I'm glad, I like the look of you pregnant. I did before too. Just have to keep you that way, I guess." He studied her small delicate feet and her slim ankles. They looked whiter than ever against the dark earth floor. "Barefoot and pregnant, like the old saying."

She started to say something, then gave up pretending that this was an ordinary conversation. Instead she shivered.

Tommy reached out and let his fingers trail over her skin. His hands had grown tough with the efforts of the past month; she could feel his calluses.

"This is what you're all about, sweetheart," he whispered. "Maybe the only thing you're good for."

The cot was a few feet behind them, and he pushed her toward it. "Lie down."

"Tommy, please don't act like this. I don't know what to think! The baby . . ."

"I'm not going to hurt the baby. I talked to that doctor in New York before we left. He says it doesn't hurt the baby until just a few weeks before it's born." He chuckled. "Like they say out here"—he mimicked the southwestern drawl—"you just rest easy in your mind about that, ma'am."

He leaned over her and put his hands on her belly and traced the outline of the slight mound. "Nice," he said. "I like the way it feels. These are nice too."

Her breasts were swollen and tender with pregnancy. The nipples stiffened at his touch.

"I hate you," she hissed through clenched teeth. "I

hate you. I'll make you pay. . . ." She was sobbing and the words choked in her throat.

With a loud groan Tommy flung himself on top of her and entered her. She felt his turgid member punishing her flesh. Quick hard thrusts assailed her, there was nothing of love in them.

"Now you understand," he hissed into her ear after his climax came. "Now you know what you are. You're a whore, sweetheart. A beautiful, pregnant, part-Indian whore. You don't want me, but you've got me. Me, not Luke. I'm going to make sure you never forget."

She woke soaked in perspiration and alone in the bed. For a few confused seconds Amy thought it had all been a nightmare. The door of the shed was open. A spill of sunlight across the floor illuminated her clothes, lying in a heap where she had dropped them, and she knew the memory was true.

She rose slowly, expecting to be sore and bruised. She wasn't. Her body exhibited no reaction to the degradation so vividly remembered. She washed and dressed and went outside to stir the embers of the cook fire. The sounds of Tommy's exercises floated over the courtyard. She made coffee and eggs and bacon in a rhythm dictated by the slap of weights hitting the patio floor.

Tommy emerged. He walked briskly with almost no limp and toweled the sweat from his face. "Don't fix any breakfast for Diego. He left at dawn."

His voice betrayed no residue of last night's anger. It was simply calm and detached. She tried to make hers match it. "Where did he go?"

"To his pueblo. He's bringing a woman back. They should be here by lunch."

"What woman? Why?" She put the eggs on a plate and the yolks broke and ran yellow over the chipped crockery.

"I don't know her name. Some aunt of his. Jesus, aren't you ever going to learn to fry an egg without breaking the yolk?"

"Why is he bringing her here?"

"So there'll be someone with you. Diego and I are riding out. We're going to check the boundary. All of it. And see what we can find of the cows. It's just a preliminary look. We'll need more men to do it right, but I want to see for myself first."

"I don't need anyone with me. How long will you be gone?"

"A week, ten days maybe. You can't be alone that long. Have to look after my investment." He reached out and patted her stomach. The gesture was almost tender. She stared at him and tried to read some explanation in his familiar face. Maybe it had all been a dream after all.

Tommy pretended not to understand the question in her eyes. "Besides," he added, "maybe this aunt of Diego's knows how to cook. We'll all die from malnutrition if she doesn't. You have charm, Mrs. Westerman, but a chef you definitely are not."

She picked at the eggs on her plate and felt nauseated. "We can't afford to hire servants."

There was a long silence, during which he set down his food with slow precise motions. "I thought we settled all that last night. I'm just going to say this once more, sweetheart, so you better listen hard. I decide what we do and when we do it from now on. You look beautiful and have babies. And while we're on the subject, stop wearing those goddamn trousers. Next time I see them I'll burn them. Do you understand?"

She looked up at him. His face had become sunburned, and his freckles stood out with greater prominence. They were the only reminder of the boy who had carved the names of her parents on the church wall in Cross River. Apart from them the man staring at her so intently was a stranger. "Yes," she whispered. "I understand."

Maria, Diego's aunt, was short and round, with long black braids and a face that betrayed neither age nor emotion. But she had kind eyes, and competence. Amy swiftly became accustomed to having her around. Maria made herself sleeping space in one of the unused outbuildings, and took over the more onerous household tasks. Amy felt relief, but had more time to brood.

Tommy wasn't drunk when he did it, she kept thinking. *He said those things and used me that way and he was sober.* It was a recurrent pain, an ache of despair and humiliation that would not go away. Two or three times each day of Tommy's absence she heated a pan of water and went behind the shed to scrub her skin; as if she could wash away what had happened. Maria expressed no surprise at this passion for cleanliness, but Amy realized that she was making more work for the woman. The water butt emptied fast, and Maria had to go to the well and haul back buckets with which to refill it. Amy returned to one bath a day.

On the evening of the eleventh day the men returned. Tommy slid from his horse, and there was a brief moment when Amy thought him drunk. It was only exhaustion. He staggered to the cook fire and accepted the mug of coffee she poured.

"How did it go?" she asked.

"Not bad. No, better than that, it went well." His face was seamed with tiredness and dirt, and his clothes were covered in a thick layer of dust. He had a cut on one cheek. "You're improving," he said as he drained the coffee.

"Not me, Maria made it. I'll heat some water for a bath."

He emerged from behind the shed in twenty minutes, refused anything to eat, and went inside. Amy followed him. He was sprawled on the cot, arms folded behind his head, eyes closed. "I'll let you sleep," she said and turned to go.

"No," he said. "I'm too keyed up for that. I want to talk to you."

She sat on a rickety stool and leaned her back against the adobe wall. Suddenly she felt tired too.

"The land is wonderful, in some places it's fantastic," he said. "There's plenty of decent grazing in the high ground to the east. The first thing we have to do is get a fence around the whole place."

"Can we?"

"Yes, why not? The only problem's money. That's one of the things I want to tell you. There's no more

than four thousand left of our working capital. I spent
the rest in Albuquerque, don't ask me how."

"I wasn't going to ask."

"The fence will cost a lot," he said. "I've decided to
sell off what cows we have."

"Did you find them?"

"We saw a couple of herds. There's probably not
more than a thousand left. The way things have been
around here they were easy prey for any two-bit rus-
tler that cared to try his luck. That's spilt milk, what
we need now is a quick sale of what we have."

"Can you get it?"

"Yes. I've been in touch with Washington. The
government is buying all the food it can get its hands
on. They'll take whatever we can round up, at thirty
dollars a head. It's not a good price, but it's fast, sure
money. Lucky for us they decided to have a war."

"And afterward?"

"We hire a crew, build the fence, and buy in more
stock. We'll keep a few of our original herd for breed-
ing. They were a great strain in their day." He turned
and propped himself on his elbow and lit a cigarette.
Every time he drew on it Amy could see his eyes in
the glow. It made him seem to approach and recede in
the dark.

"I've spoken to some men in Kansas City. In the
future we'll breed and raise our cattle, and sell them
after three years. It's the only thing that makes sense
in a country like this. The guys I'm in touch with have
feed lots. They can fatten the cows for market. The
housewife back east gets juicy corn-fed beef, and we
get a quick turnover and low overhead."

Now she understood all the hours he had spent brooding, and the unexplained trips to Santa Fe. "It's a good plan. You've spent a long time thinking it out, haven't you?"

"Yeah. Then, when I found out I couldn't drive the flivver around the spread, I thought we were beaten. Sorry about the hiccup in production."

Amy started. They were the same words the nurse had used in the hospital in New York. She pressed her hands over her belly and felt the child stir. "It doesn't matter as long as it comes right in the end."

"Agreed." He stretched and stood up. "There are places out there, miles from anywhere, so beautiful it hurts to look at them."

"I know," she said.

He lit the oil lamp and looked at her in its dull glow. "Yeah, you knew right away. From the time you saw the picture in the library book." He looked around, as if seeing the shed for the first time. "I'll get you out of here as fast as I can. But the cattle have to take priority."

Amy watched him lift a jug and start for the water butt.

"Tommy," she called softly. "The things you said the night before you left, the names you called me . . . why?"

He paused with his back to her, then continued walking; pretending he hadn't heard and limping heavily.

The next morning the gum tree bloomed.

For once Amy woke first. She slipped from the narrow bed and looked at Tommy in the gray light of early dawn. He slept on, his breath deep and even. She crept quietly to the dead embers of the cook fire. Not even Maria was up yet. Amy found a little luke-warm coffee still in the pot.

She carried the mug toward the house. It looked fine in the half-light that hid its wounds. Tommy seemed to think it could look really fine again.

The sun rose at her back. The mellow terracotta walls of the house shimmered to life. She smelled a sweet vanilla scent drifting across the morning. Amy followed the perfume to the patio, and gazed up at the mass of branches twined overhead. The leaves were a soft gray green. They hung absolutely still, as if to protect the tiny cruciform blossoms that studded length and breadth. They were white, as Diego has promised. Then, while she watched, a shaft of new sun caught them. The flowers turned to flame.

18

⁓

Sɪx MONTHS LATER, ON THE TWELFTH OF NOVEMBER, 1917, Amy's child was born.

Her labor began in an afternoon almost as dark as night, the first sunless day she had known in New Mexico. "Will it rain?" she asked Maria. They were desperate for rain.

"Not yet. Duster first. Then rain maybe."

Amy gasped with another pain and Maria led her inside the shed. Amy had fantasized giving birth under the sun. On the patio perhaps, under the gum tree. There could be no chance of that today.

Luckily Tommy was home. He'd returned the previ-

ous day after a week out on the range. He'd left Diego
to continue supervising the erection of the fence. Now
he looked at his wife and required no instructions.
"I'll take the car and go into town. Be back with
Ibañez in a few hours."

Maria made Amy lie down, then sat beside her.
"When pains come you breathe hard. No push yet. I
tell you when."

After an hour Amy heard the wind. Maria was
standing by the door, looking out. "What is it?" Amy
demanded. "What's happening?"

"Duster."

Amy craned her neck. She could see nothing but
dark. The room was filled with eddying currents. She
felt the onslaught of another contraction and tried to
breathe, but inhaled choking sand instead of air.

Maria heard her coughing. She soaked a cloth in
water, then tied it over Amy's nose and mouth. She
made the same arrangement for herself. The two women
looked at each other above surreal masks that swiftly
turned red brown and had to be rinsed and renewed
every ten minutes.

"No more water," Maria said after a while. "I get
some. Come back quick." She took a bucket and
stepped outside, hunched against the dry, debilitating
storm.

Amy felt a contraction that seemed to start at the
back of her neck and move down her spine in a para-
lyzing grip of increasing intensity. She screamed, but
the sound was lost in the screeching wind. The pain
went on and on until she had no more breath to
scream and could only moan.

Maria returned, took one look at her, and came quickly to the bedside. "Sit up," she commanded. "Open legs."

Amy struggled to do as she was told. Maria put her strong arms around the girl's shoulders and dragged her upright. "Push, señora. Push down. You squeeze out baby."

Amy pushed. She felt warmth and wetness, but more than anything else, pain. It was gut-wrenching, tearing pain, without surcease. She clung to Maria. Her mask slipped. She screamed in an unfiltered mouthful of the sand that blew all around them. It was as if the rotten walls of the shed didn't exist and they were outside in the raging elements.

Then it was over. Amy sagged against the older woman, but Maria moved away and Amy was left with only the wall for support.

Maria reached for the child and laid it on Amy's belly. Then she severed the cord with a knife. Quickly she soaked a towel in a bucket of water and flung it over the baby. Maria's hands reached beneath the protective cover.

"What is it?" Amy murmured. "Is it all right?"

"Girl," Maria muttered under her breath. She continued her efforts. A few seconds passed; then the baby cried. At the same instant the wind stopped. Maria smiled broadly. "Girl, ok," she said. "Boy next time. Even better."

Amy fainted.

When she came to, Rick was there, bending over her and smiling his familiar warm smile. "You were impatient, Amy," he said. "You started without me."

"Sorry." She smiled back. They had become friends in the months of her pregnancy. "The baby . . ."

"She's fine. A beautiful girl. You're both fine. Maria knows as much about all this as I do. She says you had an easy time of it. Quicker than expected."

Amy's eyes flew open. "Easy?"

He grinned. "Anyway, Maria's proud of you. She says you did as well as an Indian woman. From her that's high praise."

Amy looked away and didn't answer.

"Here." Rick reached into the basket beside them and lifted the infant. She was wrapped in blankets and only her tiny face showed. It was red and wrinkled and the eyes were screwed shut. He lay the bundle in Amy's arms.

She looked at the child and knew neither what she should feel nor what she felt. She was too tired, still disoriented. "She's lighter than I expected," Amy whispered. "And I can't see her eyes. Have you seen them? What color are they?"

"Blue. All babies are born with blue eyes. And she weighs six pounds. That's not too small. She's a healthy, normal baby, Amy. Don't worry."

"If you say so." She stroked the tiny cheek with one finger. Something burst inside her. Love, hope, joy— call it anything. It made her feel happy and sad at the same time, and she knew she was crying, but not why.

Rick swallowed hard and reached out his hand, but drew it back without touching either of them. "Tommy's waiting outside. I'll get him."

Tommy came in and stood by the bed, staring at his wife and child. Finally Amy stopped crying and looked up. "Here, you can hold her." She started to lift the baby toward him.

He shook his head. "No, I don't dare." He dropped to his knees and studied the little face peeking out from the blankets. At that moment the tiny mouth opened and the baby made a sound. "Jesus," Tommy whispered. "Oh, Jesus . . ." It was as if, until that moment, he hadn't believed the child was alive.

The next day he went again to Santa Fe. There was no dust storm this time, and he made it there and back in six hours. He came into the shed with a big unwieldy parcel, unwrapped it, and stood back for Amy to admire the bassinet. "I don't want her sleeping in a basket like some damned papoose," he said.

The bassinet was painted white and had a tulle skirt and lots of pink satin ribbons. It stood on wheels, and he pushed it close beside the bed and waited until Amy lay the baby inside.

"I've been thinking about her name," she said.

"Mmm, so have I. But the only thing I come up with is Cecily or Jessie, maybe both. But they don't sound good together."

"No!" She shook her head violently. "I don't want to name her for anyone. I want her just to be herself."

Tommy was slightly awed by her and by what she had accomplished, as it seemed, all by herself. "Ok. What do you want then?"

"Kate. That's all."

"It will have to be Kathleen or Catherine," he said. "Kate's just a nickname."

"No, only Kate."

"She can't be baptized with a nickname. They won't allow it."

Amy's brown eyes darted to his face. As far as she knew, he had not been near a church in almost a year. "You want her baptized? In a Catholic church?"

"Yes. You promised, Amy. Don't fight me about it now."

"I won't, I just thought you had forgotten about all that."

He laughed softly. "No, not quite." He looked at the baby and then at her. "Tell you what, pick a middle name, something ordinary. Then the Kate part will be all right. They let you do that."

Amy thought for a moment. "Mary, I suppose. That ought to fulfill the requirements." *But she'll always be just Kate to me*, she thought.

"Mary Kate. Sounds better than the other way around," he said. Amy shrugged her acquiesence. "Mary Kate Westerman it is, then," Tommy said.

He stood up and looked around the room, and at the incongruous glamor of the bassinet. "The fence is almost finished. Another month, maybe six weeks. Soon as it's done I've arranged for the crew to start on the house. With luck we'll be able to move in early next year."

"Don't feel you have to," Amy said. "Not for me or for her. If you want to wait until there's more money, it's all right."

"I had a letter from Uncle Donald," he said. "The Eighty-third Street house is sold. My share's a bit over thirty thousand. We can afford to live like human beings."

Amy thought of the New York house as she had last
seen it; covered in dust sheets, with all Cecily Westerman's beautiful things packed away. "Did they sell it
furnished?" she asked. She wanted to ask what Luke
would do with his portion of the money. What did a
Dominican do with thirty thousand dollars? She knew
better than to voice the question.

"Almost completely furnished," Tommy said. "I sent
Donald a list of a few things I wanted. He's shipping
them."

"What things?"

"Nothing much, most of it would look out of place
here. Just Dad's desk and Mother's statue. The antique from France."

"The madonna and child," she said.

"Yes, that's right."

In March of 1918 they moved into the main house.
That same day Tommy had the old shed dismantled
and the rubble carted away.

"Kate was born there," Amy said. "Maybe we should
leave it for her to see."

"Not a chance! I don't want her thinking about
things like that. I want her to know only this."

He had grown less timid of his daughter. Now he
carried her as they walked through the restored rooms
of the old hacienda. The walls were repaired and
whitewashed, and the ancient wood was sanded and
polished. The floors were tiled in dull red and covered
with bright Mexican carpets. It wasn't entirely furnished, but the rooms that were had the heavy carved

pieces that had been left behind by DeAngeles, as well as some new things in the same style. Tommy had found them in Santa Fe and Albuquerque. He had, in fact, chosen all the decoration.

Amy walked beside him and studied the ambience he'd created. "While the work was going on I couldn't really tell about it," she said. "Now, seeing it all together and with the workmen gone, it's beautiful."

"Yes," he said. "Here, hold Kate a minute. There's one more thing I want to do."

He left, then returned with his mother's statue and set it on a shelf in the entrance foyer. It looked perfect. Amy had to admit that. The wormeaten wood with its centuries old patina glowed against the white wall. When the door was open, sunlight bathed the figure and revealed shafts of gold hitherto secreted in the grain.

There had been more rain than usual over the winter. Now the desert bloomed in a riotous, fecund spring. Exotic, unknown perfumes filled the air, and Amy waited impatiently for the gum tree to have its turn. Anxiously she watched the birds that settled in its branches, afraid lest they peck the life from the closed buds. Her only other worry was that her milk suddenly dried up and she had to put Kate on a bottle.

The baby didn't seem to mind. She cooed and gurgled and grew strong and healthy in the cool, spacious house. Kate was somehow a meeting place for her mother and father. She was someone they both loved so much that she created an oasis of peace in the aridity of their tense and unhappy marriage.

Tommy no longer drank, but he grew colder and harder and more distant. He spent more and more time away from the house. For weeks at a stretch he was out riding the range, overseeing the delivery of new stock, and shaping the Indian crew to his method. Amy was grateful for the time alone. When Tommy was home they were civil to each other only in the baby's presence.

He had installed a huge bed in their room, sending east for the mattress and having the base specially built on site. It was six feet square and sat on a massive wooden frame with tall carved posts at each corner. Tommy vented his bitter anger in that bed. He did not strike or physically abuse Amy. She had no cause to repeat the threat uttered a year earlier. But he seemed to take more satisfaction from humiliating her than from possessing her.

"Why?" she whispered one May night when he returned after two weeks absence. "Why are you doing this?" She had not dared the question before. The scene they had just enacted forced the words out. He made her feel like an animal, and he cursed her with every foul word he knew even as he gained freedom between her legs.

He laughed bitterly. "Don't play innocent with me sweetheart. You know why."

"No," she said. "I don't. I keep trying to understand, but nothing makes any sense."

He was smoking, and he lazily stubbed out his cigarette and turned to her. "The lady wants to know why," he said softly. "Why it is she ain't no lady. Now that's a good question." He pulled back the sheet she was holding over her nakedness. Amy tried to push him away, but he grasped her wrists. "I'll tell you why, sweetheart, since you asked. It's got something to do with wanting things you can't have. Secretly wanting them, and thinking you're fooling everybody, even your own husband. Nice girls don't do that kind of thing."

She tried to answer, but he bent her hands back so they pressed against her mouth. Her eyes widened in fear.

"C'mon, sweetheart, what are you scared of? I'm your husband, remember, the one you promised to love and obey."

She struggled to free herself, but he was too strong for her. For a moment she thought he meant to possess her again, and she braced herself for the savage onslaught. But either he couldn't or didn't want to. Instead he suddenly let her go. "Forget it," he said. "I know you're a whore and so do you." With that he quit her bed, leaving her to spend the night alone with the echo of his bitter accusations.

19

❧

SOMETIMES WHEN HE WALKED THE STREETS OF THE
city Rick Ibañez was conscious of an echo that dogged
his footsteps. Here in the *barrio* near the creek it was
very loud. He wondered if everyone heard it. Probably not, you had to have the old ones in your blood as
he did. He was spawn of the two cultures that origi-
nally clashed in this place. Rapacious Spanish conquistadors and inbred, mystic Indians warred for supremacy
in his head. It was they who made the echo; it was
both a lament for times gone by and a hunger for all
that was new and venturesome.

He turned into an alley and heard the soft slurred

strumming of a guitar. "Spanish is a loving tongue," a girl sang from inside one of the mean and dark houses of the *barrio*. "Sweet as music, soft as rain . . ." The girl sang in English, and her melody was neither old nor Mexican. It was the lament of a Texas cowboy for the señorita he'd left "down Sonora way." But in this place at this time the singer had made it her own. Such was the genius of Santa Fe.

Ibañez left the alley and the music faded. On the slightly wider street to which he'd come the houses were interspersed with small *tiendas*. By day they sold garbanzos and olive oil and rice, and strings of fiery red chilies festooned their walls. Now the shops were shuttered tight. Only the faint odor of their wares announced their existence in the moonlit street.

There was, however, one commercial establishment dignified by a sign and a window display *Beatriz Ortega—La Ropa Especial* the lettering over the door announced. Behind the glass was an artfully arranged exhibit of bright-colored ruffled dresses, lace mantillas, fringed shawls, and exquisite fans. It was a vivid visual reminder of old days and old ways.

Beatriz opened the door as soon as he knocked. Soundlessly he followed her through the darkened shop. They went past the bedroom of old Señora Ortega, his patient and his excuse for being there, to that of Beatriz. She ushered him inside and lit candles which were protected by tall glass chimneys, and the soft light illumined dusty velvet hangings and ancient furniture. The candles were kind to the shabby surroundings and to Beatriz.

"Good evening, Don Rico."

She was always ridiculously formal with him. It annoyed him, but he'd given up expecting her to change. One battle, however, he still fought. "There's to be a shop vacant soon on San Francisco Street," he said. "It's close to the plaza and I know the owner. The rent need not be high."

Beatriz smiled and her plain features were transformed. The smile betrayed a woman of intelligence and charm behind the dull exterior; it was what had first attracted him to her. "And if I move my establishment to the center of town, I can sell dresses and mantillas to Anglo tourists. Souvenirs of old Mexico, no?"

"Yes, and you'd make twice as much money."

"But that will do nothing for the *barrio.* Here I am a constant reminder to them. It is what I want to be."

"Dreams of ancient glory," Rick said with a sigh. "It won't work, Beatriz. Those who survive and prosper will be the ones who get out of here and look to the future, not the past."

"I know that. Only I don't want them to forget the past. I want the young ones to take it with them. What is wrong with that?"

"Nothing. But you have your mother to think of." He almost added, "And yourself," but he didn't say it. Beatriz needed no reminding that she was forty-six years old, and that if she meant to salvage what remained of her life, she had to quit the *barrio.* Neither did she need to be told that the relationship between her and Ibañez was only friendship joined to physical necessity. It could never be love, and marriage was no part of it.

"My mother is doing very well," she told him, as if that was what he'd meant. "The medicine you gave her last week helps a great deal."

"I'm glad," Rick said with a small smile. In her quiet way Beatriz always won. They did not speak anymore. Beatriz turned away from him and began unbuttoning her dress. It was of plain gray cotton trimmed with black braid. It was old-fashioned and dowdy; not old-fashioned and beautiful like the clothes she made and sold. Beneath the gray dress she wore a white linen camisole and petticoat. She removed those too. Her motions were calm and efficient and without shame. Rick enjoyed watching her undress. She had done it just this same way the first time, three months after Margarita's death.

Then he had been a man in torment, living in a nightmare composed as much of guilt as of grief. He was a trained man of healing, but he had not been present when his young wife began a premature labor. Instead he'd been off in a distant pueblo treating the Indians who made him feel like God if he so much as stitched a knife wound. It took hours for the summons to reach him, and more hours for him to get back to Santa Fe. By that time Margarita was dead. There was a lot of bleeding, the old housekeeper told him, a river of blood that she and the midwife couldn't staunch. Rick forced himself to examine his dead wife. Not hemorrhage, his practiced eye said, heart failure. Digitalis might have saved her, but he hadn't been there to

administer it. So the pain of loss had been overlaid
with the ugly pattern of guilt. That duo of emotions
had held him in a vise, until Beatriz healed him.

One day he went to see his patient Señora Ortega
and the quiet, self-effacing daughter led him to her
bedroom. She had locked the door and undressed, just
as she was doing now. "You need a woman, Don
Rico," she'd said in her well-modulated voice. "And I
need a man. I am a divorcée, not a virgin, you understand that?"

He had nodded. He knew that her legal name was
Beatriz Johnson and that she'd been married to an
Anglo who took her east and eventually deserted her
for a younger woman of his own culture and background. After that Beatriz had returned to Santa Fe,
resumed her father's name and opened her strange sad
little shop. "I know," he'd said, watching with fascination the dispassionate way she removed her clothes
and revealed a full, voluptuous figure. Her body did
not seem to belong to her sharp-featured, gaunt face.
No doubt his astonishment had showed.

"I am much older than you," she had said, looking
at him gravely. "I have no wish to entrap you, Don
Rico, nor could I. I'm barren. The doctors in St. Louis
proved that years ago. But my body does not displease
you, I think. And my need is as great as yours." Then
she had smiled, and he had seen that the full breasts
and rounded hips were representative of the real
Beatriz; a woman warm, passionate, and intelligent.
"Come, take me," she'd said. "It will give pleasure to
both of us."

She had said the same thing every time since. She said it now. "Come, take me."

While she watched he took off his clothes. It had become a ritual, this manner of undressing; one after the other, with each watching in turn. Ibañez saw the pleasure in her eyes and was conscious of his tall muscular frame, slim-hipped and broad-shouldered like an old time matador, and of the heavy, swollen manhood pulsing erect between his legs. He moved toward her, and she stretched out her hand and caressed his penis lovingly. Then she dropped to her knees and enfolded it in her breasts before taking it in her mouth. Sometimes she finished him like that, and afterward he would satisfy her in the same way. This time she pulled her head away after a moment, and went and lay on the bed, legs spread and arms outstretched. "Come, take me," she repeated.

Afterward he felt a strange sadness that was not like all the other times. In the past he had been grateful to her. He admired her wisdom and uncompromising integrity. "I am not a whore, and you are neither a murderer nor a hero," she'd said after the first time. "We are human beings, with needs and weaknesses, and little bits of virtue that we exercise for mixed motives. We must learn to be gentle and forgiving with ourselves."

He'd never forgotten those words, or the way they had eased his pain. So tonight Ibañez was a little ashamed. He wasn't living up to the truthfulness that had marked their alliance thus far. This time he had lain over Beatriz with the shadow of another woman between them, more real than the ghost of Margarita had ever been.

As if she read his thoughts Beatriz said, "I am told that the young wife of the Anglo who has bought Santo Domingo is your patient. Is she a nice person?"

He reached over and found a cigarette on the table by the bed. Lighting it gave him a moment to collect his thoughts. "Why do you ask?" he said between puffs of smoke.

"My cousin Manuel owns the ranch adjoining Santo Domingo. It was his father's and his grandfather's before him."

"I know that," Ibañez said. He was sorry about the impatience in his voice. "What are you getting at, Beatriz?" he asked with more gentleness.

"Mr. Westerman," she would not dignify an Anglo with the title of don or señor, "is threatening to refuse Manuel the right to water his cattle."

"I don't understand."

"The waterhole on Santo Domingo is the only one for many miles. Always it has been shared by my cousin and another ranch to the south."

"Then it will probably go on like that. Don't worry, Westerman's a newcomer. He doesn't yet know our ways. He'll learn."

"The arrangement is by private treaty," she insisted. "It is not written into the deeds. And my cousin Manuel says Mr. Westerman is a strange man. Very hard. Perhaps he does not want to know our ways." Then, anticipating his next question: "I thought you might speak to the wife and find out her husband's intentions. I would not ask you, Don Rico, except that Manuel has seven children and ranching is the only thing he knows. Besides, that land is part of him. It would kill him to lose his ranch."

Ibañez rose and pulled on his clothes. This was the first time Beatriz had ever asked him for anything more than physical pleasure. And it was not for herself but for her cousin. Still it signaled a change. Coupled with his sad unfulfilled feeling it convinced him that the relationship with Beatriz was nearing its end. He would not come many more times to this warm dark room in the *barrio*.

"If the opportunity arises, I will see what I can find out," he said. "Good night, Beatriz."

"Goodnight, Don Rico. And thank you."

He was too restless and disturbed to go home, so he wandered the streets instead. The only sound came from Doña Zia's whorehouse near the creek. Ibañez stood looking at it for a few minutes. The windows were not shuttered. Yellow light spilled from them into the narrow dirt road. He could see the shadows of men and women behind the lace curtains, and hear the sound of a tinny piano mingled with slightly drunken laughter.

Doña Zia's establishment was an accepted part of the town. It wasn't shrouded in shame or secrecy. Her girls were clean—Rick was not their doctor, but he knew that to be true—and her business was part of a long tradition that began with the fabled gaming house of Doña Tules in the last century.

In the days when Santa Fe was the center of the

Spanish crown's Kingdom of New Mexico, an area that
included what was now Nevada and Arizona, Doña Tules
provided meñ with amusement and relief. After General
Kearney's Army of the West arrived in 1846, and
annexed the city and the surrounding territory to the
United States, there had been similar houses run by
like-minded women. Doña Zia was merely the latest
link in a long chain. She was a much more conven-
tional woman than Beatriz Ortega.

Ibañez sighed. If he ended his liaison with Beatriz,
sooner or later he would make his way there to that
house. The demands of that appendage between his
legs would insure it, whatever he thought. It was un-
likely that he would find again an alliance like the one
in the *barrio*. He was not a user of women. The
physical release he needed must be paid for somehow.
Either with shared need, as it had been with Beatriz,
or with money. He had a certain distaste for the latter,
but that was foolish. Just as foolish as standing there
in the dark thinking about history. He started on the
long walk home. He'd get little sleep that night, and
tomorrow there would be an office full of patients as
usual.

While he walked it occurred to Rick that he'd left
something out of the question he'd been pondering.
What about love? Wasn't that the best underpinning
of a relationship between a man and a woman? Not
for me, he thought. He had loved Margarita, whose
childlike innocence and simplicity had delighted him.
She was dead and he doubted that such a girl would
ever again attract him. He was older and wiser and he

wanted different things. As for Amy, that was madness. She was another man's wife. To Tommy Westerman belonged her gaminlike beauty, the intensity of feeling that spilled from her dark eyes, and her quicksilver laugh. "I hope to hell he appreciates them," Ibañez muttered into the night.

The Westermans' bedroom was high in the corner of the house that boasted a second story. One window opened onto a small balcony overlooking the patio and was curtained by the branches of the gum tree. Amy had pruned them to let in light and air. Now when she stepped out it was as if she were standing in the very heart of the tree. If Tommy was away with the range crew, she went to the balcony each morning at dawn, and remembered the gum's brief season of bloom. She watched the sunrise, and imagined that she could yet see the tree afire.

By early June she thought she was pregnant again. She had suspected as much for some time, and she drove into Santa Fe to see if Rick would confirm it.

"Yes," he told her after a simple examination. "I'm fairly certain. About three months perhaps."

"I thought so."

He cocked his head and studied her. "It's very soon after Kate. You're looking pale. I wish you had waited."

She studied her hands and twisted her wedding ring. "Tommy wants more children."

Rick gave her a tonic she was to take regularly, and made no further comment. They left the office together, and Amy was surprised to see the waiting room empty. "What's happened? An epidemic of good health?"

"I wish it was," he chuckled. "No, I go to see my daughter on Thursday afternoons. My patients know that."

He walked with her to the courtyard. His car, a Pierce-Arrow, was being repaired. Rick remarked that today he'd have to ride horseback to the convent.

"I have Tommy's flivver," Amy said quickly. "He's away and Kate's with Maria. I can give you a lift. Unless you'd rather see your daughter alone."

"No, I would love you to meet her. I'm delighted." Even as he spoke Rick cursed himself for a fool. Inviting Amy into the private parts of his life was folly. He knew it, but he was nonetheless grateful for the pleasure of the moment.

He took the wheel and they drove west into the foothills. Finally they came to a small walled convent nestled amid towering spruce trees and topped by a belltower and a cross. "It's a different world up here," Amy said.

"Yes, New Mexico is a place of many contrasts."

Inside they were greeted by soft-voiced, sweet-faced nuns, robed not in black, as Amy expected, but in dark brown. "We call them *las Carmelitas,*" Rick explained. "Officially, the Carmelite Sisters of Divine Hope. They came from Spain about fifty years ago."

They were shown into a stiff little parlor, with hard-backed chairs and a large wooden crucifix as its only adornment, and Estella was brought to them.

Amy thought it an austere setting for a four-year-old, but the little girl seemed happy enough. She was, however, sniffling and feverish, and Rick diagnosed the onset of grippe. He gave her some medicine and decreed that she must be put to bed. A shy young nun, with the face of an angel and an accent that indicated her recent arrival from Madrid, gathered the little girl into her arms and lisped small comforting words in the ancient tongue.

"Thank you, Sister Angelina," Rick said. "I will return in a day or two to see how she is." The nun dropped a graceful old-world curtsy and carried the child away.

Outside Amy said, "You're sure she's better off here than home with you and a housekeeper?"

"I'm sure," he said. "Life cannot be kind for a motherless child, but *las Carmelitas* are much better than any housekeeper I could provide. My wife would prefer it like this, I think."

"Did you love her very much?" Amy asked softly. Then, "Forgive me, that's an impertinent question."

"Don't apologize, the pain is an old one. I've learned to live with it. And yes, I loved her very much."

They stood for a moment looking at the mountains. I am replacing old griefs with new ones, Rick thought as they got into the car. Still he asked, "What are you doing tomorrow?"

"Nothing unusual," Amy said.

"It's a holiday, June thirteenth, San Antonio day. I won't have any patients." He looked at her with a trace of shyness. "I wonder if you would come on an excursion with me."

Amy's smile lit her face. Being with Rick was one of the nicest things she knew. It didn't occur to her that her reaction might not be proper for a married lady. She had too much unhappiness in her life to question small allotments of joy. "I'd love to," she said. "Where will we go?"

"I'll tell you tomorrow. I want it to be a surprise." His smile was as warm as her own, and his dark eyes danced with pleasure. "We'll have to leave very early. I'll be at your place an hour after sunup. We won't get back until late. Will Kate be all right?"

"Maria is marvelous with her. She'll be fine without me for one day."

The feast day dawned bright and sunny. Amy waited for Rick by the gate. He drove up in the repaired Pierce-Arrow and jumped out to help her in. "What's this?" he asked, spying the hamper by her feet.

"A picnic. You said we'd be gone all day."

"Marvelous! I never thought about what we'd eat."

"And drink," she said, indicating a bottle of red wine.

They drove west on deserted dirt roads that cut across a broad and featureless plateau. The morning was still, not yet too hot, and full of promise. Contentedly they shared silence. At one point they stopped at a small roadside restaurant for an early lunch. "We can save our picnic for later," Rick said.

They ate quickly, then resumed their journey. At length they came to a landscape of crags and scarps tumbling into a wide valley. "This is Chaco Canyon," Rick told her. "And what you see are the deserted pueblos of the Anasazi, descendents of the earliest people in this corner of the world. You may have heard them referred to as Basketmakers."

Amy stared around her in astonishment. It was early afternoon. The air was clear and brittle, and the sun rode high over fantastic cliff dwellings scattered across a dark, stony landscape. Rick stopped the car near one free-standing cluster of buildings. "Pueblo Bonito," he said. "Come."

The pueblo was built of neat sandstone slabs, laid with precision and an artist's eye. It rose many feet into the sky and had its back to a cliff, but did not lean against it. Access to the upper floors was by ladders. Some looked new and safe, others as if a touch would cause them to fall to dust. "Archeologists are working to restore it," Rick said. "They've been at it since 1896."

"It must be a formidable undertaking," she said softly. "It's huge."

"They say in its heyday Pueblo Bonito housed twelve hundred people in eight hundred rooms and covered close to three acres."

She arched her neck and twisted her head to look at the great semicircle of prodigious effort surrounding them. "When did they build it?" she asked. "And where have they gone?"

"It probably was started around the year 750, and reached its peak soon after 1200. As to where the builders went"—he shrugged—"that is New Mexico's greatest mystery. The Basketmakers achieved all this, and suddenly, for no reason we can discover, they packed their things and left. There is no evidence of fighting or destruction, no mass burials to signify an outbreak of plague or disease. There is only what you see."

They walked through small square rooms with hard-packed earthen floors and simple rectangular doors looking out to the courtyard and the dazzling sun. In some places the restoration was incomplete and the skeleton of the pueblo showed. It was constructed of pine timbers topped with peeled branches and split bark. The covering of earth that finished each floor was four inches thick. The whole layered assembly provided the ceiling of the room below.

"They've had to stop work here now," Rick said. "The war."

"But they'll continue when the war is over, won't they?" It pained her to think of this magnificence left to fall once more to ruin.

"I hope so. I dream that one day many people will come to Chaco Canyon. America can never be strong unless it understands all the different roots that make up the whole." He grinned and looked a bit embarrassed. "It's getting late, past time for philosophy. The *kiva* will have to wait for next time."

Reluctantly she followed him back to the car. "What is a *kiva?*"

"Next time," he repeated.

When they were driving once more Amy asked, "Are you saying that this is where Diego and Maria and all the other Pueblo Indians came from?"

"Yes. Many places like this. Pueblo Bonito is only one site. When they left, for whatever reason, they settled along the Rio Grande. I think it was water they were seeking. Maybe there was a year-long drought. Maybe that's why they deserted the cliffs for the river."

"It sounds logical," she said. "I'll bet you're right."

He glanced at her and hesitated for a moment. "While we're on the subject of water—is there any point in asking if you can talk to your husband about this current business?"

Amy took off her hat and let the breeze ruffle her hair. "What business?"

He shot her a quick look. "Don't you know?"

She shook her head.

"Tommy's got Lopez working on breaking the treaty that gives rights to the waterhole to the two ranches adjoining yours. If he succeeds, they're finished. That's one of the reasons I wanted to show you Pueblo Bonito. Because whatever you manage to achieve out here, if you can't get water, you're doomed."

Amy felt suborned. She'd thought he only wanted to share with her something remarkable and beautiful. Rick seemed to read her thoughts. "It wasn't the main reason I brought you here," he added. "I enjoy seeing all this through your eyes."

"Thank you for saying that."

"I mean it. But I meant the question too. Can you talk to your husband? There's always been enough water for all three ranches. Why must it change now?"

"I don't know. But I have no influence over Tommy any more. Partly it's his leg. He's always been at a disadvantage because of it. Now he can ride as well as any man, better than most. On a horse he's totally mobile for the first time in his life. Somehow he's drunk with that freedom."

"I understand."

"Sometimes I do too. Other times I'm not sure."

He didn't answer because there was nothing he could say. The silence between them grew awkward. To fill it Amy began telling him of Africa and Jericho and her girlhood.

Rick listened quietly and didn't interrupt until they came to a good place to stop and picnic. "I'm starved," he said. "How about you?"

"Ravenous."

It was early evening. The fierce heat of the day had spent itself, and left behind the comforting warmth that preceded the chill of night. Amy unpacked the hamper. She'd brought ham and potato salad and cornbread, and ripe juicy tomatoes and tangy pickles. "What a feast!" Rick exclaimed. Then he was too busy eating to talk. *"Estupendo,"* he said finally. "In other words, magnificent."

Amy giggled. "I'm flying under false colors. I didn't make any of this. Maria did. I can't cook."

"No! Impossible!" He laughed softly at first, then with gusto. Soon they were both laughing. "You can ride a horse and drive a motorcar, and you know all about Africa and diamonds, but you can't cook!" Rick gasped. "Only in New Mexico could such a woman survive."

"I think maybe I'm a freak," Amy said hesitantly.

Rick chuckled, then realized that she wasn't joking. He reached out and touched her cheek. "You are no freak, lovely Amy," he said softly. "What put that idea in your head?"

She would not tell him more. Never could she tell anyone about the things Tommy said and did, and the way he made her feel. Neither could she admit to the possibility of having Indian blood. These days she was so ensnared in her guilts and fears that she couldn't speak rationally of them. "Nothing," she said. "I'm just being silly."

Rick didn't take his hand away immediately. Amy could feel his strong but gentle fingers against her flushed skin for a few more seconds. Then he pulled away and they both stood up and started for home.

The next time he lay with Beatriz, Ibañez was miserable. Physically she pleased him as much as ever. But when it was over he was saddened by a sense of falseness. He lit a cigarette and stared at the ceiling and wondered what to tell her, and how.

"I saw Manuel yesterday," Beatriz said. She sat up and pulled a silk shawl over her shoulders and heavy breasts. The sweat of passion dewed her skin, and Ibañez looked away as if it was a reproach to him. "You remember," she continued. "I told you about my cousin Manuel."

"Yes, I remember."

"He came to town to see me. He is in much trouble. It is a very evil thing this man Westerman does."

"I spoke with Amy," Rick said quickly. He did not want to hear a long catalogue of Manuel's troubles. "That's Señora Westerman," he added.

"I know."

"She's very sorry about your cousin and the other rancher, but she has no influence with her husband."

Beatriz didn't meet his eyes. "That is sad for her. They cannot be happy together if this is the truth."

"No, I don't think she is happy." He didn't want to discuss Amy either. "Manuel should talk to Lopez. He'll need a lawyer."

"He has no money for a lawyer. Besides, Lopez works for the Anglo." She shrugged. "It is to be expected; they share blood. One Mexican grandfather does not make a man of one of us."

"Us and them. That attitude spells death, Beatriz."

"Yes, death," she agreed, pretending not to recognize that he was reprimanding her. "Death for us. Anyway, Westerman pays Lopez a lot of money."

Ibañez got up and dressed, and they spoke no more of the water rights and Manuel's troubles. "Beatriz," he said, "I may not be back for a while. I'm very busy at the office just now."

She lay back against the pillows, and her face was in the shadows when she spoke. "I understand. It has been good, Don Rico. Adios."

He hadn't expected it to be so easy. "It has been very good, Beatriz," he agreed. "Adios." There was nothing more to say. He would see her again because her mother was his patient. But it would be as if the many nights of athletic pleasure in this room had never happened. "Adios," he repeated.

In the alley across from the shop the girl with the guitar was singing the same song. He wondered if she was practicing, or if an appreciative and silent audience listened. ". . . I don't look much like a lover, but she may never love another . . ."

The lyric followed him home, and when he tried to sleep it still filled his mind. "Spanish is a loving tongue . . ." How did it end? Oh, yes, ". . . in her little sorry tone, *mi amor, mi corazon*." He'd never spoken such words to Beatriz. At least he didn't have lies to repent.

20

ONE DAY IN THE AUTUMN OF 1918, WHILE SHE AWAITED the birth of her second child, Amy went to Santa Fe to have a checkup and do some shopping. Warm October sun overlaid a hint of crispness in the air. It had rained the day before; everything seemed fresh and new and sparkling. Even the newspapers were cheerful. The allies were pushing deep into German-held territory— they called it the Argonne Offensive—and columnists were predicting that the war would soon be over.

"Good news at last," Rick said when her visit was over and he escorted her to the terrace door. He gestured to the folded newspaper she held.

"Do you think it really will end?" Amy asked.

"Yes." He looked pensive. "I wonder if everyone's ready for that." She stared at him quizzically and he grinned. "Nothing for you to worry about. I'm just thinking about the price of beef."

"You mean it may not be good for ranchers like us?"

"Not like you. Whatever happens, Tommy Westerman won't be caught napping." Rick's voice was hard.

"You don't like Tommy much, do you? Not since he fenced off the waterhole and bought those other two ranches."

Ibañez looked away. "I have patients waiting. We'll talk about it another time." He took both her hands in his. "Meanwhile, remember there's one thing about Tommy I admire very much. His choice of a wife."

Amy left without answering. Sometimes she felt guilty about how important Rick was to her. At other times she examined their relationship and found nothing to be ashamed of. They were both lonely. Each met a need in the other. On this occasion she wasn't thinking so much of Rick as of what he'd said, or at least implied.

Two months before Tommy had secured a court order breaking the treaty that governed the rights to the waterhole. It was on Santo Domingo land, the judge had said; henceforth it was reserved for the exclusive use of Mr. Westerman. The two adjacent ranchers promptly sold out to Tommy. It was all fairly predictable. Tommy was simply applying Wall Street business methods to New Mexico.

As Amy made her pensive way along the alameda

toward the plaza, what bothered her was the economics. Winning the legal battle took a good deal of money. Lopez and the other attorneys had, as Tommy commented, extracted their pound of flesh. The pair of ranches left waterless had dramatically decreased in value, but they commanded a high figure. Where was Tommy finding the capital for it all?

Amy thought about the unpaid bills she'd found in New York, and the sale of her diamond ring. But it didn't seem likely that this was a repeat of that situation. No shopkeepers accosted her on her trips to Santa Fe. On the contrary, they made it obvious that her credit was excellent. The name Westerman had become one to reckon with in these parts.

Her ponderings brought her to the plaza more quickly than she realized. She looked up, saw Moore's Men's Shop, and started to cross the road.

"I tell you Tommy Westerman says so, what else do you need to know!"

The words were spoken by a strident female voice. They echoed across the plaza and stopped Amy in mid-step. She stared in the direction they'd come from and saw a small crowd clustered at the door of Spitz's Jewelry Shop. The onlookers were ranchhands in town to spend their wages and have a bit of fun. They were laughing and egging the woman on.

"You tell him, Rosa!"

"An' if he don't do what you want, you can hit him. Ain't nobody 'round here gonna get the law after Mr. Westerman's woman!"

There were more shouts from inside the shop, but Amy could distinguish none of the words. She remained where she was, in the shade of a cottonwood tree, as if she too had roots.

"It's ok, boys," someone said. "Rosa's won. Spitz is givin' her the necklace."

More laughter, then the crowd of cowboys began to drift away. One of them spotted Amy and whispered something to his companion. She wasn't embarrassed. She was too deeply shocked to feel anything.

Amy stayed where she was. In a few moments a woman left the jeweler's. She was about twenty-five and her features identified her as a *mestiza*—part Indian, part Mexican. She had black hair piled high in an elaborate arrangement, and a voluptuous figure barely covered by a flamboyant red dress. Amy stared at her. This Rosa moved with a kind of insolence; as if daring any man to ignore her full breasts, her wide, swaying hips. She wore a heavy silver and turquoise pendant, and she left the plaza without glancing in Amy's direction.

Amy told herself that she must move. She must go to Moore's and get the shirts Tommy wanted. Hesitantly she put one foot ahead of the other. Then she caught sight of her reflection in a shop window. She was heavy with child. Beneath a neat straw hat her long black hair was coiled primly at the nape of her neck. Her maternity dress was of brown cotton, sedate and subdued, as befitted a young matron. "Oh, my God . . ." she whispered aloud. Suddenly she wheeled round and entered a door marked by a red and blue barber's pole.

"Afternoon, Mrs. Westerman. If you're lookin' for

Mr. Westerman, I ain't seen him today. Was he plannin' to have his hair cut?"

"No, Joe," Amy said. "I am. I want a bob. Will you do it?"

"Well, sure. If you're certain you won't be sorry afterward."

"I won't," she said firmly. She looked pointedly at the barber's chair. The cowhand sitting in it rose hastily. "Thank you," she said and took his place.

Joe Turner's scissors flashed round her head. Great handfuls of shiny hair fell unheeded to the floor. Amy stared into the mirror. Joe had draped her in a protective white cloth. It hid her swollen shape. She saw herself as a wide-eyed child. A foolish, innocent child, she thought. Reared in the African bush, tainted by the blood of a savage; a child who knows nothing of the adult world.

"That'll be fifty cents, Mrs. Westerman. Looks real nice, if I do say so."

She smiled at him, but didn't trust herself to speak. Carefully she stepped over the debris of the shearing and extracted a coin from her bag. Then she put on her hat and went out into the sunlight. Until now she'd been as if anesthetized. Suddenly Amy didn't think her legs would carry her. She had to drag herself to where she'd parked the flivver, holding on to the mellow adobe walls of the buildings of the plaza for support.

A few months ago, when she started to show, Tommy protested about her driving. Amy ignored him. The Model-T was her link with the outside world. Since Tommy had bought himself a Packard, the flivver was exclusively hers. She handled it with the same confidence she sat a horse. Now she automatically turned the starting crank, positioned herself in the driver's seat, and released the spark and throttle lever. Just as automatically she headed toward the alameda.

She was still numb when she turned north on Castillo Street. Until she pulled up she hadn't realized where she was going. The road there was narrow and skirted a deep arroyo. That's why she usually parked in the plaza and walked to Rick's office. This time she didn't care. Amy left the car on the street and pushed open the familiar green gate. Through the gathering dusk she saw Rick's nurse approaching.

"I'm sorry," the woman said as she walked down the path, "Don Rico's office hours are over for today. Unless it's an emergency." Then she recognized Amy. "Oh, it's you Señora Westerman. Are you all right?"

"Yes, but I must see Don Rico."

"I'll tell him you're here." If there was any message in the woman's ready agreement, Amy was too preoccupied to notice.

"It's all right, Elena." Rick's voice floated across the garden. "I heard." He came toward them and the nurse looked questioning. "Go on home," he said quietly. "I'm sure I won't need you." His eyes searched Amy's face, and he seemed to understand that this wasn't a medical emergency. He led her into the house and poured a brandy.

"Drink this. Then tell me what's happened."

The potent spirit made Amy cough, but it warmed her and melted some of the ice in the pit of her stomach. "I saw Rosa," she said. She studied Rick's reaction, but there was no hint of surprise, only sadness.

"I see. I suppose you had to, sooner or later."

"You know about her, don't you?"

"Yes."

"And so does everyone else in Santa Fe," Amy said. It was a statement not a question.

Rick shrugged hopelessly. "This is a small town; you know that." He led her to a chair. "Sit down. I'll get us both another drink."

They were in a pleasant high-ceilinged sitting room decorated with Rick's collection of early Indian pottery and woven blankets. He put a match to the fire. Piñon logs burst into flame. "The nights are growing cool," he said. "A fire is welcome."

Amy ignored his attempt at ordinary conversation. "Tell me about it," she said. "When did it start?"

Rick sighed. "Do you really want to know, *querida?*" He had used that endearment with her before, but it had never sounded quite so intimate.

"I want to know," Amy said.

"About a year ago, I think."

"While I was carrying Kate." Amy folded her hands over her swollen belly.

"I'm afraid so."

"Where does she live? Who is she?"

"Her name is Rosa Mandago. Her mother is from San Felipe pueblo and her father was a Mexican drifter. Rosa has always been wild."

"She's beautiful."

"If you like the type," he said with a wry smile.

"You haven't told me where she lives now. Not in the pueblo, surely?"

"No, she has a small house on the outskirts of town, near the Pecos Trail."

"On the way to our place," Amy said. "How convenient. I take it Tommy supports her 'small house' . . ."

"I believe so. I think he bought it for her."

"She was in Spitz's." Amy spoke in a high childish singsong that didn't sound like her own voice. "She bought a necklace and charged it to Tommy. There seemed to be some disagreement. You could hear her shouting all over the plaza. A bunch of hands were outside. They thought it was funny, so they egged her on. I just stood and listened. Afterward I watched her leave, but she didn't look at me."

"Stop talking about it. Stop torturing yourself. It won't do any good. Some men just . . ."

"Do you know what I did after I saw her?" Amy interrupted. "This!" Savagely she pulled off her hat and displayed her bobbed head.

Rick looked at her. The dancing fire was the only light in the room. It showed red highlights in her short, thick hair. The cropped locks framed her face and made her brown eyes more startlingly large. "You look like an elf," he said softly. "A beautiful wood nymph."

Tears filled her eyes and spilled over. Rick wiped them away, then put his hands on either side of her heart-shaped face. "Don't, *querida,*" he whispered. "Tommy Westerman isn't worth one of your tears."

She put her hands over his, then pressed his palms against her lips, kissing first one and then the other.

"That's why I'm crying," she said. "He was once. He's changed. What he is now is my fault."

"No." Rick shook his head vehemently. "You mustn't fall into that trap. Don't blame yourself, Amy. No one can take responsibility for someone else's conscience."

"It's a long story," she said as if he hadn't spoken. "I don't want to talk about it. I'm sorry for coming here like this. I just didn't know where else to go."

"I'm always here," Rick said. "Always. Do you understand me, *querida?*"

She did and the knowing burst inside her with a kind of joy that swiftly turned to fear. Amy let go of his hands and stood up. "I have to go. Tommy is away, but Maria will be worried about me."

"I'm driving you home," Rick said. He ignored her protests.

Usually Beatriz prayed in the centuries old church of Our Lady of Guadalupe on Agua Fria Street. She did this often because, despite the many taboos that she was willing to ignore, Beatriz was a religious woman. It was natural that she should take to God her problems of the moment. But troubles such as these demanded extraordinary fervor. So on that same October day when Amy saw Rosa Mandago in the plaza, Beatriz was in the nearby cathedral. She had come to ask the guidance of Santa Fe's first lady, *La Conquistadora.*

Carved in Spain sometime in the fifteenth century, the small statue of Our Lady of Victory came with the conquistadors to the new world. In 1692 she was brought to Santa Fe by Don Diego de Vargas, when he led the reconquest after an Indian revolt. Since then it was the spirit of *La Conquistadora* that animated the city, and her intercession that sustained it. Each year, on the two Sundays following the feast of Corpus Christi, she was carried through the streets in solemn and glorious procession. Thousands—people of every color—took part. In between those times she could be found to the left of the high altar in the cathedral.

Today Beatriz knelt at the lady's feet and begged for wisdom. She was utterly confident that her prayers would receive an answer. For one thing, the promise of the gospels was quite clear in this regard; for another, *La Conquistadora* must feel tender toward the man who had brought her to this place where she was so beloved, and de Vargas was an ancestor of Don Rico. The logic of it all pleased Beatriz; thinking of it almost eased her pain.

You understand, she told the beautiful lady who was arrayed in jewel-encrusted lace and a green satin cape, I have never fooled myself that I could keep him. It is not to get him back that I come to you. But I cannot bear that he leaves me for one of them. It is neither right nor fair that the Anglos take what is not theirs. First that man Westerman steals from Manuel, and now the woman steals from me. . . .

It was simple justice that Beatriz craved. The sins of Tommy Westerman cried to heaven for vengeance. He and his wife had come to this place where neither belonged, and they thought they could buy the birthright of those who did. Westerman had paid Manuel money for his ranch. It was not the amount that the ranch was worth while the treaty was in force, but it was more money than Manuel had ever before seen.

Her cousin had come to Beatriz with the check, pushing it into her hands with tears rolling down his cheeks, like a child confessing a terrible guilt. "What am I to do with this?" he'd asked. "What good is it to me if I do not have my land?"

Beatriz had ignored the second question and answered the first by immediately putting on her hat and going outside to where Manuel's wife Purisima waited with her seven children. One was still suckling. Purisima held the infant to her breast and sat silent in the buckboard. "We must go to the bank," Beatriz said, climbing aboard. Manuel drove them to the plaza.

In the bank Beatriz took charge of everything. Neither Manuel nor Purisima were idiots; they had after all managed a large ranch. But they were in a state of shock, and they were grateful if someone told them what to do. So Beatriz set aside a small amount of the money for their daily expenses. The balance she put in a savings account. At the last moment she insisted that it be so ordered that the signatures of both Manuel and Purisima were necessary for withdrawals. This precaution was prompted by the look in Manuel's eyes. A man who believes himself cut off from life is not frugal, even if he is a husband and a father.

Her premonition had been accurate. The sale of the ranch had been completed two months ago. Since then, Manuel moved like a zombie. He lived with his family in a house in the *barrio*, and supposedly he was looking for another ranch to buy. In truth he did nothing but sit day and night staring at the walls.

Purisima did her best, but it was hard keeping seven children happy and healthy in the city, after the freedom of ranch life. Purisima was thin and drawn and miserable. When she looked at her cousin's wife Beatriz felt anger burn like acid in her stomach.

She was not so much a fool as to think everything the fault of the Anglos. She knew instead that it was the particular badness of some Anglos which, brought into confrontation with the particular weakness of some of her own kind, created evil and devastation. Anglos were greedy and their natural instinct was to possess and acquire. Neither did they value sincerity of the heart the way her people did.

Faced with these things the Manuels and Purisimas of the world retreated to their stoic fatalism, and their belief that somehow *mañana* would be different. It never was, because they did nothing to make it so. Beatriz understood all this because she had learned first-hand about lies and desertion. Indeed, that lesson was the root of her fury—and the reason it had finally affected her reason.

All this anguish she laid at the feet of *La Conquistadora*. She did not actually formulate her plan in the lady's presence. When she was in the cathedral Beatriz was still trying to resist the lure of the solution that had occurred to her. But neither did she resolve against it. It stayed like a venemous snake in the back of her mind, coiled and ready to strike.

She left the church and wandered aimlessly toward the plaza, gravitating there through the ancient habit that informed her blood. Then she saw Amy Westerman walking toward her, heavily pregnant and looking pre-

occupied with cares. For a moment Beatriz considered
speaking to the girl. She would tell her all the evil
things her husband did and warn her to leave New
Mexico.

Beatriz felt the words rising in her throat. She craved
the release they would bring her.

She'd almost made up her mind to act when the
voice of the *mestiza* whore, Rosa Mandago, cut across
the plaza. Beatriz watched the whole scene. She saw
Amy's shock and pain, and when the girl half crawled
to her automobile Beatriz followed. She saw Amy set
out in the direction of the alameda and knew that she
was going to Don Rico. Anger made Beatriz tremble.
The Westerman woman had everything; a home, a
husband, a child and another coming—yet she was
prepared to steal the only thing Beatriz had.

Still quivering with rage Beatriz went into a cafe and
ordered coffee. She sat sipping it, willing herself to be
calm, and thinking about the juxtaposition of events.
She'd gone to *La Conquistadora* seeking enlighten-
ment. Immediately after she left the church she'd been
confronted with yet more evidence of the wickedness
of both Westermans. What did it mean? One answer
only presented itself. The snake inside coiled tighter.

In a few minutes she glanced at her watch. It was
past four. She must return home because the neighbor
staying with her mother could not remain later than
four-thirty. She left five cents on the counter to pay
for her coffee and stepped outside. Dusk was rolling
down the mountains toward Santa Fe. A sliver of
moon shared the sky with the setting sun. "*Hola, doña
Beatriz,*" a man said.

It was Eustaquio, an Indian from Pueblo Cochiti who supplied her with the turquoise and silver buckles she sold in her shop. Instantly Beatriz understood everything. Scraps of knowledge that she did not realize she possessed fell into place in her head. *La Conquistadora* had given her answer. "I cannot stay now because my mother is waiting," she said with breathless urgency. "But you are the very man I want to see. Can you come to my shop tonight after dark?"

The Indian shrugged. "If you wish it," he said.

"I do. Very much." The death rattle sounded and the snake struck.

"You know the boy Diego who works at *el rancho* Santo Domingo, no?" Beatriz asked.

"He is of my pueblo, I know him," Eustaquio said.

"Do you count him as a friend?" Her words were tentative, probing.

The Indian understood what information she sought, but he said only, "I know him."

Something in his eyes gave her hope. Beatriz unlocked the drawer in which she kept her money. She withdrew a small number of bills and laid them on the table. Later, when more money was needed, she would get it from the savings account of Manuel and Purisima. "I have a friend who feels deeply the needs of the pueblos. My friend is also a believer in justice and is unhappy about much that the Anglos do against the interests of my people and yours, who were here before them."

"Your friend is wise," Eustaquio said. His brown

hand lay on the table next to the money, but he didn't touch it.

"And rich. Money is available to ease the poverty of Pueblo Cochiti. Do you not think it is only fair that certain actions my friend wants performed be done in return for this money?"

"If they are possible, yes."

"Oh, they are possible," Beatriz said. "It needs only courage and determination."

"Tell me more. I'm listening."

Beatriz had chosen more wisely than she knew. Aware that religious societies and their rivalries were the true pulse beat of the lives of the Indians, she had hoped that perhaps the old man and Diego belonged to the same one. They did, but the symbiosis was greater than only that. Eustaquio was Diego's 'spiritual father.' Theirs was a sacred relationship, far stronger than ties of blood.

When the descendents of the Basketmakers left their exquisite aeries to huddle by the Rio Grande they did not re-create the extraordinary homes they'd left behind. The small clustered dwellings the Spaniards encountered when they marched north were mostly single-story adobe huts in which an entire family occupied one room. Coronado and the men of his ilk were unimpressed. These people reminded them of the poorest *campesinos* of their homeland. The Spaniards called the newfound settlements, villages—in Spanish, *pueblos*—and their inhabitants, Pueblo Indians. The conquistadors were ignorant of the mighty power which pulsed beneath the surface of the huddled shacks. They didn't know that from the subterranean pits called *kivas* there came a strength of union which would endure.

In the wake of the conquerors came the padres. Like their countrymen, the Franciscans and Jesuits and Dominicans were also seeking gold, but of a different sort. The priests wanted souls for Christ. For two bloodstained centuries they preached the gospel with words and swords. Eventually every pueblo had a church and a crucifix and a madonna and a patron saint. Probably none of the Spaniards, cleric or layman, wholly understood that the Indians had evolved a synthesis between the old truth and the new. The Most Holy Trinity ruled all, the Indians had learned. Surely that included the gods of the *kiva*? Nonetheless with the passage of time there occurred a slow but steady exodus from the pueblos. Many of the young adopted not only the white man's God, but his ways and vices.

Diego, for one, did not go often to the pueblo where he was born. Eustaquio knew this, so he sent a message to Santo Domingo. Four days later he looked up from the piece of silver he was hammering and saw his "son" standing in the doorway. He grunted with satisfaction. Diego had come quickly, so he was not entirely removed from the ancient discipline.

"You want to see me?"

"Yes, come in."

Diego was taller than most of his brethren. He had to duck his head to pass through the door. He waited a moment for his eyes to adjust to the dimness, then

went and sat on the dirt floor with his back against the
rough adobe wall. Eustaquio continued hammering.
"You should have better light to work by," Diego
said. "Next time I come I'll bring a lantern from the
ranch."

"I need nothing from that place. I have everything I
need here."

Diego bit back a sharp reply. He looked around him
and scowled. The room was a primitive pigsty. There
was a stack of pots with burned-out bottoms serving as
a chimney, no furniture worth noting, and four walls
black with smoke. It was enough for the old man, and
enough for most of them. Not him.

By happy accident he'd been spotted by DeAngeles
when he was ten and taken to Santo Domingo. From
the first Diego had considered the shabby bunkhouse
a palace compared to what he had come from. He still
thought of it as such, particularly now that Mr.
Westerman was making so many improvements. While
he watched the old man work he decided that this was
the last time he'd come here. He would cut all his ties
with Pueblo Cochiti. He was a new breed of man, and
this was a new age.

Eustaquio was busy with thoughts of his own. Ten
minutes passed in silence, broken only by the sound of
his mallet. He shaped the soft metal into the form of
an eagle with outstretched wings. He would give it
turquoise eyes. Eventually some Anglo would pay a
few dollars for it. He grunted again and lay down his
tools, thankful that there was no need to put them
away. Since his wife died and his children married,
Eustaquio had lived and worked alone in this room. It

was an unusual arrangement for the pueblo, but it was granted him because of his age and skill, and because he ranked high among the priests of his religious society.

He pondered that holy part of his life and looked at Diego through half-closed eyes. "You know who I am?" he asked finally.

Diego was startled. "Are you crazy, old man? Of course I know who you are."

Eustaquio shook his head. "No, you have forgotten." His voice was calm and betrayed no response to the insulting manner in which the boy addressed him. "If you remembered, you would not speak to me so."

"I remember," Diego whispered. Visions and old claims choked him.

"Good. Then the poison of the Anglos has not yet destroyed you. I have work for you to do. It is a sacred task and it will cleanse you."

"What are you talking about?" Diego felt the Keres language of Pueblo Cochiti a strange and oppressive thing in his mouth. "What do you want?" he repeated.

Eustaquio told him.

Diego staggered to his feet. "You're crazy," he said in English. "I'm getting out of here."

The old man sprang ahead of him to block the door. His small form was an impenetrable barrier. Diego could not violate the old taboos and push past him.

"When you were seven and the *kachina-man* beat you, was it not I who held your hands skyward and kept you from falling to the ground in disgrace? Would you be a man today if I was not your ceremonial father?"

Diego doubled over. He was soaked in perspiration,

and he shivered as if a cold wind blew through the room. He was back in the firelit *kiva* confronted by a naked figure painted in black and white stripes who whipped him with the sharp-edged fronds of the yucca plant. The sweat pouring beneath his shirt was the blood of his initiation into the ancient ways. He was marked forever. "I cannot do it," he stammered, again in English. "The sheriff . . ."

"Speak your own language!" Eustaquio commanded. "And stand up like a man!" He struck Diego in the face with caculated force. The boy did not recoil from the blow. Eustaquio knew he'd won. "If you are clever, the sheriff will learn nothing. And afterward there will be a reward. Money. You can buy a motorcar and go away," he added slyly. He was not above combining new persuasions with the old.

"Is this why you want this thing? For money?"

"No, not only that." Eustaquio looked around and his watery eyes saw more than the room that encompassed his life, or the craft that the Anglos required him to pervert to their taste. He saw a whole history, a world infringed and violated. "I have my reasons," he said simply.

Diego wanted to protest that Westerman had done nothing to any of them. The words died on his lips. He knew too much to speak such a half-truth.

"We will smoke," Eustaquio said. He went to a shelf in the corner and took down an elaborate pipe. When it was filled and lit he drew a mouthful of acrid smoke into his mouth and exhaled it in the directions of the four winds, the earth, and the sky. Then he passed the pipe to Diego.

The young man took it with trembling hands. This was the final pledge. After it there could be no turning back. He wanted to run away and deny the old man's claim on him, but he could do nothing. The chains, forged early, were unbreakable. He inhaled and did exactly as Eustaquio had.

The old man returned the pipe to its resting place and opened a small decorated jar. He removed a pinch of sacred cornmeal and carried it to the entrance, pushing aside the blanket that served as a door. Light streamed in and Eustaquio allowed the pale yellow maize to dribble from between his brown fingers. A sunbeam gilded it gold as it fell. "It is good," Eustaquio said. "You will have success."

"It will take time," Diego whispered. "I need to plan."

"There is no hurry."

Diego struggled to his feet and stumbled into the street. He spoke to no one else and set out at once on the long ride back to the ranch. He was returning to Santo Domingo charged with the duty of killing Tommy Westerman.

21

ON NOVEMBER ELEVENTH, THE DAY THE ARMISTICE was signed in Europe, Tom Junior was born. Tommy stood beside his wife's bed and grinned at her and their newborn son. He looked and sounded like the boy he'd been when Amy first knew him.

"You're marvelous, *memsahib*, and so is he. We'll have a big party to celebrate as soon as you're feeling up to it. Invite everyone. I know a guy in Albuquerque who has plenty of French champagne, war or no war."

He leaned down and kissed her forehead. Amy almost asked if he planned to invite Rosa Mandago too.

But she had decided never to mention Tommy's mistress, and she bit her lip and stuck by her resolution.

Tommy was pleased to have a son and heir, but his daughter had captivated his heart. A year old when her brother was born, Kate was a beautiful child whom everyone said resembled her father. It wasn't wholly true.

Like Tommy, Kate had gray eyes, but hers did not have his steely glint. They were mother-of-pearl eyes, luminous and iridescent and shadowed; the kind that are said to have been "put in by a sooty finger." Her hair was thick and curly like his, but lighter. More like Luke's, Amy sometimes thought.

When her father was home Kate followed him everywhere, first crawling, then toddling. Often Tommy would scoop her up and carry her around the ranch for hours, as if unaware that she weighed anything at all. It was to Tommy that Kate lisped her first baby words, and for him she pined during the days and weeks when he was out on the range. "Uncle Rick" was another familiar figure. Kate gave him affection, and an equal amount to her mother, but it was for Tommy the child reserved her adoration. He knew it and basked in it.

"Don't let her get jealous of the baby," he told his wife. Tom Junior was two weeks old, and Kate had shown nothing but indifferent curiosity toward him.

"That's up to you, not me," Amy said. She softened the comment with a smile. Amy was not bothered by her daughter's worship of Tommy. "As long as she remains number one with you, Kate doesn't worry about anything."

"Yeah, well I'm going to be gone for a while. Got to check the new south range."

That was one of the pieces of land he'd recently acquired. Amy preferred not to think about how. "Will you be gone long?"

"A week, maybe ten days. When I get back we'll have that party I talked about. Meanwhile you'd better make arrangements to have the baby baptized." He performed some quick calculations. "Set it up for the second Sunday in December. We'll have our party the same day."

Amy nodded. She wasn't sure how to do what he asked, but Rick would help her. "Are you taking the crew with you?" Visions of herself alone with the children, the new maid, and Maria flitted through her mind. She liked it when the hacienda was given over to only the gentle life-cadences of women and children.

"No. There's a lot of work to be done here and on the other ranges, Diego and I are riding out alone."

Tommy surveyed his land with satisfaction. "Good grazing," he told his foreman—as if it were a new discovery, and he'd not known how good it was when he contrived to acquire it.

"Yeah, it's ok."

He glanced at Diego. The Indian rode hunched into his saddle as if some weight pressed down on his shoulders. "You all right? You've been acting funny lately."

"I'm all right."

Tommy said nothing more. He'd allowed himself to become fond of Diego because the boy was no threat. Besides, he was an excellent foreman. All the same, he was an Indian. He has funny ideas about some things and a queer way of looking at the world. Tommy accepted their differences as a fact of life.

On the third day of the tour they made camp later than usual. Tommy had been anxious to cover a lot of ground. Now they hurried to get a fire started before the night chill penetrated their bones. Tommy watched Diego hacking with his short-bladed knife at the mesquite they'd use for firewood. He worked quickly and the blade flashed blue in the dusk. "You like that knife of yours, don't you, Diego?" He'd seen the Indian stroking and fondling it all day, like some kind of fetish. "What's so special about it?"

Diego looked up quickly. "Nothin'. It's just a knife, that's all."

"Yeah? I thought maybe it was something special," Tommy repeated. He enjoyed getting Diego to talk about the pueblos and the beliefs of the Indians. His earlier, academic world sometimes called to Tommy. Occasionally he thought about writing a book on New Mexico and the different cultures that had created it. Perhaps when he was old and rctircd. Mcanwhile he had Diego and Rosa to study first-hand. He grinned to himself. Different aspects of the Indian character, riding hard and screwing. That could be a chapter title.

Later, over the thick bitter coffee they'd brewed, he probed a little more. "I heard a weird story recently. Been meaning to ask you about it."

"What story?"

Tommy noticed that Diego didn't look at him when he spoke. He kept staring at the earth and the fire. And fondling that damned knife. Something was definitely eating the kid. "About Indians handling poisonous snakes," Tommy said. "Picking them up and petting them. And nothing ever happening to them. Is it true?"

"Yeah, it's true."

"How's it done?"

Diego shrugged. "They don't let them coil. Snakes can't strike unless they're coiled."

"I know that. But according to what I heard that's not all there is to it."

"The snake god protects them," Diego said quietly.

"Do you believe that?"

The boy turned to him and his black eyes burned in the fire's glow. "I don't know what I believe," he said fiercely

"Yes, that's your problem, isn't it?" Tommy nodded and poured them each more coffee. "You live in the twentieth century in a white man's world, but you aren't sure you're ready to give up the old superstition and magic. Not just you. All your people."

"My pueblo doesn't do the snake dance," Diego said. There was a note of desperation in his word. "It's mostly the Hopi pueblos west of here." He got up and walked away into the dark.

Tommy slept fitfully. Usually he had the best sleeps of his life out under the open sky, elated by his conquest of the one challenge that had eluded him in the past. He wasn't just clever, not any more. He was master of his physical surroundings as well. Tonight that fact didn't bring him peace. Instead he tossed and turned, and some primordial instinct made him feel fear without his knowing its source. A coyote bayed in the distance. He jerked awake and looked around. In the dying embers of the fire he could see Diego's empty bedroll.

Tommy sat up, conscious of the weight of his built-up shoe. Out here he didn't remove it at night. Now he got to his feet and looked around. The horses were tethered some distance away, grazing peacefully. About fifty yards to his right loomed the clump of mesquite scrub that had provided their firewood. He thought he saw some movement in that direction. "Diego, you out there? What the hell are you doing?" There was no reply. The echo of his voice died quickly in the vast silence.

He moved toward the mesquite and called again. "Diego! Are you ok?" There was still no answer, and he wished he carried a gun like some old-time cowboy. There was a rifle strapped to his saddlebag, of course, in case he had to deal with stray coyotes or game. Maybe he should get it. But he'd have to walk back to the fire and turn his back on the mesquite. It didn't seem a good idea. Tommy was aware of the weight of his shoe and the fact that his leg ached. Then, while he stared into the darkness, he saw Diego approach.

The boy moved stiffly, as if drugged or sleepwalking. His torso was naked and his arms outstretched. His head was thrown back in a contorted, unnatural way. It was like some parody of crucifixion. Tommy peered hard into the darkness. "Oh, Jesus," he whispered. "Oh, sweet Mother of God . . ."

Diego was carrying a snake. In the starlight to which his eyes were now accustomed Tommy recognized it. *Crotalus Ademanteus,* the southwestern rattler. The diamond markings became clearer as Diego approached. He held the creature in both hands, one at each end, and the four feet of its slender venomous body were stretched against his chest.

The thing twitched and hissed and writhed in its struggle to break free. The muscles of Diego's forearms bulged with effort. His grip did not weaken. Tommy exhaled through clenched teeth. As long as it was held thus the snake was impotent.

Diego recognized that the other man was watching him. His head jerked forward, and they stared at each other across a few yards of desert. "Ok, Diego," Tommy said quietly. "I see your point. But it's you doing the protecting, not any snake god. You keep holding it like that, and we're both safe."

"The old ways are strong," Diego said.

It sounded like an old man's voice coming from his young throat. Strange notions of possession flicked at the edge of Tommy's mind. He rejected them. Self-hypnosis more likely. "Men are strong," he said. "They decide what they'll do. God gives us free will, Diego. You know that." He wanted to laugh. He, of all people, quoting theology to a half-savage in the desert. "Get rid of it," he commanded. "You don't owe the old ways anything, Diego."

"I am one with them." More like his own voice now. And tears streaming down his cheeks.

"Not unless you choose to be," Tommy said.

Silence was the only answer. Tommy counted the seconds by the loud beating of his heart. He calculated how swiftly he could jump out of the way if the snake was flung in his direction. Not too fast, because of his leg. But fast enough probably. It would take the thing a few seconds to coil. If he'd been sleeping, Tommy realized, he'd have had no chance at all.

The two men waited on opposite sides of an abyss older than time. Suddenly Diego broke the tableau. He shouted into the night, a wordless cry of agony. Then he turned and ran into the darkness, still carrying his lethal burden.

When the Indian returned Tommy was sitting by the fire. He'd stirred it up and added more wood. And he'd made fresh coffee. He offered Diego his hip flask of whiskey first.

The boy took a long pull, then handed it back. Tommy didn't drink. He'd had his share earlier. Now the trembling in his limbs had subsided and his mind was clear. "You want to tell me about it?" he asked after a few minutes.

Diego shook his head. "No. If you want me to leave, I'll pack my gear soon as we get back."

"No reason to do that," Tommy said. He'd figured out most of the mystery while Diego was gone. The only thing he didn't know was who was behind it. The why would be related to that, and the how was obvious It had to do with playing skillfully on old fears and loyalties. Maybe that in itself was a clue to the question of who. "Like I said, Diego," he continued, "you're the one with the choice to make."

"I ain't never goin' back to the pueblo," the boy said.

"Ok. I'm glad. I'd still like to know whose idea it was," Tommy said softly. He was half afraid of the answer, and half grateful when Diego only shook his head.

"All I know is that I'm never goin' back."

Amy spun faster and faster. Her white chiffon gown floated around her legs, and her gold slippers were incapable of missing a beat of the senuous music. Rick's arms held her tight, and their bodies moved in perfect harmony. The flickering candles and the other people were the edges of a whirlpool. They receded further away as she was sucked into the vortex. She sensed the rhythmic clapping of the crowd as something in tune with her heart. It was no intrusion on this moment of pure and private joy.

"Olé!" someone shouted. "Olé! Olé! Olé!" a chorus of voices chimed in. The violins, guitars, and flutes climbed to their crescendo and then, with one last spin, it was over. Applause and laughter replaced the music.

"Fantastic!" Rick said. "I thought you didn't know this dance."

"I don't, I just followed you." She was flushed with a heat greater than that generated by the crush and the warm room. I'm so happy, she thought. Then Tommy's voice snatched it all away.

"You'd better check with Maria. The ham's running out."

"Yes." She disengaged her arm from Rick's and saw the look the two men exchanged. "I'll go right away."

The truce she and Tommy established at the birth of their son had evaporated. He had returned from the south range bitter and silent, and his eyes accused her at every turn. After Tommy got home Amy wanted to cancel this party, but it was too late. And if she had she wouldn't have experienced the precious seconds she'd just known. She hugged the memory close as she made her way through the crowd to the kitchen.

"It's like the old days," Rick said to his host.

"That pleases you, does it?" Tommy asked. He had to look up slightly because the other man was taller. He could hate him for that alone.

"It pleases me and everyone. As I've told Amy, this used to be the heart of the ranches hereabouts. These old walls have seen many fiestas like this. Maybe not quite so sophisticated," Rick added with a nod to his champagne glass.

"And the ranch wasn't as big." Tommy flung the challenge in Ibañez's face. He knew what the locals thought of his recent acquisitons.

Rick refused to be baited. "It wasn't the same," he said easily. "There was less concern with boundaries. The size of the herd was more important. Santo Domingo had the biggest and the best."

Tommy smiled. The doctor was clever and very cool. "Personally I am concerned with boundaries," he said. "What's mine is mine."

"A man keeps what he has as long as he cherishes it," Ibañez said.

Tommy's smile faded. "That's one way. There are

others." The music started again. The dance floor created by clearing all the furniture out of the living room filled with couples. Moving out of their way gave Tommy a chance to recover his poise. "Enjoy yourself, doc. I have to see to my guests. Truth is, I don't now who half of them are."

"Amy said you wanted to invite everybody." Rick drained his glass, eyeing Westerman over the rim.

"Indeed I did," Tommy agreed. "*Noblesse oblige,* and all that sort of thing. Just like the old days."

Ibañez watched Westerman limp away. It must hurt, a leg like that, but Westerman never let on. It was courage of a sort; the kind that congealed into a hard lump of defiance, and spread until every part of a man was hard. A vision of the couple alone together in their bedroom, as they must be later, came into Rick's mind and stayed to haunt him. What must Amy endure at the hands of her husband?

"You have not danced with me, Don Rico."

Beatriz's voice interrupted his thoughts. Ibañez hastened to erase his scowl. "It will be a greater pleasure for being postponed," he said gallantly. Beatriz took his hand and they began the first steps of the fandango. He felt no familiarity, no warmth at her touch. That they had once been lovers made no difference now.

Ibañez knew a moment of guilt about his indifference to a woman who had given him much, and his eyes sought hers. "How have you been, Beatriz?"

"I have been well, Don Rico, but lonely."

He was glad when the formal movements of the dance separated them for a few seconds. Unwittingly he scanned the room to see if Amy had returned. When he and Beatriz came together again he read in her face that she had noticed his preoccupation.

Beatriz held herself in strict control. They parted and came together in the measured ritual of the dance, and she made her expression a polite mask which betrayed nothing. Behind it her thoughts were seething. If she'd needed confirmation, she had it now. She'd come reluctantly to this fiesta, but it was making clear many unwelcome truths. They made a tight band around her heart and caused her to breathe with difficulty. When the fandango ended she curtsied gracefully and drifted toward the patio.

Outside it was cold, and her breath hung frosty in the air. Beatriz pulled her gray wool shawl closer. Like her black dress, it did nothing for her mouse brown hair and sallow skin, and disguised her beautiful body.

After she made up her mind to come here there had been a moment when she considered wearing one of the gorgeous gowns from her shop. Her hands had flitted lovingly over brightly colored silk and taffeta. She could wear a dress that lifted her breasts, hugged her waist, and clung to rounded hips and buttocks, one that ended in tiers of ruffles swaying around her ankles. She could pull her hair back into a coil and pin flowers behind her ear. She could carry a fan and wear a fringed shawl. What would they make of her then? But no, she had decided, it was not yet time for such revelations.

Now she was glad she'd resisted temptation. She had only to look at Diego and see the friendly inti-

macy between him and his employer to know that
Eustaquio had failed her. The Indian boy worshipped
his Anglo boss. The sight saddened her. The sadness
mixed with fury when she saw the longing in Don
Rico's face. He gazed at Amy with hunger, and Beatriz
trembled with rage that it should be so, and because
of the way her people mingled with the Anglo guests.
It was not friendship between them; how could it be
when they did not meet as equals?

Beatriz mourned because the young ones from the
barrio wore cheap imitations of the Anglo women's
clothes and mimicked their speech and their ways. The
dresses they bought from her they kept only for wed-
dings and fiestas confined to their own kind. Be proud,
she wanted to shout at them. You have an ancient
culture, a wonderful tradition. Glory in it! But no,
were it not that the musicians played the music, they
would not even perform the old dances.

Now Beatriz fingered with disgust the stuff of her
own northern-style gown. She was as bad as they. She
too was hiding behind the anonymity of foreign ways.
No more. It was time to strike a blow of defiance. It
was time for vengeance. Beatriz started back to the
house to find a place to hide.

The party lasted until dawn. The way home was
long for most of the guests. They might as well enjoy
themselves and travel by daylight. Amy had arranged
for breakfast to be served at sunrise.

In the courtyard fronting the hacienda they'd created three huge barbecue pits fired with charcoal and

fragrant piñon wood. Most of the night the ranch hands tending the fires had grilled steaks and ribs and basted them with fiery chile sauce. Now they lay flat griddles over the embers and fried flapjacks and eggs and rashers of bacon. Maria and the girls who helped her brought an assortment of hot breads and jugs of syrup from the kitchen. There was chile sauce for those who preferred it, and numberless pots of steaming coffee.

"It has been marvelous, Amy," Rick said. "You have made a fiesta that will be long remembered."

Many people had said the same thing to her, but no praise was as sweet as Rick's. "Thank you." Her heart was in the simple words, and her smile belied her tiredness.

"Now you must rest," Rick said. "Those are doctor's orders."

"I will. There are just a few more good-byes to be said; then I'm going to bed."

He looked around. "Have you seen Beatriz Ortega?"

"I'm afraid I don't know her. You added her name to the guest list, remember?"

"So I did. She must have left earlier. Too bad, I wanted you to meet her. She's a remarkable woman." It did not occur to him that there was something peculiar about introducing them. Amy and Beatriz were different orders of being in his mind.

Amy felt a surge of jealousy. There was so much about Rick's personal life she didn't know and had no right to question. That didn't keep her from asking, "Is she a special friend of yours?"

He smiled at her. "I have many friends," he said. "None are as special as you."

Their eyes caught and held for a moment, then they both looked away. No, Amy told herself. I must not love you or let you love me. She'd had enough betrayal and guilt to last her a lifetime. She would invite no more. Her eyes found his again. "You should get married, Rick," she said coolly. "You're far too dangerous single."

Ibañez recoiled. "Adios, Amy," he said stiffly. "Thank you for a lovely party."

She had to feed the baby before she could sleep. She went to the nursery and lifted him from his tiny crib and loosed the bodice of her gown, pushing it all the way down to her waist so the beaded front wouldn't rub his tender skin. Her breasts were heavy with milk, and she was grateful when the infant's tiny mouth fastened on her nipple and sucked greedily. Amy closed her eyes and drifted into a half-doze while her arms cradled the precious burden of her son.

She opened them to find Tommy standing in the doorway, studying her. "Quite a picture," he said quietly. "The nursing mother still in her party finery."

"He was hungry. I couldn't wait to change." She saw that the baby was finished and asleep and she rose. She didn't understand why everything Tommy said made her feel defensive, but it did. "Anyway," she added, "the party was your idea."

"And you did it beautifully," he said, watching while

she diapered the child and returned him to his crib. "I didn't realize you knew so many people to invite."

"Rick helped me with the guest list. I thought it was what you wanted."

"Oh, yes, the handsome doctor." He ignored the reference to his instructions. "Tell me, where does he lay you? Here or in his office?"

Amy couldn't control her trembling. "That's an ugly thing to say. And it isn't true." She glanced hurriedly at the baby, afraid their voices would wake him, but he slept peacefully. "Get out of my way. I have to check on Kate."

"Kate's downstairs with Maria, having her breakfast. She's fine."

"Then I'm going to bed."

"Yes," he agreed. "That's exactly where you're going."

When the door to their room was closed he fell on her like a rutting bull. The chiffon gown lay on the floor in a tangled crush around their twined bodies. Tommy hadn't waited for them to reach the bed. Amy felt the rough wool of a small woven rug abrading her back and her buttocks. Her arms overreached its borders to rest on the cool tiles.

"That's the way I like to see you," Tommy said, kneeling over her. "Spread-eagled and waiting." He lifted her legs and drew them round his waist. The great strength of his arms supported her weight and the depth of his sudden penetration sent a shock of pain through her body. Worse was the anger apparent on his face and conveyed by his touch.

"Please," she heard herself beg, "please love me just a little. Like you did once."

He didn't answer. All his energies were diverted to a blinding, gut-tearing climax composed as much of fury as of passion.

Amy waited, but he spoke no word of apology, not even of kindness. She stumbled into the bathroom and turned on the shower so he would not hear her weeping.

22

~

BEATRIZ PASSED OUT A FEW TIMES DURING THE NIGHT.
The air in the closet was stale and oxygen-poor, despite the louvers in the door. After the first couple of
hours she was only vaguely aware of the passage of
time and the terrible cramp in her arms and legs. She
had wedged herself into this position when she took
up her hiding place. She could not move without making a noise.

Eventually she fought her way to consciousness and
sensed that it was morning. She struggled to clear her
mind. There were no voices outside and no more party
sounds. She waited a few moments longer. Nothing
disturbed the silence.

When she'd entered the closet she'd taken the precaution of inserting a fold of paper into the door. It looked closed, but the latch wasn't engaged. Now she felt for it and inched it free. Her drawstring bag lay beside her, and she thrust the telltale sliver of paper into its depths.

Slowly, every nerve alert for danger, Beatriz pushed at the door. A gap of six inches appeared, and she waited, willing herself to patience. There was no sound except the faint ticking of a clock. She chanced another push at the door. This time it swung out of her control and fell open against the wall. There was the soft but unmistakable sound of wood striking plaster. Beatriz held her breath and squeezed her eyes shut, afraid to look at the face of her accuser. Then the need for air overcame her, and she inhaled in a loud gasp, opened her eyes and looked around. There was no one in the room except herself.

She crawled out of the closet and sat on the floor, rubbing her stiff arms and legs. She had chosen this place because of it was a library of sorts. It contained a desk and a table and numerous hard-backed chairs. Rows of books lined the walls. She'd decided last night that it was not the kind of place likely to be visited the morning after a party. Now the confirmation of her cleverness gave her courage. She stood up and examined her surroundings more closely. It was a beautiful room in the best southwestern tradition. Fury gagged her again, as it had last night. Westerman and his woman were interlopers. They had no right to enjoy such an ambience.

She faced again the question she'd debated during

the long night. What did she intend to do? She wanted to kill him, of course, maybe both of them, but she knew she couldn't. It was one thing to plan death from a distance, another to perform the act.

Beatriz went to the desk and touched a heavy paperweight fashioned of a lump of igneous rock seamed with dark green olivene. The semiprecious crystals winked up at her. Next to the paperweight was a letter-opener with a long brass blade and an onyx handle. For a moment she fondled the weapons, then pulled back. They would be impotent in her hands; she'd lose her nerve at the last minute.

Panic and indecision overwhelmed her for a few dangerous seconds. She wanted to bolt and run, and she held onto the back of a chair to prevent herself from doing so. It was true that only death could meet all the requirements of her vengeance, but if that was beyond her reach, she could still mete out some sort of punishment. She'd come this far, and she must do something. The man and his wife must be made to suffer as they caused others to suffer.

Her glance lit on a box of matches. Beatriz had a swift vision of leaping flames destroying all this elegance and richness. It pleased her only briefly. There would be risk to the servants and ranchhands who were her own kind. And to the children, the two tiny *niños* asleep in their cribs. She could not bear the thought of a holocaust claiming such innocence.

The clock continued ticking, a metronome beating out the rhythm of her deliberations. Suddenly Beatriz sighed with satisfaction. She knew what she must do. She moved stealthily to the door.

*   *   *

Maria grumbled quietly under her breath while she went about her tasks. So many people, so much food . . . and now all the cleaning left to her. Birds chattered in the early morning; apart from them, little Kate outside in her playpen, and herself, all Santo Domingo slept. Rasping snores echoed softly from the bunkhouse. The ranchhands were unconscious after the labors of the night and the bottles of whiskey Don Tommy gave them when the party ended. The girls who helped Maria were also in their beds. She herself would not rest until Doña Amy came downstairs. Someone must restore order to the hacienda.

Sighing, Maria padded from room to room. Her bare feet made no sound, and her heavy body seemed not to disturb the still air as she went about her duties. In the silent morning she carried a tray of glasses from the patio into the kitchen. The tray made a sharp tinkling sound when she set it on the table; then the quiet returned. Maria looked at the sink, but changed her mind. She would wash the glasses later. First she must look at the child. By now Kate might be growing restless.

She opened the back door and stepped into the sunlight. Its hot, harsh glare blinded her for a moment, and she moved toward the playpen guided only by instinct. It was a few yards to her left, in the shade of a gnarled old cottonwood tree. Walking toward it, Maria made the soothing, crooning sounds which she always used with the children. Her strong brown arms reached into the small wooden enclosure to gather up the little girl, but they encountered only emptiness. Surprised, Maria blinked her black eyes into focus and gazed from the playpen to the surrounding earth.

There was nothing. No tousled fair head turned toward her and no baby words were lisped in greeting. *"Madre mía!"* Maria muttered aloud. Such a wild one the tiny señorita; little more than a year old and already she had learned to give trouble to her elders!

She called the child by name and circled the area around the door to the kitchen. Still there was no sign of Kate. Puzzled, Maria returned to the playpen and stared into its emptiness.

Normally a favorite toy accompanied the little one everywhere, a stuffed bear whose brown fuzzy body was larger than that of the child herself. Maria remembered propping it in the corner when she put Kate outside. Now it too had disappeared. Even if the little girl had managed to climb over the rails, she could never have dragged the bear with her.

A sound began in Maria's throat and exploded through her gaping mouth. Shouts of pain and fury were hurled into the still morning and rose toward the sky. "See Señor Jesus, see what the devils and witches who stalk the earth have done! They have stolen her away. . . . Mercy, Señor Jesus! Have mercy on us!"

The words became meaningless cries of grief and dismay, and Maria's screams woke the sleeping hacienda to its agony.

Forty-eight terrible hours passed, but the ransom note the sheriff expected never arrived. Amy kept telling herself it was a nightmare, that any minute she'd wake up and find it was all a dream. Instead it went on and on, and the pain and the anger and the terror got worse. Kate, oh, Kate! Sometimes the words were a silent cry in her head. Other times she shouted them aloud. Then Rick would appear and give her medicine. But nothing made her sleep. She sat in the living room with Tommy and the sheriff and half a dozen strange men who came and went. They spoke in hushed despairing tones.

Once Tommy left with two of them, his face grim and his eyes colder and harder than she'd ever seen them. When he returned, the grief on his face was pitiable.

"Nothing," he said to no one in particular. "Rosa doesn't know a thing about it. I didn't really think she would."

Amy realized that he'd gone to see if his mistress had kidnapped his child, but the only emotion she felt about it was a terrible sadness because it was not so. If Tommy had come back with that small beloved form in his arms she would not have cared if Rosa Mandago was invited to live at Santo Domingo. This pain was so much greater than the other that the question of pride no longer existed.

"Amy," Rick's voice sounded in her ear, speaking quietly so the others wouldn't hear. "You've got to feed the baby."

She ran to the nursery, prodded by the irrational fear that something had happened to Tom Junior too. He was safe, but when she picked him up and held him to her breast he kept crying in hunger and frustration. Finally she closed her blouse and carried the baby to Rick, tears streaming down her face, "I can't. My milk's gone."

"It's the shock," Rick said softly, taking the child from her. "We'll put him on a bottle. I'll take him to Maria. She knows what to do."

Amy stood in the hall, her arms aching and empty and her children torn away from her. She had a desperate and crazy desire to talk to Luke. She wanted him to pray for Kate. God must be told that the little girl was innocent and mustn't be made to pay for her mother's sins. If He exists He must know, the rational part of her brain said. Reason could not erase the image of herself and Luke planning to run away together while Tommy's child grew inside her.

"But we didn't," she cried aloud in the empty hall. "Listen to me, God! We didn't do it. And that was another baby, not Kate." She realized that she'd shouted, and clamped a guilty hand over her mouth.

Tommy appeared. "What's the matter? Who were you talking to?"

"Nothing, no one," Amy whispered.

"Ok." Tommy took her hand and led her toward the living room. His touch was gentle, as it had been so rarely these last years. "Come sit down," he said. "It's going to be ok. You'll see."

"Send Luke a telegram," she whispered urgently. "Tell him he must pray for her!"

For once Tommy didn't misunderstand. "Bring on the shamans," he said wryly. "You may be right. I'll do it." He laughed mirthlessly. "No atheists in the trenches. Q.E.D."

They went back to the living room and the shadowy men who were trying to decide on a course of action. After a few minutes Rick returned. "I have to get back to town," he told Tommy. "I'll come out tomorrow and see if there's anything I can do for Amy. Perhaps by then . . ."

"Perhaps," Tommy said. He looked up and his eyes were dull. "Thanks for your help," he said. For Tommy, too, the new terror submerged all the old rivalries.

Ibañez punished the Pierce-Arrow all the way to Santa Fe. His hands were white-knuckled on the wheel, and he pushed the car to speeds over forty miles an hour. It squeaked and shuddered in protest, but he didn't notice.

When he was a medical student in Maryland the police had brought in a child who'd been kidnapped. A six-month-old baby, barely alive and covered with burns and cuts. He remembered how he'd felt at the time: sickened, furious and impotent, because vicious sadists could prey on whom they chose and so-called decent people could do nothing about it. He thought of Kate with her silvery eyes and golden hair. He thought of the way she cocked her head when she listened to him, and the grave expression that always seemed so incongruous on her baby face. Thirteen months old! A toddler who barely walked and talked and she was the victim of . . . of what?

Think, godamnit! Don't just feel, think. At seven-thirty that morning her father saw her eating breakfast in the kitchen. By eight Maria had her bathed and dressed and in her playpen just outside the kitchen door. Not until close to nine did the woman think of checking her again, because the child had seemed content. There was no noise, there was a lot of cleaning to do after the party, and Maria herself had yet to go to bed. It was all very understandable. Except that when she finally looked, Kate was gone and her playpen empty.

After that they'd searched everywhere. Maybe Kate had learned to climb out of her playpen. The crew were rousted from their beds to hunt inside and out. Diego even went down into the well. They found nothing. At ten-thirty Tommy sent for the sheriff and dispatched Diego and three others to carry the search in a widening circle beyond the house. In Santa Fe Pete Wilkins, the sheriff, contacted Ibañez. He'd been back at the ranch by five yesterday, no, the day before.

Rick passed a hand over his face and noted the stubble of beard. His eyes felt like they'd been dipped in sand. No sleep and a lot of worry was a recipe for disaster. Think, he told himself again. They'd been waiting for a ransom note, but none came. Wilkins had hemmed and hawed a lot, and finally told Westerman that the kidnapping might be personal, an attempt to get at him. So they'd made a list. Rosa Mandago and the two ranchers Tommy had squeezed out were on top. Only nobody produced results. Not Tommy and the guys who went with him to see Rosa, or the Spanish-speaking deputies who went into the *barrio* asking questions.

The *barrio*. Ibañez felt in his gut that the answer was there. Why? He didn't know. Yes, he did! Because of something Maria said. He'd had to give her a sedative because she was beside herself with guilt and worry, and just before she went under she'd said, "Her *osito*, Don Rico, they took her *osito* too." He hadn't thought about it much at the time, but it had stayed with him.

"Because," he muttered aloud, "it's so damned Spanish!" Kidnap a child, terrify her by removing her from her home and her parents, but bring her teddy bear. And it was cause for hope. Whatever the motive of the crime, they couldn't mean Kate any harm if they took her toy too.

Ibañaez pulled on the break handle, and the car came to a screeching squealing halt. For a few minutes he just sat on the road. Then he began driving again— faster than before, because he knew where Kate was, or at least who did. Not they, her.

Taking Kate was an act of vengeance—Wilkins had been right about that. Only the sheriff hadn't known all the people who had cause to despise the Westermans. Rick was able to supply the one name that had been missing from the suspect list.

Beatriz.

The shop was closed when he arrived. It was eight in the evening, so that wasn't surprising, but the fact that the shutters were bolted over the display window was. Ibañez looked around. A man lounged in a nearby doorway, "Has Doña Beatriz gone away?" he demanded.

"*No se*, Don Rico. I know only that the *tienda* has been shut yesterday and today."

He remembered that there was a rear entrance and, he started for it, picking his way through a narrow opening between two buildings. It was littered with garbage and stank of urine. The passage ended and he was in a tiny yard that belonged to the Ortegas. In this space of no more than ten square feet, Señora Ortega had created a garden. It was beautiful even in December. Spikey cacti contrasted with velvety geraniums whose flowers were insignificant, but whose leaves exuded spicy scents as he brushed past them. A lemon tree dominated one corner. Its branches were heavy with pale yellow fruit that shimmered in the moonlight. Many years had passed since Señora Ortega was well enough to tend the garden, Beatriz must be keeping it up. Ibáñez sighed and crossed to the kitchen door.

He raised his hand to knock, then thought better of it and tried the handle. Locked. No choice now. He pounded on the thick ancient wood with his closed fist. "Beatriz, it's me, Don Rico. Open up. I know you're in there." Where could she gave gone with an invalid mother and a baby?

The door swung open and Beatriz faced him, as neat and self-possessed as usual. He tried to read her expression, but the light was behind her and it was impossible. "I did not expect you, Don Rico," she said coolly. "This is not a good time to visit. My mother is well. Please return in a few days. If that is convenient," she added hastily, still playing at the old deference.

"Let me in, Beatriz. I know." His voice was thick with exhaustion, and he willed himself to think clearly.

She must be close to the edge, perhaps already over it, or she would not have done this thing. "Let me in," he repeated when she didn't move or answer. "It's much better if we discuss it between ourselves, Beatriz," he added gently. She remained where she was a few seconds longer, then stepped aside.

The kitchen was spotlessly clean. The pale light of a single gas lamp spilled in a circle on worn linoleum polished by years of scrubbing. The table was covered with a starched and embroidered cloth, and there was a potted begonia in its center. A picture of the cruci-fied Jesus hung by the stone sink, and another of *La Conquistadora* filled the space over a shelf of china. The dishes had been arranged to allow room for a candle and a tiny vase of flowers. It was all so pitifully ordinary. And now she'd torn it apart by doing this unthinkable thing. "Why, Beatriz?" he asked.

"I do not know what you mean."

"Yes, you do."

And then, as if on cue, a child's cry filled the silence between them. Beatriz started, shot him one guilty and terrified glance, then moved jerkily in the direc-tion of the summons. "I must see that she is all right," she said simply, as if merely apologizing for the inter-ruption. Rick felt a flood of relief. Beatriz's instinctive response to the cry told him Kate was safe. He fol-lowed her out of the kitchen and down the hall.

The little girl sat on Beatriz's bed, surrounded by cushions and quilts and clutching her teddy bear. She was dressed in a clean linen nightgown that had be-longed to Señora Ortega before it was hastily cut down. A candle burned on the table, and there was light enough for him to see that Kate was flushed with recent sleep. She'd wakened and been frightened by her strange surroundings. That was the only thing wrong with her.

"Hello, little pet," he said, moving quickly to reach the bed before Beatriz did. "Have you had a nice visit? I've come to take you home to Mommy and Daddy."

"Daddy," Kate repeated. It was the only word she understood, but she stretched out her arms to Rick's familiar figure, and he gathered her up with a sense of deliverance so profound that it made his knees weak.

"Has she eaten?" he demanded of Beatriz. It was the only thing he could think of.

"Of course," she said. "You did not think I would mistreat her?" Beatriz stretched out her hand and lay one gentle finger on the child's cheek. "We have had fun together, haven't we, *mi niña?*" Kate buried her face in Rick's shoulder, but it was playful coyness, not fear.

"What about your mother?" Rick asked. If the señora suspected anything, she must be beside herself with worry. Her old heart would withstand little of that.

"She is well," Beatriz said calmly, "I told her I'd been asked to look after a friend's child. She enjoyed having a baby in the house again."

Rick nodded and took a blanket from the bed. "It's a long drive back to the ranch, I'll need this to keep her warm." He wanted to ask how she'd arranged the kidnapping, but he could spare no time for questions. The agony at Santo Domingo was continuing even as he stood here. He started for the door, but Beatriz stepped into his path. Her mood had changed suddenly, and her face was contorted by fury and loathing. Rick stepped back, repelled by what he read in her twisted features.

"Do you understand why I did it?" she hissed.

He shook his head. "I could never understand such a thing. Have you any idea of the grief you've caused? The terror?"

She stared at him, her eyes black coals in her face. "Do you think there is anything I do not know of suffering?" she said. Then, when he didn't answer, "It is right that they should pay! They and all their kind."

Ibañez could think of nothing to say. Besides, there was no time now for recriminations or decisions about the future. "I must take her home," he said. "I'll come back later. We'll talk then."

She exhaled softly, and it was as if her anger was dissipated with her breath. Her muscles relaxed, and the anguished grimace disappeared. "Yes, you'll come back," she said dully. She turned and led him not to the kitchen, but through the shop to the front door. She unbolted it with calm and deliberate movements and held it open. *"Adios, querida,"* she whispered. The endearment was only for the child who slept peacefully in his arms.

Ibañez was too dead on his feet to register much of the reunion. He noted the joy in Amy's face and the way Kate clung to her father. Then he sagged against the wall and said, "I've got to go home. Sorry, I just need some sleep."

"You can't do that drive again," Tommy said over the top of his daughter's head. "It's past midnight. You'll sleep here."

"Thanks, but no." It seemed to Rick vital that he get out of this place. Besides, he'd have to talk to Beatriz and decide what to tell the sheriff. He looked again at Amy. "Tomorrow's Thursday, isn't it?" He was confused, but he was pretty sure he was right. "I'll have to see Estella tomorrow. It's better if I go home now."

"Yes, tomorrow's Thursday," Amy said. She came to him and put her hand on his cheek, unaware of her husband and the other men in the room. "I can never thank you, Rick dearest," she said softly. "I won't even try."

"Just a minute, folks." Sheriff Wilkins' voice cut through the tangled emotions eddying in the room. "I've a few questions for the doc. There's been a crime committed here."

"Not unless I say so," Tommy said. He handed Kate to Amy and went to where the lawmen stood apart. "Dr. Ibañez is in no condition to explain anything just now. And there's no question of a crime unless I press charges. That's correct, isn't it?"

"Maybe, but damn it, Mr. Westerman, we've been chasing our tails for three days! Now he just walks in and produces the baby like a rabbit out of a hat. There's got to be some questions and some answers."

Tommy walked slowly to the drinks cupboard, as if considering the sheriff's words. He poured a brandy for Rick, then a round for the rest of them, "You're a good man, sheriff," he said quietly. "I've been glad of your efficiency throughout this nightmare. Now I'm sure you'll show some common sense as well."

He didn't actually say that elections were coming up, but the fact was present in the room like a silent guest. "It's as plain to me as it must be to you that Dr. Ibañez figured out where to look for Kate. That's why he found her and we didn't."

Ibañez felt the tension disappear from the back of his neck. No more questions, thank God. Suddenly Tommy said, "Maybe you can just put the sheriff's mind at rest about that, Rick?" Westerman's eyes hurled a challenge. For a moment the two men stared at each other. Ibañez was the first to look away.

He sipped his brandy to gain a few seconds of time. Across the top of Kate's head he saw Amy watching him. Her eyes too were full of questions. He set his glass down and spoke very softly, conscious that everyone in the room was hanging on his words.

"On the drive back to town I realized that in a crazy way the kidnapping was aimed at me, an attempt to punish me through my patients and"—with another look at Amy—"through my friends."

Ibañez and the Westermans were an isolated triangle of tension in the room, but Wilkins was the next to speak. "Maybe that's the why of it. It tells us nothing about who."

Rick turned and faced him. "I'm not going to answer that, Pete. At least not until I've had a chance to think."

"You could be charged as an accessory, you know," Wilkins said.

Ibañtez shrugged.

Tommy noted the way the two men glared at each other. It was obvious that Wilkins was ready to invoke all the ponderous power of the law. The temptation to let Ibañez hang himself was strong. Just then Kate woke and squirmed in her mother's arms. "Daddy," she said, holding out her arms toward her father. The child's movement created a momentary break in the tension.

"I'll take her," Tommy said.

Amy relinquished her burden and stood with her arms hanging empty at her sides and her gaze fixed on Rick. Tommy watched the pair of them, then tightened his grip on his daughter and spoke. "Let it lie, sheriff. We all know the eminent doctor didn't snatch Kate." The words came out hard and tight, betraying what they cost him.

Wilkins sighed and moved to where his assistants stood waiting. "Ok, for now," he said. "But we'll have to talk more about it later."

Rick turned to Tommy, "Thank you," he said quietly.

Westerman shook his head. "No, don't thank me." His voice was pitched low, meant only for Ibañez, and perhaps Amy, to hear. "I've got reasons not to like you much, but at the moment I owe you a big one." He stroked Kate's silky blond curls while he spoke.

The deputies began moving toward the door, collecting the belongings they'd scattered during their encampment. Amy watched the exodus, anxious for the strangers to go and the process of forgetting to begin.

"We'll give you a lift home if you want, doc," Wilkins said. "You're in no shape to drive." Rick nodded and followed the departing men. Wilkins paused and turned back to Tommy. "Do you want me to leave a couple of guys here to guard the house? Since we don't know a damn thing about the how or why of this business, I can't say whether or not you need them."

Tommy looked questioningly at Rick. Ibañez shook his head. "No need, sheriff," Tommy said. "Thank you again. I'll find a more concrete way to express that sentiment pretty soon."

If Wilkins thought to question Ibañez on the journey back to Santa Fe, he was mistaken. Rick fell asleep as soon as he got into the Model-T, and he had to be shaken awake when they parked in front of his door.

"I'll be around to see you first thing in the morning," Wilkins said.

"Make it the evening," Rick said. "I plan to sleep all morning. Then I'm going to *las Carmelitas* to see my daughter. The evening, Pete, that's time enough."

23

Rick shook himself awake soon after ten the next morning. He'd had only six hours sleep, but the knowledge that the tragedy wasn't finished denied him any more. He showered and shaved and dressed while his cleaning woman made coffee. Then he went to his office. Elena was there, and he spied half a dozen patients in the waiting room. "Is there anything urgent?" he asked.

"Nothing. They're all well trained. They save the serious sickness for after Thursday."

He smiled at her. "Sorry you've had to cope on your own this week. There was trouble at Santo Domingo after the party."

"I know," she said. She had been at the party and she lived in the *barrio*. She was aware of the deputies who had come asking questions, and the story behind them. "I've managed ok," she said. "I put off the ones that could wait, and the others I sent to your competition."

"Not the rich ones, I hope," he said with a grin.

"You don't have rich patients, Don Quixote," she retorted. "You're too busy doing good." It was an old argument and they both laughed. "Except Señora Westerman," Elena added. "And she's too nice to be rich." Her face grew serious. "How is she?"

"They're all fine now."

"Thank God! What a terrible thing to do. Do you know who? . . ."

"I have to go out," he said, cutting off her question. "I'm sorry, but it's necessary. Tell those who are waiting I'll see them first thing tomorrow."

Elena sighed. "There are at least twenty-five people planning to see you first thing tomorrow. Don't worry, I'll work it out. Now go if you're going. Otherwise you'll never get away."

He looked for his car, then remembered he'd left it at Santo Domingo last night. He'd have to ride to the convent later. He could walk to the Ortegas, and that came first.

It occurred to him to worry about being seen. When he thought of that he realized that he didn't intend to tell the sheriff about Beatriz. Not if he was convinced she'd do nothing like this again. He was debating that when he turned into her street and headed for the shop. Then he saw Wilkins' automobile and the cluster of people standing in front of the door.

So Pete had figured it out for himself, and the matter was out of his hands. Ibañez felt a mixture of sorrow and relief. He'd have to find someone to look after Señora Ortega, a convent maybe.

All his speculations ended when he made his way into the house. Beatriz was lying on her bed. They'd covered her with a sheet, but they pulled it back when he came in. He inhaled sharply. She wore a white satin fiesta dress trimmed with emerald green ruffles. Her extraordinary figure was clearly outlined, but in death it looked hard-edged and unreal. Her hands lay peacefully at her side and two silk gardenias were tucked behind her ear. An image of them together in this same bed superimposed itself over the corpse. Rick pushed it away. He felt pity, but not guilt. In seconds the shock passed and he was in control.

"Never saw her dressed like this before, did you?" Wilkins asked.

"No. Where is Señora Ortega?"

"Don't worry, doc. She doesn't need your services. She's as dead as this one."

"How did it happen?"

"Can't say for sure. But we think it was an overdose of medicine. That strike you as possible?"

"It's possible," Rick said quietly. He'd prescribed tincture of belladonna for his patient. Enough of that would kill them both. "When did you get here?"

"About half an hour ago. The neighbor who sometimes looks after the old lady got concerned. Seems there ain't been no sign of either of them for the past week. She got her son to force the lock on the front door. Found 'em both, just like this. Murder and suicide I make it.''

"Those are ugly words," Rick said.

"Yeah. We found this too. It's addressed to you."

Wilkins passed him a note. "Don Rico" was written on the unsealed envelope. Inside it said, "Do not imagine that I did it for you. It will be a peaceful end for both of us and I am content." It was ambiguous and no doubt she'd intended it so. Rick looked up. He felt tears sting the back of his eyes, but he didn't know whether he was crying for Beatriz or her mother or himself. Maybe for all of them.

Wilkins had obviously read the message. "Any ideas?" he asked.

Ibañez shook his head. "She was a strange and very intense woman. She'd had a hard life. Perhaps it all got to be more than she could bear."

"Yeah." Wilkins produced a small bundle and held it out for Rick's inspection. It was a freshly laundered child's sunsuit made of blue and white checked gingham. "We found this in the kitchen. Seems to me it fits the description of what the Westerman child was wearing the morning she was abducted."

"Maybe. You know more about such things than I do," Rick said. "But I'd risk a guess that this sunsuit can be bought all over Santa Fe. I think my own daughter has one just like it."

"You're just bound to obstruct justice, ain't you, doc?"

"For God's sake, Pete! She's dead. Kate's safe and sound. What the hell do you want?"

The sheriff threw the sunsuit on the table in disgust. "I'm just doin' my job. If anybody'll let me."

Rick put a hand on his arm. They'd known each other since childhood. Both were products of the amalgam that made up the city. In his own way each was able to cross the invisible lines separating the different worlds of Santa Fe. "Let it be," Rick said. "It's nothing to do with anybody else, and it's not a matter for the law. Not anymore."

Wilkins shrugged. "Ok, you say so and Westerman says so. Old blood and new money in cahoots against me. I'd be a fool to buck that." He softened the words with a sour grin.

"Thanks," Rick said.

"You're not welcome."

"I'll remind you of that next time your trick shoulder acts up." He left the sheriff scowling at his back and went into the shop. A few women dressed in the perennial black of the *barrio* stood silent among the bright frippery of the display. They were ready to mourn as soon as the men left.

"What are we to do with all this, Don Rico?" one of them asked. "No one knows of any relatives except Manuel and Purisima. They have their own troubles."

"Yes," Rick agreed. "Listen, tell Purisima I think the clothes should be distributed among the girls here. Doña Beatriz would want that."

"It is a good idea," the woman said. "I will tell her. The church will not bury her, you know," she added. "The mother, yes, but not the daughter. Suicide is a grave sin."

"Leave it to God to decide what is a sin," he said tiredly.

"I will." She nodded solemnly. "And I will see that there are flowers on her grave."

On Sunday afternoon Tommy watched Ibañez ride toward the house. The Mexican sat a horse the way his ancestors had, with absolute grace and mystery. Time was when that might have made Tommy jealous, but no longer. He rode just as well.

"We expected you before this," Tommy said, taking the reins from Rick and passing them to a nearby cowhand.

"I couldn't get away. I had to see Estella, and there were a lot of patients waiting. Is Kate all right, and Amy?"

"Both fine. Come inside. They'll want to see you."

"In a minute," Rick said. He took off his broad-rimmed black hat and studied Westerman. "Have you heard?"

"About the woman who killed herself and her mother? Yes, Wilkins came to see me. He said you weren't very forthcoming."

"There didn't seem to be any point. There still isn't, as far as I'm concerned."

"Ok," Tommy said easily. "She'd tried earlier to get me killed you know. Found a way to pressure Diego, my foreman."

"How can you be sure of that?" Rick demanded.

"It figures, that's all. She was a cousin of one of the guys I bought out a couple of months ago."

"Look, Westerman, you seem hellbent on making enemies out here. There's no need. New Mexico is big enough for all of us."

Tommy cocked his head. "Are you really such an innocent, or is it an act?"

Rick realized how wide was the gulf between them. He would not try again to bridge it. "It doesn't matter now, does it? She's dead. Let her rest in peace."

"That's your choice. You earned it." They started for the house, but Tommy halted before they reached the door. "Listen, I don't know what Amy's told you, but there's some things we'd better get straight."

Rick stiffened. "What things?"

"I'll never let her get a divorce," Tommy said.

"That's between you and Amy."

"Maybe. But it concerns you too."

"I'm not your wife's lover, Westerman." Rick couldn't keep the loathing from his voice. "Whatever ideas you've got, you're wrong."

"No, I'm not," Tommy said easily. "Don't answer, just listen to me. I owe you. That's not a comfortable position for me, but it's a fact. I won't forget it as long as you follow my rules."

"You listen!" Anger was a white heat in Rick's belly and a red haze before his eyes. "Amy is too good to breathe the same air as you. And if I can do anything to get her out of this sham you call a marriage, you better believe I mean to do it."

Tommy laughed. "Too good? You've got a lot to learn, amigo. I'd like to be around when you find it all out. Come to think of it, I probably will be. I'm not going anywhere and neither is she."

*   *   *

Rick found Amy in the patio. The two children were playing nearby. "Hello," she said. Her voice sounded distant, removed from him. "I'm sorry about your friend Beatriz," she added, but the words conveyed no warmth.

"So am I," Rick said. "She was a fine person, despite what happened."

"She's the one who took Kate, isn't she?"

"Forget it, Amy. It doesn't matter now."

"No, I suppose it doesn't." She rose and went to retrieve a toy lying on the tiles beneath the gum tree. "I just keep wondering why she did it."

"She was very unhappy and confused. A lot of bad things happened in her life," Rick said. "Besides, one of the ranchers Tommy forced out was her cousin."

Amy nodded gravely. "It will be hard for you now that she's gone, won't it?"

"She was my friend," Rick said.

Amy turned to stare at him. The terrible emotions of the week still showed in her face. There were lines of fatigue and strain that had not been there last Sunday night when she joyously danced in his arms. "Were you in love with her?" she suddenly blurted out.

"With Beatriz? No," he said. "I was never that."

"But you were lovers, weren't you? That's really why she stole my child. She hated me." Amy spoke the words in painful wonder.

Rick didn't meet her eyes. "Why are you doing this? Do you just want to pick a quarrel with me?"

He saw her shiver, despite the heat of the midday sun. "I don't know," she said. "I don't know why I'm doing anything these days."

The conversation with Tommy was still fresh in Rick's mind. He had a sudden urge to say, "I wasn't in love with Beatriz, I'm in love with you," but he didn't. He said nothing.

Amy broke the painful silence. "I'm a fool to think I've any right to an explanation. Your private life is your affair." Her tone belied her words, and her jealousy was impossible to hide.

"You have a right to any part of my life that you want, *querida*." He moved toward her and took both her hands in his. The touch of her flesh burned his fingers. She leaned toward him with a movement that seemed beyond her control, a response to a magnetic field neither of them could escape.

"What am I to do?" she whispered. The words seemed more for herself than for him.

He let go her hands and took her face between his palms, forcing her to meet his eyes. "I know what I want you to do," he said. "But the decision must be yours."

She moistened her lips with her tongue, as if preparing to speak words that parched her mouth. Rick was suddenly afraid. His first instinct had been the right one. This was not the time to talk of the future. "Don't," he said. Then, because he wanted to smother a declaration that might be irrevocable, and because he couldn't resist, he covered her mouth with his.

For a moment she didn't respond, and it was as if he held a ragdoll in his arms, but suddenly she wrapped her arms around him and pressed her body against his. A shock of recognition passed through each of them. The knowledge that here was fulfillment and peace and the satiation of all hunger passed from one to the other, and welded a union that seemed, for a brief moment, unbreakable. Until Tommy's voice broke it.

He wasn't on the patio with them, they merely heard him in the house, speaking to one of the hands, but Amy pulled away with a fierce movement that bespoke rejection and fear. Rick let his hands drop to his sides. "I don't want to make you afraid," he said. "That's not the way I want you."

"I know, but . . ."

"No," he interrupted quickly. "Don't say anything. There's time, *querdia*. A better time than this one."

"Yes," she nodded. "A better time."

The memory of that moment's revelation remained between the two of them, a shared secret neither spoke aloud. Amy knew that Rick was waiting for her to choose the "better time" they'd promised each other. Sometimes she was half-wild with anticipation and hope, sometimes she despaired. Once before she'd dared to dream of a life of love. It had been pointless then and it was pointless now, she told herself. She'd made her choice and she must suffer the consequences. Whatever Tommy had become was her fault. How could she hope for happiness built on a wreckage she herself had made?

*   *   *

Two months later her evaluation was confirmed. She was pregnant again. Once more she carried Tommy's child in her body. This was a life conceived in anger and loveless lust, the fruit of Tommy's half-rape the night of the party and the kidnapping. It had to have happened then, for he'd not touched her since. But whatever its origin, it was a life. The circumstance served to convince Amy that there was no way out of her dilemma. Once more she had given a hostage to fortune, and once more she must pay the penalty and protect the innocent.

She wanted to tell Rick, but the thought that now he might cease even to be her friend was terrifying. She kept promising herself that she'd do it "next week," then the week after. The right time, a moment when her courage and her sense of honor would converge to overcome her fear, never arrived. Neither did she tell Tommy. He was away most of the time, working hard to consolidate the three ranches he'd made into one, and he seemed hardly aware of her existence. There was a kind of peace in the limbo in which she found herself, and having nothing else, Amy was reluctant to give it up.

Toward the end of April she finally accepted that she must tell both men that she was expecting. She was starting her fifth month. Few of her dresses fit, and she could not continue to disguise her pregnancy. Besides, a few days previous, Rick had been on the verge of pressing her for a decision.

They'd gone riding, one of the rare times they were together without the children, and when they stopped to admire a particularly beautiful view, he'd lifted her down from her horse and not let her go. They stood together for many seconds enjoying the silent symphony of their touching bodies. Then he'd kissed her again.

Afterward Amy needed only to close her eyes to feel once more the joy of it. His lips on hers were infinitely gentle, and the taste of him was an aching sweetness. She'd pressed close and clung to his strength and the promise of delight in his touch. She wanted to drown in the beauty of it; she wanted to melt and open to him, to deny him nothing of herself that she might have all of him. But she'd done none of those things. Instead, once more she'd pulled away.

For a few moments he'd stared at her and waited. Then he'd said, "You can't sit on the fence forever, *querida*. You've got to make up your mind."

"I can't," she'd said hoarsely, knowing even as she spoke that it was a lie. The decision had been made for her. Only she couldn't bear to communicate it to him. "Not yet," she'd whispered. "Please not yet."

So another opportunity for truth had passed. Now the end had come. She must face reality or make Rick hate her as a liar and a cheat. That would be worse than saying good-bye to him forever. Amy prepared herself to deal with the inevitable.

A golden spring Sunday dawned. Amy woke alone in the big bed and heard Tommy downstairs playing with the children. She glanced at the clock. It was after nine. If Tommy planned to ride out, he'd already be gone. Very well, she'd tell him today and see Rick tomorrow.

She stretched out her hand and felt the warm sheets Tommy had vacated. Nowadays they never touched.

Even in sleep they stayed rigidly apart, like two strangers forced by circumstances into the imitation of intimacy. Amy sighed and swung her legs over the side of the bed. It was then the pain attacked, a roaring beast whose name she knew the moment it bit. Amy felt blood running down her thighs and she screamed.

"I'm having a miscarriage. Get Rick," she cried between gasps:

"I'll carry you downstairs," Tommy said. "We can drive to the hospital in town."

"No." She couldn't say more.

Tommy looked at her, then ran from the room yelling for Diego and Maria.

When Rick arrived she was hemorrhaging and close to death. His surgery was of necessity drastic and final.

"No more children," he told Tommy when he emerged grim-faced from the bedroom. "She's had too many pregnancies too fast. We're lucky she's alive at all."

"Yes," Tommy said. "I guess we are." He looked pointedly at the other man. "Just as well, I guess. I'd never be sure if it was your kid or mine."

Rick clenched his fists, but his voice was cool. "You're pure bastard, aren't you? There's no room for truth or decency."

"What is truth?" Tommy laughed mirthlessly. "Sorry, I never can resist the apt quotation."

Ibañez wanted to punch the smug face opposite him. He didn't because he knew that would make it worse for Amy. He spun on his heel and returned to his patient.

During his wife's convalescence Tommy moved out of her bedroom. He never returned.

For a while Rick was her doctor first and the man who loved her second. He wouldn't let her talk about anything until she was again up and beginning to regain her strength. Then one day he said simply, "I want to take you away from here, *querida*. Are you ready to go?"

Amy folded her hands in her lap and looked at him with all the love in her heart. "I can't, my dearest," she said softly. "I never can."

"In God's name!" he exploded. "Why not? What else does he have to do to you?"

"It's not Tommy's fault that I lost the baby. You know that."

"All right, but you're begging the question."

She shook her head. "Don't shout at me, Rick. It won't do any good. I'm sorry if you think I led you on. I never meant to do that. But I'm Tommy's wife, and I can't change it. I made my choices a long time ago. Losing another baby, losing even the chance to have any more, just confirms it."

He stared at her in anger and pain and stormed out of the house without saying another word. Three days later he came back. "I was on the verge of transferring you to another doctor, of never coming here again," he admitted. "I couldn't do it. What we have—

what we could have together—it's too precious to give up."

"We have to give it up," she said. "Oh, Rick, please believe me. I'd give anything if it could be different, but it can't be."

"I think you're mad," he said grim-faced. "I think that bastard's bewitched you."

"I'm sane. Maybe for the first time in my life."

"What do you want me to do, then?"

"Whatever you want," she said dully. "Whatever you think you must do. But I'd be very happy if we could still be friends," she added in a small and wistful voice.

"Friends," Rick said, as if it were a foreign word. "When I touch you you tremble like a leaf in the wind. Do you think we can simply be friends?"

"I don't know. I'd like to try."

He made a wordless sound of disgust and turned away.

Amy stared at his back and saw the way his shoulders rippled beneath his shirt. She wanted desperately to go to him, but she made herself be still. Losing another baby, almost dying herself—it was a warning from the vengeful God whose face she had glimpsed in New York. Amy understood that now. Her hands remained clenched in her lap. If she reached out to Rick, they would all fall into some terrible destiny. Not just the two of them, the children as well. Amy clung to her resolve and their safety, a tenuous thing she gripped in her slender fingers.

"Very well," he said at last. "Not because I think it will work, only because I won't let you throw away everything we might have together." He turned to look at her, and he managed a smile. "I'll wait a little longer, *querida,* but I won't wait forever."

She closed her eyes in relief.

24

THE CADENCES OF SANTA FE LIFE ARE GENTLE AND slow to change. The rhythm of the city is determined by a history which, however dramatic, took place when life moved at a slower pace. Nonetheless, things were different after the war. The cowhands congregating on the plaza around Joe Turner's barbershop discussed the alterations.

"Some smart boy in New York says we're livin' in the roarin' twenties."

"Looks like they're gonna roar right by New Mexico."

"President Wilson says we ain't never had it so good."

"Don't matter what he says. He ain't runnin' again, and Harding's bound to beat that democrat, Cox."

"Ain't gonna matter none to us who's president if the price of beef keeps goin' down."

The man who knew the sobriquet applied to the times knew too why cows were suddenly cheap. "The war's over, so the federal government ain't buyin'. And they cut off the ranchers' credit, cause now we're not an 'essential war industry.' "

"You blamin' the drought on Washington too?"

"No, but I sure blame 'em for that Stock-raising Homestead Law."

Inevitably at the mention of the odious law the men fell silent and drifted apart. Some things were too painful to talk about.

In 1916 Congress promised six hundred and forty acres to anyone willing to raise cattle. After five years, if they survived, the land was theirs. Nobody mentioned that it was arid desert land and six hundred plus acres could support no more than sixteen head. If a homesteader was lucky enough to find water, it was likely to be four hundred feet deep. The cost of digging and maintaining such a well was prodigious.

They moved across the horizon of Amy's world, these land-hungry Easterners heading west. They came in beat-up motorcars and antique wagons. Eventually almost all were forced to make the return journey. It was a sad and tragic epic.

"Fifty million acres!" Rick railed one afternoon. They'd taken Estella and Kate and Tom Junior on a picnic, and were forced to watch yet another defeated family dragging themselves and their pitifully few belongings back to wherever they'd come from. "Those loco fools in Washington have no idea what this place is really like. But they've managed to take fifty million acres of it out of the control of those who could use it, and give it to people they might as well poison. Worse, poison would be quick."

It was a few weeks short of Christmas 1920. Amy had lived long enough in New Mexico to understand. In a drought every inch of grassland was precious. Ranchers who had the skill and the manpower could move their herds and find forage. But guileless homesteaders put up fences, thus taking vast tracts of land out of circulation.

"Barbed wire is going to be New Mexico's shroud," Rick said bitterly. He looked quickly at Amy, then looked away. It was one of their unspoken rules. They didn't discuss Tommy. But Amy knew what Rick meant.

Faced with numberless cows dying of starvation, many ranchers banded together and sent a delegation to Washington. Negotiations with the Mexican government followed. Recently the land south of the border had received rain when none fell to the north. Chihahua, for instance, had knee-high grass, but scarcely an animal left to eat it. To feed his rebel army, Pancho Villa had stripped the country of cattle.

So a great migration was organized. Stockmen loaded their herds onto trains and sent them south under bond. The theory was that they would feed and fatten in Mexico. When rain resurrected the American range, they would be brought home. It was a scheme born of desperation, and most who took part knew they'd never see their herds again. Tommy Westerman didn't participate.

Tommy had a different vision. He had no sentimental attachment to the old golden days. And he had water. Even with the water table getting lower by the week, the hole at Santo Domingo wasn't dry. Tommy deepened it, and covered it to reduce evaporation. He kept armed guards there day and night. His entire eighty thousand acres, a relatively small spread by southwestern standards, was fenced with barbed wire and vigilantly patrolled. It didn't make him popular, but it was making him rich.

At the end of the war three-year-old cows had brought sixty to eighty dollars a head. Now their price had dropped back to thirty. Tommy sold yearlings at twenty. "They're going to develop a taste for veal back east," he said. They did.

Amy knew all this, but she lived her life somehow apart from it; just as she separated herself from the rest of her husband's behavior. Tommy still kept Rosa Mandago in the house near the Pecos Trail. He had other girls as well. From Albuquerque to Santa Fe, Westerman was known as a womanizer and a hard drinker, and famed for his lavish parties. He didn't use the hacienda as a venue, instead Tommy would hire the entire floor of a hotel. Somehow he managed to sidestep the law of prohibition passed in 1919. There was plenty to drink and plenty to eat, and often he'd entertain all comers for two or three days at a stretch.

Stories of these bacchanals reached Amy, but she ignored them. They did not prevent Tommy from attending brilliantly to his business, thus providing security for her and the children. She had Kate and Tom Junior, and she was often a surrogate mother to Estella, whom she had grown to love. Most important, she had Rick. For a brief space of time it seemed as if he would be content to go on under the terms she'd stipulated. Only when he took her hand or gazed questioningly into her eyes did she face the fact that she'd only built a temporary barricade. The tide of passion still threatened to overwhelm them both.

One day in the summer of 1921, Rick called at the ranch after visiting patients in the pueblos. He was hot and tired, and his customary patience was frayed at the edges.

"*Hola*, Don Rico!" Maria greeted him with a smile and hurried off to summon Amy. Rick went to the living room and poured himself a drink. When Amy came he was staring into the empty fireplace.

"Rick! What a nice surprise. I was thinking . . ." Her voice trailed away when he didn't turn around. She noticed how stiff and tense he was. "What's the matter?"

He spun round and faced her. "You and me, that's what's the matter."

"I don't understand."

"I can't believe that." He tossed back the drink and put the empty glass on a table. "For God's sake, Amy, how long is this charade going to continue?"

She twisted her hands together, conscious of her wedding ring and the sapphire that had belonged to Tommy's grandmother. "I'm married, Rick. I have two children. I've told you how it must be. What in the world can you expect me to say?"

He wouldn't give in. "One thing only," he said quietly. "Go or stay."

"Now, you mean? Tonight? Tommy's away, but he might be back this evening."

"No, that's not good enough!" He crossed the room and grabbed her roughly. His lips punished hers, then they were clinging together in mutual desire. "Oh, God," he moaned. "Amy, Amy, stop torturing us both! Leave him and marry me. The two of us, the children, we'll be so good together. . . ."

She tore herself away and tried to still her trembling. "I can't," she whispered, "I can't ever leave Tommy."

"Then at least tell me why. I keep thinking about it. You can't be worried about the scandal; you must know we're already talked about." She shook her head and his voice grew hard. "Are you surprised by that? Don't be a child, Amy. Everyone says that you're my mistress. Even Tommy thinks so." He laughed softy.

She dropped into a chair. "Why are you doing this? Why do you want to hurt me?"

"Hurt you!" Rick knelt beside her and took hold of her hands. *"Querida,"* he whispered. "I would never hurt you. But you are destroying us both. You must make up your mind."

"I have made it up," she said tonelessly. "It's all tied up with things you don't know, things I can't talk about."

"You want me to go, then," Rick said. He stood up. "Very well, the choice is yours."

"I never said that!" She was suddenly desperate. The thought that he would disappear from her life was insupportable. "I couldn't survive without you! Why can't we go on as we are? Can't we be friends? Isn't that enough?"

The word no formed in his mouth, but he didn't utter it. Rick looked at her. She was beautiful, fragile, alone for all intents and purposes; she was the woman he loved. He could not say that he would go away and never see her again because it wasn't true; he did not have that much strength. "My dearest friend," he said softly, taking her face in his hands. "*Claro, mi niña.* That is all you will give, so I will try to be satisfied."

It was once more an uneasy truce, but Amy was grateful for it.

She suspected that Rick sometimes visited the house of Doña Zia, where men could buy pleasure, but she would not allow herself to dwell on such thoughts. Physical love was something she could never have, she told herself. The thought of Rick in the arms of some other woman, even a tart whom he paid for the privilige, was agony. It was worse than the surge of jealousy she'd known when she'd realized that he'd been Beatriz Ortega's lover. But how could she be angry with Rick for seeking elsewhere what she repeatedly denied him?

There was something else. Deep as were her feelings for Rick, Amy didn't trust them. She had loved Luke, and he had rejected her. Tommy had loved her, and she had married him because of that, not because she returned his love. Now she must repay that injustice with the rest of her life. It was all a painful tangle of wrong choices and what might have been. Often Amy wondered if the true flaw was in herself. Perhaps her peculiar heritage had marked her forever.

Most of the time she succeeded in burying both the past and the simmering dangers of the present. Only once, when Tommy was home and drinking more than he usually did at the ranch, did Amy lose her control.

"Have a drink," Tommy said when she went into the living room. She'd thought him in bed, but he was sitting with a half-empty bottle by his side. "Bathtub gin," he said, gesturing with his glass. "Illegal rotgut, but it's all there is at the moment. Have some."

She shook her head and murmured something about going to sleep.

"Never do anything illegal or immoral, do you?" he said with a chuckle. "Pure as the driven snow, that's my wife. Come off it baby, I know better."

"You're drunk. I don't think we'd better talk anymore. Good night."

Instantly he was out of the chair and had hold of her arm. "Don't you turn your back on me, lady." His voice was quiet, but full of menace.

Amy could not summon fear; too much had passed between them for her to be afraid now. "What do you want, Tommy?" she asked tiredly.

He cocked his head and studied her.

"Now that's a good question. How about a faithful wife? Will that do for openers?"

"You have that."

He threw back his head and laughed. "You and

your spic boyfriend just hold hands. Is that what you're saying?"

"I don't know what you're talking about."

"The hell you say! It's all right, baby." He dropped her arm and turned away. His voice began to slur, as if the quantity he'd drank had just caught up with him. "I don't give a damn anymore. You're a whore. I know it and you know it. Not even able to produce more kids. I don't give a damn what you do."

Amy fled upstairs and locked herself in her bedroom. That night she had terrible nightmares, and when she woke she remembered a dream in which Rick had made love to her, and when it was over he looked at her with disgust and loathing.

At dawn Tommy came to her door and knocked repeatedly. She had to let him in or he would wake the whole house and frighten the children.

He was pale and drawn, but sober. He didn't look at the big bed they had once shared, or at her half-clad form. "I came to say I'm sorry," he said grimly.

For a moment Amy wondered if he meant sorry about everything. Maybe they could find a meeting ground and begin again, for Kate's sake and Tom Junior's. "I'm sorry too," she said. "About so much."

"Don't mistake my meaning. I'm only saying that I understand the rules. We both do exactly as we want, as long as the kids are taken care of, and no smut gets as far as this house."

"I see," she said.

"I hope you do. You can sleep with whomever you want. My brother, the doctor—any man that takes

your fancy. Just don't do your whoring in any way
that's going to hurt my daughter or my son."

The house on the Pecos Trail was really a cabin, a
tumble-down wooden structure hastily erected by some
prospector in the last century. Tommy won it in a
poker game around the same time that he acquired
Rosa Mandago. That was in 1917, when he was scratch-
ing for every penny needed to rebuild Santo Domingo.
It was logical for him to install his half-breed mistress
in the cheapest quarters available. Since then he'd
many times offered to replace the shanty with something more substantial, but Rosa always refused.

"Will you come to see me more often if I have a
better house?" Rosa demanded every time he mentioned it.

"I come when I can. Don't start that again."

"When you find nothing better, you mean," she
said. "When your fancy wife has the big belly, or the
chicas in Albuquerque are too far away."

Usually Tommy would leave when the familiar ha-
rangue began; sometimes he would respond by kissing
her lush mouth, fondling her ripe breasts, and finally
finding peace and release between her tawny thighs. It
was all a question of his mood.

When he first met Rosa, she drove him wild. She
was so unlike any female he'd known or imagined that
the mere mention of her name enflamed him. Then
he'd ride any number of miles for the privilege of
pouring his seed into the voluptuous crevices of her
alien flesh. Eventually the novelty faded, and she be-

came just another easy lay. Still Rosa remained different from other women. She was his in a special way, one more symbol of his conquest of New Mexico. That's why the business about the Indian so enraged him.

"I just passed a redskin riding away from here," he told her when he arrived at the cabin late one night.

"*Si*, he came to see me."

Rosa sat on a sofa covered with woven blankets. It was the only piece of real furniture in the room. Her black hair was loose over her shoulders, and she clutched a red satin dressing gown across breasts which strained at the fragile restraint. Her fingers too were red-tipped, and they sported a profusion of rings which sparkled in the light of the oil lamp. "He is from my pueblo," she added with a trace of pride.

Tommy had removed his jacket and was unbuckling his belt while she spoke. He paused long enough to laugh. "What the hell do you mean, 'your pueblo'? There can't be any self-respecting pueblo prepared to claim you, my girl. Not Rosa Mandago the *mestiza* whore."

She stared at him through half-closed lids. He liked to make her angry, but tonight she wasn't going to give him the satisfaction. "That shows how much you know. My mother was from Pueblo San Felipe, so it is my pueblo. Always, no matter what."

"Yeah? Well, ok, if you say so. I still want to know why an Indian was riding out of here after midnight." Tommy was naked now. He didn't wait for Rosa to answer, but walked into the bedroom, expecting her to follow.

Even without turning around he could sense that she'd not yet risen to do so, and that she was thinking hard about the answer to his question. He began to feel real anger, and a kind of surprised jealousy. Rosa was bought and paid for years before. It was absurd to have to remind her of that yet again. He stood where he was, his back still to her, and said in a soft, aggrieved voice, "I'm waiting, Rosa."

"I'm coming."

He could hear the swishing sound made by her robe as she removed it. "That's not all I'm waiting for," he said.

She came up to him and slid her arms around his waist. Her breasts pressed into his spine, and he could smell the raw, animal scent of her skin. "For why you worry about the Indian? Is no man I like better than you. Maybe you forget that. Now I show you."

Tommy gripped her hands where they were clasped above his belly and wrenched her round to face him. "You stinking whore," he said softly. "You've been spreading your legs for some lousy heathen, haven't you?"

She shook her head, and the great mane of black hair swung from side to side. "No, no! What you think I do that for?"

"That's what I want you to tell me." He didn't release his grip on her wrists. "Talk, baby. Quickly, while I've got some patience left."

"I ain't got nothing to talk about. You making it all up in that crazy head of yours. You think too much, I always say it."

Only once in his life had Tommy Westerman hit a

woman, the night he slapped Amy when she came back from riding with Diego. There was still enough of his boyhood and his upbringing in him to make the idea repugnant. Now he wanted to punch Rosa's face. He wanted to retrieve his belt from the other room and whip her senseless. Maybe if he'd been drunk he'd have done it, but he was cold sober and self-disgust mingled with his fury. "You lousy bitch!" He pushed her away from him and she stumbled and hit the wall and slid to the floor. "You stinking cunt! What's his name?"

Rosa was moaning softly, and tears were running down her cheeks, but she only shook her head again. He moved to where she lay and stood above her, fists clenched at his sides. "You tell me his name, or I'll make you sorry you were born."

Again Rosa shook her head.

He squatted beside her and grabbed a handful of the thick black hair. "Why, for Chrissake? You've got everything you want, more money than you can spend. . . . Why?"

She tried to speak, but her mouth was parched with fear. Finally she managed to say, "You don't come so often anymore."

Tommy stared at her, incredulous. "And you can't do without it? Is that it? If you don't get laid enough, you can't stand it? Jesus!" He was trembling with rage, and the fear in her eyes made it worse. He'd treated Rosa better than any man she'd ever known in her life. And this was his reward. "Ok," he said softly. "I understand now. I'll just have to give you something you won't forget, something to let you know how things really are."

He was still holding her by the hair, and he used the grip to swing her over on her belly. Then he thrust himself into her body between her buttocks.

Rosa screamed with pain and rage. "You animal! You lousy cripple! He treat me like I somebody! Like a human being . . ."

When he withdrew his organ it was covered with blood. He used the water in the pitcher beside the bed to wash himself, then carried it to where she lay sobbing. Unceremoniously he dumped the contents of the pitcher over her quivering rump and knelt beside her to towel dry her flesh and inspect the damage. "You'll be ok," he said finally. "It's just a little torn. Put some salve on it."

He went into the outer room and got dressed. When he returned she was in bed with the covers drawn up to her chin. "If I ever hear of that redskin coming here again, I'll have you both strung up," he told her. Then he took two hundred-dollars bills from his wallet, put them on the washstand, and left.

Tommy didn't return to Rosa's for nearly a month. When he did she was docile and subdued, and he figured the incident was over and forgotten.

By December 1921 Tommy Westerman met with deference when he went to town. He heard the same greeting from the black shoeshine boy working the lobby of the swank new Hotel La Fonda or the manager of the First National Bank, "Good morning, Mr.

Westerman. Anything I can do for you, sir?" Tommy enjoyed it, but he was smart enough to be cynical. He remembered when everyone was watching him, expecting him to fail.

Tommy was thinking of that when he looked up and spotted John Hughes, the bank president, through the coffee shop window. He was crossing to the east side of the plaza where his Greek-columned temple of finance stood, a symbol of one kind of power in Santa Fe. Tommy waved. Hughes waved back. They were buddies now.

Tommy stirred his cold coffee and stared at it unseeing. A stamped addressed envelope lay on the counter next to his hand. Tommy didn't touch it. The letter was an omen of sorts, but he couldn't make up his mind if it boded well or ill.

The waitress approached and broke his reverie. "I'll just hot that up for you, Mr. Westerman." She smiled while she poured fresh coffee.

"Thanks, Lucy."

"Don't mention it. Awful mild for Christmas Eve, don't you think?"

"I do indeed."

"Must be even warmer down on your ranch. I guess you'll be goin' home today, loaded with presents for your pretty wife and the kiddies." She sighed wistfully, seduced by her vision of the good life—married and rich. She was single and poor.

Tommy removed a five dollar bill from his wallet. "Sorry there's no card, Lucy. This is just a token for the season, and all the good coffee you serve me."

She thanked him effusively and moved away. Tommy

still didn't drink his coffee or touch the letter. He did have presents for the children, just as Lucy surmised, but it was a long time since he'd bought anything for Amy. He remembered the bugle-bead purse he'd given her their first Christmas together. That was before they were married, while she was living with Lil and Warren. She'd given him a cashmere scarf. He had it still, though he hadn't worn it in years. His fingers crept tentatively toward the letter.

What would it prove? If Luke came and they were all three together in the house that Tommy had created, in the world where he was master, would it change anything? Perhaps. He would see Luke and Amy together, and he would know for himself if what he believed was true, or the lie Amy always claimed it to be. Luke was a different man now, a priest, but that would make no difference to him or to Amy.

He picked up the envelope abruptly, left the coffee shop, and made his way through the hotel lobby, stopping at the newsstand for a paper. The masthead of *The Santa Fe New Mexican* announced that it was the region's oldest daily. Next to it Tommy spotted a copy of *El Neuvo Mexicano*, the Spanish weekly. They were both published by the same company. That was the way it was in Santa Fe.

"Shine, Mr. Westerman?"

"Not just now, Jason. Thanks anyway, and merry Christmas." Tommy dispensed another five dollar bill. By the time he'd collected his packages at the desk he'd divested himself of twenty dollars in Christmas tips. The one to the bellboy who carried the presents to the Packard made it twenty-five.

Tommy stood hesitantly beside the car. He was conscious of the letter still in his pocket. For a few moments he didn't move. Finally he turned and hurried in the direction of the post office. He didn't slow down until after he'd mailed it; then he had to lean against the building and catch his breath. He had the sensation of having started a process with a doubtful outcome. It wasn't just Luke. Other truths would need to be explained if his brother came.

"Shit!" he cursed quietly. He didn't know what or who he was swearing at. Himself maybe. He pushed back into the crowd of last-minute shoppers. Once he stopped to examine a display of expensive perfume and the idea of a gift for Amy teased him. Then he saw in the glass the reflection of Rick Ibañez. Tommy turned. Rick was across the road, striding rapidly and exchanging greetings with people he passed. Ibañez either didn't see him, or didn't acknowledge him. Tommy watched until he was out of sight.

There was a sour taste in his mouth, and all thought of a present for Amy was gone. Nor did he want to go home just yet. He'd be there in the morning when the children woke. That was the only part of Christmas that mattered to him. This year Tom Junior was three and Kate was four. They'd really appreciate the tree and all the toys. He intended to be with them for that, but there was plenty of time.

Suddenly he wanted to be away from the tinsel and the hearty bonhomie of the season. He headed for a small private club where he knew he'd find a card game. Santa Fe had always been a gambling town; it still was.

The club was in a dark basement devoid of any concessions to the December madness. One table of players was full, but at another the day's big loser was happy to give Westerman his seat.

"Five card stud," a grizzled man said. "Jacks or better to open, no limit on bets."

"I'm only in for a couple of hours," Tommy said. "Win or lose I quit by four. Have to get home and spend Christmas with my kids." The other ranchers nodded agreement.

He played insanely, without caution, and he won big. "Money goes to money," one of the losers said.

Tommy scooped the pile of bills into his pockets and rose to leave. "Yeah, ain't it the truth."

He climbed the stairs into cool dusk and breathed deeply to clear away the smoke and the taste of illegal tequila smuggled over the border. Money goes to money was probably true, but only after you had your first stake. The memory of how he'd acquired his wouldn't leave him. It was there like a dull ache in the back of his head, made worse by the memory of the letter he'd mailed. "I need a couple of aspirin," he muttered. Then he realized what he really craved.

He thought of driving out to see Rosa. She was convenient and on the way home, but she wasn't what he wanted now. He got his car and drove to Doña Zia's.

"Merry Christmas, Don Tommy." The woman greeted his warmly, as befit an infrequent, but respected customer.

Tommy hated being addressed by the Spanish title, but he let it pass. "Is Claudia free?" he asked.

Doña Zia laughed. "She is not free, but for you she is available."

Tommy grinned and took out his wallet. At Doña Zia's everyone, without exception, paid before they went upstairs. He handed over twenty dollars, then put another twenty on top of it. "A little present for you."

"Thank you, Don Tommy. You are very generous. Wait a moment. I will send someone to tell her you are coming."

After a few minutes she nodded to him. He climbed the stairs and walked past many doors to the one numbered six. Ordinarily muffled grunts and groans of pleasure escaped the confinement of the bedrooms and seeped into the narrow corridor. Today the hall was quiet; neither had he seen anyone in the downstairs salon. The piano was silent and the bar empty. On Christmas Eve the ladies of joy were left alone, while their clients sampled the delights of family life.

Westerman pushed open the door. Claudia was waiting for him. She was the only girl in the house not of Mexican ancestry. Her accent was pure East-Coast. Tommy didn't know if it was real or a careful affectation and he didn't care. She was small and had long black hair and dark eyes and an expression of perpetual innocence. She was, in fact, very like the Amy he'd known in Cross River. He'd spotted the resemblance the first time he'd gone to Doña Zia's; now it was only for Claudia that he returned.

"Merry Christmas, Tommy," she said in her soft girlish voice. "I'm wearing the outfit you like."

"You're a good girl, *memsahib*," he said.

Claudia didn't know why he called her that, or what it meant. She didn't let it trouble her, anymore than she was troubled by his insistence that when he came to her she wear the pale blue negligee and nightgown which he'd bought for her. Some of the men who visited her had far crazier ideas. She waited while he undressed, then poured them each a glass of chilled champagne. That was part of the ritual too.

Finally he touched her, and his touch was pleasant. He fondled and petted her as if they were teenagers on a back porch swing. Obligingly Claudia giggled and sighed. After a few minutes she let her fingers flutter between his legs and she felt that he was rock hard and ready. She kissed him once more, her lips primly closed the way he wanted them, and got up and removed the things she wore. Then she crawled under the covers, pulling the blanket up to her neck, and waited.

Tommy lay down beside her and trailed his hands over her skin. It was nice and soft. It didn't have quite the incredible silkiness he remembered, but that couldn't be helped. When he rolled on top of her she sighed softly. Tommy fumbled for a moment, then pushed himself inside her. She didn't help, because he'd told her never to do that.

He had learned control over the years. That part wasn't like the night in the hotel in Niagara Falls. Now he used his skill to tempt her into betrayal. His thrusts were slow and ever deeper. She was small and tight, and shudders of pleasure passed through his body. Claudia did not respond. She lay absolutely motionless and compliant beneath him, the way he hoped it would be. When he grasped her shoulders and pumped his seed into her in rapid staccato bursts, she still didn't move. "'You're a good girl, *memsahib*," he whispered after it was over.

He gave Claudia fifty dollars out of the poker winnings and wished her a merry Christmas before he left.

Outside it was dark except that small fires burned everywhere and turned the night into a glittering fantasy. It was a Santa Fe tradition. On Christmas Eve people made little pyramids of brushwood in front of their houses to "light the way of the Christ Child."

The fragrant scent of piñon filled the air, and sputtering flames reached toward the vast star-filled sky. Tommy walked toward his car. He passed an open church door and saw an altar banked with poinsettias and a manger scene arranged nearby. For a moment he stood looking. Behind the altar a light burned steadily beside the tabernacle. It appeared to him as something he was seeing across a wide chasm in the earth, an abyss he could not cross. He remembered all the midnight masses of years gone by, and he thought of the opulence of St. Ignatius, and of the simple little church in Cross River where the names of Jessie and Roland Norman were carved on the wall. Then he turned and walked away.

25

IN MARCH 1922 THE DROUGHT ABATED. THE RAIN WAS not as heavy as they needed, or of sufficient duration, but it was something. Rick arrived at the ranch at eight in the morning of what promised to be the first dry day in a week.

"What are you doing here at this hour?" Amy asked him in astonishment. "You must have left Santa Fe before sunrise. What about your patients?"

"I left at five," he told her. "I couldn't sleep. I put a sign on the door saying I was taking the day off. I'm entitled to a holiday."

She grinned. "I'm glad you're here. What shall we do?"

"Go back to Chaco Canyon," he said unhesitatingly. "Five years ago we promised ourselves a return trip. It's time we took it. Just the two of us." He looked at her, trying to gauge her reaction. Sometimes Amy went out of her way to avoid being alone with him. This time Rick had reached a decision during a long sleepless night. He had no intention of bringing the children on this outing.

Amy made no protest. She wore a maroon silk dressing gown tied tightly at the waist. When she moved it betrayed enticing glimpses of skin. "Give me ten minutes to dress," she said.

"I wish you'd undress instead," Rick answered softly.

Amy acted as if she hadn't heard. "I won't be long," she said. "Go say hello to the kids. They're in the kitchen with Maria."

She returned, wearing a denim skirt and chambray blouse which made her look like a fetching feminine cowboy. Rick was on the patio with Kate and little Tom. They were laughing together under the scented shade of the gum tree. It had bloomed in the rain three days earlier. Just that morning Amy watched the sunrise set its flowers afire. Now a young maid was sweeping away the fallen blossoms.

"It lasts such a short time," Amy said wistfully. "When the war ended I wrote to my father's old lawyer in Africa. I wanted some seeds of a flame tree. He never answered."

"Too bad, *pobrecita*," Rick said gently. "Perhaps the old lawyer has also died. It happens to people as well as flowers." He scooped up a handful of the faded petals that littered the patio and let them sift

through his fingers. Tom Junior giggled and tried to
catch them in his pudgy three-year-old hands.

The morning was cool, freshened by rain and bright
with promise. They were easy with each other, and
had no need to talk. The familiar scenery rolled by the
open top of Rick's new car. It was another Pierce-
Arrow. This one was called a runabout and had room
for only two passengers.

They used Amy's flivver when the children were
with them. The Runabout, however, had all the latest
features. It boasted hydraulic brakes, and a convert-
ible roof that could be folded away as it was now. Its
lines were rakish, symbolic of the times, and they were
emphasized by the spare wheel set jauntily atop the
rear fender. The car was painted sunny yellow. "It's
your best color," Rick had said when he bought it.
Today Amy wore a yellow blouse. It was astonishing
how much pleasure she took in finding little ways to
please him.

At Pueblo Bonito a few men were working on part
of the wall. Restoration had been slow since the war,
but steady. "I'm so glad they're doing something,"
Amy said. "I'd almost forgotten how magnificent it
is."

They wandered deep into the valley, far from the
laborers. The silence was broken only by the occasional call of a bird, or the soft papery sound of a
scurrying lizard. Amy sensed a change in Rick's mood.
Earlier he'd been relaxed. Now his quiet was laced
with tension. She darted a sideways glance at his pro-

file. His rugged good looks hadn't changed in the years she'd known him. But today his jaw was so set that he looked as if he were clenching his teeth. "If something's wrong, you'd better tell me," she said finally. There was a knot of fear in her stomach.

Rick stopped walking. "It's the end, Amy," he said quietly. "Or the beginning. That's up to you. I only know I can't go on like this."

She couldn't answer. Her cheeks grew hot with more than the heat of the sun.

"I love you," he continued. "I never thought it possible I could love a woman so much. But I won't be used. Not even by you."

"I never meant to use you. Surely you know that."

"I know that you take, but you don't give," he said. His voice sounded strangled. "You've never even told me what you feel. What am I? A convenient escort? A salve for your pride?"

"Oh, God . . ." She moaned as if he'd struck her. "You don't know me. You only think you do. You don't know what I've done."

"Then tell me!" He turned and gripped her shoulders. He was shaking her and her straw hat fell off and her short dark hair bounced around her face. "Tell me, damn it! What terrible secret are you hiding? Why do you insist on staying with a man who treats you like dirt?"

"I can't talk about it." She forced the words out through chattering teeth.

Always before he had drawn back when he saw how he was upsetting her. This time he wouldn't. "No! You've used that excuse for the last time. Either you tell me everything, the whole story, or I walk away now."

She started to sob, and he relented sufficiently to lead her out of the sun into the shade of the building. There was a pile of stone slabs waiting to be used by the restorers. Rick made her sit on them and stood over her. "Talk," he said. She still wept. "Here." He held out his handkerchief. "Blow your nose. Then start telling me the truth. It's the last chance for us, Amy," he warned. "I mean every word I say. There's no going back, not this time."

"Tommy's brother Luke is a priest," she stammered. "Before he joined the Dominicans I was in love with him. He loved me too, but he wouldn't admit it until it was too late." The words poured out like water rushing over a broken dam. "I married Tommy to spite Luke. He loved me, but I didn't love him. I only knew that I couldn't have Luke, so I wanted to hurt him. I never even thought about what that would do to Tommy."

She paused for breath. "Go on," Rick said. "That can't be all of it."

"Before he took his first vows Luke came to see me. I was married by then, but Luke said we'd made a terrible mistake, that he'd leave the priesthood and I would get a divorce and we'd go away together. Only I was expecting a baby and I knew neither of us would ever be able to forget Tommy. Not with his child always there to remind us. Luke went back to the priory and took his vows. Then I saw the advertisement for Santo Domingo."

She told him about her inheritance and how at first

Tommy didn't want to buy the ranch. "Then he wanted to inspect it before we bought it. I wouldn't listen to anything. I just wanted to get as far away from Luke as possible. The war was on and I couldn't go home to Africa, so I was determined to come west. When I lost the baby Tommy blamed himself, and because of that we bought Santa Domingo."

"Was it his fault you miscarried?"

She shook her head and pressed the handkerchief to her face. It smelled of Rick, and she held it very tight. "No. We had a fight about Luke. Tommy accused me of wanting his brother to be the baby's father. I denied it, but it was true. Tommy knew. Then I fell, and he didn't realize I was hurt and he stormed out of the house."

Too long had Amy hidden from the past. She couldn't stop now that she'd started. She explained about their disappointment when they first saw Santo Domingo, and the way Tommy finally taught himself to ride and make a success of it.

"That should have been the happy ending," Rick said. "Why wasn't it?" His tone didn't soften. "Keep talking, I want it all."

"Tommy knew about Luke coming to see me that time after we were married. I never told him, but he knew. He must have wondered and wondered why I never mentioned it. Don't you see? It confirmed all his worst fears."

"Ok, so he knew you still loved his brother, even after your marriage. I still don't see how things got the way they are between the two of you. When you were first married, did he drink then? Run around with other women?"

"No, nothing like that. It was only after I . . ." She swallowed hard. This part of it she could not tell him. "I can't," she moaned. "Let me be, Rick. Please, I can't . . ."

He took hold of her shoulders again. They felt pitifully fragile beneath his hands. "Yes, you can," he said. He searched her face for the missing pieces of the tale. "What about sex?" he demanded. "How was that between you and Tommy?"

Amy shivered. "At first it was normal," she whispered.

"Normal! What does that mean, for God's sake? And what do you mean 'at first'?"

"After a while . . ." She moistened her lips and tried again. "It got so . . ."

"Tell me!" He shook her once, fiercely, then waited.

"I couldn't stand for him to touch me," she said in a small voice. "I couldn't help it. I tried to be a good wife, but I couldn't hide my feelings. Tommy knew. He said I was still dreaming of Luke and he was right." She let the humiliating admission slide into the space between them, then rushed to cover it. "He said it was because I was part Indian. I've never told you, but I had an Indian grandfather. That's maybe why I'm so unnatural. I never wanted you to find out. I didn't want to see you look at me the way Tommy did, not ever."

Rick stared at her in horrified disbelief. "You little fool," he whispered. "I don't know who's crazier, you or Tommy."

She didn't answer, just kept crying. He crushed her to him and murmured endearments. "*Mi amor, mi corazon.* It's nothing like you think. You're the victim of ignorance." She was sobbing as if her heart would break, great shuddering sobs that made her tremble from head to foot, and he knew that she could not yet comprehend the meaning of his words.

The sun had crept round and destroyed the shade in which they were sheltering. Rick looked for some place cooler to take her and spied the opening of a *kiva*. He gathered her into his arms, carrying her as if she were a small child.

"I want to show you something beautiful," he said. "Almost as beautiful as you are." He kissed her cheeks and her forehead and her eyes as he walked across the empty courtyard. He stopped kissing her only long enough to negotiate the descent into the underground cavern.

"This is the place I promised to show you," he said. "It's the heart of the Pueblo Indian world." They were in a vast pit dug out of the earth. Rick spoke to her in a low voice, more as a calmative than anything else. She didn't seem to hear. "First the *kivas* were only the scenes of religious ceremonies," he said. "Eventually they became the place where all social life of the pueblo centered."

This one was a circle about seventy feet in diameter. It was lit by a series of holes in the ceiling, and kept from collapse by four massive timbers. There were many fire pits and stone benches, and numerous niches in the walls. Once they'd housed statues of gods and saints. But even denuded of the pulsing life it had formerly know, the *kiva* remained enormously impressive and haunted by an air of mystery.

"Look around you, *querida*," Rick said. "This place was built centuries ago. Can you still think all wisdom is contained in the brain of Tommy Westerman? Or that there's some shame in having Indian blood?"

Amy studied his face as if the only answers she wanted were to be found there. Rick realized that she was emotionally exhausted, that all her strength had been used in the effort to tell him the truth. He was still carrying her. Now he laid her gently on the cool earthen floor. He knelt beside her and bent and kissed her mouth. When he lifted his head she started to say something, but he put his fingers over her lips. "Don't speak," he said. "Just close your eyes and trust me."

He had not thought about what he was going to do, but once begun, the actions came to him as naturally as breathing.

He loosened the bow at the neck of her blouse and undid its buttons. Then he slipped the garment from her shoulders. Amy lay very still and offered no resistance. When she was naked he took off his own clothes and lay down beside her. "Some men are selfish and ignorant," he whispered. "It's not your fault you felt the way you did with Tommy. And it's nothing to do with race." Gently he ran his hand the length of her small perfect form. "You are lovely, you give me pleasure. I want you to feel pleasure too."

She had been his patient; in a sense the most intimate secrets of her body were known to him. The difference was that now he saw her with the eyes of a lover, and touched her with a lover's hands and lips.

Rick kissed every part of her. He was very slow and very gentle. For long moments Amy didn't move or seem to respond. He understood that she had padlocked her feelings behind a false wall of shame, and that only love would open the gate. *"Mi amor,"* he murmured over and over. *"Mi corazon."*

Finally she sighed as though she was waking from a long sleep. Hesitantly she reached out her hand and touched his shoulder. It was the touch of a butterfly, precious and fleeting. "I . . . love . . . you," she whispered. The words were halting, as if she must relearn speech. "I've loved you for such a long time. But I was afraid."

"You will never be afraid again," he said. He stroked her silken skin and trailed his fingers along her midriff to her breasts. They were white and tipped with pale pink. He tasted them and they were infinitely sweet.

Amy put her hands on his hair. Like all of him it was dark and strong and bristling with vibrant life. She had never known a man with so much life in him, so much joy. He lifted his head, and she guided his lips to her own. Their tongues mingled in long seconds of shared promise. When their mouths parted she whispered, "Now."

Their eyes remained as much locked together as were their bodies. His movements were controlled and unhurried, and calculated to arouse.

Amy felt herself filled by him. She knew that at this moment he was exposing his soul as completely as he had demanded that she bare her own. Her body found a rhythm that matched his. Her muscles tensed and quivered, and answered the spasms that she felt in his.

They were together in flesh and spirit when they climbed to the top of the mountain and remained long seconds on its glorious peak.

All around them was the mystic past of the *kiva*. Here ancient *shamans* and rainmakers had donned their horned headdresses and danced. The men sat on one side and the women on the other, and they sang and shook their rattles and their oiled bodies gleamed in the glow of the sacred fire. Now their ghosts laughed with delight.

"When will you tell Tommy?" Rick asked on the journey home. Part of him was afraid of her answer, afraid that perhaps he'd dreamed all that had passed between them, and once more she would deny his claim.

"As soon as he comes home," Amy said. Her voice, calm and matter-of-fact, dispelled all Rick's doubts. "He's been away for over a week, so he should be back soon." She shifted in her seat so she could study his beloved profile. "It may not be easy. He'll probably fight us. For spite, if nothing else."

"We'll tell him together," Rick said. "Don't worry. Tommy's made a name for himself, but he's a newcomer. I'm Santa Fe born and bred. In New Mexico that makes a difference. He may fight, but he won't win. We will."

When they arrived at Santo Domingo it was after midnight. The house was sleeping and silent, and there was no sign of Tommy. "I won't stay the night," Rick said. "Much as I want to, it's not wise. In the morning pack the kids' clothes and your own." He took her face in his hands. "Don't take anything else, *querida*, just your clothes. Will that hurt?"

"No. There's nothing here I want."

"Good. I'll be back about noon and take you and the children to Santa Fe. If Tommy returns before I do, don't say a word to him. You must promise me that." She promised, and he kissed her good night and left.

Diego waited for his boss by the waterhole. They had not seen each other in four days. Tommy had taken one crew south while the Indian foreman led another along the eastern boundary close to the Pecos Trail. Tommy was alone when he rode up and reined in. "How'd it go?" he asked without dismounting.

"Ok. Picked up a few strays near Buggy Cliff. No sign of trouble though, and the fence is holding."

"Good. Let's make for home. I sent the others ahead."

Tommy started to turn the horse's head in the direction of the hacienda, but Diego's voice stopped him. "Boss . . ."

There was something unnerving in the Indian's tone. Tommy reined in again and waited. For a few seconds the boy didn't speak. "Spit it out, Diego," Tommy said.

"I think you should know, but I don' like bein' the one to say it."

"Too late, you've already said too much. What's up?"

"It's Rosa."

Tommy stiffened. "What about her?"

"She ain't there."

"At the cabin, you mean?"

"Yeah. I checked when I was close to the place. Like you always tell me to."

"Maybe she went into town for the day."

Diego shook his head and stared at the ground. "No, it ain't that. I met somebody told me she's gone off."

"Gone off where?" Tommy asked. His voice bespoke calm reason, but the knuckles of his hands were white where they gripped the reins.

"To her pueblo, San Felipe. They say she's gonna marry some guy from there."

"Do they indeed?" Tommy said quietly. "You go on home," he added after a moment. "Get a night's rest, then take a crew west. Somebody saw a dozen strays going in that direction."

"What about you?" Diego asked.

"I'll be along when I can."

The cabin told him little except that Rosa had left. Her clothes and her jewelry were gone, as well as a gold framed picture of *La Conquistadora* which she treasured.

Tommy made himself a pot of coffee and drank it laced with some malt whiskey he found in the kitchen. Then he went out back and washed in the tepid,

scummy water of the half-filled butt. It was his custom
to leave a clean shirt and a pair of jeans in the cabin;
they were hanging in their usual place behind the door
of the bedroom. He changed and mounted up. He
knew he should be tired, but he wasn't. He felt fine.
Even his leg didn't hurt.

Pueblo San Felipe was a dusty, impoverished chain
of single-story mud huts. They framed a small plaza,
distinguished only by a few struggling cottonwood trees.
At one end was a locked and bolted church. There
was also a *kiva*, but its opening was purposefully disguised from intrusive eyes. Tommy Westerman did
not suspect its existence. He saw only a few squat
brown people with hooded eyes and expressionless
faces. They moved aside when he rode into the plaza.

"Where's Rosa?"

The Indians stared at him and did not reply.

Tommy got off his horse and tied the animal to a
nearby tree. Then he collared a boy who stood watching. "Go tell her I'm here."

The lad looked at the expression in the eyes of the
gringo and did as he was told.

Nothing moved on the earth or in the brittle blue
sky. The houses and the people seemed part of the
landscape, immutable and covered with red brown
alkaline dust. Finally a door opened at the end of the
row of dwellings, and Rosa stepped hesitantly into the
road. Tommy shaded his eyes with his hand and peered
at her. She wore a rectangular *manta* of black cloth
with a blue border. It was belted tightly at the waist

and short enough to expose her strong brown calves and bare feet. Her hair was braided and hung down her back.

At that moment he almost turned and left. She wasn't anyone he knew, this woman. For a few seconds Tommy saw himself a stranger in an alien environment. The notion of assuaging his pride in this place struck him as absurd. Then Rosa walked toward him.

As she moved her confidence increased. Her hips swayed with the old insouciance; she thrust her heavy breasts forward. When she was a foot away from him her red lips parted and revealed her white teeth and her darting pink tongue. She laughed softly. "Go away, *Anglo*. I'm through with you."

Tommy slapped her twice. All his strength was behind the blows, and the red marks of his fingers stained her cheeks. "Get your things. I'm taking you home."

"This is my home. I'm staying here."

He raised his arm to hit her again, but from behind a hand reached out and arrested the motion. Slowly Tommy turned around. He faced a man about his own age, but shorter. Instinctively Tommy knew that it was the man he'd seen riding away from the cabin months before, the one Rosa said treated her like a "human being." The Indian face was creased with lines of fury. "Leave her alone! Get out of here. Go back to your own kind."

Tommy spoke slowly and distinctly. Only those who knew him well would recognize the controlled rage in his voice. "What makes you think you can give me orders?"

"Rosa is going to marry me," the man said.

Tommy shook his head. "No. She's a slut and a whore, but she's mine. I'm taking her back where she belongs."

The man uttered a strangled gasp of fury and lunged. Tommy straight-armed him to stop his forward plunge, then hit him with one vicious left jab. The body of Rosa's intended husband crumpled to the ground. Rosa whimpered softly.

There were about a dozen people in the street. They huddled in doorways and watched and made no sound until a youth of about sixteen bolted into the road. "What's the matter with all of you?" he shouted. "Are you going to let this pig come here and attack our women and do nothing?" He wore trousers, but no shirt. His broad shoulders rippled in the glare of the sun. He had long hair, restrained with a woven head-band, and it swayed when he dashed forward.

Rosa screamed. Tommy raised his arm to meet the boy's attack. Then a voice cut the air with authority. "Stop!"

They did. The tableau was like a scene caught by camera. Only the man who had uttered the command moved. He approached the place where Tommy and Rosa stood. "I am Pedro, the *cacique*. I make the rules here. You are not welcome. Go."

"That's what I intend to do," Tommy said. "But I'm taking her with me." He jerked his head in Rosa's direction and studied the *cacique*.

The man was about sixty years old, maybe more. He had a thin, wiry body and old, strangulated sinews that stood out on his neck and his hands. He wore a loose open weave shirt and trousers, and his hair was cut short around his face, but long at the back. He looked like every Indian Tommy had ever seen, except for his eyes. They were pale blue, evidence of some mixed blood in his ancestry, and they stared into Tommy's with riveting force.

"That is for Rosa to decide," the old man said. "Her mother was of this pueblo. She was a right to be here if she wishes."

Tommy broke the eye contact and took a step nearer Rosa. "That's not how I see it. And I don't intend to stand here talking about it." He grabbed Rosa's arm and yanked her forward. "Get moving."

"No!" she hissed. "Here I am somebody. I never go back with you."

Just then the Indian whom Tommy had knocked out groaned; softly at first, then louder. He staggered to his feet, but collapsed again instantly. Rosa gasped and tried to go to him. Tommy yanked her back. She struggled to free herself, but it was no use. Each movement was a silent pantomime in the hushed street. None of the onlookers moved or spoke.

Finally the *cacique* thrust his body between Tommy and the woman. Tommy could smell the old man's sweat and sense his surprising strength. He did not want to hit a man over sixty. He turned and shoved him instead. Then, without warning and in the split second before Pedro responded to the force of the push, Tommy felt a hot stab of pain in his back below his shoulder blades.

The knife Rosa plunged into him remained buried to its hilt. For a few seconds Tommy's gray eyes opened

wide in surprise. Then they closed, and he staggered a
moment before he fell.

The road leading to San Felipe was a rough dirt
track that cut a jagged path to the Rio Grande and the
pueblo. That's why Tommy had come on horseback.
Now the Indians hauled him away on a cart pulled by
two burros. Pedro and two other men, both elders of
the village, accompanied his prostrate form. The women
had staunched the flow of blood and administered
herbal medicine, but they did not go on the journey to
Santo Domingo.

The trip did not begin until the *cacique* and his
council met and discussed the best way to deal with
this emergency. Someone suggested keeping the gringo
in the pueblo until he either died or recovered. In the
latter case he would be grateful to them for saving his
life; if he died, they could bury him and hope he'd
never be found. Wiser heads prevailed. The gringo
was a prominent man, and his alliance with Rosa was
well known. If he disappeared, the authorities were
bound to search for him in San Felipe. No, they must
take him home, where his own kind could try and save
his life. Then they must simply wait and see what
consequences followed this evil day.

The cart reached the ranch in late morning of the
day that Amy intended to leave her husband and join
the man she loved. Her suitcase and the children's
were packed and discreetly hidden in her bedroom.
She waited only for Rick's arrival. Her heart was
singing, and she felt neither guilt nor shame. She had

paid whatever debt she owed Tommy a long time ago. And she had done all she could to make the marriage a success. It was his choice, not hers, that forced this end to the drama begun six years earlier in Cross River.

"Doña Amy! Doña Amy!" Maria's wails filled the cool serenity of the beautiful hacienda. "Come quick! Don Tommy, I think he is dead! They have killed him . . ."

Amy's sandaled feet slapped on the tiled floor. She ran out into the courtyard and ignored Tom Junior's howls of fright. The baby could not understand what was said, but he recognized the anguish in Maria's voice and was terrified.

"What is it?" What are you talking about?" Amy thrust her head into the wagon and saw Tommy's inert form. He was lying on his stomach and a blanket covered him from the neck down. She did not think he was breathing. "Oh, my God! What happened?"

"He is still alive," Pedro said. Then he quickly told her the facts. Amy did not require long explanations. She instructed them to carry Tommy to his bedroom, and then looked at her watch. It was pointless to send for help. Rick was on his way there right now. Nothing would make him come any faster than the motive he already had.

"Get hot water and more blankets," she told Maria. "Bring them to Don Tommy's room. Then see that these men have a drink and something to eat before they leave."

Amy started to follow the half-dead form of her husband. Then she noticed Kate. The little girl stood by the entrance of the patio. She was absolutely rigid, and her eyes were wide with terror.

Amy dashed to her and swept the child into her arms. The small form was hard and unyielding. "It's all right, darling," Amy crooned, stroking Kate's hair and pressing her close. "Daddy's going to be all right. Uncle Rick will be here any minute to make him better."

Suddenly Kate began pummeling her mother with tiny clenched fists. She threw back her head and screamed and screamed, and her agony was fearful to behold.

26

"WILL HE LIVE?" AMY ASKED AFTER RICK HAD BEEN with him for almost an hour.

"I don't know." He wiped his hands on a towel and accepted the drink she had poured for him. The kitchen was cool and dim, despite the midday heat. Rick extended his foot and hooked a chair closer, then straddled it. He leaned on the back with his elbows and studied her over the rim of his frosted glass.

"The knife punctured a lung. I've stitched it as best I can, but there'll probably be infection. Besides, he's lost a lot of blood. How's Kate?"

"Sleeping. Whatever you gave her worked fast."

Amy lit a cigarette with trembling fingers. "I didn't want it to end like this," she whispered. "I wanted to leave him, but not like this."

"I could say a lot of things about useless guilt for something you didn't do," Rick said. "I don't think there's much point. You know it all anyway. Here." He reached into his shirt pocket and withdrew a folded letter. "You'd better read this."

Amy took it and saw the heading of the Dominican Priory in Dover. The handwriting was familiar. It was from Luke. "Where did you get this?"

"It was in Tommy's desk. He was conscious for a few minutes. I asked him if he wanted a priest. I thought his answer was pretty strange. He said, 'Only if it's the right one.' Then he told me to get the letter. He lost consciousness after that, so I read it. There didn't seem anything else to do."

Amy looked at Rick for a long moment, then bent her head to read Luke's letter. It was postmarked a month earlier and the first paragraph was just ordinary chatter about how he was and what he was doing. Then he'd written, "I am sorry to hear things between you and Amy are past help. If you have 'bitched it up beyond repair,' as you say, that's a damn shame. Don't forget you're married in the eyes of God. He'll help you if you ask Him."

Amy suppressed a wave of distaste for this easy religiosity. She continued reading.

"As for Uncle Donald, we can leave the judgment to the Lord. Apparently he backed himself into a corner and didn't know how else to get out. May he rest in peace. When I get there we can talk more about all this. I don't mind saying I'm nervous about traveling with the extraordinary luggage you've arranged. Brother James will be coming with me and we should arrive on the third or the fourth of June. . . ." There was more, but it was unimportant.

"Does any of that make sense to you?" Rick asked.

"Some of it does. Uncle Donald is Donald Varley. He was my guardian and executor of Tommy's and Luke's parents' estate. I guess he must have died. Tommy never told me."

"What about the 'luggage' he refers to. Do you know what it is?"

"No. Tommy never said a word . . ." She broke off and looked at the calendar on the wall. "What day is it?" she asked Rick.

"Wednesday, June seventh," he said. "Your brother-in-law is at least three days overdue."

Suddenly it dawned on Amy that Luke was coming there, to the ranch. That part of his letter was absolutely clear. "How will he get here?" she asked.

"Hire a taxi at Lamy I expect." Rick stood up. He started to cross to her, but something in her face stopped him. He had finally won her away from Tommy, whom she had never loved. Was he to lose her now to a ghost from the past? A celibate ghost at that. "I have to get back to my patient," he said. His voice was grim, but Amy neither looked up nor met his eyes.

The Dominicans arrived late that same afternoon. They came in a taxi from Lamy, as Rick had predicted. Both Luke and his companion looked tired when they climbed out of the car and stood in the courtyard facing the house. They didn't wear their white habits as Amy had expected. They were in black suits with small white collars at their necks, and they were gray with the dust of the dry roads.

"Hello, Luke," she said, extending her hand. "I'm sorry there was no one at the station to meet you. I didn't know until a few hours ago that you were coming."

He held her hand a moment longer than formality dictated, then introduced his companion. Brother James was a man a little older than Luke. He had a broad smile and a decidedly Irish cast of features. Amy waited until the driver had unloaded their luggage and received payment for the trip. Only when the taxi drove out the gate did she say, "I'm sorry to greet you with bad news, but there's been an accident. Tommy is very ill, he may be dying. I'm sorry," she repeated. "There's no easy way to tell you such a thing."

Luke ignored her apologies and asked only one question. "Has he had a priest?"

"He told the doctor he only wanted 'the right one.' I think he meant you."

Luke unstrapped his single suitcase. It was old and battered, though once it had been of fine quality. His possessions were all neatly folded, and he found what he wanted right away. Then, holding a satin stole that was purple on one side and white on the other, he followed her into the house.

*   *   *

"*In nomine patris et fili et spiritu sancti.*" Luke traced the sign of the cross on Tommy's forehead. His thumb was moist with holy oil, and he bore down as if he wanted to impress the symbol on his brother's mind and soul. Tommy didn't respond. Three days he'd been like that. Seventy-two hours of heat and suppressed emotion and mystery had passed since Luke came to Santo Domingo.

He sighed and stood up. His knees were sore and his white habit was faintly soiled where it had pressed against the tiled floor. Luke had spent most of the last three days praying beside his brother's bed. He was waiting for a sign, for some symbol of remorse or awareness. Luke wanted that desperately. He wanted to give Tommy real absolution, not the conditional sort the Church permitted in these circumstances. It was only for that grace he stormed heaven. Luke did not presume to pray for his brother's recovery. Now he was too weary to pray for anything.

When he bent his head to remove the purple stole he saw the child. Tommy's daughter was standing in the doorway. Luke couldn't know how long she'd been there watching. Carefully he folded the stole and placed it and the vial of holy oil in the drawer of the bedside table; then he walked toward her. "Hello, Kate, do you want to see Daddy? He's still sleeping."

Kate didn't answer; she merely studied him with her silvery eyes. Luke took her hand and led her to the still figure of her father. "You can give him a kiss if you want, then we'd better go away and let him rest." She pressed her small rosebud mouth to Tommy's ashen cheek. After that she allowed Luke to lead her from the room.

The household had evolved a schedule for watching by Tommy's bed. When Luke and his niece left the sickroom Brother James was waiting in the hall. He nodded to them and went in to continue the vigil.

There was another vigil being kept simultaneously. Luke glanced out the window and saw the pair of Indians still poised motionless on the horizon. They had been there since Tommy was brought home. They were from Pueblo San Felipe, and they were waiting to see if the man Rosa stabbed would die.

"The people of the pueblos are very closely knit," Rick had explained. "If Rosa is indicted for murder, they will see it as a trial of the entire village. It will be too. The publicity will be awful." He'd gone on to speak of the life of the pueblos, their struggle to survive and preserve their culture, their poverty.

Luke liked Rick. He recognized in the doctor a blend of toughness and gentleness. "He knows who and what he is," he'd told Brother James. "Ibañez doesn't need to put on an act for himself or anyone else. That's rare." Luke stuck by that evaluation, but he also knew that some kind of charade was being enacted in his brother's home. Ostensibly the doctor was present because a desperately ill man required his skills. And Amy was quiet and withdrawn because her husband was teetering on the edge of death, as a result of wounds inflicted by his mistress. Perhaps it was understandable, this sense of hidden truths seething below the surface, but Luke didn't believe he wholly understood it.

A maid appeared and took Kate from his custody. Luke wandered into the living room. Amy was sitting alone and staring into space. Luke went to her and laid a hand on her shoulder. "Let me get you something," he said. "A cold drink or perhaps some tea."

"I don't want anything, thanks." She put her hand over his, almost without thinking of the gesture. "I'm glad you're here. I never would have expected it, not in a million years, but it's a blessing."

"For me too." He paused, then went on, "Amy, dear, we've got to talk. Maybe this isn't the right time . . ."

Rick came into the room, and Luke stopped speaking. Ibañez looked at the pair of them. Amy's hand still lay over Luke's, his was still on her shoulder. "Sorry," Rick said. "I didn't mean to intrude."

Amy stood up. She looked oddly guilty. "You're not intruding. We were just . . ."

She had no opportunity to complete the sentence. Brother James appeared in the doorway. " 'Tis over," he said in his soft brogue. "He's gone to God."

Rick was the first to move. He said nothing, merely hurried from the room to ascertain the accuracy of the pronouncement. Amy looked after him, as if debating whether she should follow. She couldn't bring herself to do it, and she sank back to her seat instead.

"Did he recover consciousness?" Luke asked. "Did he say anything?" His eyes pleaded for the right answer.

Brother James shook his head. "He moaned once, that's all. Then he stopped breathing. I made an Act of Contrition for him. Sure the Lord takes a soul when and how 'tis best. You'll not be doubting His mercy or His wisdom."

In minutes the fact of Tommy's death somehow made itself known throughout the house. Maria went out to the courtyard and rubbed her face with dirt and began a keening chant of formalized grief. It was unrelated to her feelings for Don Tommy; it was merely a rite she owed her employer.

Amy heard the eerie wail and ran to where Maria sat cross-legged on the ground. "Stop it! The children will hear and be terrified. Kate's already beside herself."

Maria paused and looked at her mistress. "They must know about dying," she said. "It is not a secret." Then she resumed her loud mourning. Exasperated, Amy started back to the house. She must find Kate and Tommy Junior and tell them herself. Before she went inside she looked up. The men of Pueblo San Felipe were gone.

In the hiatus between death and burial they went through Tommy's papers. A locked drawer in the desk in his bedroom contained all his vital documents, carefully filed. There were the deeds to the ranch, the original one and those representing Tommy's later acquisitions, and there was a will.

How like him, Amy thought. He was young and healthy and very much alive, but he made a will. Clever Tommy left nothing to chance, until he turned his back on Rosa.

The will was a carefully thought out disposition of Tommy's assets. The terms were clear and simple.

Santo Domingo and everything belonging to it went to his children. It was to be run as a trust until Tom Junior was twenty-one. The First National Bank of Santa Fe was the trustee. "My wife, Amy Norman Westerman," the will continued, "has the right to live at Santo Domingo as long as she wishes. Further, I instruct my trustee to pay her support and maintenance as long as she lives."

That was all, no riders, no codicils or exceptions. The ranch was Amy's home and its earnings her upkeep as long as she lived, not just until she remarried or broke some other condition of Tommy's making.

"He wanted to be fair," Rick said. Amy nodded.

There was one other thing in the locked drawer. It was a folded brown paper containing a dozen small brown seeds. Outside it was marked, "flame tree."

"Where did he get these?" Luke asked.

"From my father's lawyer in Dar es Salaam," Amy said. It was the only possibility. "I wrote to him after the war and asked for the seeds. Tommy must have intercepted his reply."

There was not yet time to ponder why he had done it, or why he afterward preserved the little package.

Two days later they buried Tommy in the old graveyard beside the mission church of Our Lady of Guadalupe. Luke made the arrangements and calmed the ecclesiastical waters. Thomas Westerman had been baptized a Catholic and died after receiving the last rites of his religion. He was entitled to a funeral mass, and interment in consecrated ground. The manner in which he had conducted the years between birth and death was something he must settle before another tribunal.

Ultimately, Luke explained, the Church does not pronounce anyone damned or saved. "She never has and never will. Not even the pope can presume to know the final dispensation of God's mercy, or His justice."

Amy found the theology obscure, but she was grateful to Luke for making the decisions.

She went through the funeral with quiet dignity, a small but erect figure behind her black veil. There were many people present at both the church and the cemetery. Most weren't true mourners. They were voyeurs come to see the end of a man who had "made a name for himself," and managed to die as dramatically as he lived. It occured to Amy that Diego was perhaps the only person present who felt sincere, unmitigated grief. He had seen it all happen and been beside Tommy from the beginning. Amy had already asked him to remain as foreman and manager of the ranch. "It will belong to Tom Junior and Kate someday," she told him. "But only you can preserve it for them. You know exactly what Tommy planned." Diego had nodded solemnly and agreed.

Rick had tried to persuade her to take the children to the funeral. "At least Kate," he'd insisted. "She needs to see the end, Amy. Unless she does there can never be a finish to her grieving."

Stubbornly Amy refused. It struck her as a monstrous idea.

"You told me how desolate you were when your parents died," Rick reminded her. "You said it was worse because they never had a funeral."

"I was seventeen," she insisted. "Kate won't be four until November."

In the end he couldn't convince her. She took both children to the nuns who looked after Estella and asked the sisters to keep them for a week or ten days. *Las Carmelitas* had come to know Amy, since she frequently visited Rick's daughter. They did not refuse her this charity.

After the burial Amy and the three men returned to the house. It was silent and cool and beautiful. Amy was surprised to find how much a refuge it seemed. She put away her widow's weeds and changed into a denim skirt and a white blouse. She had gone through the formalities required; she would not descend into hypocrisy.

She made a pitcher of lemonade and took it and a tray of glasses to the patio. Rick was there alone.

"I want you to have these tablets," he said, handing her a vial of small yellow pills. "They'll help you sleep for the next few nights. Don't take one unless you need it, but don't hesitate if you do."

"You won't be here, then?" She asked the question in a small voice.

"I can't be away from my practice any longer, *querida*," he said softly. "And I think you need to be apart from me for a time."

Amy didn't answer. She busied herself pouring the lemonade, but when he took the glass from her hand Rick didn't drink it. "I love you," he said. "Nothing has changed, but everything is different. Once more all the decisions are yours."

"I don't know what you mean."

"Yes, you do. I had one rival for a long time, *mi*

amor. I don't propose to spend the rest of my life fighting another one."

She started to say something, but Rick put his finger over her lips. "Father Luke tells me he and his companion will remain here for a few days. You and your brother-in-law have much to discuss." He looked at her closely when he said, "There's one thing that won't wait. Do you plan to do anything about Rosa?"

Amy looked at him blankly, then understood his meaning. "Please see that she has a lawyer. Not Lopez, a good criminal lawyer. She was acting in self-defense. I'm sure of it."

"Yes," Rick agreed. "I'll get someone from Albuquerue."

"Make sure all the bills come to me," Amy said.

"I will, *querida*. And I'll see the sheriff and get word to Pedro, the *cacique* at San Felipe. I doubt you'll have to testify or become involved in the proceedings."

Wilkins would be kind to the widow, Rick knew. And it would satisfy Pete's sense of justice to finish the drama Beatriz had inaugurated. Westerman was dead, all the loose ends were neatly tied. Ibañez sighed and rose to go.

Amy waited for him to kiss her good bye, but he left without doing so.

Amy went to her room and took one of Rick's pills and slept until the following morning. When she came downstairs it was after nine. Luke was waiting for her. "I'm sorry to press you, Amy, but James and I can only stay a short while. I need to talk to you."

She suspected something of what he wanted to say. She'd worked it out, along with a number of other truths, in the days since Tommy died. The thought of discussing it was unpleasant. "Perhaps tomorrow," she said listlessly.

"No," Luke insisted. "Today."

"Very well, I'll meet you in the study in an hour."

The study was the square spacious room in the rear of the quadrangle that formed the house. It had one window that looked out to the patio, and another that faced the corral. It was furnished with a big desk and a long oak writing table. The chairs were all hard-backed. They had curved arms and wide red leather seats and looked as if they might have come from the governor's palace in Santa Fe, or some Spanish library. It was a room for solitary thinking or serious talk; an appropriate setting for the business which Amy and Luke discussed.

"What bothers me," Luke said, "is that you may misjudge Uncle Donald. He robbed both our estates, yours as well as mine and Tommy's, I'm not denying that. But at the same time he tried not to see any of us hurt."

"I figured out that the reference in your letter had to mean that. But I don't understand what it signified, or how you found out. I don't even know when he died. Tommy never told me."

"Three years ago," Luke said. "In 1918."

"That's the year Tom Junior was born." Amy said.

"Well, small wonder Tommy didn't name him for Donald." It was a weak attempt at humor, but they both managed a smile. "If he hadn't died just then, nothing would have been discovered," Luke continued. "When the lawyers were sorting out his estate they found the papers relating to the purchasing of the Norman mines from you. At the same time the war had ended, and your father's attorney had written from Africa to say that he'd had an offer of half a million dollars for the diamond mines and the house. He thought that you still owned them." He paused and looked at her, but Amy didn't say anything.

"It was obvious that the sixty thousand Donald paid you was patent robbery. They probed further and discovered the banker who'd helped with the swindle. It turned out that the bank wanted to make private restitution rather than risk a scandal, and Tommy and I agreed. There wasn't much point in dragging the whole family through the dirt." He peered at her. She was pale and wide-eyed and she sat very still. "You must know all this. You had to sign the papers."

"No," she said. "This is the first I've heard of it. Tommy never told me." She was repeating that phrase so often it sounded like a litany.

"But that's impossible! Your signature was on all the documents. The loans from the bank in Albuquerque were made on the strength of them. I know that. It was all so intertwined that I had to sign a lot of things too."

She shook her head. "I never signed anything. If my name was on any papers, then Tommy forged it." She didn't wait to see his reaction to that. "This bank loan you speak of, what year was it made?"

"Nineteen-eighteen. Everybody knew it would take

a while to get the capital out of Africa. And Tommy said you needed the money right away."

Amy stood up and gripped the back of the chair. "He needed it. He wanted to get exclusive rights to the waterhole, and buy out two other ranchers. That's why he agreed to sell the mines, and Jericho. That's why he didn't mention it to me. All his hopes and dreams were tied up with this place. He was afraid that mine were still in Africa."

"And he never gave you the chance to prove otherwise," Luke said quietly. "I'm sorry," he added, as if it were his fault and he must still defend his little brother.

"So am I," Amy said. She was not referring to Jericho. That wound had healed long ago, at least as much as it ever would. But somehow Tommy had not realized that. So he had cheated her, and his guilt had been the bitter finale to whatever remained of their union.

"There was one thing that wasn't sold," Luke said. "In the light of what you've told me I don't know what to make of that fact." He reached below his scapular and brought forth a chamois bag tied with a drawstring. "Tommy has been negotiating to get this from Dar es Salaam to New York for nearly three years. It arrived a few months ago, and he asked me to bring it out here. That's why I came."

Amy took the offering with trembling fingers. She felt its weight, and the familiar texture of the velvety leather. She had held this bag before. "This belonged to my mother," she said. "It was usually kept in the bank vault in Dar es Salaam, but sometimes she had it at home."

"I see," Luke said. He had opened the bag earlier, but now he was going through the experience with Amy, seeing it with her eyes. It seemed entirely possible that some new and mysterious thing would be revealed when she looked inside.

They didn't speak while she unloosed the drawstring and spilled out the contents. Four stones tumbled silently onto the leather-edged blotter on the desk. Three of them were overshadowed by the fourth. Even in the casual heap in which they lay the Jericho diamond announced its presence as with a fanfare of trumpets.

When Roland Norman found the stone thirty years earlier it created a furor. Since then, larger diamonds had been discovered, but the Jericho remained one of the wonders of the world. It was a flawless blue-white gem. Norman had taken it to Antwerp for cutting. When the artisans were through it was seventy-two carats of fiery perfection. Amy held it. She gazed into its depths and saw all her childhood, and all that had happened since.

The only sound in the room was the ticking of a grandfather clock. Seconds passed. The clock chimed the hour. When the sound had died away Luke said. "Its extraordinarily beautiful." It was an absurd understatement, but he felt he must say something.

"It's more than that to me," Amy said.

She put the Jericho diamond down and picked up the three that had accompanied it. In the company of the great stone they were only handmaidens to glory.

Seen by themselves each would have the power to excite.

They were of graded size; ten, eleven, and twelve carats. Jessie had shown them to her daughter numerous times. "When you grow up we'll make these into a necklace for you, or maybe a tiara," she'd said. Amy had wondered where she would wear a tiara in the African bush, but she had taken part in the game with glee. "Yes, and I'll have a satin gown with a long train."

She savored the memory for a few moments, then set it aside. "Did Tommy tell you what he intended to do with these?" she asked.

Luke shook his head. "No, but I can guess. They weren't mentioned in his will. He didn't consider them his. He meant to give them you."

"I think perhaps he did," Amy said slowly. "It would have meant telling me about the whole thing, the sale of the mines and the house, and what he'd done with the money. But I think he planned to do it. And he meant to give me the seeds of the flame tree at the same time. That's why he saved them."

Amy did not talk to Luke again that day. When she came downstairs the following morning it was after nine. The two men had already breakfasted.

"The padre says his prayers," Maria told her. "The other one I do not understand."

Maria found Brother James's English too rich with brogue to be comprehensible. Besides, she didn't approve of him. He spent his time drawing pictures in an oversized book. To Maria that somehow smacked of witchcraft. Amy placated the woman by having a cup of coffee in the kitchen, though she refused anything to eat. Finally she went to look for Luke.

He was slowly pacing the length of the patio. He held an open leather-bound breviary with colored ribbon markers, and he was muttering softly to himself in Latin. Amy waited until he looked up and noticed her.

"I'm sorry, am I interrupting? I can come back later."

"No, don't go away. I was saying my office. I just finished." He closed the book and made the sign of the cross. Then they sat together under the gum tree.

"Where's Brother James?" Amy asked.

"He went out to make more sketches of the local flora. He's a remarkable botanist and a fine artist. That's one of the reasons Father Prior selected him as my companion."

She had spent many hours thinking of Luke, and the incredible fact of his presence. "Were you sorry to have to come here?" she asked.

He didn't look at her. "Not sorry. Frightened, maybe. Things were pretty bad between you and Tommy, weren't they?"

"As bad as they could be." She took a deep breath. "I want you to know the truth. The day they brought him home, after he'd been wounded, I was getting ready to leave him. If they had come an hour later, I would already have gone."

"I'm not surprised," Luke said. "Tommy wrote me a little bit about it. Then, when I got here, it was obvious you weren't grieving in the ordinary sense."

"I had done all my grieving for Tommy a long time before," she said quietly.

"He'd changed that much?"

"Yes. I suppose we both had."

He turned to her. His smile was as sad and as devastatingly beautiful as it had always been. "You've grown up, little Amy, but if you're changed, it's for the better."

"Not really," she said. "A lot of our trouble was my fault."

"No," Luke said. "It was mine. I've never forgiven myself for going to see you that day in New York. Or for the things I said."

She rose and walked a few steps away. A branch of the eucalyptus hung by her head and its gray green softness brushed her cheek. She could no longer postpone the question most in her mind. "If I had agreed," she said. "If I had said I'd leave Tommy and go away with you, would you have gone through with it?"

His reply was so low that she had to strain to hear. "Yes, God help me, I would have." He gripped the breviary and his knuckles were white. "It would have been a choice I regretted the rest of my life. I don't think I'm much of a priest, but it's what I was born to be."

She nodded. "Thank you for being honest. I needed to know." There was no reason to tell him that Tommy had found out about the clandestine visit, or that it put the seal of doom on their marriage. She had decided earlier to keep that secret. Nothing Luke said had changed her mind.

They were silent for a while. Finally Luke spoke.

"We'll be leaving tomorrow. Unless you need me for anything more."

"No." she smiled gently. "I don't need you anymore."

She felt a deep longing to be by herself, and she turned and left the patio. Luke let her go without a word.

Amy wandered the house, but it seemed suddenly confining and oppressive. She changed her clothes and went to the corral and saddled Sheba. The gray was getting old, but she remained Amy's favorite mount.

When she rode out the gate she saw Brother James sitting beside a cactus. He was sketching, and he wore a wide sombrero. It made a queer contrast to his black and white habit. He looked up and waved when she passed him, but Amy didn't stop

In a few minutes the ranch buildings were a speck on the horizon behind her. She was alone and free and at one with the tawny earth and the blazing sky. She rode hard and fast, confident of her skill and her knowledge of the countryside. The wind whistled past her face, and the distant mountains filled her eyes. She did not think. She allowed herself only to feel, and to be healed.

It was nearly nightfall when she returned. The two Dominicans were nowhere to be seen. Maria had left a cold supper for her. She ate it, then went up to bed, and she did not need Rick's tablets to send her to sleep.

Amy's bedside clock said 5:00 A.M. when she woke. Dawn was only a promise in the gray night sky. Suddenly she knew that she could wait no longer. She had intended going to Santa Fe after Luke and James left, but there was an urgency in her blood now. She bounded from the bed and showered, and washed her short black hair. Her hands were trembling when she rifled through her clothes closet, but it was the quiver of joy and anticipation, not fear.

She chose a yellow silk dress because it was Rick's favorite color, and because the rippling pleats of the skirt and the deep ruffle at the neck were intensely flattering. It wasn't a widow's dress, not a sign of mourning. For Rick's sake, and the children's she would be discreet in the next few months. But not today.

The Model-T started without hesitation. Amy covered the distance to town in two and a half hours. The car would probably never be the same. It was just eight-thirty when she arrived at Rick's, and there were no patients waiting in the office. She tried the front door and found it unlocked.

The smell of fresh-perked coffee filled the house, and there were sounds of occupancy coming from the kitchen, but the dining room was empty. So was the sitting room and Rick's small study. She raced up the stairs. Her feet were encased in patent leather pumps with high thin heels, but they made no sound on the carpeted floor. Rick's bedroom was at the end of the hall and the door was ajar. She caught sight of him buttoning his shirt in front of the mirror over the dresser. Amy pushed the door open wider, and stepped into the room. "Good morning, my love," she said softly.

He looked up and saw her reflection in the mirror, then turned and opened his arms. Amy rushed to them, and when they closed around her, everything in her world came into harmony.

"I love you," she said. "Oh, my Don Rico, I love you so much."

She was laughing and crying, and he could feel her pounding heart and her cheeks wet with tears. His eyes filled too, and he held her very tight and they swayed slightly to the rhythm of their happiness. *"Mi amor,"* he whispered. *"Mi corazon."*

Generations of intrigue, romance and murder in these family sagas by...

Beverly Byrne

14